THESE
DEADLY
GAMES

ALSO BY DIANA URBAN

All Your Twisted Secrets

THESE
DEADLY
GAMES

....

DIANA URBAN

WEDNESDAY BOOKS
NEW YORK

First published in the United States by Wednesday Books, an imprint of St. Martin's Publishing Group

THESE DEADLY GAMES. Copyright © 2022 by Diana Urban. All rights reserved. Printed in the United States of America. For information, address St. Martin's Publishing Group, 120 Broadway, New York, NY 10271.

www.wednesdaybooks.com

Book design by Michelle McMillian

Library of Congress Cataloging-in-Publication Data

Names: Urban, Diana, author.
Title: These deadly games / Diana Urban.
Description: First edition. | New York : Wednesday Books, 2022. | Audience: Ages 14–18. |
Identifiers: LCCN 2021037758 | ISBN 9781250797193 (hardcover) | ISBN 9781250797209 (ebook)
Subjects: CYAC: Video games—Fiction. | Treasure hunt (Game)—Fiction. | Hacking—Fiction. | Brothers and sisters—Fiction. | Revenge—Fiction. | Murder—Fiction. | LCGFT: Novels. | Thrillers (Fiction)
Classification: LCC PZ7.1.U73 Th 2022 | DDC [Fic]—dc23
LC record available at https://lccn.loc.gov/2021037758

Our books may be purchased in bulk for promotional, educational, or business use. Please contact your local bookseller or the Macmillan Corporate and Premium Sales Department at 1-800-221-7945, extension 5442, or by email at MacmillanSpecialMarkets@macmillan.com.

First Edition: 2022

10 9 8 7 6 5 4 3 2 1

To Mom and Dad,
for always believing

THESE
DEADLY
GAMES

CHAPTER 1

I was going to kill Zoey.

Heat simmered in my belly as I crept up behind her. She was oblivious to my presence, gazing over the stone balcony toward the forest. Rotting tree stumps littered the field below, but nobody lurked in the shadows.

Now was my chance to take her out.

My fingertips tingled as I slinked closer, the desire for vengeance flooding my veins. How should I do it? I could shove her over the balcony's edge, but that wouldn't guarantee a kill. We weren't high enough from the ground, so it would depend on how she landed. I could shoot her, but my trembling fingers couldn't guarantee my aim. And I needed her to die.

I sounded like some homicidal maniac, didn't I?

Well, trust me—she didn't deserve my mercy. Not after what she did.

A dagger should do it. Sinking a blade into her back would be the most gratifying way to take her down, anyway. God knew she'd stabbed me in the back enough times that killing her now wouldn't even the score.

I unsheathed my blade and closed the distance between us, steps stealthy and silent. Zoey was still except for her long blond tresses fluttering in the breeze as she stared into the distance. Focused. Unwavering. What the hell was she waiting for? It didn't matter—I inched closer, raised the dagger, and plunged it into her back.

"Dammit, Crystal!" Zoey shouted from the squishy recliner. She threw off her pink gamer headset that matched her blond hair's pink ombre tips as the alert *ShardsOfGlass eliminated DaggerQueen29 with a dagger* popped up on-screen. My cat, Whiskers, leaped from the nook between her socked feet and zoomed upstairs. Poor fuzzball—it was bad enough my esports team had invaded her turf in our basement den at the crack of dawn.

I rubbed my lips together, trying to suppress a grin and failing miserably. I couldn't decide which was more satisfying: the fact that I was the last player standing in this round, scoring fifty extra MortalBucks on top of ten for killing Zoey, or that it was one last chance for *her* to earn them before the statewide MortalDusk tourney on Sunday.

I couldn't believe it was only two days away. Two days until we'd know who'd win the tourney's solo and team prizes, each $250,000. Two days until we'd know who'd advance to the annual MortalDusk Crown in New York City next month along with the other states' winners. I could see it now: standing onstage at the tourney with my friends in our costumes, accepting the prize in front of a cheering crowd and all those cameras—not to mention the all-expenses-paid trip to New York for the crown and the sponsorships that'd roll in. Sponsorships I'd *kill* for.

And did I mention the crown's solo and team prizes were $3 million? That's right. Three. Freaking. Million. Dollars. Can you imagine having that kind of cash at sixteen years old? You'd be *set*. I mean, sure, I personally had no shot at winning the solo competition, and if we won the team prize, it'd be split five ways. Still, though! I was no math whiz, but even I knew that amount would change my life.

We had a legit shot at winning the team tourney, too, and not just statistically speaking, since Vermont had the fewest competitors. We'd monopolized our state leaderboard for *months*.

Problem was, only five of us could play on a team at the tourney . . . and all six of us wanted in. So we'd decided to compete for it: the first five to earn twenty thousand MortalBucks would claim a spot.

And I refused to be the rotten egg.

"Welp, Crystal's not messing around," said Dylan, our newest recruit. We sat cross-legged on the couch, his knee an inch from mine—not that I'd noticed or anything. Was he complimenting my badassery, or implying I was a traitor? He met my gaze over his tortoiseshell-rimmed glasses and lifted the corner of his mouth, revealing a dimple in his cheek. God, why was he so hot—I mean, so hard to read?

"Well, we *are* down to the wire—"

"Guys, get down here!" Zoey screeched. The rest of our team was upstairs; Dylan had been the only one to stick around to watch after getting killed in this round. "Next round's starting—"

"Shhh," I said. "My family's still asleep."

Zoey's sharp features twisted into a scowl, our main form of communication these days. Ugh, I hated competing like this. But winning the tourney would be the difference between my family living in this house and, well, not. My parents' divorce last year had been quick—too quick—and Mom had been struggling to pay our mortgage ever since. It was my fault Dad took off so fast, so I *had* to win that prize money. I couldn't let Zoey keep me from competing. We'd do fine without her blade combat skills, anyway.

My bestie, Akira, was first down the stairs, her heart-shaped face so flushed you could've fried an egg on it. "What happened?" I asked, but she wordlessly curled up on my other side, stuck her headset over her chin-length, shiny, jet-black hair, and perched her laptop on her hip. In MortalDusk, she was our top architect, a harbinger of death to anyone who got lost in her structures. But right now, she looked like she wanted to erect a fort around herself and hide until the end of time.

Her boyfriend, Randall, came downstairs next, chuckling as he raked back his shaggy light-brown hair that looked sun-kissed at the ends—a blatant lie, like his tan complexion, as he hardly ever got a lick of sun.

"It's not funny," Akira snapped.

"Oh, it's plenty funny," said Randall, tossing her a granola bar, though his own cheeks were a bit rosy.

I flicked Akira's arm. "Kiki, what *happened*?"

But she just flicked my arm back as Matty hustled downstairs last, Diet Coke in hand, honey-brown eyes glimmering with amusement under his backward blue baseball cap. "Your mom caught them necking in the pantry," he told me.

Randall shoved him playfully. "Yeah, whatever, man." Somehow Akira got even redder, even the tip of her nose.

"Oh, God." I laughed. "Did she try giving you 'the talk' or something?" Wouldn't put it past her.

"Nah, she was cool," said Randall.

"Unlike Akira's face." Matty flopped into his seat at Dad's old L-shaped desk.

Akira covered her flaming cheeks, but said with a smirk, "You're one to talk." Matty always blushed easily.

He guffawed as he hunched over his laptop to reload the game. He was built like a basketball player—tall, broad-shouldered, and lean—though the only sports he'd ever play were pixelated. His sparkling brown eyes, round cheeks, and oversize brown sweatshirt gave him teddy bear vibes, a stark contrast to his vicious mage avatar, best at conjuring sparks and fireballs.

"What happens if none of you hit twenty K?" Randall changed the subject as he took his seat next to Matty. He was our top archer, whose aim made everyone seem like inept storm troopers. It was no surprise he'd already hit twenty K, as had Dylan, those bastards.

"I love you guys, but we are *not* rock-paper-scissoring this shit," Matty groaned. None of us wanted to leave this up to chance.

"We'll get there," I said. That's why we were meeting so early on a Friday morning before school. We needed every spare minute to rack up MortalBucks. We only counted earnings at meetings; Randall couldn't exactly play while ringing up customers at Food Xpress.

"We could call it now," Zoey piped up.

Of course she'd suggest that—she had only slightly more MortalBucks than Akira, who was in last place. But she was lucky she still had a shot at playing in the tourney at all. If I hadn't kept my mouth shut—if everyone knew what she'd been doing the past few months—she'd be thrown off the team in a millisecond. She was good at pretending she hadn't done anything wrong.

To be fair, we all were. Except Dylan. He was free from the memories that plagued the rest of us. The memories that made me wake up screaming in the middle of the night five years later.

"Can we not?" Akira bristled, jarring me back to reality.

I glared at Zoey. "That would be fair . . . how, exactly?"

She scowled again. "I'm just saying—"

Matty grabbed a pencil from the desk and chucked it at Zoey, missing by about a mile. "Can you *stop* saying? Rules are rules." I grinned at him, and he rolled his eyes at Zoey, though pink spots colored his cheeks.

Zoey was still sulking as our dragons dropped us off on a fresh map. She always joked she had resting bitch face—though Akira and I referred to it more as *ax-murderer face*—but now she looked pointedly miserable, her full pink lips set in a pout, a line furrowed between her angled taupe eyebrows.

After a few minutes, Dylan nudged my elbow. "I've got a stockpile of health potions."

"No, thanks," I said, emptying a treasure chest. "Just found plenty."

He smirked. "I wasn't offering."

I snorted in response and met his gaze for a moment, catching the glint in his eye. He thought he was so freaking clever. Or cute. And maybe both of those things were true. But really, if it weren't for Dylan, we wouldn't be in this mess.

Over the summer, rumors swirled in the MortalDusk Discord about the annual championship. The tourneys in March would be statewide instead of regional, they said. Teams of six would compete instead of five, they said. More prizes than ever. A bigger New York City crown than ever. But we'd need another teammate to qualify. So we held tryouts the first week of junior year and recruited Dylan, the new boy in school. By the time MortalDusk announced the rules—statewide tourneys, but with teams of *five*—we couldn't exactly kick him out. Besides, he did boost our odds. He was a fierce enchanter, nimbly crafting potions and spells to eliminate our foes, with solid aim, speedy reflexes, a sharp jaw, defined cheekbones, tousled chestnut hair, and these steel-gray eyes—

Oh, crap. He started pounding on his keys, clearly in a firefight with Randall, who was also annihilating his space bar.

"We got company," said Randall.

"Dude," said Matty, "please don't tell me it's Fishman."

"It's Fishman." Dammit. Jeremy Fischer, alias Fishman, had dominated the top spot on the Vermont leaderboard for years—at least, until recently.

"Gah. Why's he playing this early?" Matty was especially determined to beat cocky streamers like Fishman who already had about a zillion followers and made plenty of cash.

"When is he *not* playing?" said Akira, tucking back a loose strand of black hair.

Ever since Fishman realized a group of bona fide competition lived one town over, he'd made it his personal mission to seek and destroy us. His audience thought it was a riot. He'd be at the tourney on Sunday, but fortunately, his teammates were a master class in mediocrity. Still, he'd give us major trouble in the solo competition.

Zoey glanced at her phone. "I *knew* I saw an alert that he went live."

"Thanks for the warning, boo," said Randall. He ran our team's YouTube and Twitch channels, though today Akira convinced him not to livestream while groggy as hell, pointing to his hair sticking up every which way.

I hurtled into the woods. "Where are you guys?"

Randall scratched at the hint of stubble on his square jaw. "Just north of Blackpool Lake."

"On my way."

"You don't have to," said Matty. I knew he wanted me to focus on landing more kills, to secure my spot on the team. But it'd be easier to kill Fishman together.

"If we don't take him out pronto, he'll hunt each of us down." Across the forest, I found Akira's elf sorceress building a wooden fortress on Blackpool Lake's shoreline. I preferred peasant garb for my avatar—lots of players mistook me for a newb, but I was a lethal assassin who'd shock them with my stealth prowess and deadly aim.

Matty was already on the roof, powering up his staff. "You got him, bro?"

"His shield's way up," said Randall. As I slinked from shrubbery to shrubbery, fire arrows flew between Randall's knight and Fishman's fisherman. But Fishman had the high ground and lunged at Randall.

Fishman854 has eliminated Ran_With_It with a flame rod.

"Gah!" Randall tugged back his unruly hair. "I hate when he

pulls that medieval Jedi shit. Where'd you go, man?" he asked Dylan.

"I had to brew more shield potions," said Dylan.

Zoey also seemed to be keeping her distance, probably hoping we'd take care of this.

Matty sniped one of Fishman's buddies with a bolt of lightning. "Nailed it." But Fishman deflected his next blast and danced as Matty powered up again, taunting him. "Son of a butthole."

I snuck behind Fishman. "I got him."

"No way. He's mine," said Matty. He used to be such a Fishman fanboy. Then everything changed. Suddenly, Matty's thick brows shot up. "He has a hellfire launcher!"

"Run!" said Akira. They leaped from the fortress as Fishman set it ablaze, narrowly escaping into the woods.

Matty cursed. "Crys, you got this."

Heck yes, I did.

I whipped out my shock staff and stalked Fishman, avoiding grazing the trees to remain undetected. My stomach did mini-somersaults—knowing his massive audience was watching was almost like getting stage fright. When I got close enough, I lined up my shot, fingers tingling with anticipation—

The basement door burst open with a crash. Startled, I missed my shot, my lightning bolt barely grazing Fishman. Mom thundered downstairs as she tied her disheveled curls into a messy bun. "Crystal, have you seen my keys?"

"Ugh, *Mom*—"

"I can't find them anywhere!"

Fishman spun and blasted me into oblivion. "Dammit." I

wiped a hand down my face. "They're not in your purse?" Akira had gone rigid, cheeks flushing again, still clearly embarrassed from earlier.

"No, obviously not." She mocked my voice, and we stuck our tongues out at each other, as per our ever-so-normal mother-daughter relationship. But stress lines deepened on her forehead.

"What's going on?" I asked.

"I was just called in for an emergency surgery. Two of the nurses are down with some stomach bug, so I've got a double shift now, and I have to drop off Caelyn at school first."

"Can't she take the bus—ah, crap," I said, remembering. "Frost Valley." It was the first Friday of March, so my little sister had to be dropped off two hours early today; her eighth-grade class was taking an overnight field trip to a mountain lodge for a full day of sledding, zip-lining, and cheesy team-building exercises.

"Yup," said Mom. "Everything always happens at once."

"Murphy's law," Randall chimed in.

"No, it's synchronous," said Zoey.

"Literally no one cares," said Randall, deadpan. Zoey glowered, but Akira chuckled and seemed to relax a bit. Randall's chest puffed slightly—he loved making her laugh. The others were busy casting ice spears at Fishman, who'd finally stopped gyrating over my dead avatar, gloating for his audience.

Mom sighed. "Either way, it's craptastic."

Lately, Mom struggled to squeeze much of anything between all the extra shifts she took to cover the bills. Still, the late-night screaming matches she used to have with my drunk of a father were even more craptastic. I'd gotten good at distracting Caelyn from those. When they started a few years ago, she'd slip into my room and crawl into my bed, and I'd helplessly clutch her skinny, trembling body close as we listened to them hollering. But then I started sticking huge headphones on her head and playing Mario Kart until it was over.

Video games were reliable like that. They can distract you from the pain. They can make the tears stop.

Now, Mom's pretty face seemed more haggard by the day, with purple half-moons like shiners under her eyes. Sometimes I thought she looked more stressed than before Dad left. *My fault my fault my fault.* My chest tightened.

"I'll drive Caelyn to school," I volunteered.

A collective grimace stretched across my friends' faces. We were running out of time to earn MortalBucks.

But Mom sighed gratefully. "Oh, *thank* you. But I still have to find my keys . . ." She started back upstairs, then paused. "Oh, and Caelyn forgot her inhaler in her locker. It's her last one, as usual. Make sure she runs in and grabs it before getting on the bus, okay?"

"Got it."

As she raced upstairs, I shut my laptop and smoothed down my mussed auburn curls. Those MortalBucks would have to wait. "I'm sorry, guys. We've still got tonight and all day tomorrow—"

"We can hold the fort until you get back," said Zoey, her amber eyes calculating. I'd be gone for half an hour. How perfect for her.

"You know what? I want Starbucks, anyway," said Akira,

seeing the anxiety on my face. Starbucks was right next to school. "Then we can meet up at the computer lab and play till first period."

"I'm down for S-bucks," said Randall.

"But the internet's faster here—" Dylan started. Distracted, his avatar collapsed. "Welp, so much for that." He shut his laptop.

"Sorry . . ." I said again, digging my phone from the couch cushions between us. My knuckles grazed Dylan's jeans, but he stood before he could see me blush.

"Yeah, what gives, Crystal?" Matty screwed up his face exaggeratedly. "Way to be a good daughter."

"Ugh, good daughters are the *worst,*" said Randall.

"Disgusting, honestly," said Matty. His and Randall's eyes twinkled mischievously, as they always did when the two were bantering. If we were streaming, our audience would be eating this up.

"Your face is disgusting," I shot back.

Matty grinned. "Nailed it." He stretched his arms overhead, nearly touching the ceiling. "Alright, I'll drop you guys off at Starbucks, then I gotta shower." I knew that was just his excuse to avoid Starbucks. A few months ago, I ordered a soy Frappuccino, and they gave me an almond milk Frappuccino instead. Then Matty took a sip, and, well, it wasn't a good day. There were lots of needles involved. I couldn't blame him for being traumatized. Even trace amounts of peanuts or tree nuts caused an allergic reaction, and he was sick to death of it.

"Gross." Randall cringed. "Were you not going to shower today?"

"What?" Matty sniffed his pits. "I don't smell, do I?"

"You always smell," said Randall.

"Like roses," said Matty.

"Dead roses," Dylan joined in. Randall guffawed and offered his fist for a bump. Dylan had been quick to pick up on our particular brand of humor, though I could always tell when the others were joking. I was never sure with him.

By the time we trooped upstairs, Mom was gone—she must've found her keys—and my sister, Caelyn, was leaning against the coat closet, fidgeting with her handcrafted lightning bolt charm necklace that matched the one hanging from my neck.

"Hey, li'l twerp," I teased, still in banter mode, fumbling my boots on. "Aren't you a troublemaker?"

She remained silent, refusing to look at my friends as they streamed out the front door, even when Akira gave her arm a friendly poke. Caelyn's messily braided auburn curls created a frizzy halo around her face in the dawn light, and her thick purple glasses magnified her huge hazel eyes, identical to mine except for the fact that all she could see were blurred blobs. She'd begged Mom for contacts, but Mom said she had to wait until she was sixteen. Though it wasn't like contacts would be any cheaper when she turned sixteen.

"Let's go." Not bothering to zip my coat, I dashed down the front walkway to my car, a decade-old Prius Dad left me as a parting gift—well, more of a bribe, actually—before moving to Las Vegas. Caelyn and I hadn't heard from him since, which honestly suited us fine.

As Akira and Randall climbed into Matty's car, Zoey bolted to her house next door. "What the hell's she trying to pull?" I muttered, realizing we'd forgotten to tally our MortalBucks totals. Would she skip Starbucks to sneak in an extra round?

Dylan chuckled, waiting by his Jeep since Matty's car blocked him in, hands stuffed into the pockets of his blue-and-white-plaid jacket.

"What's so funny?" I called over.

"You are. Paranoid much?"

I made a face. Easy for him to say—he'd already secured his spot at the tourney. But he was probably right. Maybe Zoey was checking in with her super-strict parents. They only let her come over so often because they thought our esports team was a study group.

As I grabbed Caelyn's duffel and chucked it into the back seat, she muttered, "I'm sorry."

"What're you sorry for?" I slammed the door.

"I'm trouble . . . and you were busy . . ."

"Oh, I was kidding. It's not your fault. Let's make it snappy, though, okay?" I hurled myself into the driver's seat and clucked my tongue, waiting until Caelyn was buckled in before backing down the driveway.

Since the roads were empty, I surged past the speed limit, desperate to make good time. I had to get more kills—more than Zoey, at least. But I quickly hit a red light. Dammit. There were only so many traffic laws I was willing to break.

I drummed my fingers on the steering wheel and glanced at Caelyn. Her nose was pink, a telltale sign she was holding back tears. Shouldn't she be brimming with excitement? Did she really think I was mad at her?

"I'm not mad," I said.

"I know," she mumbled. But she kept moping.

My heart sank. Maybe I shouldn't have called her a twerp. I was only joking. Sure, sometimes Caelyn annoyed the heck out of me. But I loved her to death. She had this way of brightening a room with her boundless energy, always showing off some funky new fashion creation, always a willing opponent when I wanted to play a game. When Dad made her go quiet and small, I hated him for stifling her spark. It blazed again once he left, thank God. But now she was acting all weird.

"Hey." I flicked her arm. "What's wrong?"

Her cheeks flushed to match her nose. "Nothing."

"Liar, liar, pants on fire."

She merely snorted.

The light turned green, and I hit the gas, giving us both whiplash. Oops. "Sorry. Aren't you excited about Frost Valley?"

"I don't want to go on this stupid trip."

My jaw dropped. "Um, excuse me? A sleepover a hundred miles away from any parentals is basically a thirteen-year-old's dream come true." She only shrugged, so I went on, "There'll be sledding! And zip-lining!"

Caelyn cringed. "I'm afraid of heights."

"Since when?" *She'd* dragged *me* onto every roller coaster at Six Flags last summer. I still had flashbacks of my feet suspended over blue skies, and that terrible drop in my stomach after cresting each peak. I'd sucked it up to make her happy. But now her eyes were brimming with tears. Something was bothering her . . . and it wasn't the prospect of dangling from ropes.

"What's really going on?" I whipped around a curve, imagining Zoey smugly cracking her knuckles after landing a kill.

Caelyn shook her head. "I don't want to get into it."

"Aw, c'mon, Cae. You can tell me anything."

She rubbed her eyes and sighed. "Tessa and her friends are gonna pull some prank on me. I know it."

Ah. Tessa was the ringleader of a group of catty girls in Caelyn's grade. Caelyn had been so excited to turn thirteen and create an Instagram account—she dreamed of being an influencer with her chic handcrafted creations—but Tessa quickly ruined it for her, commenting with mockery and insults on each photo.

Yet another spark stifler. The world was full of them.

"Did you overhear her planning something?" I asked.

"No . . ."

"Well, then, you're probably being paranoid." Just like I was with Zoey. "Don't worry about Tessa. Just stick with Deja and Suki." They'd been a steadfast trio since kindergarten.

"They're going next weekend."

"Oh, shoot." Since Frost Valley was only so big, they split the eighth grade into three groups to go on consecutive weekends. "Did you ask to switch groups?"

Caelyn nodded. "Yeah. But they wouldn't let me. Then they'd have to let anyone who wanted to switch, switch."

I floored the gas to make a yellow light. We were only a couple of blocks from Caelyn's school now. "Well, if Tessa tries anything, laugh it off."

Caelyn screwed up her face. "*What?*"

"I'm serious. Think of it like a game. The more she upsets you, the more points she gets—"

"Oh, please."

"No, really! And the more points she gets, the meaner she'll get. But if she sees you don't give a shit, she won't get any points, and she'll get bored and move on to someone else."

"It's not a game." Her voice trembled as she wiped away a tear. "She's always picking on me."

"Yeah, well, she can probably read you like a book. Whenever you get upset, you turn bright red or start crying right away. That's, like, the mother lode of points."

"Shut up."

"I'm serious, Cae. If she does anything to you, just laugh and walk away."

"I can't." Caelyn raised her voice.

I stopped at a stop sign across the street from her school. "Well, why not?"

"Because I can't just laugh it off. Not everything is a game. She's so mean, and all her friends egg her on. Maybe *you're* a good actress. Maybe *you* can pretend like everything's fine when it's not. But I can't."

Her barb sucked the wind from my lungs, and I froze, gawking at her. Did she *know*? How could she know about that? She was only eight years old when it happened, and I never told her the truth—I never told a soul.

"We're going to have to move soon," she went on, "you know it. I heard what Mom told you. One more missed payment, and the bank will take the house, and we'll have to move in with Grandma Rose. And all you can think about is your stupid video game."

I let out a deep exhale, my heart pummeling my rib cage. She didn't know. But since when did she resent MortalDusk? Video games were my refuge from the guilt that would otherwise slither through my mind like a serpent eager to feed. I thought games were a distraction for Caelyn, too. But maybe I'd buried my head in the sand so deep I didn't realize how they affected her.

The car behind me honked, and I jumped. "Dammit." I drove into the school parking lot. "Well . . . think of it this way." I kept my tone light as I pulled up behind the lineup of cars dropping kids off. Two huge coach buses stood at the front of the line, and kids and teachers clustered next to them, white puffs of steam escaping their mouths as they chattered excitedly in the crisp morning air. "If we *do* move, you'll be rid of Tessa forever—"

"Are you serious? I don't want to move to Maine! I don't want to leave my friends. Do you? Do you even care about *anything* in the real world?"

My stomach clenched. Of course I did. I wanted that prize money to help Mom and Caelyn, so we wouldn't have to move. So I wouldn't have to leave my friends. I adored them, the way we slipped into our easy banter, the way we could spend hours together playing games and never get bored, the way we stuck together no matter what. I couldn't imagine ever finding another group like them. That's why I *had* to win the tourney.

Before I could reply, Caelyn pushed her door open. But we couldn't leave it like this. It would kill me to leave it like this. "Wait—" I started.

"No." She was already climbing out. "I have to get my inhaler. I can't just *laugh it off* if I have an asthma attack." She grabbed her duffel from the back seat and slammed the door, and I watched helplessly as she headed toward the school, avoiding the crowds, her bag bumping against her hip with each step.

Resolve coiled around my heart. I had to win that money for

our family. I had to prove to my sister that I cared about way more than MortalDusk—and that a video game could amount to something *real*.

Something more than a way to hide from the terrible thing I did. Something more than a way to escape from my own memories.

I had to win that prize. And first I had to get those kills.

CHAPTER 2

I didn't get those kills.

My stomach roiled just thinking about it. When I got to the computer lab at school, my friends were already there, waiting for me, but Zoey was missing. Zoey was staying home from school "sick" today. Zoey would get to play MortalDusk all day. Zoey was a horrible, sneaky, selfish, two-timing—

"You're gonna take someone's eye out with that," Dylan whispered as he poked my shoulder blade. I flinched and dropped my pencil, which I'd been aggressively twirling between my third and fourth fingers, a habit I'd picked up years ago.

"Shit," I said way louder than I'd meant to. Our whole history class turned to look at me—even Mr. Richardson, who'd been droning on about the United States electoral college. Dylan chortled under his breath while Matty, sitting at the desk beside mine, threw me a sympathetic look.

"Yes, actually." Mr. Richardson nodded. "Many would agree with you that the system is quite flawed. But . . . please watch your language, Crystal."

"Sorry." I scooped up the pencil and twirled it again. Whenever I was bored or antsy, my fingers groped for a pen or pencil, eager for the soothing rhythm.

And I was antsy as hell right now.

Not only would Zoey gain an advantage today, but my sister was furious with me, and there was absolutely nothing I could do about it until she got home tomorrow afternoon. There was no signal at Frost Valley, and the kids were supposed to turn in their phones for a technology-free two days, anyway. And then I'd be at the MortalDusk tourney in Burlington on Sunday. *All you can think about is your stupid video game.* God, what a mess. I hated leaving arguments unresolved. The tension mounted in my gut until I wanted to throw up. Ugh, how was I going to get through forty more minutes of this lecture, and then two more classes?

I must have looked a bit green, because Matty leaned over and whispered, "You look like you're about to yak."

I shook my head. "I'm fine."

"Don't worry. You'll make the team. You only need, what, ten more kills?"

"Eighteen," I said.

Matty shrugged. "No sweat. You got this."

"It's not just that . . . It's my sister . . ." I bit my lip and glanced at Mr. Richardson, who clicked to the next slide in his Power-Point as he drawled on.

"What about her?" Matty's golden eyes searched my face.

"We had this big fight this morning . . . She totally hates me right now."

He snorted softly. "Oh, please. She wouldn't know how to hate someone if they were chucking hamsters at her face."

I bit back a laugh. "Mm, she'd actually love that." Caelyn adored all fuzzy creatures. "No, but seriously . . . she's angry I play MortalDusk so much."

"No way. She made your tourney costume, didn't she?"

"Yeah . . ."

"You're just chomping on nothingburgers," Dylan chimed in.

I swiveled in my chair. "Can you not right now?"

"Can I not what?" said Dylan, adjusting his glasses, feigning innocence. Was he trying to mock me or reassure me? His tone and steely eyes made it impossible to tell.

I narrowed my eyes at him, and he stared right back, lifting the corner of his mouth slightly. My heart did this weird little flutter, and I faced forward again. God, I could not figure that kid out. He was a walking contradiction—he aced every exam, yet barely studied; he killed at MortalDusk, yet never wanted to stream; he ranted about social media being society's downfall, yet wanted to study algorithms and AI at MIT.

And I could never tell when he was serious or throwing me shade. All I knew was that his acerbic wit and razor-sharp snark sent a strange thrill down my spine. That his quizzical, almost unnaturally gray eyes made the butterflies in my stomach flip out. But I hated how I couldn't read him. How I couldn't stop my insides from going all mushy around him. How Zoey had thrown herself at him at Lucia Ramirez's party the other weekend.

She must've known about my mushy insides.

It was like everything she did, she did to beat me.

I shook away the thought and focused on the lesson, taking thorough notes to distract my brain from replaying over and over the image of Caelyn slamming the door in my face, or Zoey's smug look warping her sharp features, or Fishman dancing over my dead avatar. It was like anxiety had permeated every neuron in my brain.

The sound of Dylan *tick-a-tick* typing on his keyboard behind me wasn't helping. Most people took notes on their school-provided Chromebooks, but I preferred handwriting my notes. Otherwise I'd end up playing the unblocked games I'd downloaded and miss the entire lesson. There's always a way to get past the school's IT team.

And the temptation was too real.

After a few minutes, someone's phone buzzed nearby. I glanced around, but nobody moved to check theirs. Was it mine? I thought I'd silenced it. We were allowed to keep our phones with us as long as we kept them silenced and tucked away during class. Mr. Richardson was staring at his presentation, waiting for some animation to load. A quick peek wouldn't kill anyone. I dug my cell from the front compartment of my backpack and surreptitiously dropped it onto my lap.

Sure enough, there was a notification on my screen. *An-0nym0us1 sent you a message.* Huh. The notification showed the app's logo—a silver serpent wrapped around a red microphone.

I didn't recognize it. Curious, I tapped the notification and unlocked my phone.

A message flashed across my screen.

React to this, and she dies. Show this to anyone, and she dies.

I scrunched my brow. Before I could question it, a video message started playing. The sound was off, but the visual alone made
my heart lurch into my throat so fast I thought I might choke.

The video showed Caelyn gagged and bound to a chair, struggling against the restraints.

No. That couldn't be her. It couldn't be.

The camera panned closer. Her auburn curls were no longer braided, but hung loose around her face, shrouding her in
shadow. Her thick glasses were slightly askew. It was unmistak-
ably my baby sister.

My chair made a loud screech as I reflexively scooted back
and hit Dylan's desk, and a cry threatened to escape from my
lips. *React to this, and she dies.* I just reacted, didn't I? What did
that mean? What the hell did that mean?

"A problem, Crystal?" Mr. Richardson asked. Everyone in
class had turned to stare at me again. Matty gave me a question-
ing look.

"I, uh—" My heart ricocheted off my ribs like a rabid animal
in a cage as panic flooded my veins. I wanted to show Matty the
video. I wanted him to assure me it wasn't real. But if it was, I
couldn't show him. What should I do? What the hell should
I do? I gripped my stomach. "Bathroom?"

Lucia Ramirez giggled in the front row.

"Food poisoning isn't funny!" I yelled without thinking. Her smile collapsed.

Mr. Richardson raised his eyebrows. "Go, take the hall pass. And then, erm, go to the nurse's office, if you need to."

I didn't need to make a show of swallowing hard—the lemon loaf Akira had brought me from Starbucks was threatening to escape, food poisoning or not. "Thanks."

I grabbed my backpack, barreled down the aisle, and tripped on the front leg of Lucia's desk. I caught myself before biting it. A few more people laughed, and my cheeks caught fire as I grabbed the hall pass and scrammed.

Out in the hall, I darted into an alcove between lockers leading to a supply closet, turned up the volume just enough for me to hear it, and watched the video again. It replayed the same fifteen-second loop over and over. Caelyn couldn't say anything with the gag in her mouth, but she let out these garbled sobbing noises that tore my soul in half. I couldn't make out where Caelyn was—the room was dark, the only light source seemingly coming from the camera itself. This couldn't be real. This absolutely could not be real.

Suddenly, the video disappeared, and a message replaced it, red text on a stark white screen.

Let's play a game.

A *game*? What game? There was no text box in which to type a reply. I glanced around, but the hall was deserted.

You have 24 hours to win. If you break my rules, she dies. If
you call the police, she dies. If you tell your parents or anyone
else, she dies. If you don't respond to my messages within a
minute, she dies. If you lose or forfeit, she dies.

I clasped my mouth as my throat gurgled with a suppressed
scream.

Are you ready?

Was I *ready*? What the actual fuck?

I leaned back against the closet door, trying to catch my
breath. Breathe. Breathe. I had to breathe. I had to think.

First of all, this couldn't possibly be real. It had to be some
sort of prank. Yes, that was it. An extremely well-executed prank.
I glanced at my Fitbit, which Mom got for free at the hospital. It
was just past 1:00 p.m. Frost Valley was almost a two-hour drive
from here, so Caelyn would've arrived hours ago. Maybe she was
getting back at me for this morning. Yes, that made sense. She
got one of her friends to tie her up and record this . . .

Nope, said a voice in the back of my mind. *She'd never do this.*
But what about that bully of hers, Tessa? Caelyn was specifically
afraid of her—afraid she was going to pull some prank on her.
Yes, that had to be it!

I tapped the text box that appeared and typed, Haha, very
funny, Tessa.

This is not a joke. This is not Tessa. If you don't play my game,
your sister dies.

I banged the back of my head against the door. If this was Tessa, she *could* be lying. But wouldn't she have turned in her phone by now? Still, there was no way this was real. I dropped Caelyn off at school this morning. She got on the bus to Frost Valley. She was with her class now, enjoying the crisp mountain air.

I never saw her get on the bus.

Oh, God. I cringed and covered my eyes. Last I saw her, she was running into the school for her inhaler. I should have waited. I should have made sure she left the school and got on the bus with everyone else. What if she really was kidnapped? What if some sociopath really wanted to torture us?

I typed, my fingers trembling, Caelyn's supposed to be on a field trip. Her teachers will know she's missing. So will my mom. You won't get away with this.

Her teachers think she's home with the flu.

Dammit. Who the hell could this be? I stared at the username, An0nym0us1. No clues whatsoever. Whoever it was must have called in sick for Caelyn, pretending to be Mom. If this were real, I couldn't call the emergency contact at Frost Valley to confirm that's what happened. This anonymous person might know, and I'd be breaking their rules. And all the while, Mom would think Caelyn was safe on her field trip.

That meant nobody would suspect a thing, at least not until tomorrow afternoon when Caelyn was due home. Someone *had* to have spotted her outside the school. A teacher, or a classmate. Someone had to have seen she wasn't really home sick. Someone had to suspect *something*.

Before I could type anything else, a new message flashed across my screen.

If you think I didn't think of everything, your sister won't survive.

My God. I blinked away tears and shook my head. I had to stay calm and figure this out. But I still couldn't believe this was real. **Let me talk to her.**

I'm the one who gives the instructions. Are you ready to play?

I tapped everywhere on the screen, trying to navigate back to the video of Caelyn. But all I could do was close the app and re-open it, and it would only show the most recent message. Each message vanished as soon as a new one arrived. Were they deleted? Maybe it just wasn't obvious how to find older messages.

Maybe I could google it.

I closed the app to see what it was called and found the silver serpent icon on my third home screen; the most recent app installed. I hadn't installed it. How'd it get here? Did someone hack my phone or something? There was no text label below it, only three periods. No app name to look up.

An alert from the app popped up atop my screen. **She dies in 5.**

I opened the app.

4.

Oh, God.

3.

Oh no. I had no choice. I had to do this. Frantically, I typed my reply.

I'm ready.

CHAPTER 3

Once last year, when Mom and Dad were having yet another screaming match, Caelyn and I waited it out in my room, huge headphones glomming our skulls as we played Mario Kart with the volume turned all the way up. Caelyn was winning because I was letting her, and as she whipped around a bend to finish the second lap, there was a shriek down the hall so loud it pierced through the music and fanfare blasting in my ears. I slipped my headphones off one ear as footsteps pounded toward my room, my father's drunken drawl growing louder and louder.

"Danny, no!" Mom yelled. Caelyn's eyes were trained on the screen as she dropped a trail of bananas behind her kart, like she didn't hear any of it. But when our parents crashed against my bedroom door, she heard. Her eyes widened and welled with tears. I tugged her close, burying her face in my chest as Mom protected us from the monster booze turned Dad into. *This is it,* I thought. *This is the night he'll finally turn his fists on us.* My heart pounded in terror, and helplessness sucked the air from my lungs. If Mom couldn't stop him, I certainly couldn't. I wasn't strong enough. There was nothing I could do to protect my baby sister from such inexplicable rage.

That's how I felt now, my pulse thrashing in my ears as I awaited An0nymQus1's instructions. The image of Caelyn bound and gagged burned in my memory. If this was real . . . if she was tied up, alone with some psychopath in some isolated place . . . she must be terrified. And there was no way to know where she was. No way to save her, to assure her that everything would be okay. There was absolutely nothing I could do—except play her kidnapper's game.

Finally, a message appeared.

Let's play *The Number Thief*. Next week's key is locked under a desk upstairs in a room that adds up to 5 in its prime. Deliver the key to a locker double plus 9. You have 20 minutes. Ready? GO!

What? I reread the message twice more, but it felt like my brain's synapses were exploding without relaying any signals.

I had to find a *key*? Why different keys for different weeks? And why would it be locked up? Wouldn't you need a key to unlock the thing itself? Unless they meant . . . an *answer key*?

Holy hell. Someone kidnapped my sister and was holding her hostage so they could *cheat on a test*?

I tapped the text field, fully intending to send a response in the vein of, *Are you absolutely out of your fucking mind?* But I hesitated. Obviously, this person was out of their fucking mind.

So insulting or provoking them probably wasn't the best idea. But this had to be some sort of joke, or a prank, or something.

But what if it wasn't?

I wiped a trembling hand down my face. What the hell should I do? I had to think for a minute—though apparently, I only had twenty of them. *Think, Crystal. Think.*

Alright. The way I saw it, I had three options. Option one, do nothing. See what happened when the time ran out. But if this was real . . . my sister would die. Okay, so option one was out.

Option two, get help. Call the police, or call Mom. But she was probably in the middle of assisting a surgery. Dad was useless out in Vegas, probably in some casino blowing the cash he used to pay the mortgage with. But again, if this was real, and this lunatic somehow found out I told someone . . . my sister would die.

Option three, play this "game." If this were just a prank, okay—I'd swipe some stupid answer key, and Caelyn would be fine, and everything would be fine. But if it wasn't a prank, her life hinged on me being stealthy. Sneaking around in a video game was one thing. But in real life, I was a total klutz. What if I couldn't do it?

I typed out: What happens if I get caught?

She dies.

No hesitation. It was like a sucker punch to the gut. I was really going to have to do this, wasn't I?

At the same time . . . games were literally my life. If there was anyone who could win—well, whatever the hell this was—it was me.

They'd picked the wrong opponent.

I studied the clue, which had reappeared. Next week's key is locked under a desk upstairs in a room that adds up to 5 in its prime. Deliver the key to a locker double plus 9.

Video games had taught me to think fast and logically, even as adrenaline flooded my veins. I got this.

Okay, so—our school had three floors, and if the room was upstairs, it had to be between 201 and 399; actually, 326, since the room numbers didn't go higher. *Adds up to 5*—meaning its digits? The number 212 worked. So did 203, 221, 230, 302, 311, and 320. *In its prime*, though. A prime number? Even numbers were out, then, but were the others prime? Ugh, math. I pinched the bridge of my nose. Thirteen times seventeen was 221. That left 203 and 311 . . . damn. I scrolled to my calculator and quickly did some random-ass division to find out 203 was divisible by seven. So 311 was the only other option. And the locker—*double plus 9*—double what? Double the room number? If so, 631. Easy.

Or was it *too* easy?

Maybe it was easy on purpose, if they wanted that answer key. Anger simmered in my veins; nothing made my blood boil like cheaters.

Room 311 was in the math wing. I only ever looked at the room numbers on the first day of school when finding my new classes, but I was pretty sure that was my precalculus classroom.

And we did have an exam next week—not that I'd planned to study this weekend. That could wait until Monday; the Mortal-Dusk tourney was my top priority.

Well . . . it *had* been my top priority.

Just a few hours ago, I was stressed about Zoey scoring twenty thousand MortalBucks before I did. How the hell had I gone from that to *this*?

Balling my hands into fists, I headed for the stairwell, but Mr. Richardson's door opened behind me.

"Crys!"

Crap. It was Matty. And I was walking toward the ladies' room, where presumably I should have already been, er . . . experiencing food poisoning. I turned to face him.

Concern etched lines across his forehead. "Are you okay?"

"Yeah, just, uh"—I gripped my stomach—"not sure it's over."

"Want me to take you to the nurse's office?"

I waved him off. "No, I'll be fine. You go ahead." I motioned toward the men's room down the hall.

"Nah, I left to check on you." He adjusted his baseball cap over his short, ashy-blond hair, but couldn't hide the way his cheeks flamed like he'd just chowed down on a bucket of jalapeños.

I bit my lip and averted my gaze.

Dammit. Randall was right, wasn't he? Two weeks ago at Lucia Ramirez's party, I'd been moping on the sectional after Zoey dragged Dylan to the beer pong table—wishing I were so bold, wishing I'd worn the cute outfit Caelyn laid out for me instead of my THIS PRINCESS CAN SAVE HERSELF hoodie, wishing the music were loud enough to drown out Zoey's flirtatious laughter—when Randall flopped down beside me. Next thing I knew, we were sipping God-knew-what from red Solo cups, placing bets on how long it would take Jasmine Chopra to make a move on Matty. The gorgeous cheerleading captain had been flirting with him for weeks, to the shock of no one—Matty was a good-looking, charming nerd. A winning combo.

I'd eyed them chatting by the fireplace. "Five bucks on five minutes from now."

"No way," said Randall. "Twenty."

"Bucks or minutes?"

"Both."

I winced. That was a lot of cash. "Does flirty touching count?" I caressed his arm to demonstrate.

He snorted. "Fine."

Unable to resist a good bet, I tapped my cup against his. "You're on."

As we surreptitiously watched them, I asked, "Why do you think he won't ask her out already? Or Sara? Or Maddy?" Matty never wound up dating the girls who fawned over him.

"You're kidding, right?" He scoffed like he thought I was being deliberately obtuse.

Was this still a sore point for Randall? He and Akira had been dating for months. "Uh . . . no?"

Randall looked me square in the eye and said, like it was the most obvious thing in the world, "Because they're not *you*."

You'd think a revelation like that would make my heart drop, or my breath catch, or my face go beet red. But nope. Nada. I loved Matty and all, but we'd been friends since we were diaper-bound. I'd never even considered becoming more; if anything, I'd assumed the thought of kissing someone he'd once seen puke all over herself in a bouncy castle would make him a bit cringey. So I felt . . . nothing. Instead, my eyes flicked to Dylan—the brooding snark factory—lining up his next shot at the beer pong table. He's what made my heart wobble. Randall had laughed. "And Matty's not *him*. Funny how that works."

Matty moved closer, snapping me from the memory. "Crys, you're shaking. What's going on?" Of course he'd know something was wrong. He knew my tells. He knew when I was lying. But I didn't have time for this. I had to get to room 311.

"I'm sick, Matty," I snapped. "That's what happens when you're sick. You get all shaky and stuff. Just go back to class, okay? I can take care of myself." I spun toward the ladies' room.

But he took my hand before I could disappear inside. "Wait!"

I gasped and yanked my hand back. He hadn't grabbed it hard or anything—it was just a reflex—but he knew why I reacted like that, and his eyes widened with regret.

"Oh, geez, I'm *so* sorry. I'm the human equivalent of a fart."

"No, it's fine." It wasn't his fault I was so uptight.

He rubbed the back of his neck. "It's just, when you left class . . . you looked *terrified*. I haven't seen you look like that since . . ." He trailed off, and a dark look crossed his face. I swallowed hard. I knew what he was thinking.

I wanted to confide in him so badly. If there was anyone I could trust, it was him. But if I told *anyone* what was happening, and Caelyn's kidnapper found out—no, I couldn't risk it.

"Yeah, I was terrified to hurl in the middle of class—" I

gripped my mouth, pretending a new wave of nausea was surging up my throat. Casting him an apologetic look, I sprinted to the ladies' room, slammed the door, and made some convincing retching sounds.

After flushing the empty toilet, I checked the time. Fourteen minutes left. I had to move. I inched open the door and peeked into the hall to make sure the coast was—

Someone shoved open the door, and I flailed backward.

"Oh, God, I'm sorry—oh." As soon as Lucia Ramirez laid eyes on me, her face morphed from apologetic to agitated. What, had she come to cackle at me some more?

Lucia had been bitter since she didn't make the cut for our esports team. I felt terrible for how tryouts went down, but honestly, what did she expect? As Zoey's biggest competition for class valedictorian (much to Zoey's parents' chagrin), Lucia was clearly smart, but she had no aim whatsoever. It's not like the varsity softball team would recruit someone who couldn't catch a ball. But then she tried to get revenge. Key word: tried.

"Are you okay?" Lucia asked. Did she mean after nearly whaling me in the face with a door, or my supposed ailment?

"I'm fine," I huffed. Why couldn't everyone just stay in class? She awkwardly blocked the door, just like at her party when she'd stopped me on my way out. "Your sweater's adorable," she'd said, her sweetness fake as aspartame. She'd totally invited us as a bribe of sorts, not because she genuinely wanted us there. I'd shot back, "Oh, please. Your brownie points are rancid."

We hadn't spoken since, but I didn't have time for her drama right now. "Excuse me." I brushed past her and out into the hall, where the coast was, in fact, clear, and hustled to the third floor.

Yep, room 311 was Mrs. Chesser's precalc class, which I had next period. Was there a class in there now? I crept past the door, craning my neck to see through the window.

The room was deserted.

I dashed inside and shut the door, trying not to think about how getting busted would land me a suspension. That was the penalty for cheating or plagiarism—there were no slaps on the wrist at Newboro High. You cheat, and it goes on your permanent record. And if I failed, Caelyn would pay the steepest price. My heart was officially trying to eject itself from my chest cavity.

Next week's key is locked under a desk . . . A file cabinet was nestled under the teacher's desk. If I was right about the clue, the answer key must be in there. Oh, God. I'd never so much as stolen a lip gloss from CVS. Was I really going to do this?

Caelyn's gurgling scream flashed through my memory.

Yes.

Yes, I was.

I tugged the file cabinet's top drawer, but it wouldn't budge. Locked. Because of course it was. The bottom drawer was locked as well. I glared at the keyhole in the top-right corner. I knew how to pick locks in plenty of video games, but in real life? Forget it.

Maybe Mrs. Chesser kept the key nearby.

I slid open the top desk drawer and scanned the impeccably organized contents—neat rows of pens, pencils, chalk, calculators . . . and there was the key. Which was really dumb. Someone really ought to tell Mrs. Chesser how dumb that was.

It took me a few tries to get the key in the lock thanks to my trembling fingers, but eventually I managed it and yanked open the top drawer. It was stuffed with manila file folders, all labeled in Mrs. Chesser's neat cursive. The first one had next Tuesday's date on the tab. I grabbed it and set it on the desk. She'd already made copies. I quickly scanned the first one. Yes, this looked like what would be on next week's test. But where were the answers? I slipped out the last exam in the pile.

Sure enough, it was marked up with how we should "show our work" to arrive at each solution. The answer key. That woman was organized to a fault. I could only imagine her house—carpets freshly steamed, kitchen counters clutter-free and gleaming, bank account passwords neatly listed on the fridge.

I returned the folder, locked the file cabinet, and left the key in the exact position I'd found it. How did An0nym0us1 think they'd get away with this? Surely Mrs. Chesser would notice her answer key missing before next Tuesday—she'd probably notice a single paper clip out of place. And once she knew, she'd probably create a new test.

Shaking my head, I started stuffing the answer key into my backpack.

At that exact moment, someone opened the door.

CHAPTER 4

Mrs. Chesser walked in, and my heart actually stopped. According to science, I should have died.

"Crystal!" She tucked her blunt-cut shoulder-length hair behind her ear as she glanced at her phone. "Don't we still have twenty minutes till next period?"

Thinking fast, I shoved the answer key deeper into my bag and whipped out my math binder. "Yeah. I'm not feeling well, so I'm heading home early. I just wanted to drop off my homework first." I tried to keep my voice steady as I found yesterday's homework assignment, which I'd rushed through between classes earlier this morning before my world turned upside down. It was probably mostly incorrect, but that was the least of my worries.

She frowned. "Oh, honey, you could've just handed it in on Monday." She took it from me and glanced over the sheet, her frown deepening. "In fact, maybe you should take the weekend—"

"Cool, thanks." I snatched back the paper. "I'd better go! Really not feeling well."

Before she could say anything else, I darted out the door and down the hall. Now, where the heck was locker 631? I glanced at the nearest locker: 3135.

My locker was . . . I didn't even remember the number, just that it was right next to the water fountain in the history wing. It was mainly a glorified coatrack, since most of my textbooks were online this year.

My phone buzzed. It was a notification from An0nym0us1.

5 minutes until she dies.

"I know, I know," I whined and typed out: I got the test.

4 minutes, 40 seconds until she dies.

Jesus. Okay, the locker had to be downstairs. I raced down to the second floor—nope, the lockers by the stairwell were in the mid-thousands. It had to be on the first floor. I went all the way downstairs and down the hall, past my locker, breathing fast as I scanned the numbers.

There it was. Locker 631. Right near Mr. Richardson's class.

While most lockers were assigned, there were random empties scattered throughout the building. The combination locks were built into each locker, so I had no clue whether this one belonged to anyone. I tried the handle, but it was locked.

I sent a message to An0nym0us1: Locker 631, right? What's the combo?

2 minutes until she dies.

What the hell? I pressed a palm to my forehead. *Think.* I had to think. I glanced up—the vents at the top of the locker extended nearly the full width of the narrow metal door. I dropped my backpack and yanked out the exam, folded it in half, and slid it through one of the vents, prodding the edges until they no longer peeked out.

I typed another message: It's done.

No response.

The test is in the locker.

No response.

Oh, God. What was going on? Was I too late? Did he—or she—whoever it was, had they already killed my sister? I did what they said to do. I did it within twenty minutes. Why weren't they answering me?

Let me talk to my sister.

No response.

I paced in front of the locker, glancing down the deserted hall. If anyone walked by, they'd think I was a total freak show. I dodged into a nearby stairwell to continue my frenzied pacing in private.

Finally, my phone buzzed.

Let's play *Concentration*. Get the package from locker 499. The combination is 17–35–23. You have 10 minutes. Ready? GO!

Um. So much for riddles—

Suddenly, my screen flashed, and a picture appeared. A gloved hand gripped a chef's knife in front of Caelyn, who was out of focus in the background. The blade gleamed from the camera's flash, and the glove was black and thick, like an insulated ski glove. My heart plummeted so aggressively I thought my organs would reshuffle. Caelyn must be petrified. What if she had an asthma attack during all this? Would the kidnapper let her use her inhaler? Would—

A new message appeared.

Did you concentrate?

Tendrils of heat snaked up my neck. Damn. This was a memory game. That photo was a distraction, and I fell for it like an anvil. I'd forgotten everything—the locker number, the combination, all of it.

Okay, wait. I squeezed my eyes shut, struggling to remember. Locker . . . 499, right? And the first number was 17—I remembered because Akira just turned seventeen last week, and my brain had involuntarily made the association.

But the rest? Gone.

Well, I could at least find the locker.

I slipped back into the hall. There were still twelve minutes left in this period. I skittered past Mr. Richardson's room and found locker 499 close by. Leaning against it, I strained to visualize the remaining numbers. The second was 25, maybe? But the third number may as well have been in hieroglyphics.

I shot off a message: I don't remember the third number.

8 minutes until she dies.

Frustrated, I wiped my forehead. If I was right about the first two numbers, there were forty possible combinations. Could I try forty combinations in eight minutes? Blowing air between my lips, I turned the dial with trembling fingers, accidentally going past 17. Guh. I tried again, this time accidentally going past 25. I shook out my hand. *Get a grip. You can open a lock.*

I tried each permutation, starting with 0 for the last number. Each time I tugged the handle, it wouldn't budge. Finally, I got to 39. This had to be it. The last possibility. I spun the dial and jerked the handle.

Nope.

Alright. Think. I must have been misremembering 25, because I was 100 percent sure the first number was 17.

I tried again, shaking my head each time the handle stayed rigid. Tears of frustration welled in my eyes. I must have been out of time by now. An0nym0us1 hadn't said anything. Were they hurting Caelyn? Were they plunging that knife into her body? My chest tightened. What should I do? Should I call for help? Should I keep trying to get the locker open? I jiggled the handle as hard as I could, but I couldn't bust the door open, or magic it open, or—

Our school principal, Mr. Chen, turned down the hall, heading straight toward me. I gaped at him, still thumbing the lock. Oh no. He knew about the exam, didn't he? I was done. And that meant Caelyn was done. No, no, no.

But Mr. Chen stared at his phone, expression tense, until he reached Mr. Richardson's door. He poked his head in. "Hey,

Paul. Everyone. Sorry to interrupt, but could I see Dylan for a sec, please? Bring your things."

My phone buzzed with another message.

Shame you need to use your Get Out of Jail Free card so soon. 27–35–23. Bring the package home. Then you can talk to your sister.

Relief flooded my veins. I didn't realize I had a Get Out of Jail Free card, but I'd take it—though something about it unnerved me. Usually, I'd reserve shield potions and other protections until the end of a game, when I'd need it most. What would I wish I had this for later?

I squinted at the numbers: *27–35–23*. Wait. I was *sure* the first number had been 17. Absolutely sure of it.

At least, I thought it was . . .

I swallowed my confusion and spun the knob, letting out a bitter laugh as I swung the door open. A nylon bag dangled from one of the hooks. I went to grab it but stilled as Dylan joined Mr. Chen in the hall. He spotted me and threw me a baffled look.

"What's up?" Dylan asked Mr. Chen, clutching his backpack strap on his shoulder.

"Come with me, please." Mr. Chen glanced at a sticky note he pinched between two fingers and led Dylan a few doors down. "This is your locker, correct?"

My heart froze. That couldn't be . . . Was that the locker I just slipped the answer key into?

Dylan's posture relaxed. "Oh, this is one of those random locker searches. For drugs, right?"

"Can you open it for me, please?" said Mr. Chen. The bell rang, making me jump. I gripped the edge of the locker door so hard my knuckles turned bone white.

"Yes, sir," said Dylan. "No worries, I'm clean."

Mrs. Chesser rushed past me as students spilled into the hall, her heels tapping on the scuffed tiles. She joined Mr. Chen and Dylan, clutching her phone to her chest. Dylan glanced between the two of them before spinning the lock. He was probably wondering why two teachers needed to be present for a random drug search.

My breath caught in my throat as that helpless feeling tightened my chest again. Mr. Chen knelt and poked around Dylan's notebooks. He stood and patted down his jacket. And then he reached into the top cubby and pulled out the folded exam. He raised his eyebrows. "Sandra, is this—"

Mrs. Chesser snatched it from him. "These are the answers to next week's exam . . . How did you get this?" As though she'd had it in some high-security vault.

Dylan's eyes widened, and his face went beet red. He shook his head. "I . . . I didn't . . ."

Mr. Chen touched Dylan's elbow. "Come with me, son. We'll discuss this in my office."

"But that's . . . that's not mine."

"No, it certainly isn't," said Mrs. Chesser, her mouth settling into a grim line. She didn't look angry—just incredibly disappointed.

As Mr. Chen led Dylan past me toward his office, he nodded at me and offered a tight-lipped smile. Dylan caught my gaze

for the briefest moment and cringed. He must have been mortified, and confused as hell. And probably scared—if he couldn't
convince Mr. Chen he didn't steal the test, he'd be suspended.
Colleges would see this on his transcript when he applied in the
fall. He dreamed of going to MIT . . . Oh, God. What the hell
had I done?

But I didn't do this. Not really.

Right?

Mrs. Chesser headed back toward the stairs, staring at her answer key as she snaked through the crowds. I tried edging out
of her way, but she bumped into me, anyway.

"Sorry, Crystal." For the briefest moment, she narrowed
her eyes at me, tilting her head. Did she suspect me? I was *just*
in her classroom, right at her desk. She shook her head ever
so slightly. "I hope you feel better soon." Then she continued
down the hall.

I could imagine her thoughts. *No, Crystal wouldn't have
anything to do with this. She'd never steal a test.*

But neither would Dylan. He aced every test, barely having to
study. He'd never have to cheat. But he was technically caught
red-handed, the stolen exam in his locker.

A chill skittered down my spine. What if the first number AnOn-
ymOus1 gave me was wrong on purpose? What if they wanted to
make sure I stayed here long enough to see Dylan get caught?

But how did they know the exact moment to send me the
right combination? I scanned the halls as swarms of students
passed me by, and my eyes settled on one of the security cameras dotting the ceiling. No way. A rock settled in my gut.

They wanted me to see this. They wanted me to know this wasn't just about stealing an exam or cheating on a test.

They wanted me to know I'd hurt Dylan.

I glanced inside the locker at the nylon drawstring bag dangling from the coat hook, waiting for me and whatever the hell I'd have to do next to keep my sister alive.

5 Years Ago

Zoey's parents were evil.

It was bad enough they only let her invite five friends to her eleventh birthday party—Akira, Matty, Randall, Brady Cullen, who I'd convinced her to include, and me—but they wouldn't let us play Manhunt outside. Instead they quarantined us to their basement den to watch Zoey open presents, bash an Olaf-shaped piñata filled with—no joke—sugar-free gum, and play her favorite movie, Frozen.

I mean, *how old did they think we were? Six? At least they still let us have coed sleepovers. That wasn't going to last much longer.*

"Don't forget, stay down here," Zoey's mom reminded her as she bid us good night. "Your grandmother's trying to sleep. You know she isn't feeling well." Their fancy den was soundproofed so Zoey could play the violin her parents made her practice without bothering anyone.

"*Sorry,*" *Zoey mumbled, like she'd already done something wrong.*

We sat on our sleeping bags in front of the couch as Zoey watched an anthropomorphic snowman serenade us, entranced like she didn't already know every word. Matty and Randall were in their own little universe playing some card game, while Akira and I toyed with Zoey's new LEGO set. I sorted the pieces while she built a castle sans instructions, her skills boggling my mind, as always. Brady leaned over, reaching for a stack of colorful blocks, but Akira swatted his hand away. "Don't! You'll ruin it." He pouted and backed off.

Brady lived in the house on the other side of Zoey's. He was a year younger than we were, but so creative; I loved hanging out with him. Sometimes during the summer we'd set up a lemonade stand in front of his house, or collect stones, paint fun designs on them, and sell them door-to-door. We'd often compete to see who could earn the most cash by the end of the day. Sometimes his older brother, Andrew, would buy stuff just so he'd win, which was totally cheating, but whatever. I always tried to include Brady in our group, but he didn't fit in for some reason. I didn't get it—he wasn't shy when it was just the two of us.

Antsy, I threw a handful of popcorn at Zoey. "C'mon, let's go play Manhunt!" I'd been hooked on the idea ever since we'd seen the older kids in Matty's neighborhood playing. We tried to join, but one of his moms stopped us—she didn't want us running around the main drag, as though straying farther than their yard would instantly get us run over by a car or snatched into a van.

I never said Zoey's parents were the only evil ones.

"Hey!" Zoey frantically scooped up the popcorn. "Don't, my mom will kill me—"

"I'm in," said Akira, almost out of LEGO bricks, as Matty and Randall scrambled to their feet. I bet she just wanted to get away from that creepy wood-paneled door in the back corner—she'd been throwing glances at it all night. It led to a run-of-the-mill storage room, but when we were little, Randall told Akira a dead body was buried in there. Ever since, she was convinced it was haunted, and for a long time, she refused to sleep over at Zoey's.

Zoey's eyes boinged out of their sockets. "We're not s'posed to go outside after dark."

"We could sneak out through the kitchen," I said.

"No! I'll get in so much trouble."

"Well, fine," I huffed. "But let's play something."

Randall practically lunged at Zoey's pile of presents on the pool table and dug out his. "Ouija board?"

Akira crossed her arms. "No way."

"Aw, c'mon, Akira." Randall's eyes twinkled. Teasing her was his favorite game. I bet the present was more for her than Zoey. "Ghosts can't hurt you."

"Um, poltergeists definitely can."

Randall snorted. "No, they can't."

"No?" Akira quirked her brow, pointing to the wood-paneled door. "Well, why don't we lock you in there for a while and find out?"

Zoey and I chortled as Randall's grin collapsed, and he set down the Ouija board. Matty pulled out a board game called Sanctuary. "What's this?"

"I brought it," said Brady. "Thought it looked cool."

Randall scoffed. "Yeah, but you think Dungeons & Dragons is cool—"

I grabbed the box and peeled off the plastic wrap. "Let's try it." It wasn't Manhunt, but excitement bubbled in my belly, anyway—I loved playing new games, learning all the rules, seeing how they worked.

Matty scanned the instructions. "We need teams of two."

I glommed onto Akira's arm, claiming her as my partner. Zoey's eyes flicked to us. "Uh . . ."

And Matty and Randall were already bumping fists.

That left Brady.

He stared at Zoey expectantly, a half smile puffing out his cheeks. But Zoey screwed up her face. Ugh, did she have to be so obvious?

Brady wasn't the best at most games. He ran the slowest and had zero hand-eye coordination. As a klutz myself, being on his capture the flag or softball team guaranteed a loss. But this was a board game. That didn't matter now.

"Zoey—" I started.

"It's my birthday," Zoey said. "I get to pick the teams. Me and Kiki, Matty and Randall, and Crystal and Brady." Brady stuffed his hands into his pockets and stared at the carpet.

Heat simmered in my belly. "Hey, you didn't pick new teams. You just took my partner." There'd been this weird tension between me and Zoey lately. Like whenever she, Akira, and I walked down the halls at school, she'd shift in front of me and slow, so she'd walk next to Akira while I trailed behind. Or whenever she made her origami fortune-tellers, she'd only ask Akira to pick numbers *and colors. I'd tried brushing off these little snubs, but they were piling up, and I didn't know what it meant.*

Matty glanced at me. "We could do boy, girl, boy, girl?"

"Or we can draw straws," Akira suggested.

Brady gripped his stomach. "Actually, I'm not feeling well. I'm gonna go home." His voice shook. Were those tears glimmering in his eyes?

Zoey's eyes filled with regret. "Aw, Brady, don't go."

"I didn't mean—" I started, matching everyone's chorus of protests.

"No, really, I don't feel so good. I'll . . . I'll see you." He sprinted up the stairs, leaving his sleeping bag and backpack behind.

Nobody chased him.

About ten minutes later, I mustered the guts to bring him back from his house next door.

Later, we'd all wish I never did.

CHAPTER 5

I **made a beeline toward the** parking lot, my jacket forgotten in
my hurry to get outside. You were supposed to get approval
from the school nurse to leave early, but I was beyond caring
about school rules at this point.

I had a new set of rules to follow.

But who was setting them? Who the hell would kidnap my
sister? And why would they want to get Dylan suspended?
None of this made sense.

Meager clusters of students occupied the picnic tables on the
lawn bordering the lot. As I passed them, my attempts to look
calm and collected must have been laughable—my already-
big eyes were probably bugging out of my skull, and the crisp
breeze was making me convulse with shivers. I glanced in the
nylon bag, unable to resist satiating my curiosity any longer.
There was an old-school flip phone and something that looked
like a walkie-talkie—

"Crys!" someone called.

Well, crap.

Akira and Randall huddled at one of the tables. They must've had this period free. I hesitated as they waved me over, wanting to get home per An0nym0us1's instructions. And the sooner I got home, the sooner I could make sure Caelyn was okay.

But it was more than that.

As much as I hated to admit it, even to myself, I was itching to find out what came next in this game. Because here's the thing: Whoever would hold a thirteen-year-old hostage clearly had a twisted mind, but when they made sure I was in the right place at the right time to see Dylan get busted, I knew I was dealing with a mastermind. Chills had swept through me, and not just from terror.

From *intrigue*.

For me, there was nothing so tantalizing as a cunning opponent.

Guilt mangled my heart. Of course I was terrified for my sister. Of course I wanted to play this game to get her back. But I also wanted to outsmart its creator. I wanted to *win*.

Ignoring my friends would set off alarm bells, so I jogged over. "What're you doing out here?" I tried to keep my voice steady and failed miserably. "It's freezing."

Akira frowned and brushed her windswept chin-length hair from her eyes, taking in my lack of a coat. "It's not that bad." But she was siphoning Randall's body heat while polishing off a PB&J sandwich. Despite everything, I was relieved to see her eating. Akira had been in recovery from anorexia for over a year now, but I still worried about her constantly.

Randall tugged the hem of my sweater. "Hear about Dylan?"

My insides lurched. "How'd you know about that?"

"You didn't see Matty's texts?" Akira brandished her phone. I glanced at mine and saw I'd missed a string of notifications from our dormant texting chain from before Dylan joined our group.

"He saw it go down," said Randall.

"So did I," I said.

Akira leaned forward, breathless. "Oh my God. What did he *do*? What did he *say*?"

I shrugged. "He seemed freaked out. He denied it."

"He would." Randall chuckled.

My breath caught. "You think he stole that test?"

"They found it in his locker. I don't need to *think* anything." He poked my side, eyes glittering with amusement. "Damn, you've got it *bad* for him."

"I do not." I swatted him away, but my face flushed. Akira grinned—she'd been shipping me and Dylan hard, though I'd made her promise not to intervene like I did for her when I'd cornered Randall at the public pool the last week of summer.

It had been a rare day outdoors to appease our parents, who thought we'd disintegrate or something if we didn't get some vitamin D before school started. When Matty, Akira, and Zoey dashed off to see who could make the biggest cannonball, I spotted my chance and slinked into the lounge chair next to Randall. "So, when're you gonna ask her out?"

"Ask who out where?" he'd said absentmindedly, watching TikTok on his phone.

"Kiki. On a *date*."

That got his attention. The corner of his mouth flicked up. "Oh, come on. We're having *this* conversation again?"

"I've been coerced," I admitted, watching Matty plunge into the water butt-first.

Randall chortled, then froze, eyes widening. "Wait, coerced by who? *Akira?* Does she know . . . How . . . You told her I like her?"

"Nope." I laughed. "Your secrets are always safe with me."

"So . . . she *wants* me to ask her out?" He shook his head, baffled.

I shoved his arm playfully. "Why wouldn't she?"

He hesitated a moment, clucking his tongue. "Because she knows I liked Matty."

My smile dissolved. Randall had told us he was bi ages ago, and Matty—well, who *didn't* like Matty? But Matty was straight, and the thought of Randall unrequitedly thirsting after him when they'd been best friends forever shattered my heart. I used to gently nudge Randall toward other people, but he'd always say, "Nah . . . he's not Matty." After a while, he'd just say, "Nah . . . ," glance at Akira, and go all quiet. It didn't take a psychic to figure out his feelings had shifted.

"So?" I asked.

"Well, doesn't that bother her?"

I screwed up my face. "Why should it? She was obsessed with Blake Thatcher literally all of ninth grade. But she's over him now. Doesn't matter who you liked once as long as you like each other now."

Over Randall's shoulder, I spotted Akira climbing out of the pool. For a moment, I could see the stress on her face, the self-conscious part of her that wanted to wrap herself in every towel within eyesight. But then, seeing Randall's back to her, she grinned mischievously, snuck up behind him, and shook out her dripping wet hair. "Augh! Watch the phone!" But he laughed, cheeks flushing, and tossed his phone to me before chasing her back to the pool, where she shoved him in before cannonballing next to him.

By the following week, they only came up for air to play MortalDusk.

Now Akira wanted to return the favor, but I wouldn't let her. Besides, Dylan always threw me so much shade, I knew my little crush was one-sided. For whatever reason, he thought I was obnoxious. Maybe Zoey had poisoned his ear when I wasn't looking.

I gripped my stomach and edged away from the picnic table. "Anyway, I'm heading home early. Not feeling so hot."

Akira furrowed her brow in concern, and Randall scooted down the bench. "Eek, you catch whatever Zoey has?" Oh, God, he was so gullible; Zoey was totally playing hooky. But our friends were oblivious to the level of deception to which Zoey had stooped. I couldn't tell them—I had no choice.

But Akira noticed my expression. "Dammit, will you spill the tea already?" She hated that Zoey and I weren't getting along, but she hated not knowing *why* even more. She usually managed to wheedle out my secrets but couldn't siphon this one from my skull.

"Kiki, chill. There *is* no tea," I insisted for the zillionth time. Akira gave me a skeptical look, but I changed the subject. "Anyway, I don't think I have anything contagious, but I want to nap it off."

"We're still coming over, right?" Akira asked. School let out in an hour and a half, and I had no clue what An0nym0us1 would make me do next. But Akira knew how stressed I was about making the team. If I canceled our plans entirely, she'd know something else was wrong.

"Sure . . . but maybe come over around five instead?"

"Works for me," said Akira. She'd probably spend the extra time working on her re-creation of New York City in Minecraft. Last year she re-created the Magic Kingdom and recorded a tour, and the video went viral.

"I can't come over anyway," said Randall.

Akira pouted. "I thought you didn't have any more shifts till next week."

"My parents are in Burlington for some meeting, and Nessa's babysitter's booked, so I gotta do it."

"Ew," I said. "Good brothers are gross."

He cackled.

"But you're coming over *later,* right?" Akira gave him a meaningful look. Her parents were in California visiting her older sister at Stanford for the weekend. She'd begged them to let her stay home so she wouldn't miss the tourney, promising to stay at my place. Judging by the box of condoms she'd dragged me with her to buy at CVS—not that I'd contributed an iota of knowledge throughout my giggle fits—there'd be no sleepover at my house tonight.

Randall smiled coyly. "I wouldn't miss—"

"Alright, I don't need to hear your sex plans," I said.

"Oh my God." Akira threw the balled-up Saran Wrap from her sandwich at me.

I swatted it away, faking a laugh. "I'll see you later." I rushed toward my car before she could see how the laughter didn't reach my eyes.

Before she could piece together that my life was falling apart.

CHAPTER 6

After pulling into my driveway, I shot a message to AnOny-
mOus1. I'm home. Let me talk to her.

How would this work? Would they call me? Did this app have
something like FaceTime? As I waited for a response, I ran my
fingers over the passenger seat. Caelyn sat here only a few hours
ago. This whole situation was too surreal—like something that
would happen to Liam Neeson in an action movie. But I wasn't
a former FBI agent, and I hadn't the slightest idea how to track
down Caelyn's kidnapper.

I glanced at Zoey's house—her second-floor bedroom window was just visible, facing mine. Our houses were inset in a
hill, so we used to keep our windows unlocked and climb in
and out to visit each other. Until that time her mom caught her
with one leg out the window. She screamed bloody murder and
grounded Zoey for a month. I never understood why she found
exiting through windows so much more offensive than doors.
Either way, after that, I did all the climbing. We'd spend hours

trying new video games, hiding from our guilt, losing ourselves in virtual landscapes—but at least we got lost together. We'd discovered MortalDusk before it went mainstream, and convinced the rest of our friends to play together.

Then she went and ruined everything.

I hated keeping what happened bottled up, the stopper under lock and key. Akira clearly knew *something* happened, and I was pretty sure even Matty and Dylan suspected something thanks to my slipup in chemistry class a few weeks ago.

I cringed at the memory. Mr. Ferguson had started class with his usual bonus question. "Alright, folks, first person to tell me eight risks of carbon monoxide poisoning gets five points—"

Zoey and I had shot our hands into the air before he could finish. Weeks earlier, I would have let her have it. After what she did? Forget it.

"Zoey was first," said Dylan.

I threw him a scathing look. He winked, and something sparked in my chest. But Zoey's smirk quickly smothered it.

"You seeing time backward, bro?" Matty chimed in behind me. "Crys was first."

Mr. Ferguson chortled and rolled up his sleeves, revealing the dorky electron tattoo on his dark skin. "Looks like we've got ourselves a sudden death. Ladies! Paper out. Pen out. First to write down all eight wins."

As our classmates drummed on their desks, I frantically scrawled: clogged chimneys, space heaters, dryers, stoves, water heaters, portable generators, fireplaces, and . . . and—

"Got it!" Zoey grinned triumphantly.

"Fucking cheater." I'd meant to mutter, but the jocks in the back row crowed, clearly having heard. Heat crept up my neck.

"Whoa, language," said Mr. Ferguson as Zoey exclaimed, "What? No! I didn't cheat." Then she (successfully) muttered under her breath, "Paranoid jerk."

I scowled. Screw her. Like I didn't have a good reason.

As Mr. Ferguson scanned her answers, Dylan watched me like he was trying to puzzle something out, and Matty squeezed my shoulder. "It's only five points." But it wasn't about the points.

"You got it," Mr. Ferguson confirmed. Zoey folded the page, looking defeated despite her victory. Then he tapped the next blank line in my notebook. "Car exhaust!"

I groaned. "Obviously."

"Sometimes the most obvious answer is the one that eludes us." He quirked his brow. "You gonna apologize to your friend or what?" Shame burned my cheeks as I mumbled my apologies. Zoey said it was fine, but her glassy eyes told me it wasn't. She knew why I'd really snapped.

My phone buzzed, jolting me from the memory, and I gasped. But it was just a text from Mom to say she was heading into a long surgery, and there was leftover Chinese food in the fridge. No word yet from An0nym0us1. That's when I noticed Mrs. Rao watching me, two driveways down, wheeling a garbage can from next to the mailbox. Her family had moved in after the Cullens moved to California. I babysat her kids a lot—she paid way better than Randall's grocery store shifts—but it was always weird going into Brady's old house. It felt like something was sitting on my lungs the whole time.

Mrs. Rao smiled and waved, and, afraid she'd try to strike up a conversation, I slipped from my car and rushed inside, pretending I hadn't seen her.

Wanting to look up this bizarre app on my phone, I raced down to my laptop in the den, sank onto the couch, and searched. All I had to go by was the icon: a silver serpent wrapped around a microphone. I googled a bunch of variations of "app icon snake microphone." Nothing came up. Next, I checked the App Store, scrolling through the endless icons. Filtering by messaging apps didn't help—eventually, my eyes glazed over.

Maybe An0nym0us1 had coded the app and manually installed it. But *how*? I couldn't remember anyone else holding my phone, or my clicking a suspicious link recently.

Still no new messages. What the hell were they waiting for?

Maybe there'd be some sort of clue in Caelyn's room. I bolted upstairs. Her room was in its usual state of disarray—purple blankets tangled on the bed, clean laundry in heaps on the floor, fabrics piled next to the ancient turquoise sewing machine Grandma Rose had given her, in-progress jewelry and beads scattered across her desk. I spotted my denim jacket dangling from a bedpost. She was always swiping the few items from my closet that passed as fashionable, even if they were big on her. I didn't mind; if anything, I was flattered she thought them worth filching.

Her laptop was missing, but she probably took it with her, even though she wouldn't have internet access at Frost Valley. Nothing seemed particularly out of place except for Whiskers, curled up like a fuzzy orange cinnamon bun on Caelyn's pillow.

She usually camped out in the den. Could she sense something was wrong?

I petted her and stared at the corkboard above Caelyn's desk, at the picture of Caelyn and me snuggling Whiskers as a kitten. I'd wanted to name her Bowser but was overruled three to one. My eyes lingered on the selfie of all four of us at Hanover Lake a few years back, Dad's arm taking up a quarter of the shot. It was our last family outing before Dad found out the news that would change everything—news I remembered had felt like the end of the world to him.

Little did we know how much more our lives would fall apart.

Finally, my phone buzzed. An alert from An0nym0us1. My lungs constricted as I tapped on it, and a video started to play.

Oh, God. Caelyn's gag had been removed, and her curls hung around her face as she looked wide-eyed into the camera. "Crystal—" she managed before letting out a sob. I bit my lip to keep from making a similar noise. Her glasses were askew; with her hands tied behind her back, she couldn't fix them. "Help me. Please, help me."

Seeing her was both comforting and horrifying. She was alive, but this killed any possibility that this was all some epic prank.

This was real.

My sister was a hostage.

And she was truly terrified.

The video lasted fifteen seconds and looped back to the beginning. Panicking would get me nowhere, so instead I scoured the footage for clues. Caelyn sat against a faux-brick concrete wall on either a low-backed chair or a stool, since I couldn't see it behind her. The lighting was shit and caused a vignette effect, so I couldn't tell if the room had windows or not. I guessed she was in a basement. Eventually, text replaced the video.

You can send one video message back.

I tapped on the video icon, and my own face filled the screen. A fifteen-second meter stretched beneath the Record button. So that's how this worked—short bursts of video back and forth. What should I say?

My reflex was to make sure Caelyn was okay. I could ask if she was hurt. I could comfort her, assure her that everything would be fine. But my brain whirred with other possibilities. This was also a chance to get her to reveal information about who took her, or where she was. How could I ask her the right questions without being obvious?

I bit my thumbnail, pondering this, but I couldn't think straight—her voice looped in my mind. *Help me. Please, help me.* Despite my efforts to stay calm and focused, fear enveloped my heart. My baby sister was tied up in some dark, dingy basement, terrified, awaiting my reply. The agony of leaving her alone with her kidnapper for another moment drove me to hit Record.

"Caelyn . . . I . . . I love you." My voice shook, and my tongue felt thick in my mouth. But I had to get more words out. "Just hang in there. Everything's going to be fine—"

A notification appeared over the recording screen.

A text from Matty.

Just wanna make sure you're okay.

I frantically swiped the notification away. But the video had stopped recording. My fifteen seconds were up.

Apparently, there were no do-overs. I let out a frustrated cry. I didn't get to ask any questions. "Dammit, Matty!" It was 3:00 p.m.—school had just let out. If Matty hadn't texted right then, I could have finished my recording. Instead, Caelyn would see that useless video of me getting distracted. I could *kill* him.

But it wasn't Matty's fault. He'd had no idea what he was interrupting.

Gripping the edge of Caelyn's mattress, I took a deep breath, trying to temper my boiling blood. Whiskers had perked up at my outburst and stared, primed to flee if necessary. But I needed to stay calm. I bit my lip, staring at Matty's text. I had to keep playing the sick card. If he knew the truth, he'd insist on calling the police. I texted back.

I'm fine. Gonna nap now. See you later.

Then I scrolled to my notification settings and turned off alerts for everything except for An0nym0us1's mystery app.

An alert popped up—a new video of Caelyn. "Crystal, please," she said. "If you don't do everything"—either the audio was garbled, or she struggled to catch her breath—"they tell you to do . . . they said they're going to *kill* me . . ." Before I could search for more clues, the screen went black.

Dammit. I really needed to start taking screenshots.

They, Caelyn had said. Was there more than one kidnapper? That could explain the perfect timing with Dylan, if someone watched me at school while someone else held Caelyn hostage.

But would two people be in on such a depraved stunt? Maybe the kidnapper instructed Caelyn to use gender-neutral pronouns as to not reveal anything about their identity. She'd hesitated, and the audio got all fuzzy—like she was correcting herself.

Or was I overthinking this?

A new message replaced the video.

Time for our next game.

What? That hardly counted as a conversation. But there was no text field where I could argue.

Instead, I cracked my knuckles, and the tips of my toes tingled with adrenaline. Whatever game they'd throw at me, I was determined to win. "Bring it on, asshole."

CHAPTER 7

Let's play *The Great Crystal Bakeoff*. Bake a batch of brownies using the recipe below. You have 30 minutes to get the batter into the oven. Ready? GO!

What the actual fuck?" I said to no one.

I had to bake *brownies*? Shaking my head, I tapped the link below the message, and it opened a brownie recipe on some random lifestyle blog. While Mom loved to bake, I'd never so much as turned on the oven before, so I couldn't tell if the ingredients list was standard: all-purpose flour, unsweetened cocoa powder, white sugar, eggs, melted butter, vegetable oil, vanilla extract, salt, and chocolate chips. Seemed legit.

But *why*? This was so ludicrous, I almost wanted to laugh.

Yet time was ticking.

I sprinted to the kitchen. Did we even have these ingredients? Where did Mom keep things like vanilla extract? There suddenly seemed to be, like, a gazillion cabinets in here.

That was Dad's doing. Back when he was an ad agency executive, home renovation was a hobby of his. Caelyn and I used to
love helping him sand and paint, and he even let us help knock
down the wall between the living and dining rooms to make it
one expansive space. We took turns with the sledgehammer,
pummeling the drywall with satisfying thwacks.

That was before Dad started pummeling Mom.

Once he got laid off, everything changed. He'd spent his entire career clawing his way up the corporate ladder, and then
one day, he got the news—after his company's CEO (and his
mentor) suddenly passed away, new management wanted to
downsize. The job he loved was gone in a flash. He transitioned
to freelance work and we survived, but he'd lost his dream job
and monthly NYC trips over something utterly out of his control. His nightly glass of whiskey turned into four or five, plus
beer. Soon after, booze and online gambling replaced his home
renovation hobby. For some reason, alcohol turned Dad into a
different person—belligerent and violent. In his presence, this
enormous room felt positively claustrophobic.

Now, as I puzzled over the ingredients, it felt like the cherry-
wood cabinets stretched infinitely—like in one of my nightmares,
where the door I'm racing toward shrinks ever smaller in the
distance as something terrible chases me, and my legs grow
heavy, too heavy, before I startle awake.

Wait. Deep breaths. I had to take this one step at a time, just
like a game with a multipart puzzle.

First, I had to preheat the oven. The dials on the fancy retro
oven range might as well have controlled a spaceship. Mom tried
teaching me to cook after Dad left and she took more nursing

shifts, but I'd managed to botch even the most basic dishes. I'd tilt runny eggs into a plate, afraid to overcook them, or boil pasta for too long, letting the noodles get bloated and mushy. Instead, we stocked up on takeout or frozen meals. The microwave, I could handle. Baking, on the other hand, seemed like rocket science. One of the middle knobs went up to 500—that must've been for the oven. I dialed it to 350 and peered through the oven window. Um. I guess that worked?

Now for the ingredients. We had eggs and butter in the fridge, and fortunately, Mom was organized—all the baking supplies were in the same cabinet above the stove, even a sealed bottle of vanilla extract. I pulled out Mom's favorite green mixing bowl and an aluminum baking tray and laid out the ingredients on the counter.

Okay. I got this.

I measured the ingredients and poured them into the bowl. Maybe the brownies were a clue. Maybe An0nym0us1 *wanted* me to figure out who they were. In some video games, rewards like food or health kits were sprinkled like bread crumbs toward the final boss, or a villain's hideout. And didn't some serial killers send clues to detectives, wanting credit for their crimes, like each murder was a trophy?

My insides tied in knots. Hopefully An0nym0us1 wasn't a serial killer.

But who the hell would *do* this? I stirred it over in my mind as I mixed the batter. It had to be someone from school—someone who knew my and Dylan's class schedules and where Mrs. Chesser kept her exams. Or did it? If they could remotely hack my phone to install that app, they might've been able to hack the school network to access our schedules. Before sophomore year, Zoey hacked into it to tweak our schedules so we'd have more classes together, without triggering the school's defense system. "It's not like I'm changing our *grades* or anything," she justified. "It's totally harmless." So it was possible.

And technically someone could've broken into school one night or weekend, gone into Dylan's classrooms, and searched for something worth stealing. Something that would get Dylan in trouble. Without any vandalism or stolen computers to raise any red flags, the security guards might not have noticed a break-in.

So it didn't necessarily have to be someone in our school.

The thermostat light on the oven turned on as it reached the right temperature. I'd mixed the batter enough, right? It's not like I cared about quality here. How would An0nym0us1 judge the brownies? Would they come over and take a bite? This made absolutely no sense.

Next, I had to line the pan with wax paper. That seemed weird. Why not grease the pan? Whatever. I tugged open a drawer containing aluminum foil, parchment paper, Saran Wrap, and . . . aha, wax paper!

I tore off a sheet, lined the pan, poured in the batter—getting globs all over the counter—and slid the pan into the oven. I wiped my hands on my jeans and searched the oven for a timer. It didn't seem to have one, so I set the timer on the microwave for thirty minutes.

Finished with ten minutes to spare. Perching on a barstool at the kitchen island, I rattled off a message to An0nym0us1. **The brownies are in the oven.**

Good. Let's play *Time Trial.* You have 30 minutes to get to the gazebo at Hanover Lake. Bring the package from locker 499! Ready? GO.

My toes went numb. I knew exactly what gazebo they were referring to, but that part of the lake was past Mount Morgan in Lakecrest. I couldn't possibly get there in thirty minutes unless I drove like an absolute maniac, and that didn't even include the time it'd take to hike to the gazebo.

I glanced at the timer on the microwave. Our old-fashioned oven wouldn't automatically turn off after a set amount of time. I hopped off the barstool and headed for the oven to switch it off, but my phone buzzed.

TURN OFF THE OVEN AND SHE DIES. OPEN THE OVEN AND SHE DIES.

I gasped and nearly dropped my phone. My brain hurled into overdrive, processing too many emotions at once. Shock from being all-caps screamed at. Panic for Caelyn. Terror over the implication *they were watching me.*

How else would they know what I was about to do? I peered out the window, but didn't see anyone outside. Remembering the security cameras in the hall at school, I scanned the ceiling, the spaces above the cabinets, the countertops. No cameras. Nothing.

But somehow, they were watching.

Unless they'd *guessed* my next move. Because obviously you'd want to switch off the oven before leaving the house. If going to the gazebo would take *at least* an hour round trip—plus whatever I'd have do there—the brownies would burn by the time I got back.

Maybe that was the idea. The hairs on my arm stood on end.

I knelt to peer into the oven's window, but the wax paper peeking over the edge of the tray blocked my view of the batter. The brownies might burn, but they wouldn't catch on *fire,* would they? Surely baking wasn't *that* dangerous. The wax paper, though—that part of the recipe was bizarre.

I scrolled back to the recipe. The page had automatically refreshed and now only showed a 301 error. It was gone. The whole blog was gone. A tinny buzzing noise filled my ears as I searched Google for "wax paper oven burn" and clicked the first result, *Can you put wax paper in the oven?*

The article began: *The short answer is a resounding no! Wax paper is not heat-resistant; the wax will melt at high temperatures and the paper itself can catch fire.*

Holy hell.

The brownies weren't a clue. They were a fire starter.

I gaped helplessly at the pan lined with my own stupidity. I'd been so busy mulling over who An0nym0us1 might be, I hadn't even second-guessed the recipe. I never stopped to think that blog might not even be real.

My fingers shook as I shot off a message. I'm not burning my house down.

Then you'd better hurry.

CHAPTER 8

My entire drive to the lake was basically a near-death experience. I swerved around cars on the single-lane highway, blatantly blew red lights, and forget the speed limit—the trip to Caelyn's school earlier was a turtle stroll in comparison.

Our local police force was MIA, thank God. Setting speed traps was the most action they ever got in this Podunk town. I kept imagining burly Chief Sanchez clutching his radar gun, cruiser obscured behind a shrubbery, ready to pounce. Maybe he was busy giving one of his lectures at the middle school about how "drugs are bad, mmkay?" Heck, he'd probably leap at the chance to work a kidnapping case. But An0nym0us1's first messages burned in my mind: *If you call the police, she dies.*

Whiskers mewed from the back seat. "We're almost there, Whiskey—" The word soured my mouth; that's what Dad used to call her. His favorite drink.

I'd stuffed her into her carrier crate, which she'd resisted by sticking her legs out in every direction, the little twerp, taking up five whole minutes. But like hell I was letting her stay in a house that might burn down. She was a pampered indoor cat and wouldn't know which way was up if I plopped her outside.

Only a few cars dotted the parking lot when I tore in and zipped into the spot closest to the trail leading to the gazebo. The lot would fill up later when joggers, dog walkers, and kids hankering to get high took to the trails wrapping around Hanover Lake to catch the last of the daylight.

I cracked open the windows before turning off the engine. "Wait here, okay?" I said to Whiskers. Like she could go anywhere else.

"Five minutes left," I muttered as I grabbed my phone and An0nym0us1's nylon bag from the passenger seat. "I can do this." I'd have to sprint. I slammed the door shut and started toward the trail.

"Crystal!"

I whipped around. Leaning against a boxy clunker of a car was none other than Jeremy Fischer.

Fishman.

The pro gamer with five million YouTube and Twitch followers—the one who used to dominate the Vermont leaderboard. Now the top three spots shuffled among him, Matty, and Randall, and once I even bumped him down to number four. I knew it made his blood curdle to have a bunch of high school juniors wreck his status.

"What are *you* doing here?" I asked.

"Hello to you, too." He meandered over, rubbing the dark scruff on his cheek and chuckling to himself—over what, I had no idea. Maybe he was remembering how he'd annihilated my team this morning.

My mind reeled, caught off guard by his appearance. I'd only met him IRL once before. And it was a complete disaster.

Soon after we recruited Dylan, all six of us had been squished into a red-cushioned booth at Happy Grillmore, sipping milk-shakes and cracking open the new kid, when in walked Fishman, basically the Harry Styles of the online gaming community. Zoey let out an odd squeak, and Matty's jaw practically hit the table. "Holy shitmonkeys."

"Is that . . . ?" said Randall, breathless.

"Yep." Zoey's cheeks flushed with excitement. "Fishman."

Fishman slipped off his hat and shook out the rain, sliding into a nearby booth. A pretty Black girl peeled off her raincoat and sat across from him, adjusting her braids and gold-hoop earrings as the server handed them menus.

"He's even hotter in real life," Akira cooed.

Randall nodded. "Way hotter."

"You know who Fishman is, right?" I asked Dylan as he sipped his vanilla shake.

"Mm, no." He set down his glass. "Where I come from, we all live under these gigantic boulders, so." He kept his tone flat, without cracking a smile. When he finally met my gaze, only the slightest twinkle in his eyes gave him away.

Before I could think of a clever retort, Matty exclaimed, "We have to go over there, bro," practically hyperventilating. "We have to *say* something."

Randall nodded aggressively, for once speechless. He insisted we livestream almost every day, but despite climbing the leaderboards, our Twitch and YouTube channels had been slow to grow. A shout-out from Fishman would make our subs skyrocket. We'd tried initiating challenges with him, but he'd ignored us. He was a few years older—maybe he wanted nothing to do with a bunch of dorky teenagers.

Akira looked wary. "I dunno. This whole thing reeks of nope."

"Yeah," I agreed. "Don't celebs hate that kind of thing?" But Matty already stood, bouncing on his toes.

Zoey tugged me from the booth. "Oh, c'mon. He's not, like, Chris Evans. He's just a *person*." I'd argue Chris Evans was *just a person,* too, but I let her take my hand and drag me over.

Fishman's date noticed the group of us hovering first and froze mid-laugh. "Um . . . d'you know these kids?"

"I only just moved to Lakecrest," said Fishman. "Don't really know anyone yet. Can we help you?" he asked us, quirking his brow. Was there a hint of recognition there?

Matty and Randall looked ready to pop like balloons, and Zoey squeaked again, completing her transformation into a chipmunk. So much for Fishman being *just a person.*

Oh, geez. One of us had to say something. "Hi," I said. "Sorry to bother you—"

"We recognize you from Twitch!" Matty spouted. "We're big fans! We play MortalDusk, too! I'm Mattastic15! We were in the same round last week! I don't know if you remember! I shot someone on your team at Calamity Castle! And then you killed me!"

Wow. Zero chill whatsoever. People at neighboring tables turned to look. I cringed, and Akira muttered, "Oh, God."

Fishman's eyes darted between us and his date. "Sorry, you got the wrong dude." Uh-oh. Was she oblivious to his online persona?

"No way," said Randall. "You're Fishman, right?"

"*Fishman?*" His date sneered and crossed her arms.

"No!" said Fishman. "I dunno what they're talking about." He snapped his fingers. "Ah, you know what? I bet I was catfished."

"Catfished?" Matty repeated incredulously.

I grabbed Zoey's wrist. "Guys, let's go—"

But she shook me off. "We watch you stream, like, every day. You can't fake that."

Did they not see how intrusive this was? Akira did—she was plucking at the back of Randall's shirt, trying to pull him away. Dylan held a fist to his lips, stifling laughter. If he had second thoughts about joining this clown factory, I wouldn't blame him.

Fishman let out a defeated huff and narrowed his eyes at Matty. "Who'd you say you were?"

"Matty Wilson—"

"I'm Randall Lewis," Randall interrupted, eagerly extending his fist for a bump. "Ran_With_It in MortalDusk—"

"Oh, fuck." Fishman rubbed his scruffy cheek, leaving Randall hanging. "You're those pesky little dipshits . . ." he muttered. Yikes—he *did* recognize us. Had he noticed us climbing the leaderboard, encroaching on his turf?

"Wait," said his date, "these kids know you from a video game?"

"And his streams," said Matty uncertainly, thrown by Fishman's reaction. "He's got, like, five million subs."

"You got time for that? It said on your profile you ran a tech start-up—"

"I do, babe." Jeremy cleared his throat. "Well . . . not a conventional start-up, per se. More like . . . a game influencer . . . start-up . . ."

"Don't call me *babe*." She grimaced and stood, grabbing her jacket. "Talk about *catfishing* someone. You know what? I don't date liars." She paused in front of Matty and said, "Thanks for clueing me in, cutie," then stalked outside.

"Fuckturnip," said Matty, watching Jeremy chase after her, though it was clearly a lost cause. "Next time I try to meet a pro, please punch me in the face."

I hadn't seen our nemesis since, but now here he was in the flesh, standing between me and the game that might get my sister killed.

"Crystal Donovan," Jeremy said. "It seems we have a traitor in our midst."

Conflicted, I glanced back at the trail. I only had four minutes to get to that gazebo. I imagined some sadist sinking his knife into Caelyn if I was late. I imagined the wax paper's edges browning and curling over the tray, wax oozing, paper flaking off, mingling with the grease below, catching aflame.

But I had to know what in the actual hell Jeremy was *doing* here. The day after we'd accidentally sabotaged his date, his team ambushed us in MortalDusk. Zoey assured us it was impossible to stalk us from map to map without a hack. It had to be a coincidence. After all, we were on a regional server, and there was some skill-based matchmaking going on—we *were* pretty much at Fishman's level now. But then Akira found a plug-in that listed who was on your map, somehow without violating MortalDusk's terms of service. Soon it was clear: Fishman was out for pixelated blood. Whenever he landed on our map, he was hell-bent on taking us down in front of his audience of millions. The joke was on him, though—we fought back hard, and soon the MortalDusk community was picking sides, giving us a massive jump in subscribers. After losing the top leaderboard position, he must've felt humiliated; I bet he absolutely loathed us. Was he stalking us IRL now, too?

"What do you mean?" I asked. "Who's a traitor?"

He grinned. "Who do you think? *You* are." I cringed, confused. Jeremy stepped closer, peering at me. "Huh. Your eyes really are as green as they are on Instagram." *What?* I could have sworn my profile was set to private.

"They're hazel. And ew, are you hitting on me?" I backed away. "How old are you? Like, twenty-five?"

"Twenty-one. And no, I'm not. Aren't people allowed to make observations anymore?" He snorted. "Girls always use filters and shit to make their eyes look like that." He waggled his fingers in front of his own eyes.

"Why were you stalking my Insta, anyway?" I rarely posted selfies, and when I did, I was always mid-laugh or sticking my tongue out. You don't have to worry about lighting or looking pretty if you're goofing off. Caelyn was more self-conscious, so we smiled normally for our pics together, though I'd often sneak in bunny ears.

Jeremy smirked. "I had to see what kind of person would turn against her friends like that." My stomach dropped. "So two-fifty K's your number, huh?"

I scrambled to make sense of this. The solo and team prizes at the tourney were $250,000 each. Was he insinuating I'd framed Dylan for stealing that exam . . . for *what*? To take him out of the running? "How'd you even know about that?"

He scrunched his brow. "You're the one who made the first move, sweetheart."

I shook my head, completely lost. Three minutes left.

"So what'd you have in mind?" he asked. "You want me to help you pick them off?"

My mouth dropped open. *"Pick them off?"*

"Well, yeah. But you're gonna have to sell me on this. I mean, if I agree to meet you somewhere—say, Calamity Castle—how do I know your whole crew won't be waiting—"

"Hang on. Are you talking about forming an alliance at the tourney?" Matty and Randall would be Fishman's biggest threats in the solo competition. Aligning with me to take them down would boost Fishman's chances for sure. But why'd he think *I* initiated this conversation?

"No shit." He threw up his hands. "Listen, if you're getting cold feet, fine. But don't pretend like you have no clue what the fuck I'm talking about. Don't waste my time like that."

"I *have* no clue! How'd you even know I was going to be

here?" Only one person in the world knew I was going to be in this parking lot right now.

An0nym0us1.

My breath hitched, and I skittered back a few steps. No way. I glanced at Jeremy's car—it didn't look like anyone was in the back seat. What about the trunk?

"What the hell do you mean?" asked Jeremy, frustrated— whether genuine or good acting, I couldn't tell. "*You* emailed *me*. You told me to meet you here."

Unease prickled my skin. "No, I didn't."

"*Seriously?* Oh, man. You've got to be kidding me."

Even if Jeremy wasn't An0nym0us1, they had to be pulling the strings, just like when Mr. Chen knew to check Dylan's locker for the answer key. Maybe they'd phished my email address or something.

But why involve *Fishman*?

I glanced at the trail again, remembering An0nym0us1's memory game. Jeremy had to be another distraction. Anyone who paid attention to the MortalDusk streaming community would know about our rivalry. He was the perfect obstacle to keep me from getting to the gazebo in time. To keep me out of my house even longer, giving the wax paper more time to burn.

An0nym0us1 had set a trap, and I'd fallen into it face-first.

And I only had two minutes left.

"Listen . . ." I edged toward the trail. "There's been some mistake. I can explain another time."

"Oh, come on!"

"I'm sorry. I have to go." I looped the nylon bag over my

shoulder and sprinted toward the dirt path leading to the gazebo.

"You're going to regret this!" he called after me.

Little did he know, I already regretted everything.

By the time I reached the gazebo, I was gasping for air, and a metallic taste filled my mouth. God, I was out of shape. I shot off a message to An0nym0us1—I'm here—and collapsed onto one of the benches.

The small gazebo was nestled at the corner of Hanover Beach—more an outcrop of stones and sludge than actual beach. And in the shadow of Mount Morgan, you couldn't exactly get much sun here. It was a poor attempt at convincing us landlocked folks otherwise.

My phone buzzed, and I gasped to see a photo of Caelyn's forearm with red text stretched over her pale skin as though etched in blood.

> You cut it close. I almost cut her.

Black cloth bound her wrist to the chair, and the chef's knife was menacingly positioned next to her arm. If the letters weren't so perfectly aligned, it might've fooled me. *Bzzzz.* A fly buzzed near my ear and, already on edge, I jumped and swatted at myself. "Fucking hell." The next moment, my phone buzzed.

> Let's play *Prank Caller*. On the burner phone, call the favorite contact. Read my script with the voice changer. Ready? GO!

"Yeah, let's go, bastard." I had a feeling another game was coming—otherwise, they wouldn't have made me bring the bag from the locker. I emptied it. The thing that looked like a walkie-talkie must've been a voice changer. I switched it on, raised it to my lips, and pressed the large red button. "Hello, hello." It deepened my voice and changed the tenor, making me sound a bit like Dad. My throat constricted.

But then I pictured smoke billowing from the kitchen stove, flames licking the surrounding cabinets. I had to do this fast.

I set my phone on the bench to read the script while holding the burner and voice changer, then navigated to the Favorites contacts screen on the burner and tapped the only one there: Call Me. These games were bizarre. What would they possibly make me say? Maybe they'd have me hurl insults at—

Someone picked up. "This is 911. What is your emergency?"

My heart jolted, and I reflexively pressed End Call.

What the heck? I thought I wasn't supposed to call the police, *or else.* I stared at the burner. Would they call back?

Once, during a visit to Grandma Rose's when we were little, Caelyn and I discovered an old rotary phone still working in the basement. We started dialing random numbers, fascinated by the archaic wheel. Somehow it turned into a competition to see who'd get more people to pick up. We giggled into our palms as people shouted, "Hello? *Hello?*" But then Caelyn dialed 911 before I realized what she was doing. "This is 911—" I'd heard the operator say before grabbing the phone and slamming it into the receiver. "Why'd you *do* that?" I'd asked Caelyn.

Her doe eyes widened behind her thick glasses. "I don't know! I was curious—" The phone rang. We both screamed.

911 had called back. We stared helplessly, like ignoring Caelyn's mistake would somehow make it go away. But Grandma picked up upstairs, and we got in buttloads of trouble.

Now a message flashed across my own phone.

> **You already used your Get Out of Jail Free card. Call back NOW.**

How did they know I'd ended the call? The base of my skull tingled, and my eyes snapped up to the woods. Just then, something crunched over the crisp, dead leaves.

A twig snapped. The brush rustled.

And I braced for someone to lunge at me.

5 Years Ago

I rang Brady's doorbell and bit my lip, hoping he wasn't already holed up in his room crying or anything. I hated seeing people cry—it made my own tear ducts instantaneously burst. But I had to come get him. Being in a fight was the actual worst. I couldn't stand the tension—it made me all queasy, and it was all I could think about.

Brady's mom answered the door, giving me a tight-lipped smile. "Crystal." Brady had clearly told her what had happened. Her curly, red hair was tied in a loose bun atop her head, short ringlets framing her face like fire tendrils. I always wished my curls were that defined, but they were more of a messy blob.

"Hi, Mrs. Cullen. Can I talk to Brady?"

She widened both the door and her smile. "Of course, hon." She probably thought it was cute I'd come over to apologize or whatever. "He's in the living room."

"Thanks." I dashed past her to the living room. It was warm and stuffy inside. Brady and his older brother, Andrew, sat cross-legged *on either side of the coffee table next to the crackling fireplace, working on a jigsaw puzzle. Andrew was two years older than I was, with the same round features as Brady's, friendly but quiet—whenever I spotted him at school, he had his nose buried in a book or laptop.*

"Hey, Brady," I said.

"Hey." He refused to look at me, pinching a puzzle piece as he scanned the edge he was working on.

"Listen, I'm sorry about before. Come back and—"

"Can't you see we're busy?" Andrew snapped, surprising me—he was usually so soft-spoken. He glowered at me and motioned to the board like I couldn't see for myself what they were doing. I winced, guilt building in my gut. Brady must've told him, too.

If Zoey were here, she'd say something like, "Um, chill, Brady's been here for, like, two seconds." She didn't mind confrontation so much. In fact, she kind of relished it.

I simply ignored Andrew. "Brady, I'm real sorry. I want to be on your team. Come play with us." Brady finally glanced up.

"You really wanna be on his team?" Andrew asked skeptically. Brady watched, eyes wide and hopeful.

"Yes! What happened before . . . I was just mad at Zoey about something else. She's been all weird lately . . ."

Brady tilted his head. "Weird how?"

He wouldn't understand. It suddenly seemed so petty to worry over Zoey inching me out in the halls. Although . . . if Brady felt shunted out before, maybe he would get it. Maybe I could confide in him.

But I didn't want to get into it with his brother listening. "It's no big deal, I'll tell you later. But c'mon, we have to get back over there. We can't let them form an alliance!"

At that, Brady leaped to his feet. There's nothing worse than an alliance in which you're not included.

If only that were true.

If only that were the worst thing that would happen that night.

CHAPTER 9

had no idea I'd get murdered in the woods twice today.

And by the same person, no less. Jeremy must've followed me here. He'd lied about that email before to mess with me. Now he'd get to reenact his MortalDusk slaying in the flesh—sans fire staff, obviously.

The rustling got closer. I imagined a hooded figure in shadow clutching a knife, bearing down on me. I had to run, to at least find a branch or something I could use to defend myself. But my legs were locked up, frozen in fear—

A chipmunk darted from some nearby foliage and up a tree.

Gah! I clutched one of the gazebo's wooden beams, slowing my breathing. Paranoia was practically oozing from my pores. I had to get a grip. Just then, my phone vibrated with a photo message.

A gloved hand clutched a knife in front of Caelyn, and a black cloth covered her mouth and nose. Jesus. The blade wasn't the only danger—if she panicked, and couldn't breathe . . . "She has asthma, you son of a bitch."

Thinking fast, I tried taking a screenshot. Nothing happened. I frowned, pressing the usual buttons on the side of my phone again.

The image disappeared, replaced by red text on white.

No screenshots. Call again, or I won't let her use her inhaler.

So they knew about her asthma. They'd found her inhaler on her—wait . . . Had they heard me say that? If they'd disabled my screenshot functionality, they must've had complete control over my phone. I glanced at the front-facing camera.

And that tiny black dot peered back like the eye of fucking Sauron.

Shudders tore through me. That's how they knew my every move. My phone's cameras. It seemed so obvious now.

They were always watching.

Always listening.

I was so creeped out I raced to the lake's edge and wound my arm back, about to chuck my phone into the sparkling water. But I stopped myself. Tossing my phone would sever my only connection to Caelyn. And it might count as forfeiting the game. I couldn't risk it. I had to go through with this call. To save her. To keep my house from burning down. I had to get it over with, like tearing off the world's stickiest Band-Aid.

I returned to the gazebo, raising my phone in front of my face. "Fine. I'll do it." No point typing out messages anymore. I swallowed my fear and redialed with shaking fingers.

"This is 911. What is your emergency?"

A script appeared on my screen as one long text block. I held the voice changer to my lips and read. "Yeah, hi. Uh . . . my name is Lance Burdly." Even the *uh* was in the script. "I'm at 379 Pearson Drive in Newboro. I need an ambulance. But no cops. My mother and sister were having a fight, and my mom was getting violent. So I grabbed the gun from her nightstand—"

I clasped my mouth. *No.* No way. I couldn't read the rest. But I had no choice.

No. There was *always* a choice.

Option one, hang up. Refuse to play this twisted game any longer. But then Caelyn would die.

Option two, tell the operator the truth. Get the police's help. But would the cops even believe me? Either way, then Caelyn would die, and my house would burn.

Option three, read the script. Get this over with. Then somehow outplay An0nym0us1 and find my sister.

You can't outplay your opponent if it's already game over. I had to choose option three.

But then I'd fight back.

"Hello?" said the operator. "You said you had a gun?" Despite her persistence, her voice was calm and steady, like she'd talked to dozens, maybe hundreds of people in domestic abuse situations before.

The voice changer masked the tremor in my voice as I read, "I grabbed the gun from her nightstand, and I shot her. I shot my mother. She isn't breathing."

The operator took a moment to absorb this. "You said you had a sister? Where is your sister now?"

A new text block appeared. I read, "I locked her in the basement. And I doused the house in gasoline. If you send the cops, I'll set the house on fire."

Oh, God. What had I done?

My pulse roared in my ears, drowning out the 911 operator's words. She was asking me something, trying to get me to stay on the line.

A new message from An0nym0us1.

Hang up now.

I scrambled for the End Call button and let out a choked sob. I'd chosen wrong. Some innocent person was about to get swarmed by the police. Once those words left my lips, they ignited a fuse. Now I had to stamp out the flame before Lance Burdly's life exploded. I had to warn him, whoever he was.

Something else niggled at the back of my mind. A sister locked in a basement. A mother shot and killed. Caelyn was locked in some basement. I'd gotten that one text from Mom, but what if it was fake? Had An0nym0us1 taken her, too? What if the subtext of this call was a threat?

No way. I was overthinking this, jumping to illogical conclusions—

My phone buzzed.

Put the burner and voice changer in the bag, fill it with rocks, and throw it into the lake.

They wanted me to get rid of evidence. Like I'd just committed a crime.

I quickly scooped glittering white gravel surrounding the gazebo into the nylon bag, scrambling to figure out what to do next. First, I had to warn Lance. I could go to their house . . . dammit, what was the address? I couldn't even remember the street name. It was lucky enough I remembered his name: Lance Burdly.

What was the worst that could happen, anyway? The police would show up and have nobody to save, because none of that was real. Nobody had been shot. Nobody's house was being set on fire—

Oh, God. The brownies.

The wax paper smoldering, smoking, setting the kitchen aflame.

I had to get home. *Now.*

I cinched the bag, chucked it as far as I could over the lake, and bolted before it even hit the water.

I scanned the sky for wisps of smoke as I pulled into my driveway, but it was clear—blue and cloudless. And when I raced inside, the decadent smell of freshly baked brownies filled my senses. There was no smoke or acrid smell of burning paper. I switched off the oven, threw on oven mitts, and yanked out the pan. The brownies' edges looked slightly charred, but otherwise delightful.

Weird. They were in the oven for more than double the time they were supposed to be.

I examined the edges of the wax paper. It hadn't burned or melted at all. Had that article been mistaken? Had I freaked myself out for nothing?

But the way AnOnymOus1 had sent me that all-caps threat to stay away from the oven . . . they'd clearly wanted to make me think the brownies burning was a real danger. I set the tray on the counter, took off the mitts, and pinched the wax paper. Huh. It didn't feel particularly waxy. Oh, well. Crisis averted.

I rushed outside to grab Whiskers's carrier from the back seat and let her out in the foyer, where she gave an indignant huff before racing down to the den. "Hey, at least you're not a cat-kebab." I started after her to grab my laptop and google Lance Burdly, but . . . wait.

Back in the kitchen, I set my phone on the counter and yanked the box of wax paper from the drawer, and felt the roll inside. It matched the stuff in the tray. Curious, I pulled out the parchment paper and ran my fingers over the edge of the sheet poking out.

It felt . . . slippery. Waxy.

The temperature in the room seemed to plummet. Had Mom accidentally swapped the two at some point? She was always getting discombobulated. Had she unwittingly foiled An0nym0us1's plan to start a fire?

I glanced at my phone, at the tiny dot next to the ear speaker. Watching. Always watching. Fuck that shit. I grabbed a roll of Scotch tape from the junk drawer and started layering tiny slivers of tape onto the selfie camera, intending to do the same with the back camera, when the phone vibrated. An0nym0us1.

I don't think so. Take it off, or she dies.

Dammit. My fingers shook as I begrudgingly peeled off the tape, and a new message appeared.

Congrats on winning the first five games! The next game will be later tonight.

Huh. Not the reaction I expected to their plan going awry. Maybe they were trying to save face and needed time to scheme.

In the meantime, enjoy the brownies. They're your reward.

Like hell I was going to eat those brownies. Besides, I wanted a different reward. "How's Caelyn? Can I talk to her?"

She can't exactly come to the phone right now.

Dread snaked through me. A moment later, a video appeared. Caelyn. Hands still tied behind her back. Head lolling forward. I sucked in air, but it was like my lungs wouldn't take in oxygen. Was she unconscious? I couldn't see her face. I tried zooming in, but the video wouldn't expand—

A loud knock.

I jerked my head up.

Someone was at the front door.

CHAPTER 10

Sometimes I'd kill for the chance to travel through time and undo my mistakes. Other times a sound or smell triggers such a vivid memory, it almost seems possible.

Pound, pound, pound.

The knock on the front door hurtled me back into my bedroom over a year ago as Dad pummeled the door. At first, his fights with Mom were mostly hurled accusations—he drank too much; she didn't understand. He blew too many Bitcoins at poker; she wasn't being fair. "You don't get it!" he'd shouted once. "You haven't lost everything you ever worked for. You still fucking *matter.*" Eventually, their bickers became brawls.

Pound, pound, pound.

I could almost feel Caelyn trembling against me, burrowed under my covers. But it was only the tingling sensation of fear spidering through my veins. Whoever was at the door now, it wasn't Dad. He was clear across the country.

I'd seen to that.

I glanced at the clock—4:46. I'd told Akira and Randall to come over at 5:00, and now I needed every second of those fourteen minutes to Google-stalk Lance Burdly. Frustrated, I set my phone on the counter, then thought better of it and shoved it into the silverware drawer before scurrying to the door. Through its floral stained-glass window, I recognized Dylan's plaid jacket. He was alone. Last I saw him, Mr. Chen was leading him to his office after finding the answer key I'd stuffed into his locker.

Palms sweating, I opened the door. "Hey."

Dylan leaned against the doorframe, an olive-green beanie covering his chestnut hair. "Hey." He stuck his hands into his pockets all casual-like, but worry creased his brow. "Your doorbell doesn't work."

"Obviously." Mom hadn't had a chance to call someone about it. "You're early."

"Obviously."

Cool. So we established we could both observe things.

His lips twitched into a grin, and I let out an awkward chuckle snort.

"Dork," he said with continued accuracy. "Akira said you already went home, and, uh—I wanted to . . . I had to tell you . . ." He rubbed the back of his neck, smile gone. "I didn't do it, Crystal. I didn't steal that test."

I reeled, surprised. Why'd he give a rat's ass what I thought? But the earnest look in his eyes told me he did. I almost said, "*I know.*" But I wasn't supposed to know. I had to pretend that for all I knew, he *did* steal that answer key.

Or was it cruel to feign suspicion, especially with this new-found knowledge that he cared what I thought of him? It made my heart simultaneously wobble and constrict with guilt. Confused, I motioned for him to come inside, mustering an empathetic smile. "Well . . . listen, I'm sure everything will be fine—"

"I got suspended."

My stomach dropped. "Oh *no.*"

"Newboro has a zero-tolerance policy. And it's going on my record. MIT will see it on my transcript. I'm screwed beyond belief."

Dammit. This was all my fault. Sure, I hadn't known that locker was Dylan's. And if I hadn't stolen that test and slipped it into his locker, I would've put Caelyn's life in jeopardy.

But my actions might've put Dylan's future in jeopardy.

Oh boy. I had to sit down.

Dylan followed me into the kitchen and slid onto the barstool next to mine, dropping his backpack on the floor. "I can't believe this." He slipped off his beanie, strands of hair flopping across his forehead. "You know when something so absurd happens, you think you must be dreaming, because there's no way in hell it could be real? Almost like you're watching shit go down from someone else's perspective, because it can't possibly be happening to you?"

I almost laughed. Accurate description of my day. "I know exactly what you mean."

He adjusted his glasses and sighed. "Wow, this smells good." He pinched the edge of the brownie pan and slid it closer. "Did you *just* bake this?" He must've felt its warmth.

My heart jolted. "No! I mean, yes. I did. I, uh . . ." I scrambled for a lie. "I thought you could use some comfort food." He met my gaze, and a strange expression crossed his face. Was he amused? Surprised? My cheeks flushed. "But they're no good."

"Why not?"

"A fly landed on it." I internally face-palmed. That was the best I could come up with? Really?

He quirked his brow. "You're going to throw out all this gooey goodness because of one fly?"

I cringed. "Don't flies puke on whatever they land on?"

"Aw, but you baked me brownies. I'll suffer some microscopic puke."

"Gross." But my heart did that weird little wobbly thing again. The brownies *were* technically fine. I handed him a spatula, and he dug in. "So Mr. Chen really thinks you took the test?" I asked.

"Yup." He freed an uneven brownie square and took a bite. "I told him math's my best subject; I don't even *need* to cheat. Didn't matter, though. The evidence was in my locker, so, you know, guilty until proven innocent."

"Huh," I said, remembering the security cameras dotting the ceiling in the hall. Would Mr. Chen eventually think to check the footage? "Maybe you could talk him out of putting it on your record, at least. Everyone makes mistakes."

"But I didn't *make* a mistake. I can't admit to something I didn't do. Anyone could have slipped that test in through the vents."

My heart seemed to stop beating. *Feign ignorance. Just feign ignorance.* "What, you think someone planted it in your locker or something?" Okay, so that was like the opposite of feigning ignorance. My cheeks scorched as he gaped at me.

"Oh, geez. I thought maybe someone was trying to get rid of it. You think someone was trying to *frame* me?"

I glanced warily at the silverware drawer where my phone was, hoping our voices were too muffled for An0nym0us1 to hear. "Er . . ."

"Wow." He chuckled. "And I thought *I* was being paranoid."

I crossed my arms, feeling myself get defensive, but I couldn't stop myself. "Well, that'd be *some* coincidence otherwise, no? Oh, so you just *happen* to be taking that test next week. Right."

His brow crinkled. "Good point. But who would *do* that?"

I'd been asking myself that all afternoon. Who would hate Dylan enough to get him suspended? Who would hate me enough to kidnap my sister?

There was only one person in our school I could think of . . . but that was ridiculous. She'd *never.*

"What is it?" Dylan prodded, seeing my expression.

"No . . . it's nothing."

"Tell me. Who are you thinking?"

I blew air between my lips and, throwing caution to the wind, I whispered a name.

CHAPTER 11

Lucia Ramirez hated our guts, and it was totally my fault.

In our frenzy to recruit a sixth player for our esports team, we'd held tryouts the first week of school. Only two people signed up, including Lucia. She was more of a floater than a loner, flitting from clique to clique depending on her mood. We were never exactly friends—she seemed to care more about getting into Harvard than anything—but she was pleasant enough, sort of like hydrangeas brightening a room without drawing your eye. *Just like Brady,* I'd thought with a shudder.

Still, her interest in joining our geek squad baffled me, especially when she fluttered into the computer lab, balayaged hickory-brown waves shimmering under the fluorescent lights, wearing this chic floral dress, a stark contrast to my Zelda Triforce T-shirt and the pink pajama pants Zoey wore to school, zero fucks given.

But then Lucia made googly eyes at Randall the whole time Matty interviewed her, and suddenly it all made sense.

When Randall reciprocated with a lopsided grin, Akira threw irked looks at Zoey and me, and Zoey glared at Lucia like she was already silently plotting her takedown. Something in my chest went cold. We couldn't recruit Lucia. I didn't trust her not to tear our group apart as much as I didn't trust us not to rip her to shreds. I couldn't let either of those things happen.

As it turned out, she couldn't last more than two minutes in her MortalDusk tryout rounds without getting burned to a crisp or vaporized—at least not until Randall started landing beside her, playing bodyguard. Even then, she was hopeless. But after her last round, Randall said, "Nice job that time." Nice job, what, lasting five whole minutes?

"Yeah, sick shooting," said Matty. More like *shit* shooting. "Thanks for trying out." He couldn't be serious.

Zoey scrunched her nose like there was a turd on her desk, and Akira looked positively murderous. That cold thing in my chest snaked through my veins. I had to stop this—to save us all from clawing at each other's throats. I had to make sure Lucia didn't even *want* to join us.

A hopeful smile stretched across Lucia's face. "When will I find out?"

"Find out *what*?" I said.

"If I made the team?"

Matty started answering, but my *pfft* cut him off. "Do you honestly think we'd let you onto the team after that? You were absolutely pathetic. My seventy-year-old grandma could play better than you just did."

Lucia's mouth dropped open, and her eyes watered as she searched each person, hoping someone would jump to her defense. But nobody did. As she fled into the hall, I knew I'd made a mistake.

Randall gaped at me. "What the hell was that?" My cheeks flamed.

"A sick burn is what it was," said Matty, though he looked conflicted.

"She *was* horrible," said Akira.

Zoey glared at the boys. "And you two were lapping it up."

"We were being nice, boo," said Randall.

"What, to hurt her later when we don't pick her?" said Zoey. "Better to be up-front." I gave her a grateful look, and she nodded. But I was so mortified, I barely paid attention to Dylan's tryouts. I'd been so afraid we'd do to Lucia what we did to Brady that I'd done exactly what I was protecting her from, humiliating her in front of everyone.

And I must've really hurt her, because she tried to get revenge. And if she tried once . . . maybe she'd try again.

"*Lucia.*" Dylan considered this as he polished off his brownie. "Because I made the team, and she didn't?"

"That, or everything that went down after." I wiped a hand down my face. But she couldn't be An0nym0us1—she was in class when I got that first video message. Although . . . she *did* follow me into the bathroom. That was kind of weird.

"But I barely had anything to do with that," said Dylan.

Little did he know, *I* was the primary target here. I bit my lip and glanced in my phone's direction. It was too dangerous to speculate aloud like this.

Dylan mistook me averting my gaze. "Ugh, you're just humoring me, aren't you?"

Oh no. He thought I thought he was guilty. He looked so distraught, I reached out and clasped his hand. "No, I'm not—"

"Hey." Matty stood in the doorway between the kitchen and foyer, eyes trained on our hands.

I snapped mine back. "Hi."

"Uh, sorry . . . The door was open." Oops. I must not have closed it behind Dylan. Mom always lectured me for forgetting to lock it, and then I'd remind her of the latest time she forgot where she put her phone or keys.

"It's fine," I said. The rest of the group streamed into the kitchen. Zoey slinked in last, looking a bit off-kilter.

"Dude! You stole a test?" Randall shoved Dylan's arm playfully. "Everyone knows you gotta snap pics and put it back."

Dylan's jaw clenched. "I didn't steal anything."

Matty and Randall snickered. "Sure, sure," said Randall. Akira elbowed him.

"I didn't!"

Zoey gave Dylan a sympathetic look. "You could tell us if you did. We wouldn't judge." My eyes nearly rolled to the back of my skull. She *would* love another con artist to commiserate with.

"But I *didn't*!" Dylan slumped his shoulders, defeated. "Dammit. If you don't believe me, how will anyone else? How will MIT?"

"Them's the breaks." Randall chortled some more, already helping himself to a brownie, relentlessly teasing as always.

"I believe you," I said.

Dylan's head snapped up. "Really?"

"Really?" said Matty at the same time.

Heat rushed into my cheeks, and I swallowed hard. "If he said he didn't do it, he didn't do it. Why would he lie to us?"

Matty's eyes darted between Dylan and me, and something twinged in my chest. Did he know how I felt about Dylan? I trusted Akira and Randall to keep my feelings on the DL. But Matty had seen me storm from Lucia's party after Zoey kissed Dylan. Was he putting two and two together?

"Cuz he knows he shoulda snapped pics!" said Randall, mouth full.

Akira flicked Randall's arm. "Will you stop?"

"Aren't you supposed to be home babysitting?" Dylan snapped at Randall.

"My parents got home early. I'm a free boy," Randall said in a Pinocchio voice. He shook Dylan's shoulder, getting crumbs all over the place. "Chill, dude. I'm just giving you a hard time."

"C'mon." I slid off the barstool. "Let's go play." I needed to distract my friends with MortalDusk so I could google Lance Burdly. Hopefully the police hadn't already busted down his door . . .

Dylan grabbed the tray of brownies, and Akira took a plate from the cabinet and tugged open the silverware drawer. She always nibbled at her desserts, savoring them for as long as possible. "Um . . . ?" She picked up my cell.

My heart jolted. "Oh, that's where it went." I grabbed it and headed for the basement, ignoring how she watched me as if I were an alien.

Downstairs, I settled into the recliner Zoey usually took. She gave me a confused look before plopping down in my usual spot on the couch next to Akira, but I needed this spot to research Lance Burdly without Akira or Dylan noticing.

"So your dad was chill about it?" Randall asked Dylan.

"Uh . . . no?" Dylan set the tray on the desk before sitting next to Zoey. Whiskers leaped off her perch on the armrest next to him and dashed upstairs to find some peace and quiet.

"Well, you're *here,*" said Randall. "He didn't ground your ass?"

"Oh. He still doesn't know. Mr. Chen couldn't get in touch with him . . . He's at some book festival in New York." Dylan and his dad moved up to Vermont when their old New York City landlord skyrocketed their rent, and they couldn't swing it on his dad's publishing salary. He got a job at a small local publishing house but had to travel to conferences and festivals all the time. And since Dylan's mom was dead, he was on his own a lot.

"Lucky break." Matty took a brownie and passed the tray to Zoey.

She waved him off. "No, thanks. Still feeling queasy." Huh. Zoey was a chocoholic. Maybe she really had been sick today.

"So, Crys, let me get this straight," said Matty, distracting me from starting my search. "You yakked at school, and then, to celebrate yakking, you baked brownies?"

"Uh . . . well . . . I wanted to make Dylan some comfort food."

Dylan chuckled. "Nothing like chocolate to make you forget your life's been destroyed." There was that snark again.

"Your life hasn't been destroyed," I said. "We'll figure this out together, okay?"

Dylan's eyes snapped to mine and held, almost like he was trying to puzzle out something. My cheeks warmed, and by the time I finally broke eye contact, my face probably matched Zoey's pink hair.

She and Matty both stared with sour expressions.

I couldn't care less what Zoey thought. But Matty's expression made cracks spider through my rib cage. I couldn't let our mismatched feelings destroy us. I had to talk to him. I had to make sure he knew how much he meant to me, and that I'd never do anything to risk our friendship—though he'd probably point out how Akira and Randall were making it work . . .

Yet as our eyes remained locked, the thought of discussing this with him physically pained me. *Why?* I was scared to hurt Matty's feelings, sure. But there was something else. For some reason, I'd closed myself off to the possibility of *us,* pulling away whenever he leaned too close, inviting the others whenever he asked me somewhere. Was I being foolish?

Ugh, how had things gotten so messy this year? Nothing discombobulated a good friendship like hormones.

"So, who's streaming today?" Randall asked. Akira cringed. Though we'd all be on audio, we rotated which two of us streamed our screens and webcams each day. Akira hated being on camera and despised when it was her turn, especially ever since we got trolled—though, to be fair, we'd all felt a bit wary after that. But her therapist encouraged it as part of the exposure therapy to bolster her self-esteem. So lately she'd been sucking it up. Dylan was the only one who flat-out refused, in his rebellion against social media. "You and me?" Randall poked Matty's arm.

"Let's do it," said Matty. Akira's posture relaxed.

As we loaded MortalDusk, Matty asked Dylan, "You got suspended, right, bro?" Dylan nodded morosely. "Shit. Does that mean you're technically suspended from our team?"

My stomach dropped.

Everyone stared as Dylan blanched, and Zoey straightened hopefully. Ha. She'd even throw Dylan under the bus for a spot at the tourney—if he couldn't play, that meant the rest of us could.

"The tourney's not a school event, though," I said. Many players were older, like Fishman and his Vermont-based team he'd scrounged up since his usual buddies were scattered around the world. All I knew about them was they lived up near the Canadian border.

"Yeah, but it's technically a *team* activity," said Matty. I squinted at him. Was he really concerned over this technicality? Or was he being a jealous doofus?

"Mr. Ferguson hasn't said anything yet," I said. Back when Matty officially established our esports team at Newboro High—his moms insisted he play a team sport, and they couldn't argue that esports didn't qualify—Matty recruited Mr. Ferguson as our supervisor. But Mr. Ferguson was so busy running the Science Olympiads, he pretty much left us to our own devices. "So until he does, let's assume Dylan's good to play. We've got a better shot at winning with him on the team."

I thought Dylan would appreciate this, but his jaw clenched. Did he think I only cared about his gameplay, not *him*? Caelyn's voice echoed in my head: *Do you even care about* anything *in the real world?* My heart went rigid. Oh, God. None of this mattered. I had to warn Lance Burdly. I had to find my sister.

As soon as my dragon dropped me off at Bewitched Bay, I let some random elf kill me without fighting back. "Dammit!" I cried. Not exactly an Oscar-worthy performance, but Zoey smirked. Ugh. Well, I couldn't worry about that now. Fat chance I'd get to play in the tourney, anyway—God knew what would happen before Sunday.

I tabbed over to Google.

No results found for "lance burdly."

None at all? Huh. I switched to searching on social media— tuning out Randall and Matty's witty banter and the occasional grunt in battle like humming in the background—but there were no Lance Burdlys anywhere. Weird. Well, not everyone had profiles. Dylan didn't. Whenever someone asked for his handle, he'd say, "I'm not giving corrupt corporations access to my brain." And whenever he caught any of us doom-scrolling, he'd say, "Those algos have you addicted." All valid points.

Next, I checked every directory site I could find, but still, nada. My stomach sank. How could a person not exist online *at all*?

"Nailed it!" Matty cried suddenly. I jumped out of my skin. "And that's twenty K." Oh, snap—he'd secured the third spot at the tourney. Randall whooped, but Zoey scowled—I could tell she hated that the boys got there first. I returned Matty's mimed high-five, but Akira threw me a worried look. She wanted the prize money for college. Her heart was set on Cornell, which had one of the top architecture programs, but since it was Ivy League, there was about a snowball's chance in hell she'd get a scholarship. And none of us wanted to be buried under student loan debt like our parents.

At least Akira knew what she wanted to do with her life. Sometimes I thought maybe I could become a video game developer, to create the lush landscapes and stories I loved escaping into. But did I even have the design chops? Would I need to learn to code? Zoey had tried to teach me some stuff, but none of it stuck. Could I devise intricate puzzles and rules? I hadn't thought it through, and let's be real—I could barely think further ahead than next month.

Matty happily scarfed down the rest of his brownie. "Too bad you crapped out so early, Crys."

"Too bad your face crapped out," I shot back reflexively.

He chortled approvingly—our audience loved that kind of banter—scratching the back of his neck, then covered his mic so the livestream wouldn't hear, "It's just nice having a Fishman-free round."

"Ugh, I know." But I had bigger problems. And so did Lance.

In the next round, I had to stay alive long enough not to arouse suspicion, so I half-heartedly hunted for treasure chests. "Hey, Matty, I got a fire staff. Want it?" That was his favorite weapon. I preferred a shock staff since its lightning bolts reached farther, and I could sneak onto rooftops and snipe people.

"Nah." He scratched his neck again. "Already got one."

"'Kay." As I sped toward Calamity Castle, I heard footsteps thud nearby, so I veered toward a cottage and dashed upstairs to peek out a window. An avatar with long, flowing blond hair in a pink gown sprinted across the dirt path. I hovered my cursor over them and right-clicked. *DaggerQueen29.*

Zoey.

Might as well. I lined up my shot with the fire staff, aiming for her head. But the fireball whizzed past her. She spun, searching for the flame's source, and sprinted toward me. Dammit. I couldn't help caring—I didn't want to give her the satisfaction of killing me. I lined up my shot again, but before I could fire, lightning streaked across the screen, and her avatar vaporized.

"No!" she shouted as her health potions scattered. "Ugh, I thought I had you."

"That wasn't me," I said. Matty cleared his throat. For a moment, I thought he was claiming credit, but then the feed in the corner reporting the most recent kills updated.

Icy tendrils wrapped around my heart.

An0nym0us1 took out DaggerQueen29 with a shock staff.

CHAPTER 12

Every hair on my body stood on end. An0nym0us1 had found me *in the game*. How?

I glanced at Zoey, who watched her screen, nibbling on her pink-lacquered fingernail. She'd once said it was impossible to stalk a specific user onto a map without hacking MortalDusk. And even though we were livestreaming, there was no way for anyone to join a map once it was already in play. But An0nym0us1 clearly had hacking skills.

Zoey threw me a baffled look. "You gonna move?"

She was watching my avatar, which meant An0nym0us1 could see me, too. After dying, you got to watch the person who killed you until they died, then the person who killed them until *they* died, and so on. We rarely stuck around to watch; dying early was a chance to get homework done.

But one time a couple of months ago, I did watch. Zoey had blasted me with a fireball through a window, and when my vantage point switched to hers, I did a double take. She was way over on Crescent Hill. "Whoa, you blasted me all the way from there?" I gaped at the feed: *DaggerQueen29 eliminated ShardsOfGlass with a fire staff.* Maybe a pro archer like Randall could pull off that kind of shot with a fire arrow. But with a staff? Impossible.

Her cheeks flushed. "Sorry. Didn't realize that was you."

"No worries, but *how*?" Zoey kinda sucked at aiming, relatively speaking. She usually preferred blade combat.

"Lucky shot, I guess." She clamped her lips together so tight all the pink disappeared. I narrowed my eyes. Was she lying to me?

Dylan chuckled. "Don't be a sore loser."

Now it was my turn to blush. "I'm not! I'm just . . . surprised. Whatever, forget it." I tabbed over to my English essay, trying to ignore the niggle at the base of my skull. But Zoey kept getting lucky, racking up MortalBucks faster than anyone. I couldn't help it—it bugged me how good she got so fast. I *needed* to play in the tourney. I needed that prize money to help Mom pay the mortgage. Zoey's parents were already loaded. They'd foot her college bills, no question, and once she joined their dental practice as an oral surgeon, she'd make bank. Her future was laid out before her like a red carpet dotted with silver platters. The works. She didn't need the money. She wouldn't have to move if she lost.

I tried casting aside these resentful thoughts, feeling like a crap friend. But something felt *off*. Like when you see a blur move in your peripheral vision, but nothing's there. Or when you feel your phone buzz in your pocket, but nobody texted. A glitch in the matrix.

I started watching the feed like a hawk—DaggerQueen29 was knocking people out with all sorts of weapons and spells. Players usually mastered two or three, but Zoey was suddenly good at *all* of them. So the next time we sparred, I let her kill me and pretended to tab over to my homework with a huff. Instead, I watched her play. She chased her next victim out in the open—reckless, like she felt immune—and drew a fire arrow while sprinting. The white aim dot fluttered around the enemy's back, then bounced up to their head and stilled. Even when they darted behind a tree, the dot remained where their head would be, like Zoey had X-ray vision or something. And the split second they reemerged, she loosed her bow and landed a fatal head shot.

My stomach curdled like sour milk. She was totally using an aimbot—software to automatically aim at other players' heads. A high-profile streamer recently got banned from MortalDusk for aimbotting—username, IP address, everything—for life. Why would Zoey risk it? How dare she betray us like that! I glared at her over my monitor, wanting to smack that smirk right off her face.

But the thought of calling her out in front of everyone made me want to curl up like a pill bug. I hated conflict. And what if I was wrong? She'd accuse me of being a jealous bitch—and rightfully so. I needed *proof* she was cheating.

"Why are you just standing there?" Zoey demanded as Matty started coughing, snapping me from the memory as I gaped at An0nym0us1's username in the feed.

But I didn't need to move. A figure dressed in black from head

to toe stepped into my line of sight, stopping directly in front of
the cottage. I right-clicked the avatar. But I already knew.

An0nym0us1.

"Easy kill," Zoey said bitterly.

They didn't fire at me. They simply stared me down as though
to say, *I'm watching you everywhere.* My headphones amplified
my pulse thrashing in my ears, drowning out everything else. It
felt like the walls were closing in.

"Yo." Randall shoved Matty's shoulder. "That's enough,
dude."

Matty laughed through his cough. "Egads, I'm choking on
my own spit here—" But he started hacking again.

"Do you need some water?" Akira asked. Matty waved her
off, shaking his head. But his face was going red.

"I'll get you some," I said, slamming my laptop shut. I had to
get away. An0nym0us1 was everywhere. *Everywhere.*

I bolted upstairs to the kitchen. Dots the color of mud
blinked into my vision, blinding me, and I gripped the edge
of the granite counter. My heart raced so fast I thought my
rib cage might burst. Caelyn's kidnapper was watching, always
watching, in reality and in MortalDusk. They didn't just want
me to play their twisted game. They wanted to *scare* me. To
torment me.

Akira pounded upstairs, looking distraught. "Are you getting
that water or what?" she asked, then noticed my expression. "Are
you okay?" She knew I had panic attacks every so often, sometimes for no reason at all. So if I ever slipped away, she'd come
check on me. Last time it happened, she lay next to me on the
carpet, letting me grip her hand even though I was crushing it,

waiting out the waves of tremors that racked my body. Sort of like when I noticed she wasn't eating more than an apple each day at school, how her face went gaunt and her eyes dimmed, how she shivered in warm rooms and clutched at nearby surfaces when she stood, dizzy, unfocused. I'd convinced her to tell her parents, held her hand as she did, told her she was safe and wasn't alone every day. We secretly soothed each other's pain when it seemed nobody else would understand.

But this time, she hadn't come upstairs for me. Without waiting for a reply, Akira spun and grabbed a glass from the cabinet. "Something's wrong with Matty." My blood ran cold as she filled the glass at the sink. I followed her back downstairs. Matty was hunched over, coughing into his hands, face beet red, the game forgotten. Randall's and Matty's laptops were shut—the fastest way to end the livestream. Akira passed him the glass. He took it but couldn't stop coughing long enough to take a sip, and water sloshed over the edge. As she took it back, Zoey and I exchanged a worried look.

"Are you choking on something?" I asked, frenzied, ready to leap into position for the Heimlich maneuver, like Mom taught me.

"No . . ." he croaked, then kept hacking. Shaking his head, he jabbed a finger toward his backpack. That's when I noticed the round, reddish bulge on the back of his hand. There were two on the back of his neck, too. Were those *hives*?

"Oh, God. His EpiPen. He needs his EpiPen." I dived at his backpack and searched inside for the bright orange case.

Randall gripped Matty's shoulder. "He's having an allergic reaction?"

"I think so," I said.

"But from what?" asked Akira.

"The brownies?" Zoey pointed to the half-eaten tray.

I froze, and my chest tightened again. "No, that's impossible. I baked them myself . . . there were no nuts in the recipe . . ."

"Are you *sure*?" Zoey asked.

"Yes!" I kept digging through Matty's backpack with shaking fingers. "We don't even have nuts in the house." Mom kept the house nut-free since Matty came over all the time, much to Caelyn's chagrin—whenever she went to Deja's or Suki's houses, she gorged on Reese's Peanut Butter Cups.

The veins in Matty's neck bulged as he wheezed between coughing fits, gasping for air. The EpiPen would shut down his allergic response, reducing the swelling and relaxing the muscles that were keeping his lungs closed. One time, Matty's mothers corralled us all in their living room so Mom could teach us how to use it—remove the cap, place the tip against his thigh, swing, and push it in, and it'd auto-inject. It was supposed to be so easy, Matty could do it himself.

But it could only be easy if you could find the damn thing.

I frantically fished through each compartment. "I can't find it. Matty, are you sure it's in here?"

He managed a nod.

"I'm calling an ambulance." I grabbed my phone, dialed 911, and held it to my ear, biting the inside of my cheek so hard I tasted metal.

Randall raced over and turned the backpack upside down, shaking it vigorously. Notebooks, pens, pencils, gum, and various school supplies went flying everywhere, but there was no sign of the orange case. "Where the hell is it?"

Akira knelt at Matty's side, rambling reassurances, but Zoey stood back, cheeks shining with tears of fear.

Dylan perched on the edge of the couch, gripping his mouth and staring at his laptop. "Yup," he said suddenly, "anaphylaxis can set in within three to thirty minutes."

Why didn't I hear ringing? I glanced at my phone screen again. It wouldn't connect the call, and after another moment, it gave up and went back to the home screen. "My phone . . . something's wrong with my phone. Someone call 911!"

Randall dug out his phone and placed the call. "Yeah, hi, we're at . . ." He looked to me.

"Five-five-two Radcliffe Drive," I said. Matty had his head between his knees now, violently coughing and clutching his throat.

Randall repeated my address. "We need an ambulance, fast. My friend's having an allergic reaction. He can't breathe!"

Why could Randall's call connect when mine couldn't? I was pretty sure we had the same service provider, and I never had signal problems at home. I checked the screen—yep, full bars. So why couldn't I call 911?

An0nym0us1. They'd hacked my phone. They'd blocked me from making the call, hadn't they? My stomach dropped like I was falling off a cliff. Did they tamper with the brownies some- how? They'd sent me to the park. They'd gotten me out of the house.

And the brownies didn't burn.

Holy hell. Had they been *inside my house*?

Just then, Matty tumbled from the chair to the ground. "Matty!" I raced to his side. Getting Dylan suspended was one thing, but would An0nym0us1 make me kill someone?

They *had* kidnapped Caelyn. Now they were holding her hostage, taunting me with threats of sinking a knife into her flesh . . .

"Yeah, anaphylactic shock, exactly," Randall said to the 911 operator. "And he doesn't have his EpiPen."

Akira knelt on Matty's other side. "It's okay, everything's going to be okay." But to me she said, "What do we *do*?"

I couldn't let this happen. "Turn him on his side!" I said, remembering Mom's training. Akira helped me roll him onto his side. Mom had seen so much preventable stuff at the hospital, and since I babysat all the time, she'd taught me basic first aid and CPR. She was also paranoid that one day we'd discover an allergy we never knew about, so she kept—

"EpiPens." I scrambled to my feet. "My mom keeps emergency EpiPens upstairs."

"Go!" Randall cried, his eyes bugged and panicked.

As I flew up the stairs, I hoped our EpiPens were still good. There were two per case, but didn't they expire every year or something? Mom was so frazzled lately, she depended on us to remind her of these sorts of things—like when Caelyn's inhaler cartridges ran low.

I reached the upstairs bathroom and swung open the medicine cabinet. The orange case was always in the bottom right-hand corner for easy access.

But there was nothing there.

Letting out a frustrated growl, I groped at the empty space, like the case had fallen into some hidden panel or something, then dug through the drawers. Had An0nym0us1 tampered with the brownies, knowing about Matty's allergy, then searched the bathrooms for anything that might save him?

The mere thought was creepy as hell.

But there was no way that's what happened. No *way*. I was just being paranoid. The EpiPens must've expired, just as I suspected, and Mom threw them out, meaning to replace them soon.

By the time I raced back downstairs, Matty was convulsing as his lungs strained to suck in air, and his eyes were closed.

"Do you have them?" Randall said.

"No, I couldn't find them," I said, and he cursed. "Did he pass out?"

"Yeah," said Dylan. Akira was still kneeling next to Matty, keeping him on his side.

"Where's the fucking ambulance?" Zoey cried.

"They're coming—" Randall started.

But suddenly, Matty went quiet. And still.

"What happened?" asked Zoey. "Is he breathing again?"

I fell to his side and held my hand under his nose, hoping to feel a rush of air on my fingers. But there was nothing. Nothing. "He's not breathing."

"He's not breathing!" Randall repeated into the phone. After listening for a moment, he asked, "Does anyone know CPR—"

But I was already on it. I rolled Matty onto his back again

and pressed an ear to his chest, listening for a heartbeat. Mom had mentioned that anaphylaxis caused some people to have heart attacks. But I couldn't hear anything but Zoey's sobs.

I held back sobs of my own. "No. This was too fast. This happened too fast." I began chest compressions, clasping my hands and pushing hard and fast in the center of Matty's rib cage, tears streaming down my cheeks as I counted to . . . what was it supposed to be? Thirty? I frantically wiped my face with the back of my hand so I wouldn't get tears all over Matty. I couldn't lose it. I had to keep it together.

Matty's mouth was already open, lips pink and swollen. I pinched his nose, pressed my lips to his, and blew in. His lips were somehow dry after all that hacking, and still warm. But his chest remained flat. I wasn't doing it right. I tilted his head back and lifted his chin, placed my lips more firmly over his, and blew.

But nothing happened.

His chest should have risen as his lungs filled. Was his airway completely closed? Or was I doing this wrong? I choked back a sob as I started another round of compressions. If air wasn't reaching his lungs, his brain would be deprived of oxygen. There could be brain damage, if his heart hadn't already given out.

Dylan knelt next to me. "How can I help? What can I do?"

I shook my head and tried blowing air into Matty's lungs again. Still nothing. I let out a strangled cry, and everything went blurry like in a nightmare, where everything had warped, fuzzy edges. This couldn't be happening.

"Oh my God," said Akira as Zoey clung to her, sobbing. There was a muffled voice coming from Randall's phone—

someone was clearly asking for an update—but he was too shocked to speak.

Dylan pressed his fingers against Matty's neck and said something, his words distorting in my mind as sirens wailed in the distance. The ambulance was coming. Help was coming.

But was it too late?

5 Years Ago

"Hang on," I whispered to Brady. We'd just snuck back into Zoey's house, quiet as mice. The lights were still off except those in the kitchen. Upstairs, Zoey's parents' bedroom door was closed, and all was silent and still.

I gave Brady a mischievous grin and raised a finger to my lips. He nodded conspiratorially. As we crept downstairs, everyone was laughing over something, oblivious to our return. I took my phone from my pocket and readied the flashlight, heart pattering with giddiness. At the bottom of the stairs, I flicked the light switch, plunging the den into darkness.

Akira gasped.

"What the—" Matty started.

Creeping closer, I held the phone under my chin and turned on the flashlight, setting my face aglow, and made a raspy growling noise. Zoey squealed, but the shriek that came out of Akira would've been loud enough to wake the whole neighborhood if the basement wasn't soundproofed.

Matty and Randall hooted as she burrowed into her sleeping bag.

Zoey stood and lunged at the light switch. For a sec, I was afraid she'd be mad, but she was laughing. "Kiki, it's just Crystal."

Akira peeked out, eyes darting toward the creepy door in the back corner. "I thought . . . I thought . . ." She fully reemerged, pursed her lips, and chucked an Olaf stuffed animal at me. "Fool!" Then she succumbed to a fit of giggles with the rest of us.

Brady stood to the side, chuckling awkwardly. Nobody acknowledged his reappearance. Hopefully, we could just forget what happened earlier and have fun.

"You guys," I whispered excitedly. "Everyone's asleep upstairs. Let's go play Manhunt."

Zoey's smile collapsed. "No. I told you, my parents'll kill me if we sneak out."

"We were just outside." I pointed between me and Brady. "And they had no idea."

"You were gone for, like, five minutes, though."

"C'mon, Zoey," said Randall. "Don't be such a chicken."

Matty squawked.

"What about Sanctuary?" said Brady.

"We'll play it after," said Akira.

Zoey stretched her sleeves over her fists, looking torn.

"C'mon, Zoey." I shook her arm. "Your parents won't murder you on your birthday. Nobody's going to die. It'll be so *much fun."*

After a moment, her eyes sparkled with rebellion. "Alright. Let's go."

As everyone scrambled into their coats, Brady moaned, "Ugh, I forgot my jacket at home."

"Oh, farts." Matty dug an oversize red sweatshirt from his duffel and tossed it over. "Here."

Brady pulled it on—it had a Minecraft creeper design and came nearly to his knees, and he had to bunch up the sleeves to free his hands.

Zoey disappeared into the storage room. Akira grimaced, like some ghosts might hack Zoey to bits, but she quickly reemerged wearing a pink pom-pom hat and matching gloves, wielding flashlights. "We only have four."

As Matty and Randall wrestled over one, I said, "I'll use the one on my phone," passing a flashlight to Akira. She and Brady didn't have smartphones yet.

I led everyone upstairs and held the side door open as my friends slipped out into the crisp night air. Akira and Randall laughed giddily as they dashed up the hill toward the swing set behind the house, and Zoey followed, shushing them. I quietly shut the door and started to run, not wanting to be left behind, and stumbled over the step down from the stoop.

My arms shot out, and I gasped, bracing for impact.

Someone grasped the back of my jacket and yanked me back. Once I regained my footing, I saw it was Matty. He'd been waiting for me. "That was almost a fiasco," he said.

I laughed and straightened my jacket. "Totally. Thanks."

"Maybe try not to be such a klutz." A coy smile blossomed across his lips.

I tried to shove him, but he angled out of reach. "Maybe try not to be such a futz."

"Maybe try not to be such a butt!"

Giggling, I chased him across the backyard toward the others.

The night was ours.

CHAPTER 13

There were two men in this world I fully didn't trust—well, not including politicians and stuff. Men I knew personally. And one of them was in my kitchen.

Chief Sanchez hunched over the counter, sniffing the tray of brownies I'd brought upstairs after a pair of paramedics whisked Matty away. They'd detected a faint heartbeat. Gave him a large dose of epinephrine. But he remained unresponsive, and they wouldn't let any of us in the ambulance with him. Akira went into eternal optimist mode, trying to convince us all he'd be fine. But how could she possibly know that? God knew what was really happening.

Now we gathered in my kitchen, Sanchez dominating the space, tall and broad-shouldered, with side-swept ebony hair flecked with gray, and a dark, scruffy goatee. A gun protruded from his holster, black as night. Did it bother him to carry death on his waist? Did it weigh him down? My eyes kept fluttering to it, just like they had that time at Food Xpress last year.

Sanchez had gotten in line behind me as Mom unloaded groceries from our cart onto the belt at Randall's register, clutching a wrapped sandwich and a Coke bottle, scrolling through his phone. I'd reflexively glanced at his gun, feeling a stab of unease.

But maybe he could help us. That's what cops were supposed to do, right? Help people who were getting hurt.

"Mom," I'd whispered, grabbing a carton of milk from the cart. "Tell him."

"Tell who what?" She didn't bother keeping her voice down before glancing up and spotting Chief Sanchez behind me. Blanching, she tugged down her sleeve, covering the small bruises that bloomed on her forearm like sour grapes. "No."

"But he's right there—"

"*No.* He won't believe me."

I pouted. "Why not?"

"Good morrow, Mrs. Donovan!" Randall called out, handing the customer ahead of us her receipt. He often used fake accents and teased customers to keep from dying of boredom. "How art thou presently—"

"Yeah, hi." I waved him off. To Mom, I whispered, "Show him the bruises," pointing at her arm.

She batted my finger away and reached for the frozen peas. "No. We can talk about this later."

"Well, then, I'm telling him—"

I started to turn, but Mom grabbed the hem of my sweater, tugging me back. "No!" She sighed. "Crystal . . . this happens to women all the time. I see them come into the hospital—" She cut herself off, eyes tortured, like she didn't want to say too much.

Like she was trying to protect me from life's harsh realities, though our reality at home was already hell. "It'd be *his* word over mine."

"And mine. And Caelyn's—"

"I daresay, thou art troubled," said Randall, dragging items over the scanner. "Pray tell?"

We both ignored him and glanced back at Sanchez, who stared down at his phone. If only he'd look up. If only he'd see the bruises for himself, the frightened look in Mom's eyes, the desperation in mine. He'd *have* to believe us. "I don't trust him to trust me," Mom whispered. "And if your father finds out . . . I can't risk it. I *can't.*"

He'd been *right there.* Someone who could help. But he didn't bother to look up. And if Mom didn't trust him, how often did the police ignore battered women? How often did they let victims suffer?

Sanchez motioned to the brownies, jarring me from the memory. "These the culprit?" he asked, voice gruff. I was suddenly very aware of my cell in my back pocket. *If you call the police, she dies.* This didn't count, did it?

"Probably." Zoey scowled at me. "Crystal baked them."

"Zoey—" Dylan started.

"I told you, there aren't any nuts in them!" I frantically pointed to the ingredients scattered on the counter next to the stove, nearly clobbering Akira, who winced. "Sorry. That's everything I used. No nuts. Nothing with nuts." Randall sat alone at the kitchen table, gripping his head, face hidden. Matty was like his other half, and he loved him more than Matty ever knew. Seeing him so distraught was almost as unsettling as what happened in the basement.

"Mmkay. I'll tell you what, though." Sanchez peered into the open bag of flour. "Sometimes there can be contamination at the factory. Could've been any of these." He shrugged, like it was no matter.

"You should test all the ingredients," Mr. Bloom piped up. Zoey's parents had come straight from work and hovered in the doorway like Secret Service agents, mouths set in matching grim lines, hands clasped in front of them. I honestly wouldn't have been surprised if they had a code name for Zoey. Dark-haired Mr. Bloom towered over his wife, who had wispy blond hair like Zoey's, but shorter and without pink ombre tips. I remembered how furious she was the first time I helped Zoey dye her hair; one act of rebellion she was brave enough to pull off. Now Zoey kept glancing at them, conflicted, like she was simultaneously mortified and comforted by their presence. "If there's contamination," said Mr. Bloom, "and no warning on the packaging, his parents could sue."

My throat tightened. I wished Mom were here. She hadn't picked up her cell—she must've still been in surgery. Sanchez had contacted Matty's mothers, who'd headed to the hospital. If Mom saw them or Matty, or heard about this before I could reach her, she'd flip.

Sanchez gave Mr. Bloom an appeasing smile. "I hear ya. But those tests are expensive, and we don't actually know it was the brownies that did it. Could've been something he ate earlier. Sometimes it takes an hour or two for a reaction to kick in."

"What, so you wouldn't even try to find out what did it?" Zoey asked.

"Matty didn't eat anything right after school," said Akira morosely. "I remember because he said he was hungry, and we talked about ordering in pizza later."

"That's right," Randall croaked.

Dylan stayed quiet, withdrawn.

"And it happened right after he ate a brownie . . ." Zoey's eyes went misty again.

"Yeah, that's how it happens sometimes." Sanchez smoothed down his black mustache. "It's not the first time it's happened. It won't be the last. A real shame he didn't have his EpiPen."

"How the fuck didn't he have his EpiPen?" Randall slammed his fist on the table. "How could he be so fucking *stupid*?" I flinched.

"Is it like him to forget something like that?" Sanchez asked. Forgetting was one theory. Another was that An0nym0us1 swiped the case from Matty's backpack somehow, and the one from our upstairs bathroom. They *wanted* Matty to die.

"No, actually," said Akira. "He panics if he ever leaves his backpack at home and runs back for it."

"Maybe it fell out in his room or something," said Zoey.

"The *one* time he needed it . . ." Randall's voice wavered.

Akira sat next to him and clasped his hand.

I bit my lip and glanced at Sanchez, wishing I could tell him what was *really* happening. But An0nym0us1 was listening, always listening. I couldn't risk Caelyn's life.

Besides . . . what if Sanchez didn't believe me? If he wouldn't believe Mom when her arm was covered in welts, how would

he believe me without any of An0nym0us1's messages? I had no
real proof they even existed.

"Take the ingredients," Mr. Bloom insisted again. "Send them
to the lab. Let the boy's parents decide about the cost." If there
was some ingredient in the brownies I hadn't used, I'd know An0n-
ym0us1 tampered with them while I was at the park. But how
long would it take to get the lab results?

"I mean, sure," said Sanchez, though he shook his head
slightly like he thought it was pointless. He flipped over the bag
of chocolate chips and read the ingredients, then twisted open
the bottle of vanilla extract and sniffed. He frowned, scanning
the label. "You know this is almond extract, right?"

Exactly all the blood drained from my face, and my body
went rigid and numb. I half expected to look down and see a
pool of red around my feet. It couldn't be almond extract. That
was impossible. *Impossible.*

Randall's head snapped up. "*What?*"

"No," I said. "It's vanilla extract—"

Sanchez turned the label to me. *Pure Almond Extract.* But
that was impossible.

That's when everyone glared at me, like what happened to
Matty was entirely my fault.

CHAPTER 14

"**Y**ou knew about Matthew's nut allergy, correct?" Sanchez asked me.

"No!" My voice came out an octave too high. "I mean, yes, I did, but no, I didn't use *that*. I used vanilla extract, I'm sure of it. It said vanilla in the recipe, and I followed the recipe *exactly*." I dashed to the cabinet where I'd found the ingredients. "Here." I grabbed the vanilla extract. "I used this. I know it."

Zoey's eyes drilled into my skull. "Then why was the almond stuff out?"

"I thought something tasted strange . . ." Akira muttered.

"*What?*" Randall released her hand. "Why didn't you *say* anything?"

Akira's eyes widened. "I didn't realize it was nutty at the time . . . It just tasted weird; I couldn't put my finger on it . . ."

As they argued, I breathed hard, clasping my forehead, scrambling to make sense of this, to remember if I'd made a terrible mistake. "I don't know, I don't *know*. I never would have used the almond extract on purpose. I never would've let Matty eat those brownies if I did."

Wasn't there only one bottle here earlier? I didn't even know we had almond extract. But maybe in my rush earlier I'd spotted the word *extract* and assumed it was vanilla. *Was* this my fault? Was Matty's allergic reaction a total coincidence? Maybe An0nym0us1 never meant to kill Matty. The brownies had already served their purpose in their game—to make me think a fire would start. While scrambling to gather the ingredients, I might've grabbed the wrong bottle of extract. If only I could *remember.*

Suddenly, the two-way radio on Sanchez's shoulder crackled. He tilted his ear toward it, somehow understanding the staticky voice on the other end, and went into the living room to reply.

"You killed Matty," Zoey spat. I flinched like she'd slapped me.

Akira gasped. "Don't say that."

"Zoey," said her mother in a soothing tone, "I'm sure the doctors will do everything they can to save him." She threw me a troubled look, though.

Sanchez returned looking somewhat frazzled. "I've gotta run. Another emergency." He eyed the brownies and ingredients. "Listen . . ." He wiped a hand down his face. "Okay, look—I'll take the brownies and ingredients for analysis, and we'll continue this conversation later or tomorrow. But I'm sure this was an accident." He dropped all the ingredients into a big ziplock bag, grabbed the tray, and was out the door. Zoey's parents went after him, peppering him with questions I couldn't hear over the pulse roaring in my ears.

My fault. My fault. *My* fault.

Zoey rounded on me. "How *could* you?"

"I didn't do it on purpose!" My God, how could this be happening? "This can't be real," I said.

Matty was fine just an hour ago, playing MortalDusk in the basement. And now he was unconscious, connected to tubes in the ambulance or hospital, in *actual* mortal peril.

"Well, it is real," said Zoey. "Matty might be dead because of you. You *knew* how careful Matty had to be, and you—"

"Hey, that's enough," Dylan cut in. "If he had to be so careful, he should have asked what was in the brownies before he ate one."

"He didn't ask because he *trusted* her," Zoey fired back, her voice trembling.

"Will you stop trying to blame Crystal?" said Dylan. "This is traumatic enough." My heart clenched. Did he really believe this wasn't my fault? Or was he repaying me for believing he didn't steal that exam?

Zoey crossed her arms. "Of course you're taking her side. But she basically fed Matty poison. It's more blood on *her* hands."

My heart went cold, and Dylan's dark eyebrows shot up.

"Zoey!" Akira shouted, her eyes darting to Zoey's parents, who'd just returned.

"Guys, stop it," said Randall. "This isn't anyone's fault."

"Bullshit," said Zoey.

"Zoey, watch—" her mother started scolding.

"I know, I know, *watch my language*. Because that's really what *fucking* matters right now." Zoey stormed from the room, and her mother followed, yelling after her. A moment later, the front door slammed.

Mr. Bloom hung behind awkwardly. "Crystal, when does your mother get home?"

"I . . . I'm not sure. She's working a double shift today."

"Ah." He rubbed the back of his neck. "Well, can I give anyone a ride home?" Randall, Akira, and Dylan all shook their heads. After waffling a bit, he said to me, "If you need anything at all, come right over," before slinking out.

I clasped my chest, struggling to breathe, like the room had run out of oxygen. Zoey was right. It *was* more blood on my hands. Whether it was an accident or a trap, I was the one who'd baked those brownies.

Akira wrapped her arms around me. "This wasn't your fault, Crystal."

"Maybe it was," I croaked, tears drizzling down my cheeks.

"Maybe," said Randall. My eyes snapped to his, but he didn't look angry. "Maybe you picked up the wrong bottle. But Matty forgot his EpiPen. We didn't call 911 sooner. And I told him to shut up when he started coughing . . ." His face screwed up, and he brought a fist to his mouth. I'd only seen him cry once before. We'd sworn never to talk about that night again.

Now it might be a secret Matty literally took to his grave.

"It was an accident," said Dylan. "A horrible accident."

Was it, though? If Randall was right, so *many* things had to coincidentally go wrong. Technically, it was possible. But technically, An0nym0us1 could have broken in, drizzled almond extract over the batter, left it on the counter, swiped everyone's EpiPens, and disabled my phone from calling 911.

Which was worse?

I dropped into the seat next to Randall, my chest heavy, drowning under the weight of all this uncertainty.

"Shit," Randall said suddenly, gaping at his phone, "I missed *seventeen* calls from my mom."

I'd vaguely wondered why his parents hadn't come over yet. Akira's were still in California with her sister, trying to move their flight up to tomorrow night, and Dylan's dad was taking a train back from New York in the morning.

"Did she find out what happened?" Akira asked.

"I dunno, she didn't text. And she's not picking up," Randall said, phone to his ear. "I should go home. Er . . . Matty was my ride."

"Mine, too," said Akira.

"I can take you both—" Dylan started offering.

"No, I'll drive them," I said, heart jolting at the thought of being left alone. AnOnymOus1 had promised a new game tonight. Once I was alone, God knew what they'd make me do. I still hadn't found Lance Burdly. I needed time to *think.*

Dylan frowned, like that didn't make any sense.

"I . . . I don't want to be alone. Not yet." It was the truth, but he didn't have to know *why.* Though I hated sounding like a scaredy-cat.

Dylan covered my trembling hand, his fingers warm over mine. "You can come. But I'm driving."

"So, who's first?" Dylan docked his phone on the dashboard and pulled up his navigation app.

"Randall," said Akira from the back seat. Randall sat next to her, uncharacteristically quiet, his anxious face glowing in the dark from his phone screen. I couldn't tell what he was more worried about—Matty or his mother.

"Remind me where you live?" said Dylan.

Randall lived on the other side of Hickory Farms, where we went to pick apples and pet the goats when we were little. I'd only been to Randall's a couple of times, and not in several years; we gravitated to those of our houses with basement dens (and therefore less parental interference), which his lacked. He cleared his throat. "It's 379 Pearson Drive."

Pearson Drive. The peculiar familiarity made a chill settle at the base of my spine. It couldn't be . . .

As Dylan turned out of my driveway, I twisted to see Randall. "Do you by any chance know anyone named Lance?"

He frowned. "Should I?"

"Is he one of your neighbors?"

"Definitely not the ones next door. But I don't know everyone on the street, so maybe? Why?"

"Never mind, just curious." I faced forward, swallowing the unease creeping up my throat as Dylan switched on the radio. Some hip-hop song blared so loudly I jumped out of my skin. Akira and I clapped our hands over our ears.

"Dude!" Randall yelled as Dylan scrambled to turn down the volume.

"Sorry," said Dylan. "When I get stressed out, I, uh . . ."

"You try to murder your eardrums?" I said.

He chuckled. "It takes my mind off whatever."

I shook my head, and as Randall ragged on him for this strange ritual, I pulled up my phone's browser and started typing Lance

Burdly's name, but froze. An0nym0us1 would see whatever I searched for on here. With a shudder, I stuffed the phone into my pocket; well, Mom's pocket—I'd swiped her old puffer coat since mine was still at school.

Before I could bury myself too deep in my thoughts, Akira raised her voice over the music. "So, what're the chances we play in the tourney now?"

Oof. MortalDusk. The prize money. Our mortgage. A stab of regret pierced my gut. I couldn't imagine life piecing itself back together in time to play in thirty-six hours.

Randall shook his head, like he couldn't even think about that right now. I turned down the radio volume even more. "I'd give it around a zero percent chance."

"Good odds," said Dylan. "I was thinking more like negative fifty percent."

I sighed. "Zoey'll probably still want to go."

"No way," said Akira. "We can't play without Matty."

"Jesus," Randall muttered.

She squeezed his hand. "No, he'll be fine. I'm just saying, I doubt he'll feel well enough to go by then." She bit her lip and glanced at me. "She'll say he'd want us to play anyway, you think?"

I shrugged. "Or she'll say we were always going to leave one of us out. Now we don't have to compete for it."

"God, that's terrible." Akira smacked the back of my seat. "What's the deal with you two lately?"

I crossed my arms and stared at the window. "Now's not the time for tea." Now, or ever. I still couldn't tell. That hadn't changed.

We endured the rest of the ride in an awkward silence, but as soon as we turned onto Pearson Drive, my insides went numb. Blue and white lights flashed ahead of us, police cruisers and unmarked black cars blocking the road.

Suddenly it all clicked into place. An0nym0us1's endgame. I knew it now. Panic flooded my veins, searing the nerve endings in my fingertips.

Dylan slowed to a stop. "Uh . . ."

"What's going on?" said Akira.

Randall craned his neck to see around my seat. "Are they in front of *my house*?"

Yes. They were. Of course they were.

Before I could respond, Randall was out the door. I unclipped my seat belt and followed, ignoring Dylan, who called my name. Randall raced across the lawn toward the cluster of officers milling by the front stoop. Bronze numbers above the door marked 379.

379 Pearson Drive. The address from the script. I *knew* it.

A police officer spotted Randall and rushed over, stopping him. I couldn't make out what she said. My heart pounded so hard I could hear it thudding in my ears.

"But this is my house!" Randall shouted.

The officer shook her head. "I need you to stand back—"

"Mom! Dad!" He tried going around the officer, who set a firm hand on Randall's shoulder. Like the other officers, she wore a bulky black uniform and a helmet strapped under her chin. The word POLICE stretched in bold white letters across her chest and arm. The porch was illuminated by electric sconces on either side of the front door, which stood wide open, its frame splintered and mangled.

This wasn't just the regular police.

A SWAT team had busted into Randall's house.

CHAPTER 15

It all happened so fast." Randall's mother perched at the edge of her seat in the hospital waiting room, face ashen and taut, absentmindedly tearing a tissue into tiny pieces with quivering fingers and letting them pile in a mound on her lap.

"*What* happened?" Randall wiped a sheen of sweat from his upper lip. It was about a zillion degrees in here—or maybe it felt that way because we'd sprinted from the parking lot, or because Akira had my arm in a vise grip as she gaped at Mrs. Lewis. Zoey was on FaceTime on Akira's phone since her parents refused to let her leave the house, even after she told them Randall's dad had a heart attack.

"I was upstairs in the office, and your dad was in the living room with Nessa, setting up Netflix for her." Mrs. Lewis spoke in a voice so low she was almost whispering, though nobody was close enough to overhear. "And all of a sudden, the front door crashed open. There was yelling. So much yelling. The police were screaming for your dad to put his hands up. And Nessa was screaming bloody murder." She visibly swallowed and glanced down at her six-year-old daughter curled up beside her, head practically buried in Mrs. Lewis's armpit. "By the time I got downstairs, he was already having a heart attack—well, cardiac arrest, I guess. But, my God, seeing those officers pointing their guns at your father as he collapsed—I thought they'd *shot* him. I'll never get that image out of my head." She clasped her forehead.

Randall cupped his mouth, eyes darting back and forth really fast, like he was trying to picture the scene she described. I imagined gangly, balding, cheerful Mr. Lewis—always cracking dad jokes and teasing his kids—crumpled on the floor in agony. *My fault.*

"Shit," said Dylan, blowing air between his lips.

"Did they have the wrong address or something?" said Akira.

Nope. Not what happened.

What happened was, An0nym0us1 had me call in a fake tip. They'd swatted Randall's family. They were making me hurt my friends in exchange for my sister's life.

There was no point clawing for some other explanation. This was exactly as deranged as it seemed.

Now that I knew, a confusing mix of fright and fury churned in my chest. As much as I wanted to curl up into the fetal position under one of these hospital chairs, I wanted to find An0nym0us1 and set their face on fire. How *dare* they do this to us?

Before Mrs. Lewis could answer Akira, Randall asked, "How's Dad?"

Nessa whimpered, "Daddy," and Mrs. Lewis hugged her closer, checking her watch. "I haven't gotten an update in a while. He's been in surgery for over an hour."

"Why didn't you call me back?" Randall demanded.

"My phone ran out of battery. I tried calling you from the nurse's station." She motioned vaguely toward it. I glanced over and saw Chantel, one of Mom's nurse friends who often came over for coffee and gossip, bustling around doing paperwork. When I'd first walked in, she'd waved and mouthed, *She's in surgery,* maybe thinking I was here to visit.

Randall scrolled through his phone. "Oh, that's what that number was . . ."

Mrs. Lewis gave him a shaky side-eye. "Well, I figured you'd be safe at Crystal's, anyway."

Wrong again. None of my friends were safe with me, apparently.

"Uh . . ." Randall rubbed the back of his neck, like he didn't know whether to burden his mother with more terrible news. The four of us exchanged wary looks, and Mrs. Lewis frowned. "What is it?" she asked.

But before any of us could explain what happened to Matty, Chief Sanchez strolled in. Mrs. Lewis's expression hardened, and she sat straight in her chair. He immediately spotted us and ambled over. "Mrs. Lewis. I'm real sorry about what happened. Can we have a word without the kids for a minute?"

Randall tried coercing Nessa to come with us, but she refused to unbury her face from her mother's armpit, so Mrs. Lewis snaked her arm around her again and waved us away.

Across the room, Randall plopped down next to Akira, white as a sheet. "What the fuuuuuuck?" Dylan sat across from the rest of us, elbows on his knees, pale and shell-shocked.

"Randall, that's all so messed up, I'm so sorry," said Zoey, her face filling Akira's phone screen. Randall grunted in reply. "Have you guys seen Melanie or Kenna?" Matty's mothers.

"Nope," said Akira. "No sign of them."

"Maybe they're in another waiting room," I suggested, though a sinking feeling pressed on my insides.

"Or maybe—" Randall's voice caught in his throat.

"Don't," Akira snapped. "Don't even think it. He's going to be fine." She clasped Randall's hand. She knew as well as I did that losing both his father and Matty in one night would destroy him. *Matty.* My eyes fluttered closed, and I focused, like maybe I could sense his presence somewhere in the hospital. But there was nothing. Nothing. My heart ached for him, and in that moment, I wished I'd given him—us—a chance. I'd denied feeling anything for him, but clearly, that wasn't true. So why had I resisted so hard? Maybe because I was scared. Or maybe . . .

I opened my eyes, immediately meeting Dylan's. He'd been watching. A current ran through me so fiercely it felt like I'd been zapped by a shock staff in real life. I quickly averted my gaze, my cheeks going warm.

Yeah. That'd explain it.

"I don't get it." Randall raked back his mussed waves. "Why would the cops bust down our door like that?"

"Your parents aren't, like, under investigation for anything, are they?" said Akira.

Oh, damn. My friends still didn't realize it was a swatting.

They didn't know anything about the fake tip. Of course *I* knew—I'd made the call. Someone wanted to take us down, one by one, and was making me do it.

But *why?*

It had to be the MortalDusk tourney. Someone wanted to take us out of the running. The timing was too big a coincidence— that *had* to be it. But I couldn't say a word. My phone was as effective a gag as the one binding Caelyn's mouth. An0nym0us1 was always listening, and I couldn't ditch my phone to speak freely. *If you don't respond to my messages within a minute, she dies.* I couldn't risk missing one. I had to hope my friends would puzzle this out.

Akira's question hung in the air for a long moment, until Randall burst out laughing.

"What the hell's so funny?" I asked, shocked.

"*My* parents? Under *investigation?* I mean, c'mon, they're a couple of website designers who watch Netflix every night. They're as vanilla as it gets."

"We always think we know everything about our parents," said Dylan. "But anyone can have a dark side." A haunted look darkened his slate-colored eyes. Was there something painful in his past he hadn't told us? I wanted to reach for his hand, but he was too far, and I was frozen in place.

"Dude," said Randall, "my parents are way too basic to have a dark side."

A few minutes later, Sanchez lumbered over and sank into a seat next to Dylan. Akira positioned her phone so Zoey could see him.

"Long time no see," said Sanchez, keeping his tone light. We all stared at him blankly. "Yeah, sorry." He cleared his throat and flipped to a new page in his notebook. "So. I'm gonna need to ask you kids a few—"

"Did those cops have a warrant?" Randall's nostrils flared. It took a lot to get Randall angry. This classified as a *lot*.

Sanchez grunted. "We don't need a warrant for emergency services."

"Emergency? What the hell was the emergency?"

"I'm the one asking the questions now, alright?" said Sanchez. When Randall glanced toward his mother, he added, "She said it was okay."

"Well, you know what's not okay?" said Randall. "Cops busting into my house, guns out, for *no reason*."

"Yeah, that's some grade-A bullshit right there," said Akira. Dylan nodded aggressively.

Sanchez wiped a hand down his face. "We received a troubling tip about your address, and my guys were doing their job."

"What kind of tip?" Randall asked skeptically.

"We'll get to that. But listen . . . I'm real, real sorry about what happened to your dad. Real unfortunate. But right now we gotta find whoever called it in."

My chest cavity fizzed like someone had opened a can of shaken soda in there, making it impossible to swallow the heat creeping up my neck.

"Now, I know you've had a rough night, so I'll try to keep this brief. Do any of you know a Lance Burdly?"

I grimaced. On the car ride to Randall's, I'd asked him if he knew anyone named Lance. But he just shook his head, looking as dumbfounded as Akira and Dylan, who apparently didn't remember, either—though after a moment, Akira tilted her head, like the name rang a bell. Sanchez noticed this as well. "Sound familiar?" he asked.

"I don't know." Akira tucked her hair behind her ear. "I don't *think* so?"

"It doesn't to me," I said with an air of finality.

"Mmkay." Sanchez directed his next question to Randall. "Do you know anyone who has something against you—some reason to pull a prank on you?" My pulse quickened, and I leaned forward, watching Randall expectantly. Come *on*. Figure it out.

But instead, Randall guffawed. "A *prank*? No way. Who'd even want to prank my parents?"

"Oh my God, Randall." I couldn't help it—it seemed so freaking obvious. I clamped my lips shut, but everyone looked at me expectantly. Guh. I lowered my voice, hoping my phone mic was muffled enough in my jacket pocket. "*You* were supposed to be home babysitting. It was supposed to be *you.*"

Me, Randall mouthed, his eyes widening.

"Holy—" said Zoey. "Randall, you got *swatted.*"

There we go.

Sanchez did a double take at Akira's phone, which apparently he hadn't noticed before. "Er . . . I'm gonna have to ask you to hang up. You can call your friend back later."

"Wait, I'm not recording or anything—" Zoey managed to shout before Akira hung up.

Sanchez flipped to an earlier page of notes from his conversation with Randall's mom. "Your parents were supposed to have a meeting in Burlington, correct?"

"Yeah, with some potential client," said Randall, dazed, maybe wondering what I was—what would've happened if he'd been home alone with his sister? Would the SWAT team have arrested him? Would they have *hurt* him? "The dude was a no-show, so they came home early."

Some potential client. I thought of Fishman at the park, claiming I'd asked him to meet. Had Randall's parents really been stood up, or was it another trick from An0nym0us1?

"Had they ever met this guy before?" I whispered.

Randall shook his head. "No clue."

"No," Sanchez said, his tone flat. "They hadn't." He suspected what I did—that it was all a setup. "Now, you kids have a big video game competition this weekend, that right?"

Akira gasped. "You think this is like what happened to Jason Tardis last year?" Yikes, I'd almost forgotten. Sanchez nodded solemnly—apparently, he knew about this. A few days after Jason won the MortalDusk Crown, a SWAT team busted down the front door of his Florida home as he livestreamed. He'd gone upstairs to investigate, so everything happened off-screen, but thousands of people heard the crashes and muted shouts. Later, Jason revealed that one of the cops had recognized him and called off the operation, realizing it was a hoax. But Jason was so rattled, he hadn't streamed since. I hadn't bothered looking into the details. I never imagined something like that would happen to us.

"Did they ever catch Jason's caller?" I asked, hoping my flushed face didn't give me away.

"Nope," said Sanchez. "They have other times, though; it's been happening a bunch, and we're getting smart to it."

"The caller pretended to be Jason, right?" said Akira.

"Yeah," said Dylan. "They said he shot his father, and had his mother tied up in the garage." Just like An0nym0us1's script. A rock lodged in my throat.

"What, so someone pretended to be *me*?" said Randall, his tone still skeptical.

"No, actually," said Sanchez. "Slightly different MO." He didn't elaborate, but I already knew. *Lance Burdly.* Whoever the hell that was. Probably no one at all.

And whoever was doing this wasn't just after Randall—they were after our whole team. I needed everyone to connect the freaking dots already. Matty's allergic reaction. Dylan's suspension. Did they think it was all a coincidence?

With Sanchez focused on Randall, I nudged Akira's elbow and mimed taking a bite of a brownie.

But she just looked confused. "What're you doing?"

Sanchez gave me a weird look, and my cheeks flamed even more. Emulating a game of charades would look suspicious as hell. I covered my mouth and coughed. "Nothing." Sanchez glanced back at his notes again. I looked to Dylan, hoping he'd caught on, but he was staring at the floor, hands clasped with his elbows on his knees, deep in thought. God, this was frustrating.

"Anyhow," said Sanchez. "Can you think of anyone who'd swat you?"

"Pfft, no," said Randall. "Some fuckbucket must've gotten the address wrong." Everything was always a joke with him. Even now. I let out an exasperated huff. "What?" he asked.

"Not everything's a joke," I snapped. "This is serious." It must've been a defense mechanism—he'd rather kid around than confront the fact that someone disliked him enough to hurt him.

"I know it's serious," he said. "My dad's the one in surgery right now—"

"What about Fishman?" Dylan interrupted. "Seems most likely to me."

Sanchez rubbed his cheek. "Say what now?"

"Jeremy Fischer," Akira explained. "Another MortalDusk gamer. He's competing on Sunday, too. He lives nearby, and he hates our guts."

"Not enough to do *this*," said Randall.

"You sure about that?" I prodded in a low voice. I wished Matty were here. He would've been quick to remind Randall how their biggest hero had disappointed them.

But Dylan was almost as quick. "You were first to knock him off the top leaderboard spot," he said to Randall. "And the way he's lost subscribers to us—to the channels *you* manage— his earnings could've taken a hit, for all we know." My breath hitched; I hadn't thought of that. Was that possible? I didn't track our numbers as closely as Randall did. It's not like we were suddenly making bank.

"No way—" Randall started.

"And we totally sabotaged that date of his," said Akira. "Not on purpose, but still."

"What happened there?" Sanchez asked, and Akira recounted the incident. "Mmkay," Sanchez said when he finished scribbling notes. "Anyone else?"

"I mean," said Dylan, adjusting his glasses, "technically, it could be anyone else on Fishman's team. Or anyone playing in the Vermont tourney. Anyone else after the prize money could have a motive."

I nodded, but Randall's eyebrows shot up.

"What're their names?" asked Sanchez. "The other people on . . . this person's team?" We screwed up our faces—we knew their streamer names, not their real names. But Dylan rattled them off, anyway.

There was someone else, too—someone with a grudge against us all. I glanced at Dylan, who clenched his sharp jaw as he watched Sanchez jot his notes. Did he realize the answer key in his locker was connected to all of this? Did he remember my suggestion that Lucia might've done it? What about Akira and Randall—didn't anyone remember how she'd tried getting revenge? I had her name on the tip of my tongue, ready to risk it all, when Sanchez flipped his notebook closed.

"Alright," he said, "I'll check out these gamers, see if any of them have a track record for this kind of behavior. It's a start."

A start wasn't enough. Sanchez didn't have all the information, and by the time he made any progress, An0nym0us1 might make me hurt someone else. They might hurt my sister. I watched helplessly as Sanchez crossed the room to talk to Mrs. Lewis again.

If he didn't know the whole truth, how much could he really help?

CHAPTER 16

Once Sanchez was out of earshot, Akira whipped out her phone again and tapped the screen. "You get all that?" she said softly.

"Most of it," said Zoey.

"Oh, damn," I said. "You didn't hang up?"

"No." Akira gave me a sheepish look. "I just turned off the speaker volume—"

"Guys, what the *hell* is going on?" Zoey said so shrilly Akira almost dropped her phone. She lowered the volume. "This can't be a coincidence. It *can't* be."

My heart leaped into my esophagus. *Finally.*

"What can't be?" Randall asked.

"What happened to Matty!" said Zoey. "Is someone trying to pick us off or something?"

Akira exclaimed, "*What?*" and Dylan's mouth dropped open.

"Zoey, that's *nuts,*" said Randall. "Speaking of which," he glanced at me, "I mean, no offense, but the brownies were—"

"Don't put that on Crystal," said Akira.

"—an *accident,*" he finished. "I'm not saying it was her *fault.* But that's all it was. An accident."

Of course, he had no clue An0nym0us1 forced me to make those brownies. That they'd driven me from my house, leaving the brownies unsupervised, supposedly burning in my oven— yet when I got home, they were miraculously perfect.

What a fool I'd been.

"I, uh . . ." I fiddled with the lightning bolt necklace Caelyn made for me, too terrified to speak. But I needed my friends to piece this together. I clamped down on my phone in my jacket pocket, hoping to muffle my voice. "I was upstairs while the brownies were in the oven."

"Why are you whispering?" Randall said loudly. I shushed him, and Dylan watched me like I had an antelope growing out of my neck.

"Kiki, what'd Crystal say?" Zoey asked.

"She was upstairs when the brownies were baking." Akira gnawed at her lower lip for a moment, considering this. "So, what, you think someone came in and tampered with them or something?"

Randall laughed. "I'm sorry, but that's insane. You know that's insane, right?"

I shook my head. His denial was staggering.

"Is it, though?" said Zoey. "Even Sanchez seems to think it has to do with MortalDusk."

"He also said it was a different MO. I was serious before," Randall said pointedly to me, "maybe whoever called in the tip got the address wrong."

"That's not it," I said quietly. "Zoey's right. This isn't a co-incidence."

"Okay. Let's say, for the sake of argument"—Randall waved his hands around as if he were casting a spell—"it's not a coincidence. Let's say it's about the tourney. What the hell's the point of picking us off? We're not the only legit competition. What, is someone going to take out the entire Vermont leaderboard?"

"We *are* at the top," said Akira.

"I still say it's Fishman," said Dylan.

Akira nibbled her lip again, looking unsure.

"But maybe it's not someone who wants to win," said Zoey. "Just someone who wants to keep *us* from winning. Someone with a grudge."

Akira nodded, but Randall shook his head. "No. No way. Nobody's picking us off—"

"Well, how do you explain Matty's missing EpiPen?" said Zoey. *Yep. Connect those dots.* I wanted to hug her through the screen. Though something niggled at the back of my mind . . .

"It fell out of his backpack," said Randall.

"Or someone *took* it out," said Dylan. I made a mental note to hug him later, too.

"Jeez," said Randall. "I didn't realize you guys had been training."

I pouted. "For what?"

"For goddamn mental gymnastics."

"Oh my God, Randall," I said, frustrated. "Why are you in such denial?"

"I'm not! Nobody would *do* this."

"You thought nobody we knew would troll us, either," Akira

said bitterly. "But *that* happened. And you know what? Maybe it's the same person."

A few months ago, someone started leaving crude comments and slurs on our videos. Deleting and blocking didn't help; they kept creating new accounts. Randall laughed it off, but Zoey obsessed over it, keeping a file of screenshots, reverse-image-searching their profile pics, tracing them back to stock photo sites. One day while Randall and Zoey livestreamed our MortalDusk game, Zoey snapped her fingers and tapped her headset, signaling for us to mute ourselves. "Our troll's back at it." She threw Akira a wary glance.

Akira stiffened. "What? Did they say something about me?"

"About *us.*" Randall patted down his disheveled waves. "It's no biggie. I'll ban them again—"

Akira leaped up, then hesitated. "Is your camera off?"

"Hang on—there, paused the stream."

She leaned over Randall, clasping his shoulder as she read the chat pane, and winced. "Ugh."

My heart sank. "What'd they say?"

"I don't even want to read it out loud."

Matty turned his baseball cap backward and read over Randall's other shoulder. "Oh, geez. Whoever said that's a steaming sack of horse vomit."

"Social media sucks." Dylan cracked his knuckles. "Can't we just play without streaming?"

"No way, man," said Randall. "We're finally making some cash here." We'd made about $800 between YouTube and Twitch last month, our best month yet, and he wanted to be able to quit his cashier gig. Too bad $800 split six ways barely made a dent in our mortgage. "Guys, chill, alright? I'll just delete and block. It's probably some Russian bot or something—"

"The Russian bots don't care about our stream," said Zoey. "They're on Twitter attacking Democrats. This is personal."

"D'you think it's Fishman?" said Matty as Akira plopped down next to me again.

I shook my head. "Fishman gets off on hunting us in the game. He wouldn't bother with this." My stomach twisted as I read the comment on my phone. "Wow. It's gotta be someone who knows you're together. I'll bet you ten—no, twenty—bucks it's someone from school." People said things online they'd never say IRL. Just like that snotface brat Tessa in Caelyn's grade who bashed her on Insta, but apparently never said more than two words to her at school.

Zoey nodded. "I agree."

Randall laughed. "You guys are being ridonculous." Akira cringed, looking hurt.

"Randall, this isn't funny," I snapped. "They're insinuating the reason you're together . . . well, they basically accused you of fetishizing Akira." Akira nodded.

Randall tilted his head, rereading the comment. "You mean, because . . ."

Akira raised her chin. "Because you're white and I'm Japanese American, yeah. It's gross."

"It's fucking racist," said Zoey.

"Yep," said Akira. I clasped her hand, wishing she didn't have to read that horrible comment, wishing I could reach through my screen and flip off whoever left it.

"Oh, shit." A regretful look crossed Randall's face. Steeped in his own privilege, he hadn't even spotted it. "I'm *so* sorry."

"It's . . ." Akira started, like she was going to say, *It's fine.*

But it wasn't.

Randall tentatively rolled his chair closer. "Can I . . . ?" He held out his arms. Akira nodded, and he gave her a long hug. "I love you for *you*," he murmured into her hair.

"I know," she said. They finally broke apart at the shutter sound of Zoey screenshotting the comment.

"Is there any way to track down this asshole?" I asked once Randall rolled his chair back over.

"I dunno," he said. "I don't think so."

Matty nudged Randall's shoulder. "Can you see a commenter's IP address on Twitch? Or YouTube?"

"Nope," said Randall. "If it was a comment on a blog we hosted or something, sure. But we'd never get that info from Google or Twitch. Not unless we were, like, the FBI."

"Even if you could," said Dylan, "the troll could be using a VPN to hide their location. They could make it look like they're in another country—"

"Oh!" Zoey's eyes lit up. "I have an idea . . ." Without another word, she slammed her laptop shut and raced home.

The next day, she showed us a widget she'd coded. "It's real simple. You just upload two photos, and the widget embeds code in each one that'll register the user's IP address wherever it loads. We'll send one photo link to the troll, and one to people we think it might be. If someone's IP matches the troll's, we'll know it's them."

Dylan raised his eyebrows. "Even if they're using a VPN."

"Exactly," said Zoey. "The IP addresses would still match."

"Nice," said Dylan, clearly impressed. Something funny lodged in my throat. But then his eyes flicked to me. "Twenty bucks?"

I gave him a tight-lipped grin, ignoring my wobbly gut. "You're on."

We compiled a list of classmates who might have a grudge against us—people like Dave Wisla, the quarterback who'd flipped out when Randall imitated him strutting down the hall; Lucia Ramirez, who I'd humiliated at our esports team tryouts; Maddy Curtis, who'd been dejected after asking Matty to Homecoming. We split the list among us, and each sent emails asking for help on our homework with a link to a screenshot of the assignment. Randall DMed the troll a link to a picture of his middle finger.

Our jaws collectively dropped when Lucia's IP matched the troll's. And I was twenty bucks richer.

Akira understandably didn't want to come with Zoey and me when we cornered Lucia at her locker the next day (let's be real—Zoey did all the talking). But Lucia denied everything. I figured confronting her would be enough to stop her from trolling us again, even if she didn't fess up and apologize. And as furious as I was, guilt soured my stomach. I'd been a bitch to Lucia at tryouts. This was, in a way, my fault.

But then Zoey snarled at Lucia, "I have receipts. I screenshotted all of it, and I have proof the comments came from your IP. I'll put it all online and make sure it ranks first on Google for your name. It won't just be everyone at school who'll see what you did. Colleges will see it. Future employers will see it.

Everyone will know you're a troll, and it'll follow you around *forever.*" For a moment, Lucia's wide, panicked eyes met mine, like maybe I'd step in, be a voice of reason—but her expression hardened as she likely remembered I'd started this. And as shocked as I was by Zoey's rancor, I wouldn't challenge her in front of Lucia. Protecting our friends mattered most. So I stood by Zoey's side and let her threaten Lucia.

Later, I did manage to talk Zoey down. But the unresolved conflict hovered over us like a swarm of starving mosquitoes. Lucia started being extra nice to us, even inviting us to her party, likely terrified we'd forever destroy her reputation at any moment. We'd gone to scope out the scene—we didn't exactly party much—but none of us spoke to her save for our little spat on my way out the door. The tension was palpable. Sometimes I wondered if we should've just deleted and blocked like Randall wanted to. But we'd flicked a domino, and now the pieces were falling.

"Would Lucia really try to pick us off, though?" said Dylan. Akira eyed Sanchez across the waiting room, like she wanted to run this theory by him.

"No way," said Randall. "Just because she screwed up once doesn't make her a *murderer.* I mean, Jesus . . ." Akira pursed her lips.

"It's not just how she screwed up . . ." I trailed off, glancing toward Zoey on Akira's phone. What if Lucia wanted to make sure we never made good on Zoey's threat?

"You guys," said Zoey, her voice wobbling in a telltale way. "What if this has something to do with—"

"No." I nearly screamed, making everyone jump. Even San-chez glanced over. But I couldn't let her say it. I couldn't let her dredge up the past. Not in front of Dylan. "It has nothing to do with that."

"But maybe Brady's—" Zoey started.

"Hang up," I instructed Akira, my body going rigid, pan-icked. Randall blanched, too. Dylan furrowed his brow at our reactions. But he couldn't know about this.

Akira leaned away from me. "What? Why? Zoey, you think this is about *Brady*?"

My stomach plunged into my uterus. "No."

"Who's Brady?" Dylan asked.

I edged forward in my seat, raising my palm. "No one. It's nothing."

"Why would they wait five years, though?" Akira asked Zoey. Dylan's eyes leaped among all of us like a bouncy ball nobody could catch.

I changed tack, laughing, playing it off like it was no big deal, pulling a Randall. "Guys, you're being ridiculous. Nobody waited for anything, because it obviously has nothing to do with that."

"Nothing to do with what?" Dylan tried again.

"Honestly, it's stupid." I waved him off. "It doesn't even matter."

"It's not stupid—" Zoey insisted.

"Listen, it can't be that," I said desperately, "because Dylan wasn't involved. And he was the first victim." Akira tilted her head, confused. "You know, the test. The test in Dylan's locker—"

I cut myself short, realizing what I'd done. I was the only one who knew the test was connected—that it was part of An0nym0us1's game. Clenching my fists, I braced like my phone might explode in my pocket or something. But nothing happened.

Akira's eyes widened. "Oh, shit. I forgot about that."

Dylan scoffed. "Thanks."

"Well, I mean . . ." She gestured wildly around the waiting room, implying worse things had happened since. "Wait—you think that's connected? That someone *framed* you or something?"

"Well, I sure as hell didn't steal that test," said Dylan. Randall quirked his brow. "No, really, man, I didn't."

"But Mr. Chen *knew* it was in your locker, right?" said Zoey excitedly. "Someone must've tipped him off. Another fake tip!" Randall's mouth dropped open. "So it has to be someone from school, right? Someone who knew where Dylan's locker was. Unless someone like Fishman had help from someone on the inside. I'm sure he has a bunch of fanboys at school."

I'd taken the focus off Brady, at least, but that niggling in my brain intensified, and I narrowed my eyes at Zoey. She was awfully quick to throw around these theories . . .

Just then, my mother burst into the room, interrupting my train of thought.

Her baby-blue scrubs were covered in blood.

"Crystal!" She dashed across the waiting room, seemingly oblivious to the gore splatters on her shirt and right pant leg. Her hair was still in its disheveled bun, and the purple shadows under her eyes had darkened since this morning. "Honey, I . . . I'm so sorry I missed your calls—"

Tears sprang to my eyes at her presence. I wanted nothing

more than a hug, but as she reached for me, I cowered away. "Your scrubs, Mom."

She glanced down at the stains and cursed. "Oh, God, I'm so sorry . . . I was in a six-hour surgery, and as soon as I got out, Chantel told me you were here, and I . . . I saw Matty's parents . . . and . . ." Her breath seemed to catch in her throat, and then she croaked, "Oh, honey . . ."

Out of the corner of my eye, I saw Randall grip his seat's arm-rest, and Akira clasped her mouth. My entire body went frigid, like I'd leaped into the lake. The way Mom's face screwed up, she didn't have to say the words for me to know.

Matty didn't make it.

5 Years Ago

"How do you play Manhunt?" Brady asked as we huddled next to Zoey's swing set, shining his flashlight into the woods. I could see pinpricks of light glowing from the houses on the other side, but clouds hid the moon and stars tonight, making the dark stretch of trees seem almost infinite.

"It's like hide-and-seek," said Akira.

"Yeah, but reversed," Matty explained. "So, instead of everyone hiding and one person being 'it,' in Manhunt only one person hides and the rest of us have to find them."

"Don't people usually play in teams?" Zoey asked.

Brady's shoes squished as he shifted uncomfortably—the last lingering snow from a recent storm had thawed in the unseasonable warmth today, leaving the grass soggy above frozen ground. I glanced at him warily. "Let's not do teams. I think that's for bigger groups."

Matty nodded. "Yeah, and we can make our own rules."

"Cool," said Akira. "It'll be more fun hunting as a group."

"Yeah, right," said Randall. "You're just afraid to be alone in the dark." Akira shoved him.

He had a point, though. Zoey's flashlights weren't all that bright, and now that we were out here, the woods seemed dark and dangerous. But it was too late to get cold feet.

"So let's take turns hiding," I said. "And whoever keeps everyone searching the longest, wins."

"I like that," said Matty. "I'll keep time."

"Do we have to do this?" Brady rubbed his arms. "It's so cold."

"Yeah, let's go back inside," said Zoey, teeth chattering. "We can play something else—"

"Zoey, your parents won't know we're gone," I reassured her.

"Yeah, stop being such a wuss," Randall chortled.

Zoey jutted her jaw and muttered, "I'm not a wuss. I'm just cold." Akira passed over her thick gloves, and Zoey put them on over her thin pink ones, disgruntled.

"So, should we set a boundary?" Matty asked, like playing was no longer up for debate.

I grinned. "Yep. Let's stick to all the yards that touch this stretch of woods, up until the Nelsons' property." I motioned toward the west. The Nelsons were an elderly couple who lived in an eighteenth-century colonial nestled back in the woods. Their property was several acres wide, and the dense woods would be pitch-black. I was putting on a brave face, but imagining ambling through them made me shiver.

"No streets, right?" said Randall.

I nodded. "No streets, and no Nelsons'. That's the cutoff." Everyone's heads bobbed in consent.

"So who's hiding first?" asked Randall.

"I'll go first." My heart leaped in anticipation. "Close your eyes and count to a hundred."

"And stay quiet," said Zoey. "And no pointing your flashlights at the houses." Paranoid as ever.

After Matty set his timer and everyone shut their eyes, I dashed alone into the woods, only the faint glow from my phone lighting my path.

CHAPTER 17

I sat numbly at the kitchen table, watching Mom through a foggy membrane as she served Whiskers dinner and made tea for me. It felt like I was encased in a vat of jelly. Nothing felt real.

Matty was dead. *Dead.*

The sound of him gasping for air played on a loop in my mind, and no matter how hard I squeezed my eyes shut, my eyelids were like IMAX screens showing his ever-reddening face, the bulging cords in his neck, the look of sheer terror in his eyes. So much for falling asleep in our house again—or anywhere, ever.

Akira and Randall's plans to spend the night together had gone out the window at warp speed. Mom had wanted to bring Akira home with us so she wouldn't have to be alone, but she'd refused, wanting to shower in her own bathroom after getting violently sick in the waiting room. And since Randall went catatonic after Mom broke the news, Dylan volunteered to take Akira home, vomit-covered coat and all. Before we parted in the parking lot, Dylan had hugged me, pressing his cheek against mine, and murmured into my ear, "It wasn't your fault, Crystal. Everything's going to be okay." But he was wrong on both counts.

Everything was my fault. And nothing was going to be okay.

"So what do you think Caelyn's doing right now?" Mom asked, setting a mug of caramel-and-vanilla tea with a splash of milk in front of me. It was her go-to comfort beverage for me and Caelyn—her equivalent of hot chocolate, sans sugar.

"What?" My heart jolted at Caelyn's name.

"In Frost Valley." She was obviously trying to distract me with a comforting thought, but my pulse picked up speed. I'd checked my phone at least seventeen thousand times since we'd gotten home. But An0nym0us1 was quiet. Every time I remembered how they'd said the next game would be later tonight, my heart jolted nervously.

"Oh, um . . ." I wrapped my fingers around the mug. "I dunno. It's after ten, so . . . maybe she's asleep."

"You think she'd go to bed this early? *Psh,* nerd alert." She stuck out her tongue, clearly trying to lighten the mood, but right now, the joke fell flat.

"Maybe not. I think she mentioned there'd be games and stuff . . ." I gingerly sipped my tea, forcing the bland, hot liquid down my throat, and stared at the table's wood grain, slipping back into my hazed silence. I couldn't speculate on a reality Caelyn wasn't experiencing. I couldn't even look Mom in the eye. Some maniac had kidnapped one daughter and was blackmailing the other, and I couldn't tell her any of it.

She grabbed my hand. "Oh, honey, I'm so sorry about Matty. I'm so sorry I wasn't there for you. Again."

Her words soured the steam rising from our mugs. "Don't do that, Mom."

"No, it's true. I've been taking so many shifts lately, I'm hardly ever here for you—" She screwed up her face and cupped her mouth, holding back tears.

"But you're working so much for *us*. So we can keep living here. You literally can't be in two places at once."

Mom choked back a laugh-sob. "Always so practical. But maybe living here should never have been what mattered. It's just a house. There are others. What mattered should've been keeping you girls safe . . ."

I frowned, my mind snapping to An0nym0us1. "What d'you mean?"

"I should've kicked him out sooner," she said in a small voice. "I should've *protected* you."

Oh. Dad. "But you did," I said. Mom was a perpetual people pleaser who let others guilt-trip her all the time. But I didn't want her to feel guilty about this. She'd been through enough—we all had. "You stopped him from coming in—"

"That wasn't enough, and you know it. You said it yourself."

Yeah. I couldn't say I hadn't laid it on thick.

The morning after Dad nearly burst into my room fists-first, Caelyn and I burrowed under my covers until sunlight streamed through the blinds, casting white bars up and down my bedroom door.

Steeling myself, I'd crept over and edged it open, peeking into the hall. "Wait here," I'd instructed Caelyn, her eyelids droopy and pink from exhaustion. In the hallway, a picture frame was missing—sunlight had faded the surrounding paint, leaving a darker teal square in its place. That'd explain the shattering noise we'd heard. I'd almost dialed 911. But if the police wouldn't believe Mom, why would they believe *me*?

I half expected to find Mom's lifeless body sprawled across my parents' bed, but the floral quilt was neatly tucked under the mattress, and nothing was out of place. Instead, I found them downstairs. Both of them, sitting at the kitchen table—Dad slurping the last dregs of cereal from his bowl, Mom nibbling on toast while scrolling through her phone.

Like nothing happened.

Like everything was fine.

"Mom," I'd said, spotting the edge of a bruise blooming over her collarbone. She tugged up her shirt and rested her chin on her fist to hide the motion.

"Morning, sleepyhead." She kept her voice light.

Dad's lips curled into a smile that didn't reach his eyes—eyes that used to twinkle when I walked into a room. Now they bored into mine like a challenge. *Don't you see? Everything's fine.* He was probably the one to clear the glass from the shattered frame in the hall, to make the bed, to pick out the high-collared shirt Mom wore now. *Nothing happened. You didn't hear a thing.*

But I knew what I heard. He'd almost barreled into my room, drunk off his ass, fury leaching off him like steam. And what would've happened if Mom hadn't stopped him? What would he have done to me? To *Caelyn*? It made my soul ache, like a bruise so deep it could never fully heal. If I couldn't trust my own father, how could I ever trust anyone?

I summoned Mom upstairs, pretending to have a question about my period so Dad wouldn't follow. "What the hell?" I rasped, shutting the bathroom door.

"Don't use that tone with—"

"Screw my tone. Enough is enough. How could you sit there and act like nothing happened last night?"

"It . . . it *was* nothing . . ."

I pointed at the bruise peeking out under her shirt collar. "That's not nothing." Under the bright lights over the sink, I could see she'd tried to cover it with makeup. "When are you going to the police? They'll believe *that*."

I loved Dad. I really did. Problem was, the man downstairs wasn't Dad anymore. Alcohol and something else—addiction, a midlife crisis, some chemistry change in his brain I couldn't understand—had turned him into someone entirely different. It shattered my heart—but my entire soul would crumble if anything bad happened to Caelyn.

"Crystal." Mom rubbed the bridge of her button nose. "I can't go to the police. If your dad leaves, we're screwed. We'll lose the house. My two shifts a week can't cover the mortgage, not to mention the rest of our bills."

"So take more shifts."

"I've already asked to work full-time; they don't have it in the budget right now."

My throat constricted. "But . . . but what if he gets into my room next time? What if—"

"He would *never*," said Mom, her voice tinny and unsure.

The truth of the matter was, he might. He nearly did last night, that bruise evidence of the Mom-shaped barrier that stopped him. "He promised it wouldn't happen again."

By now, I was trembling with frustration. "He promised that last time, too."

"But this time he said he'll stop drinking. Cold turkey." She cupped my cheek. "This time will be different."

I stared, flabbergasted. She was in such denial—like if she *believed* hard enough, the problem would go away. The ache in my soul returned, but sharper, like she'd just slapped me across the face. Dad wasn't the only one hurting us. Mom was, too . . . because she was letting it happen.

But now it was over. Now he was gone.

Because of me.

If she wouldn't do it, someone had to.

"You were right," said Mom, squeezing my hand. "But I promise, from now on, you won't have to be. I'll take care of us." She still had no clue what I'd done. And sometimes I wondered if I did the right thing. Mom still had bruises; she just wore them under her eyes now. It was my fault she was so sleep-deprived and stressed, taking too many shifts at the hospital, still unable to pay the mortgage and skyrocketing taxes for a house that was too big for us. My streaming and babysitting cash didn't help enough. Now Grandma Rose was guilt-tripping Mom to move in with her in Maine if we sold this house, and if that happened, we'd be torn from our lives, our friends. What I did to protect my baby sister might hurt her even more. I needed to win the MortalDusk tourney. I *needed* to.

But now Matty was dead, my sister was a hostage, and everything was in a shambles. All thanks to some maniac. I had to find them. I had to beat them at their own game. I had to get Caelyn back, whatever it took.

If only I had a clue what it'd take.

Seeing the stress on my face, Mom stood. "You know what? Tonight calls for chocolate. Lots and lots of chocolate."

"We don't have any," I mumbled. Chief Sanchez had taken the bag of chocolate chips, and Mom didn't buy lots of sweets.

"Oh, please. I keep a secret stash for emergencies." She went into the kitchen and knelt next to the stove, revealing her hiding place. She pulled herself up by the edge of the counter, and her fingers came away coated with flour. For a moment, she looked confused. "What's—"

Her eyes widened, realization dawning on her. In the car ride home, I told her how I'd baked the brownies that killed Matty. She quickly rinsed her hand under the faucet, obviously avoiding the subject for my sake. Because she thought it was my fault.

Was she right?

I pictured An0nym0us1 as a shadowy figure standing in this very spot hours ago. Had they brought the almond extract, drizzled it over the batter, and left it on the counter for someone to find? A kernel of doubt lingered in my mind. I had to know *for sure.*

"Mom," I said, trying to keep my voice steady. "What do you usually use almond extract for?"

"My lattes." She unwrapped a bar of chocolate. "I like to add a dash for flavor. You know, it's healthier than those sugary syrups." My heart clenched—so she did keep almond extract in the house. It could've been my mistake. She sighed, shaking her head. "I figured you'd never use it for anything. I guess I wasn't careful enough."

"It's not *your* fault." I raked back my curls with trembling fingers. "And what about the EpiPens?"

"What about them?"

"The ones we keep upstairs. Did you throw those out recently? Did they expire?"

She frowned. "No. I replace those once a year, right after the new year so I remember. They're just a couple of months old." Vertigo ravaged my body, like I was teetering on the edge of a cliff. "I was going to ask why you hadn't used them . . ." She trailed off, throwing me a wary glance.

No. *No.*

Without a word, I bolted up the stairs, taking them two at a time. Mom was on my tail. "Crystal, what's wrong?"

I switched on the bathroom light, for a moment catching my panicked expression in the mirror before swinging open the medicine cabinet. The hinges screeched so loud it made me cover my ears. But it wasn't the hinges—it was a feral shriek. The sound pitched me back against the wall, the towel rod digging into my spine. Mom gripped my arms, saying my name over and over. That sound—that shrill, penetrating sound—it was coming from me. From my lips.

I was screaming.

Because the bright orange EpiPen case was on the first shelf of the cabinet.

Right where it should be.

CHAPTER 18

Matty's death was my fault. I'd mixed up the bottles of extract. I'd missed the EpiPens in the medicine cabinet.

Negligent.

Careless.

Like that time I passed Matty my Frappuccino without tasting it first. Almond, not soy. Thinking about my own problems, it never crossed my mind that something with nuts could wind up in the brownies. Almond, not vanilla.

It was my fault the boy who loved me was dead.

I'd tried to hold it together all day, to maintain my grip on reality, to keep from falling apart. But everyone has a breaking point. And as my chest tightened and my limbs went numb, when the words and sounds coming from my lips were unrecognizable, unstoppable, I knew I'd reached mine.

"It's all my fault. All my fault," I repeated over and over.

"It's not your fault—" Mom cried over my sobs, but the roar in my ears drowned out her words. My vision filled with brown

speckles, and I couldn't see, couldn't hear, couldn't think anything besides the fact that I'd killed Matty.

Unable to keep my balance, I backed against the wall and slid
to the floor. My muscles tightened painfully with each rasping
breath, and I clenched the shaggy bath mat in my fists as fierce
spasms racked my body. Jumbled, nonsensical words tumbled
from my lips as Mom knelt next to me, trying to calm me as I
curled into the fetal position, gripping the mat so hard my fingertips felt like they'd been cut off. Warm, fat tears dripped from
my eyelashes and nose, splotching the bathroom tiles. "Matty's
dead . . . He's dead . . . I did it . . ." I choked on the words as
fresh spasms overwhelmed me.

Mom stood, slid open the bathtub's glass door, and twisted
the faucet. I had my first panic attack when I was eleven years
old, after what happened to Brady. After what we'd done to him.
I'd collapsed in the backyard, unable to breathe, and Dad had
carried me inside, filled the bathtub with hot water and lavender
bath salt, and dropped me in, fully clothed. The soothing floral
scent and the sensation of my clothes billowing around me in the
warm water had lulled me back to reality. Not that reality had
been easy to face. But at least I had control over my own body.

Now I was too big to carry. "Come on. Try to stand." Mom
helped hoist me to my feet, and I managed to scramble into the
tub. She clutched my hand as I sank into the rising water, my
jeans bloated around my legs, salty tears mingling with the lavender salt she poured into the water. The heat and steam quelled
my trembling, at least.

Mom knelt next to me, rubbing my upper back, absentmindedly humming something she might've thought comforting,

though she couldn't carry a tune worth a damn. But finally, my mind slowed. My chest felt raw and sore from the spasms, but I could breathe again. My head was pounding from sobbing so hard, but I could think again.

Matty was dead. *Dead.*

I tried pushing past that, to make sense of the EpiPen's reappearance. Now that I had my wits about me, I distinctly remembered opening the medicine cabinet earlier, as Matty strained for breath in the basement. In my mind's eye, I could *see* the empty space in the medicine cabinet. My fingers had groped at the space. I'd felt cool metal under my fingers.

"It wasn't there earlier." I gripped Mom's hand. "The EpiPen case. When I looked for it. I swear to God, it wasn't there earlier."

Mom stood to examine the medicine cabinet. There was no empty space—just neat rows of face creams, nail polish, toothpaste, bottles of medicine, and of course, the bright orange EpiPen case.

It was An0nym0us1. They'd broken into my house, tampered with the brownies, and stolen the EpiPens. They must've slipped back inside at some point to put the case back. Maybe they wanted me to lose my grip on reality. Maybe they wanted me to think everything was my fault. And it almost worked. But I knew the EpiPens weren't there earlier. I knew, I knew, I *knew.*

"Crystal," Mom knelt next to the tub again, "I know everything hurts right now. And it seems like the world is ending. But you need to know that none of this was your fault."

I knew, I knew, I knew. She was the one who didn't.

"When you're in a panic," she went on, "it's easy to miss

things that are right in front of you. There have been actual studies on this—when your frontal cortex is overstimulated and distracted, it doesn't select all the visual stimuli to focus on. It leaves things out. It's the same thing that happens when you're in a rush to leave the house, and you can't find your keys, even though they're right in front of you. Like me this morning—the keys *were* in my purse the whole time."

I cringed, choking back a sob. Of course she would think the EpiPens were there the whole time. She had no idea about Caelyn, or An0nym0us1, or any of it.

But they did this. An0nym0us1. I *knew* it.

I had to find them. I had to get my sister back. I had to—

Oh *no*. I left my phone on the kitchen table.

By the time I rushed down to the kitchen, dripping and wrapped in a towel, I could almost sense that a message was waiting for me. But Mom hovered like a gnat, so I couldn't look at the screen—she'd see my reaction and insist on knowing what was wrong. Instead, I held off until she went to bed around eleven. She'd taken another nurse's double shift today, and still had her own shift in the morning. She offered to call in sick, but I assured her I'd be fine.

Back in my room, I changed into a cozy pair of leggings and an oversize sherpa-lined sweater—with my phone tucked into a drawer for some semblance of privacy, thank you very much—then took a deep breath and looked.

You're playing with fire. You already used your Get Out of Jail
Free card, remember?

There was no time stamp on the message. I couldn't tell how long ago An0nym0us1 had sent this, or how many messages they'd sent before. My stomach roiled with worry for Caelyn.

Before I could shoot off a message or say anything aloud, a new message appeared.

There you are. It's time for a new game. Are you ready?

I squinted at the screen, head still pounding from my panic attack. Mom had offered some of my prescribed meds for when I got attacks—sort of like a megadose of Benadryl to calm me down. But it'd make me too drowsy, and I needed to stay awake. Alert. I needed to find whoever was doing this.

But now I wouldn't have a chance.

Anger and agony tightened my throat, stifling the accusations I wanted to hurl. *Why would you kill Matty? How* could *you?* But they'd be wasted words; they'd never say. Instead, I had to think of some way to outsmart them. To get them to reveal some clue that would lead me to Caelyn. Maybe I could get them to send me another photo.

Wait, how's Caelyn? I asked.

She's still alive. Are you ready?

Still alive. Implying that at one point, that may no longer be the case.

Holy hell.

Well, hopefully playing this next game would help me get

more clues out of this asshat. I cracked my knuckles. Alright, fine. Let's go.

Let's play *Grand Theft Auto.* Steal the minivan from the garage at 212 Sherborne Way. You have 30 minutes. Ready? GO!

My mouth dropped open. This time, I knew the address. That was Akira's house.

Akira didn't have a car ("Why bother? You guys always schlep me around"), but her parents each had one. They only would've needed one car to get to the airport, assuming they hadn't called an Uber or something. Either way, they must've left Mrs. Saito's minivan behind.

But how was I supposed to get the car out of the garage without Akira noticing? Sure, she was a heavy sleeper—she'd overslept so many times her mom had to get her one of those alarm clocks on wheels you had to chase around the room to turn off—but like hell she'd managed to fall asleep already. Surely she'd hear the door groan open.

Oh, God. What would happen if I got caught? Wasn't grand theft auto a felony?

Well, at least it wasn't murder.

By the time I reached Akira's street, I was clutching a sharp stitch in my side, the taste of metal thick in my throat. I usually biked to Akira's house, but if I'd be stealing a car, leaving my bike behind or stopping in the driveway to chuck it in the trunk wouldn't exactly make for the smoothest getaway.

I knelt beside one of the straggly shrubberies lining Akira's backyard to catch my breath, shivering, white puffs of condensation thick with each exhale. The neighboring yards were empty, and moonlight snuck fleeting glimpses between clouds in an otherwise starless sky. Hopefully, nobody would spot me in my all-black ensemble.

The garage was on the other side of the house. But even if I magically knew the code to open the garage door, I'd still need the car keys. Was hot-wiring a car still a thing? I'd only ever seen that happen in older movies.

No, I'd need to search Akira's house for the keys. I always did love a good scavenger hunt. If only the prospect of losing wasn't so fucking terrifying.

My stomach tied in knots as I peered up at the looming house. All the windows were dark except for a faint blue glow coming from what I thought was Akira's upstairs bedroom, but that could have been anything—a night-light, the tiny lights on a router, or Akira scrolling through her phone in bed, unable to fall asleep. There was a crooked old tree next to another window, but this was no game; climbing a tree in real life would lead to broken bones, at the very least. Maybe one of the downstairs windows would be unlocked.

A sinking feeling spread through my chest as I thought of the last time I snuck into someone's window.

Once I'd suspected Zoey was using an aimbot to cheat in MortalDusk, it needled my mind like an obsession. Watching her in the game wasn't enough—I had to see the files on her laptop. I had to know for *sure*. So, with a clear view into her bedroom from mine, I spied on her like a total creeper, until one time last month she left her room with her laptop open, unsecured. Refusing to give myself a chance to chicken out, I climbed from my window and into hers. Growing up, we always kept our windows unlocked for each other, and apparently, she still did.

Adrenaline had tingled my fingers as I searched her hard drive. Thanks to some dark gamer forums, I'd learned cheaters would download an open-source file and modify the code to evade MortalDusk's cheating detectors, playing cat and mouse with the developers who regularly patched the game. So I knew what files to search for. *MortalDuskAimbb.exe.* Nothing. *MortalDuskHackAB.exe.* Nada. *MDaimbot.exe.* Zilch. *MDaimhack.exe.*

A result.

I'd gaped at the file, then examined its properties. Installed two months ago. Last opened earlier tonight, when our team played together. I didn't know what I expected to feel if I found proof—maybe vindication, or red-hot fury. Instead, I'd felt anguish. How could Zoey *do* this? It was so unfair. Did our friendship mean *nothing* to her? But suddenly, there she was, standing in her doorway. "What the *hell* are you doing?" Her face had twisted in fury, like *I* was the criminal.

If I wasn't a criminal then, I certainly would be now. I'd been inside Akira's house hundreds of times, but breaking and entering was still breaking and entering. Come to think of it, I vaguely remembered Akira once sliding a spare key from under one of the potted plants on the back stoop. Was it still there?

I glanced in either direction. The coast was clear, but that didn't stop my pulse from racing a mile a minute as I sprinted across the yard. The windows in the back of the house were dark.

So far so good. But as I climbed the back stairs, a floodlight illuminated the backyard. I gasped and froze like a deer in headlights, squinting against the sudden onslaught of brightness.

Any of the neighbors could spot me now. A dog yipped a couple of yards down, and my stomach seemed to lurch with each bark. I glanced back toward the shrubberies, where I could hide in relative safety. But I was running out of time. Biting my lip, I eyed the potted hydrangea next to the back door. I couldn't wimp out now.

I tipped the pot to peek underneath, and a key glinted up at me. Oh, thank God. I wouldn't have to climb any trees tonight.

I unlocked the door and slipped the key back under the pot.

But when I opened the door, an alarm blared loud enough to wake the dead.

CHAPTER 19

I scrambled into the mudroom, nearly tripping over the jumbled pile of boots next to the door. The alarm panel was backlit, making the space glow red. Exasperated, I clutched my forehead. I hadn't even considered an alarm. But I couldn't just bolt—the police would get an alert and head over, and I could forget about stealing any cars. I'd lose the game. What would happen to Caelyn if I lost?

An0nym0us1 would kill her, that's what.

Okay. I had to *think*.

Usually, you had sixty seconds to enter the right code. We had the same alarm at home, but Mom always forgot to set it. Frantic, I racked my brain for a possible code and entered 0–3–1–5—Akira's birthday, March 15—followed by the pound key. The panel gave a high-pitched chirp, and the shrill alarm continued.

"Dammit." There was no way Akira was sleeping through *this*.

I tried Akira's birth year. Pound key. More screeching. Then I tried her sister's birth year. Pound key.

The beeping stopped.

I stared at the panel, stock-still, holding my breath. I did it. I guessed the right code! Akira must be out cold, thank God—

Footsteps.

Upstairs.

"Hello?" Akira's voice croaked as the stairs creaked.

Crap. I could slip out the back door, but then she'd see a shadowy figure bolting across the yard and call the cops. At least, that's what I'd do.

I could reveal myself, pretend I came over to talk. But that wouldn't explain why I didn't text first, or why I wanted to drive off with her mom's minivan, for that matter. Oh, God, I couldn't think fast enough. I couldn't let her catch me.

So, like any sane person would do, I dove behind the kitchen island.

Remaining in a low crouch, I peered around the corner as Akira switched on the foyer lights. "Hello?" Her voice was shaky. I slipped back out of view as she padded into the kitchen, leaning back against the cabinet containing the garbage can. The knob dug into my shoulder blade, but I held still.

Finally, Akira's footsteps moved to the short hallway off the kitchen leading to a half bath and laundry room.

I let out a breath I was fully aware I was holding.

The garage door creaked as she opened and closed it a few seconds later. Then she shuffled away, pausing at each room downstairs. "Huh," she muttered somewhere near the front door. A few beeps sounded. *Oh, no.* She was rearming the alarm

system. Well, I'd worry about that later. Right now, I needed a
better hiding place; if she checked the kitchen any closer than a
mere peek, she'd find me. This wasn't MortalDusk—I couldn't
slink around as she searched, silent and stealthy. Knowing my
luck, I'd knock over one of the barstools. Crouching low, I
dashed to the small bathroom Akira had already checked, and
hid behind the door.

Didn't think I'd be playing Manhunt tonight.

My skin crawled at the memory of the last time we'd played.
I shook it away and checked my phone. Ten minutes left to steal
this car. I silenced it—the last thing I needed was it buzzing with
a notification from An0nym0us1 right now.

Akira padded back into the kitchen. "What the utter fuck
is going on?" she muttered. A mood, honestly. I watched her
through the gap in the door hinge. Her eyes were red and puffy,
and strands of damp black hair fell lank around her face. She'd
probably cried herself to sleep soon after showering.

My heart ached, and the temptation to reveal myself was real.
She'd be confused for a sec, but then she'd make us hot chocolate with marshmallows, and we'd curl up on the couch under
her favorite fleece blanket to talk and cry together. We hadn't
even had a chance at the hospital to hug, to sob, to mourn. I
desperately wanted to confide in her—to tell her *everything*. But
An0nym0us1 was in my pocket, listening to my every move.
Maybe I could step out, finger to my lips, and write a note
explaining what was happening. But what if Akira shouted in
fright? What if An0nym0us1 was outside, watching through a
window? I shuddered at the thought. I couldn't risk it.

Akira poured herself a glass of water, muttering something

unintelligible—I could only make out the words "imagining things." Then she shuffled back to the stairs, switching off lights as she went. Her footsteps creaked up the stairs, and finally, a door clicked shut.

Okay, keys.

Which literally could be anywhere. Eight minutes left.

I scrambled back into the kitchen and quietly slid open drawer after drawer, rifling through them. This reminded me of that escape room game Matty got me to download on the bus ride to a maple farm for a class field trip. You had to find a key to unlock the door, first searching for other items in the room to solve a series of puzzles. I got stuck on this one pirate shipwreck level and started tapping every millimeter of the screen.

Matty had swatted my hand. "Whoa, chill. What're you looking for?"

"A crowbar," I'd huffed, frustrated. "I need to open this barrel."

"You *sure* you need a crowbar?"

"I dunno . . . There was one in the last level."

He scoffed. "What're you, some sort of newb?"

"Hey!" I shoved him, and he flailed, pretending to fall into the aisle. I tugged him back before Mrs. Chesser in the front seat noticed our shenanigans.

Well, if not a crowbar, what else could open the barrel? Behind the piles of broken wooden beams and sparkly treasure was a plaque with two crisscrossed swords mounted above the door I'd assumed was part of the background. I tapped the swords, and one appeared in my inventory. "Aha!"

Matty grinned. "There ya go. Always think like a game designer."

Hearing Matty's voice in my head made my stomach clench. It seemed unfathomable that I'd never hear his voice again. Surely tomorrow he'd be back at my house, ready to play MortalDusk, tossing around his witty banter like always. Tears welled in my eyes. No. I couldn't think about that now. I had to focus.

Too bad Matty's advice wasn't relevant now—this time, I knew what I was searching for. Car keys. And I knew to look where Akira's parents might keep car keys.

I glanced down at the silverware drawer I'd just slid open.

Okay. Maybe I did need to slow down and think more logically. Like a game designer.

Mrs. Saito probably kept her main set of car keys in her purse, and a second set with her husband's somewhere else. Hence my instinct to check these drawers, but really, they could be anywhere. But if Akira's mom was like mine, she had a second purse she used just for travel, filling it only with what she needed for the trip. She wouldn't need her car keys in California. So they might still be in her daily purse, which was likely in her bedroom, or bedroom closet. Upstairs.

Remembering how Akira's footsteps creaked on each step, I took off my sneakers and crept upstairs in socked feet.

Akira's room was at the top of the stairs, and from within, I heard a faint hum and whir—like a white noise app. Maybe that was why she didn't hear the alarm right away. I continued down the hall to the master bedroom and used my phone's flashlight to scan the space. Mrs. Saito kept things neat and tidy, so there were no purses strewn about, though on the dresser I could make out the angular shape of the LEGO Eiffel Tower Akira had built for her years ago. I made my way to the closet. Inside, below a shoe rack, was a familiar beige purse. I practically lunged at it and dug through the front compartments until my fingers found a metal loop.

Keys! I angled the flashlight on them, making sure. Yep, there was the Toyota logo. Relief streamed through my veins like a rush of cool water. *Thank you, Matty.*

But then I remembered what I had to do next. Steal the car. My stomach lurched, and I switched off my phone's flashlight as it buzzed with a new message from An0nym0us1.

Good job finding the keys.

Goose bumps bristled my arms. I'd turned off my alerts downstairs. That was no compliment—it was a reminder that they were watching.

That they had *control.*

I crept back downstairs, slipped on my sneakers, and headed for the garage. An alarm panel next to the garage door blinked at me, and I deactivated the alarm again, cringing with each beep. After the final long tone, I froze, waiting for footsteps on the stairs. But Akira mustn't have heard. Wow. That white noise app deserved a five-star rating.

As I twisted the doorknob, it occurred to me that I was leaving my fingerprints all over the place. Dammit. I wasn't exactly used to being a criminal. I was so hyper-focused on completing each game to keep Caelyn alive, I hadn't stopped to think through the potential repercussions. What *would* happen after this?

If I got away with the minivan, Akira's parents would report the theft. The police would investigate, and they'd take fingerprints of obvious things like the freaking doorknob. And I'd touched all those drawers in the kitchen, the alarm panel, and the purse and closet doorknob upstairs.

Shit.

But wait. Sure, that might be the logical fallout. But each of An0nym0us1's games had completely unexpected consequences. What exactly would they make me *do* with the car? What if they'd tampered with the brakes or something? What if they made me get hurt? A cold sweat broke out on my neck like tiny pinpricks of ice. My phone buzzed.

Two minutes left.

Jesus. Well, I'd have to take it slowly. Hopefully I was just being paranoid.

Using my sleeve as a glove, I twisted the doorknob and quietly shut the door behind me. The garage smelled like the inside of a toolshed, musty and damp. One of the storage shelves was filled with Akira's LEGO structures—the ones she didn't have room for upstairs. She refused to take apart her favorite creations to reuse the LEGO bricks, which drove her parents up the wall. Those tiny plastic blocks cost a fortune.

One of the cars was missing—Mr. Saito's sedan, probably parked at the airport. The security light on the dashboard of Mrs. Saito's minivan blinked.

Get in the car now.

"Okay, okay. I'm going." I unlocked the car and cringed when it gave a friendly chirp. But the house remained still. I climbed into the driver's seat and dropped my phone into the cup holder in the armrest. The dashboard's wood detailing gleamed, unlike Mom's, which was coated with dust.

Turn on the car.

"Alright, alright!" I shouted. "What, are you gonna tell me when to breathe?"

I stuck the key in the ignition, and the engine purred to life. Clipping in my seat belt, I found the garage door opener Velcroed to the visor overhead. I bit my lip and glanced through the rearview mirror. The garage door was right under Akira's room. She was going to hear this, white noise machine or not.

But I had to do this. I pressed the button to open the door. Nothing happened. Frowning, I pressed it again.

My phone buzzed.

Akira's parents came home early! They're pulling into the driveway! RUN!

5 Years Ago

"Gotcha!" Matty tugged Zoey out from under a gardening table nestled against a neighbor's shed.

My heart clobbered my lungs—Matty and I had sprinted to find Zoey before she beat my time. He tapped his timer as Akira, Randall, and Brady caught up to us. "Nine minutes, thirty-five seconds."

Zoey stomped her foot. "Darn it." I was still in the lead—it took everyone twelve whole minutes to find me.

"Where was she?" Randall whispered.

"There." I beamed my phone's flashlight past Zoey and Akira, under the table.

Randall gasped and pointed at Akira's jacket. "That spider's huge!"

Akira let out an earsplitting shriek and swatted at herself. "Where? Get it off, get it off!" Brady smacked her jacket with his long sweatshirt sleeves, trying to help. Matty hunched over, howling with laughter.

"*Get it off, get it off!*" Randall mocked, flapping his hands.

"*You turd!*" Akira shoved Randall so hard he stumbled and fell on his butt with a grunt. But instead of complaining, he looked up at her like he was impressed.

Zoey glanced nervously at the nearby house, still worried about getting caught, and I shushed everyone. We all stilled for a moment, half expecting the house's floodlights to switch on. But the yard remained dark. Whew.

"Whose turn is next? Brady, why don't you go?" I suggested, wanting him to feel included. I still felt bad about earlier.

His eyes widened. "Nah, it's okay, someone else can go. Akira?" But Akira had already gone—we'd found her hiding behind a shrubbery within three minutes.

"No, you go!" said Zoey encouragingly. "You can hide best." She glanced my way, like she just wanted someone to beat me.

Brady's brow pinched. "Why's that?"

"Uh . . ." Zoey mashed her lips together, realizing her unintentional backhanded compliment.

Randall piped up, clapping dirt from his hands, "Cuz you're a shrimp." He and Matty burst out laughing again. Randall didn't mean anything by it; we all teased each other relentlessly, knowing it was just for fun. But Brady cringed. To him, an insult was just that.

"Guys, stop it," I said.

Brady glanced back toward his house. "I don't want to be 'it.'"

"Think something's gonna getcha in the dark, scary woods?" Randall taunted, wriggling his fingers.

Akira rolled her eyes. "There's nothing scary in the woods."

"*You don't know that,*" said Zoey. "*Remember the bear they caught prowling around here last year?*"

"*Maybe the bear's hungry for some shrimp.*" Randall clawed at Brady's arm.

Brady shoved him away and bunched the extra material from his sweatshirt sleeves in his fists. "*Fine. I'll be 'it.'*" He raised his chin. "*I hope you losers are ready to search till morning.*"

I hooted, and Matty clapped Brady's back. "*Look who's talking smack now.*"

"*Yeah, right,*" said Akira. "*We're gonna find you in two minutes flat.*"

"*No, you're not,*" Brady faltered. Should've quit while he was ahead.

Randall opened his mouth to retort, but I flicked his arm. "*Let's count it down. Ready?*"

Akira gripped my hand. "*Ready!*"

I grinned encouragingly at Brady and made a mental note of his bright red sweatshirt, which should be easy to spot, before closing my eyes to count to a hundred.

It would've been so easy for any of us to cheat—to peek through our lashes in the dark and see where he went.

But cheaters never win, and winners never cheat. So we all squeezed our eyes shut.

Later, I'd wish I'd cheated.

CHAPTER 20

grasped for the door handle, desperate to get out of here.
Maybe Mr. Saito and I had pushed the remote buttons at the
same time, and that's why the garage door hadn't opened. But it
would any moment. Akira's parents would catch me in the act.
I threw open the door and fumbled my phone, and it clattered
to the concrete floor. "Shit," I hissed.

Hang on. Something wasn't adding up.

How had Akira's parents flown back from California so
quickly? I thought they'd changed their flight to tomorrow night.
Besides, the flight back was at least six hours, plus about an hour
drive from the airport.

Each of An0nym0us1's games had unexpected consequences.
The exam. The brownies. The 911 call.

The garage door hadn't opened yet.

Think logically.

Why had An0nym0us1 micromanaged me? *Get into the car.
Turn on the engine.* Both before I'd opened the garage door.

Think like a game designer. Each task served a purpose. *Sometimes the most obvious answer is the one that eludes us.*

It hit me like a shock bolt to my skull.

Car exhaust in an enclosed space was a leading cause of carbon monoxide poisoning. It was the answer I'd missed in chemistry class a few weeks ago—when Zoey beat me for those bonus points—despite the horrific story Mr. Ferguson told us the day before. Five teens in Florida had driven to a hotel to celebrate one of their birthdays and accidentally left the car running in the bottom-floor parking garage. The next morning, they were all found dead around the bed in their room on the second floor, still dressed, food half-eaten, poisoned by carbon monoxide fumes.

Now, the engine of Mrs. Saito's minivan purred softly, like a tiger getting cuddly. And I was about to bolt, leaving it running with Akira upstairs like a snoozing gazelle.

No.

They wanted me to kill Akira. *Kiki.* My best friend. I thought of all she'd been through, battling her own mind to eat without thinking food was turning her into a monster. I thought of all the beautiful things she'd created, of everything she had yet to build. I thought of all her progress, her grit, her hopes and dreams and kindness snuffed out as she slept.

No way.

I was being paranoid. This was too much. But sometimes the answer stared you in the face, and all you had to do was stare back. The exam. The brownies. The 911 call.

I was right. I knew I was right.

And I could stop this.

In one fluid motion, I turned off the engine and scrambled to pick up my phone, making lots of scraping and scuffling noises to hide the absence of the engine noise. Not bothering to see if the screen was cracked, I stuck the phone into my jacket pocket, blinding An0nym0us1 if they were watching.

Who was I kidding? Of course they were watching.

I tiptoed back into the kitchen and out the back door as fast as I could. The floodlights blazed again as I dashed back to shrubberies at the edge of Akira's lawn. For a moment, I gripped my knees, catching my breath, then slinked toward the front of the house to get a clear view of the driveway. It was dark. The floodlights above the garage door hadn't turned on. No car had turned in to the driveway. Akira's parents weren't home.

My phone buzzed. I pulled it from my pocket. A crack splintered from the corner of the tempered glass screen protector from the drop in the garage, slashing through An0nym0us1's latest message.

Go home.

All the little hairs on my neck stood on end. I was right. The point was never to steal the car. They'd tried to get me to leave with the engine running. They'd tried to get me to murder another one of my friends. Maybe they'd disabled the garage door remote sometime after Akira's parents left, and that's why the door never opened. But I'd killed the engine. I'd outsmarted them. Ha!

Wait . . . I couldn't act all triumphant. If An0nym0us1 realized

Akira was no longer in danger, they might force me to go back inside and finish the job. I had to act *terrified*.

I had to pretend to realize Akira was in mortal danger. I had to pretend to try to save her.

I fixed my face into what I hoped was a fearful expression and gasped, then spun and sprinted to the back door, trying to keep the camera somewhat steady. The dog in the neighboring yard started yipping again, and as I reached for the doorknob, my phone buzzed.

Go home. NOW.

I raised my phone to eye level, like I was taking a selfie. "I left the engine running," I whisper-shouted and screwed up my face—from real or fake terror, I didn't know. "I have to turn it off."

If you don't go home RIGHT NOW, your sister dies.

Instinct clashed with dissent. Part of me wanted to bolt. But part of me wanted to test An0nym0us1—to stretch them as taut as possible before they snapped. It reminded me of a recurring nightmare I'd had for years—I'd spot myself in a mirror, and despite knowing there was something evil within, I'd approach it and screw up my face, testing it, watching as the reflection turned monstrous.

"But it's dangerous," I whispered. "She could get poisoned."

Seconds later, a picture appeared—the edge of a knife flush

against Caelyn's cheek. Her hazel eyes were wide with terror, her glasses missing.

GO. NOW.

Terror sliced my insides. Whoever was doing this was pure evil. And by the time Akira awoke in the morning, they'd realize I'd outsmarted them. They'd realize I was a worthy opponent.

Before that happened, I had to find them—to discover who they were and confront them in real life. It was the only way to end this twisted game.

CHAPTER 21

It was 1:30 a.m. by the time I slinked up the hill alongside my house to my bedroom window. I'd snuck out that way so Mom wouldn't catch me creeping downstairs. I was about to hoist myself up when I heard something shuffle behind me and whipped around, breathing fast. Did something just move in Zoey's window? She'd kept her shades closed ever since I snuck in, but now there was a narrow gap between her shades and windowsill. I could've sworn I saw something brush against it. Had she seen me sneak out earlier? Was she watching me now? Either way, she'd raised the shades for the first time since I'd caught her red-handed.

And now I had an idea for catching An0nym0us1 red-handed, too.

Once I climbed back inside and shut the window, I powered off my phone and tossed it onto my bed. An impulsive move, for sure—An0nym0us1 had warned if I didn't reply to their messages within a minute, they'd kill Caelyn. But I needed a minute to *think*. The phone was almost out of battery—I could claim it dropped dead or got damaged when it fell in Akira's garage.

As I waited for my laptop to boot up, I glimpsed the cosplay dress hanging from my closet door. Zoey had bought an expensive princess warrior dress online for the tourney, and Akira would be wearing an old Halloween costume, but Caelyn had insisted on designing my costume herself. "I know you're supposed to be a peasant," she'd said as she handed it to me the other day, flushed with pride, "but I couldn't help adding a little sparkle." She'd pointed out the beads embroidered in crisscross patterns along the brown bodice's edges next to the tie strings, which hugged an off-white chemise over a dark burgundy gathered skirt. "These are *crystal* beads." I'd been so impressed by her handiwork, my mouth dropped open in awe. Now, tears sprang to my eyes, and I grasped the lightning bolt charm hanging from my neck. She'd made us matching ones because she knew shock staffs were my personal brand in MortalDusk.

I had to get her back. I had to figure out who the hell was doing this to us.

My only real clue so far was Lance Burdly. Had An0nym0us1 plucked the name out of thin air? Or did it *mean* something?

I clutched my forehead, still feeling the aftereffects of my panic attack. My skull pounded so hard I thought it might crack to match the broken rest of me. I was tired, so damn tired. But I had to stay awake. I pulled up Google and was about to type when I yanked my fingers from the keyboard like it was a scalding stovetop. If An0nym0us1 had hacked my phone, had they hacked my laptop, too? My eyes flicked to the webcam dot above the monitor.

Well, fuck.

I slammed the laptop shut. Dammit, what now? Mom's laptop was probably safe to use, but it was in her bedroom with her.

I could at least organize my thoughts and whittle down a list of suspects. I pulled a notebook from my desk drawer, flipped to a blank page, and scrawled Lance Burdly's name. Though at this point, I doubted he was real. I'd seen this true crime documentary once where a serial killer left extra evidence at the crime scenes to throw off detectives. That's probably what Lance was—a false clue. An0nym0us1 wanted me to waste time researching someone who didn't exist.

Clearly, it worked. And it had distracted me so effectively I'd let Matty eat those brownies without thinking anything of it.

Letting out a low growl, I turned to a blank page to start over.

In my mind, Jeremy Fischer was suspect number one. "Pesky little dipshits," he'd called us in Happy Grillmore—and that was before we'd finished sabotaging his date, wrecked his leaderboard standings, and humiliated him on his own livestreams—not to mention Dylan's point that we might've siphoned enough subscribers to eat into his earnings. And now we'd be his biggest competition at the tourney. His appearance at the park was also suspicious as hell. He could've easily lied about getting an invite from "me" to discuss forming an alliance. More likely, he was there to watch his *Prank Caller* game in action. He could've taken the threatening pictures of Caelyn beforehand and zipped over—he lived in Lakecrest, which bordered Newboro by the park. As far as I knew, streaming was his only job, and he set his own schedule. He had oodles of time on his hands.

But there was also Lucia Ramirez. Sweet as pie on the outside, troll on the inside. After Zoey threatened to expose her trollish ways to the world, I'd catch her staring in class, in the cafeteria, when we passed in the halls. Maybe it was guilt. Maybe it was fear I'd sink her reputation. Maybe it was hatred. Either way, it made my skin crawl—not just because of what she did but because it reminded me of what *I* did. Of how I'd treated her, even after what happened to Brady. Even at her party, I'd snapped at her when she tried complimenting my sweater. *Your brownie points are rancid.*

Brownie points.

The brownies.

No. No way.

Was she really a plausible suspect? She *did* follow me into the bathroom right after I got An0nym0us1's first message. Did she coincidentally have to pee? Or was she keeping an eye on me as I played the first game? She could have taken that first video in the morning, right after kidnapping Caelyn, been late to school, then sent me the recording from the front row of history class.

I twirled my pen, antsy. It seemed like such a stretch. But Lucia might've been desperate to keep us from derailing all her hard work, all her plans for Harvard, for the future. Any admissions board who googled her would see Zoey's exposé and yeet her right off the application pile.

But something else niggled at my mind . . .

Biting my lip, I glanced out the window. Was it my imagination, or were Zoey's shades drawn even higher than before? Goose bumps prickled my arms.

The way she'd acted on FaceTime at the hospital reminded me of when we used to play Among Us on our phones. The game was simple: Crewmates raced to complete tasks around a space-ship while an Impostor, pretending to be a Crewmate, committed murder and sabotage. After each murder, we'd guess the Impostor's identity and throw someone off the ship. If we were right, we won. If the Impostor blended in too well and we were wrong, there'd be another round of tasks, murder, and finger-pointing.

Whenever Zoey was an Impostor, she'd be the first to hurl accusations, trying to throw everyone off her scent. But whenever she was a Crewmate, she'd quietly watch everyone argue, trying to suss out the Impostor. She was so predictable, I hated when she was an Impostor—her rounds were too easy to win.

Back in the hospital, she acted like an Impostor. Overly vocal. Quick to suggest theories.

And unlike our friends, I knew she was willing to steal a spot at the tourney. But was she really willing to *kill our friends* for it? I knew she resented Randall's and Matty's MortalDusk skills, and their popularity on our streams. But what about Akira? Was Zoey so jealous of our closeness that she'd resort to murder to tear us apart? Not to mention kidnapping my sister and torturing me—did she hate me that much for catching her cheating? How would she have managed it?

Well, she *was* MIA all day, supposedly home sick. She could've followed me and Caelyn to the middle school. Snatched Caelyn before she could get on the bus. Hidden her in that creepy storage room in her soundproof basement—the one that always freaked out Akira. Taken those disturbing videos and pictures all day.

But once her parents got home from work—damn, that'd be

so risky. Also, An0nym0us1 had shown up in MortalDusk right before Matty died and zapped Zoey's avatar. Was that enough to rule her out? Or was it a clever in-game alibi? Zoey was a hacker. She'd hacked the school's network to tweak our schedules, busted Lucia, and circumvented MortalDusk's cheating detectors. Surely she could figure out how to run two instances of MortalDusk on her laptop.

Adding Zoey's name to my list broke my soul in two. But it was plausible, however unlikely, and I couldn't rule it out. Matty dying today was absurd, yet it had happened. Randall's dad being ambushed by a SWAT team was inconceivable, yet it had happened. This entire scenario was completely unbelievable, yet—

Suddenly, my phone buzzed on my bed, the sound nearly sending me into cardiac arrest. *No.* I'd turned it off. It couldn't have buzzed.

I swiveled in my chair and gawked at my phone like it came from another planet. That was the only explanation. Once, Mom lost her phone while it was off, so calling it wouldn't do any good. As she tore the house apart, I googled how to remotely power on a phone, but nope, it was impossible. You had to physically press the power button to supply power to the phone's chip.

I hadn't pressed the power button. I'd been clear across the room.

So, aliens.

Oh, God. I was going delirious. *Think logically.* There had to be another way. To turn off my phone, I'd held down the power button and toggled the Power Off slider on the screen. An0n-ym0us1 could have overridden that toggle to turn down the screen's brightness instead of controlling the power.

I'd never turned off my phone to begin with.

Swallowing hard, I inched to my bed and flipped the phone over. A message from An0nym0us1 was waiting.

The more of me there is, the less you see. What am I?

Before I could puzzle it out or consider the subtext of the riddle, my room plunged into darkness.

CHAPTER 22

I gasped and stared at the light fixture hanging from the ceiling as though it might offer some explanation. Did we lose power? No—the tiny light on my laptop's power cord was still lit. The light switch next to the door was already in the on position, but I flicked it anyway, back and forth. Nothing happened.

The riddle. You saw less in the dark. The answer was *darkness*. Dread spread through my chest.

The lights turned on again.

I leaped away from the light switch like a ghost was hovering there.

But, no, it wasn't a ghost. There was one other way to control the lights. When Dad was obsessed with home renovation, he'd replaced all our light bulbs with smart ones so we could use an app to control them, dim them, and switch to fun colors. Zoey had asked her parents for one after I got mine, and we'd created a code to communicate via our lights—purple meant *game night,* blue meant *have to study,* green meant *come over ASAP,* pink meant *love you,* and so on. The novelty wore off fast, since we could text each other—

The lights turned red.

"Jesus." I backed against the wall, goose bumps coating my skin like a rash as my room glowed like an old-school darkroom. This was unreal. I glanced out the window at Zoey's. Was *she* doing this? Was she watching me now, laughing her sadistic ass off? The thought made my blood boil, and I navigated to the lights app, switching them back to normal.

That's when I noticed the slew of notification icons atop the screen. Oh, God. Word about Matty's death had clearly spread like wildfire—tons of classmates had sent me sympathy messages across several social apps. *No.* He couldn't be dead—not really. I was so used to our avatars dying and regenerating in MortalDusk, over and over again, it was almost like part of me expected Matty to come over tomorrow like nothing had happened—

The lights turned red again.

My chest compressed, and I scrambled onto my bed and hugged my knees to my chest, burying my face in my arms to hide from both the onslaught of red light and the messages. Looking would only make everything more real. Nothing about today could be real. Matty couldn't be dead. He *couldn't* be. An0nym0us1 couldn't have this much control over my life, down to my freaking *lights.* This couldn't be happening. I rocked back and forth, back and forth.

Eventually, I calmed down, and curiosity got the best of me.

I wiped my face, took a deep breath, and looked at my notifications. The most recent message caught my eye. From Dylan,
about an hour ago.

Hi.

That's all he said. What were the chances he'd be asleep by
now?

The low-battery warning flashed, but I ignored it and replied.
Hi.

Three dots.

You awake?

I shot back: Obviously.

Then he sent the wink emoji sticking its tongue out.

I stared for a long moment. It was clearly in response to my
auto-snark, but it seemed out of touch, somehow. Would I ever
be able to send a wink emoji, or joy emoji, or anything express-
ing anything other than pure terror?

My life had become an endless scream emoji.

Can I come over?

My eyebrows shot up. Any other night, I'd have considered
this an interesting development. He'd texted *me*. He wanted to
see *me*. Not Zoey. Though for all I knew, he had pinged Zoey
and either gotten shut down or couldn't reach her.

I sent back, Now?

Obviously.

I couldn't help it—something fluttered deep in my belly. Mom was asleep. We could sneak into the basement to chat. Would An0nym0us1 be pissed, though? It technically wouldn't break any rules. And maybe they'd stop messing with me if Dylan were here. I longed for some semblance of safety, even if only for a little while. Sure. Text me when you get here.

OK.

My stomach roiled with nerves. In the weeks since Lucia's party, I'd replayed Dylan and Zoey's stupid kiss in my mind—the moment Zoey landed the winning beer pong shot, snaked her arms around his neck, and brought her lips to his—so many times I wanted to plunge a screwdriver through my skull.

My brain liked to torture me like that. Why wouldn't it replay the hilarious stuff instead? Like, for example, the moment Dylan yanked himself back so suddenly Zoey tumbled against the table and knocked over several cups, making beer slosh down her butt.

That memory was way better.

I shook both from my mind and switched the lights back to normal, then stared at the fixture for so long neon bulb shapes imprinted my vision. I waited, almost willing them to change again. But nothing happened. And there were no more messages from An0nym0us1.

Maybe they'd proven their point. *I am everywhere, and you can't stop me.*

The low-battery warning flashed again—I had only 8 percent power left, and it always shut off around 5 percent. I crossed the room to plop the phone on its charging pad, then froze.

There were two ways to make sure my phone was truly off. One was to force-shut it down by holding the power button for ten seconds. The other was to let the battery drain. Then I'd be free from their watchful gaze for a while.

I couldn't let them toy with me anymore. I had to figure out who they were.

Letting the battery drain seemed like the surer bet. Using the phone would make it drain faster, so I scrolled through my notifications, reading the names atop each one. *Dave Wilcott. Jasmine Chopra. Blake Thatcher. Lily Chang. Maddy Curtis.* Some I'd known since kindergarten, others I'd only ever exchanged five words. Yet all of them suddenly, inexplicably, wanted to be a part of Matty's tragedy.

There was even a message from Lucia Ramirez.

Crystal, I know we haven't exactly gotten along lately, but I just wanted you to know how very sorry I am. Matty was such a sweet guy, and nobody deserves to lose a friend like that. If you ever want to talk, I'm here. XO

I reread it, tugging my lower lip. That didn't sound like a message a sadistic monster would send. But it didn't sound like a message an internet troll would send, either. Was she faking kindness?

My God, this was maddening. I raked back my curls and read the other messages, thoroughly torturing myself. Talk about doom-scrolling. I was wasting time drowning in messages of sorrow when I should've been trying to find whoever killed Matty. But how could I search for someone who was watching both my phone and laptop? If they knew I was onto them, they could easily evade me—

Suddenly, I thought of it. A life raft. I dug through one of my desk drawers and fished out the Kindle Dad gave me years ago in a futile effort to get me to read more. He thought he could entice me away from video games with yet another screen, but the joke was on him—I preferred paperbacks.

Still, this thing had one of those experimental browsers, right? I could connect to Wi-Fi and continue my search. There was no way An0nym0us1 could've known about this, let alone hacked it.

Its battery was completely drained. I found the right cable and plugged it into the outlet next to my desk, under the window, then sat next to it on the floor with my notebook. It took an eternity for the Kindle to turn on, but finally, it connected to Wi-Fi and I loaded the browser.

Okay. Where to start?

Suspect number one. I googled "Jeremy Fischer address Vermont," clicked the top search result, and waited about a billion years for the page to load. Once it did, the address was right up top: *845 Camden Street, Allentown, Vermont.*

"Well, that's disturbing," I muttered, scribbling the address next to Jeremy's name in my notebook. Was it really that easy to find someone's address? Was it that easy to find where *I* lived? I searched for "Crystal Donovan address Vermont," and bing, my home address popped up. "Lovely."

I tabbed back to Jeremy's results and frowned. Didn't he say he lived in Lakecrest? I was about to pull up Google Maps when I spotted another couple of names—Susan Fischer and Richard Fischer, listed at the same address.

Oh. This was Jeremy's parents' house. He'd moved since then. Of course this wouldn't be that easy.

Resting my chin on my fist, I tapped the back button and pored over the search results. Jeremy Fischer was a common name, even just in Vermont. The name appeared in obituaries, news stories about a sexual assault, Realtor listings, and doctor directories.

I'd have to refine my search—

Tap, tap, tap.

I gasped. The sound came from right above my head.

I twisted around to see out the window and clapped a hand over my mouth to stop myself from screaming.

5 Years Ago

"My mother's going to murder me." Zoey checked her watch for the gazillionth time as we huddled near the gardening table where we'd found her earlier. We'd been searching for Brady for over an hour—it was after 1:00 a.m. now—and Manhunt was officially not fun anymore. He'd clearly won. Why wouldn't he come out already?

"I'm sure she still doesn't know we left," I said, shivering.

Zoey threw me a dirty look. "Well, if I'm dead meat, it's all your fault."

Guilt and fear coursed through me. She was right—I was the one who pushed us to play Manhunt. Maybe this was a bad idea after all. I didn't want Zoey to be mad at me. I'd just wanted us to have fun.

"Should we split up?" Randall suggested.

"No, let's stick together." Akira's scarf muffled her voice, and she clenched her flashlight under her armpit, burying her hands in her pockets.

"We already looked everywhere, though," said Matty.

Zoey yawned widely. "You guys, I'm so tired."

"Same. And it's freezing." Akira let her teeth chatter extra hard for emphasis.

"Yeah, let's go back," said Zoey.

"We can't just leave him out here," I said. After we'd made Brady feel like chopped liver earlier, he'd be extra hurt if we abandoned him now.

"Try calling his cell again?" Akira suggested.

Matty shook his head. "I mean, I already called five times."

Randall scanned the woods with his flashlight. "You know what, dude? I bet the li'l shrimp went home. He said he wanted to keep us searching till morning."

Matty shoved Randall playfully. "Calling him things like 'li'l shrimp' is what got us into this mess."

Randall guffawed. "Yeah, yeah."

But I frowned. "I don't think he'd cheat. That's not like him . . ." But then I thought of how his brother, Andrew, would buy Brady's painted rocks, so he'd win our summertime sales competitions. Maybe he would cheat.

"Yeah, well, he did this time," said Randall.

"Can we please go home?" said Zoey. "This is ridiculous." Everyone nodded.

"But—" I started.

Zoey stomped her foot. "Come on, Crystal. Brady's probably home asleep, sticking it to us. Let's just go."

As they trooped back toward Zoey's house, I lingered behind, scanning the nearly pitch-black yards once more. My phone was out of battery, so I no longer had a flashlight. "Brady?" I called, though not loudly, not wanting to wake anyone. Shadowy blobs littered the yards—swing sets, toys, hedges, tree stumps—and I tried to find a flash of red in the dark, trying not to imagine some creature slithering closer. But eventually, the darkness drove me to follow my friends.

CHAPTER 23

The last thing I expected was to see someone standing outside my window, nose practically pressed against the glass, staring down at me. I was already on edge, and my heart jolted fiercely enough to send shock waves to my toes.

Sorry, Dylan mouthed, grimacing remorsefully, though there was laughter in his eyes.

I scrambled to my feet and slid the window open. "What, like today hasn't been terrifying enough?" I clutched my chest, willing my heart to slow, reminding me of poor Mr. Lewis's cardiac arrest.

"Sorry, sorry! Didn't mean to scare you."

"I told you to text—"

"I saw your light on and figured this was your room." He passed me a thermos before hoisting himself inside. "Why were you on the floor?"

"Oh . . . just . . . reading?" I motioned to the Kindle.

He examined the space behind my desk chair. "Your reading nook isn't very nooky."

"Your face isn't very nooky." I cringed. That didn't work.

My phone buzzed. *Shit.* My heart went berserk again as terrifying possibilities flooded my mind. For some reason, I'd assumed An0nym0us1 would leave me alone if Dylan was here. But this was too dangerous—I should never have agreed to let him be alone with me. What the hell would An0nym0us1 make me do?

Whatever it was, I couldn't ignore it. As Dylan slid the window closed, I flipped my phone over.

Let's play *Truth or Dare.* If you tell him the truth, I'll dare you to kill him.

Oh, God. A shiver ran through me with such force I visibly shuddered. Dylan locked the window, turned around, and frowned. "What's wrong?"

A new message replaced that text.

See you in the morning.

I flipped the phone facedown again, trying to keep my fingers as steady as possible. Trying not to show that Dylan's life could be in my hands. "Nothing, just . . . got a chill. From the window being open. Anyway . . ." I jiggled the thermos, making the liquid inside slosh around. "What's this?" As long as I didn't tell Dylan what was happening, he was safe. At least, I hoped he would be.

"Hot chocolate. Er . . . I wanted to return the favor. You know, comfort food. Drink. Whatever."

The brownies. He still thought I baked those for him. Some "favor" that was, though—those brownies ended up killing our friend. Thinking of Matty again, my eyes reflexively watered like someone had punched me in the stomach. Dylan's face fell. "I'm sorry, I didn't mean . . ." He seemed about to reach for me, and I remembered how he'd hugged me in the hospital parking lot, his cheek flush against mine. I wanted that again, to be comforted, safe. But it felt wrong, somehow.

So I turned from Dylan, blinking away my tears. "No, it's fine." I twisted off the plastic mug and cap and inhaled the rich scent, triggering a memory of hiking the trails near Hanover Lake with Dad, our Sunday morning tradition. I loved the fresh pine tree smell, the satisfying crunch of dead leaves under my boots, the way the sun shimmered off the lake like scattered crystals when we topped Mount Morgan. I loved how Dad would spout these outlandish facts, like, "Watch out for the ants—they'll stink if you squish 'em!" and "Every few years, the trees conspire to make extra acorns so squirrels can't gorge on them all, and more trees grow." I'd try to argue ("Trees don't *conspire!*"), but then I'd google it later, and he was always right.

But once on the cusp of winter, I shivered so hard my teeth audibly chattered. Dad suggested drinking some hot chocolate to warm my belly, so we stopped to dig my thermos from my backpack. I took a sip and cringed, slapping my lips. "Ugh. It tastes funny."

He narrowed his eyes, yanked the thermos from my grip, and sniffed. "You packed *my* thermos, you little shit." I flinched like he'd slapped me. He'd never called me anything like that before. Once we traded thermoses, he took a swig from the soured one. Then another. Then another. I watched, confused, so naive it took me a hot minute to realize the problem wasn't sour milk. He'd spiked his hot chocolate with booze. For a morning hike. Then he drove us home, buzzed.

After that, I didn't mind Mom's tea so much.

"So, how are you?" Dylan asked as I reached for a mug on a high shelf on my bookcase. It was the clay one Caelyn made for me in art class, bedazzled with rhinestones she'd glued on.

"Oh, you know." My voice wavered from the recent threat of tears. "Worst I've ever been." I wiped the inside of the mug with a tissue. "You?"

"Pretty close."

"What could possibly top today?" Dylan's face hardened at some memory, and my face went hot. "Oh, sorry, I didn't mean—"

"No, it's fine." He poured hot chocolate into our mugs. "But . . . well, today wasn't the first time I'd seen a dead body."

I shuddered. Matty wasn't already dead when the paramedics took him away, was he? They'd said they detected a heartbeat. But I envisioned his gray pallor and purple lips, and my stomach lurched.

Dylan handed me Caelyn's mug, watching me closely, waiting for a reaction that never came. I didn't know what to say. I didn't want to pry or dredge up bad memories for him when everything was already so miserable.

"Welp," he finally said, raising his plastic mug. "Cheers—the most morbid cheers ever."

"Is there a depressing version of *cheers*? Like *boo* or *ugh* or something?"

"I dunno. Let's go with *boo.*"

We booed and tapped mugs, and I took a tiny sip. The liquid was lukewarm, yet smooth and rich as it slid down my throat. I tried ignoring the unsettled feeling creeping up my spine like a spider—it must've been from the lingering memory of Dad. Or the image of Matty's possibly dead face.

"Damn," I said, setting down my mug, "I can't believe just this morning, everything was fine."

A strange look crossed Dylan's face. "It only takes an instant for life to turn completely upside down." Was he thinking of his worst day? I wondered what happened.

"I think about those instants a lot." I sat at my desk as he leaned against it.

"Yeah?"

"Yeah, like . . . maybe big events cause a rift in reality, and it splits into alternate dimensions."

He raised his brows. "You believe in multiverses?"

"I don't know. Maybe. It's kinda hard to imagine infinite versions of ourselves running around. But I like to think that at some point this morning, our timeline split in two, and somewhere out there, everything's fine, and Matty's still alive, and none of this ever happened."

He laughed bitterly. "What a strange thing to find reassuring." Even after everything today, his tone was as biting as always.

"I'm sorry, but did you come here at—lemme check my notes—two in the morning to be an asshole?"

His eyes widened. "No! I—sorry. I couldn't sleep. I was worried about you . . ." His expression softened, and I felt myself blush again. "It just makes me jealous of our other selves, that's all. It's not fair that they get to live in that timeline and we don't."

"Oh." Maybe his snark was a coping mechanism. I shouldn't have leaped down his throat. We were both on edge.

"Did I ever tell you how my mom died?" Dylan asked.

"No." She must've been the dead body he'd seen.

"Car accident. She was driving drunk, as cliché as that is. She swerved into the wrong lane, and—" He snapped his fingers. "It only took an instant. The exact wrong instant."

My heart lodged in my throat, making it hard to swallow. Of course it'd pain him to think of an alternate dimension where he got to keep his mother. How long ago did this happen? Was he in the car? Did he see her die? What happened to whoever was in the other car? But my questions clung to the tip of my tongue. I'd always avoided discussing death at all costs—I didn't know which questions to ask, or which were too much, too morbid. "I'm so sorry," was all I could manage.

"It's fine. It was a long time ago." He started toward my bed, maybe to sit there, but stepped on my notebook. He picked it up, spotting my list of names. "What's this? A list of suspects?" His eyebrows shot up at the last name. "Why's *Zoey* on here?"

My stomach dropped, and I slammed my palm on my phone's mic. *No.* We couldn't talk about this. It was too dangerous. I couldn't bear to lose him. I couldn't bear to be the one to do it. Plus, if Zoey *was* An0nym0us1, the last thing I needed was for her to know I was onto her.

Dylan looked at me like I'd lost all my marbles.

I checked the screen, but it remained dark. The battery

must've drained. It was safe to talk. I just had to be careful not to mention Caelyn or anything that would trigger Dylan to call the cops. "Sorry. Thought I saw a bug." I snatched the notebook and set it on my desk, facedown. "And, uh . . . that's nothing."

"It's not nothing." He flipped it back over. "You've got our two prime suspects, then *Zoey*. I mean, I know things have been weird between you two for a while, but . . . really?" So he *had* noticed.

My mouth went dry, like I'd been sucking on a sponge or something. I couldn't tell him about this. I *couldn't*. "I . . . I was just . . . doodling?"

He gave me a look that said, *Bullshit*.

I groaned. My head was swimming in pain and exhaustion, and I couldn't think how to talk my way out of this. I crossed the room and collapsed on my bed. Dylan brought over my mug, and I scooted to give him space, tucking my legs under me.

I took a small sip. Maybe I could tell him at least part of what Zoey did, and see if he thought my theory had merit based on that alone. "Alright, fine. But this stays *between us,* okay? You can't tell anyone."

"Okay."

"Promise?"

"Scout's honor."

I tilted my head. "Were you a Boy Scout?"

"No." He lifted the corner of his mouth. "But I promise. I won't say a word." He held my gaze, looking earnest. Caring. Like he wanted to help. But I had to be careful. If I told him too much, he'd never look at me the same way again.

CHAPTER 24

Being in denial that someone's betrayed you doesn't make it any less true. I wanted to believe I was wrong about Zoey, even as I sat at her desk after sneaking in through her window last month, gaping at the aimbot file.

She even tried to deny it. "You're so fucking paranoid," she'd hissed, closing her bedroom door behind her.

"I'm not!" I'd motioned to her screen. "I'm literally looking at the aimbot file on your laptop right now. Don't lie to me!"

"Shhh! I'll get in trouble, I'm supposed to be studying. Can't we talk about this tomorrow?"

What, and give her time to weasel her way out of this? As much as I hated confrontation, we needed to hash this out. "No. *Now.*"

"I . . ." She slumped her shoulders. "I don't know what to say."

"Did you really think none of us would notice? I can't believe

you. Mr. Ferguson will throw you off the team for this. And
MortalDusk . . . they'll ban you for *life*—"

"No! *Please* don't tell anyone."

"But you've been cheating! You *betrayed* us." It sounded so
overdramatic. On one hand, MortalDusk was just a video game.
On the other, it was a ginormous part of our lives. We'd all
trained for months. We all dreamed of winning the tourney. We
all deserved a fair shot.

Zoey's eyes got all misty. "You don't know what it's like."

"What *what's* like?"

"Your mom lets you do whatever you want. She'll let you *be*
whatever you want. I don't want to be an oral surgeon. I don't
want to stare into people's gross mouths all day, to cut into their
gums, to smell their disgusting breath."

Wait, what? "Since when?"

"Since always. I know what you all think—I'm a privileged
brat, right? Everyone's worried how they'll pay for college, and
you might lose your freaking house, and then oh, poor Zoey
doesn't want to be a surgeon. Boo *fucking* hoo. But I need that
money, too. I need to get out of this perfectionist-seeking hellhole."

My heart clenched. I wished she'd confided in me sooner. I
knew her parents pressured her to study a ton and get into a college
with a great dental school, but I thought she *wanted* to join their
practice. I thought it'd be a relief never to have to worry about
interviewing for a job or competing with anyone else. If she'd told
me the truth, I wouldn't have thought, *Boo fucking hoo.* There
was nothing whiny about wanting to choose your own future.

"I'm sorry. I . . . I didn't realize." I raked back my curls, wavering a bit. But I was so *mad.* "Still, that doesn't make it okay to cheat. Like you said, we *all* have reasons to want to win."

Zoey's bottom lip quivered. "Please . . . I can't be thrown off . . . I *can't.* You can't tell anyone." I wiped a hand down my face. Maybe I could convince everyone to keep this from Mr. Ferguson and MortalDusk, and let her stay on the team so long as she didn't play in the tourney. But she must've mistaken my hesitation as a refusal to reason with her, and before I could say anything else, she balled her hands into fists. "If you tell, I'll tell everyone what really happened to Brady. I'll post the whole story online. I'll tell everyone it was *your* fault. That you're the one who made us lie."

Her words chilled me to the core. It was like every fiber of my being froze, and my heart couldn't pump crystalized blood. "You wouldn't."

"Yes, I would. And it'd all be true." This was just like how she'd threatened Lucia.

Now I was the one getting panicky. "*You* were the one who wanted to go back—"

"You made us go out there in the first place, and then *lied* about what happened."

"To protect *you*! To protect all of us."

"It only made things worse." Her eyes bored into mine like daggers. "I never wanted to go along with it."

"But you did. We all did. You can't hold that against me now . . . We were *eleven.*"

"And now we're sixteen, and you still haven't confessed."

"None of us have."

"Well, I *will* if you tell anyone about this."

My God. When I realized she was cheating, my heart had started to crack. But this? Blackmailing me with the most traumatic thing I'd ever—*we'd* ever—experienced? This made the fissures break wide open. And right then, I knew.

Our friendship was done.

I told Dylan everything except what Zoey did to keep my mouth shut. I couldn't tell him that part. Then I'd have to tell him what we did to Brady.

"So that's why she's on my list," I told him. "She wants to win that prize money and get away from her parents badly enough to cheat. Maybe she's gunning for the solo prize." Anyone could play in the solo tourney, even if they weren't on a team. "It's a hell of a lot more than the team prize split five ways . . ." I trailed off, parched. Had I really been talking that long? I downed the rest of my hot chocolate and set the mug on the dresser behind me. What I really wanted was water.

But then I caught Dylan's expression. Now he was *really* looking at me like I'd lost my marbles, plus a few bouncy balls. "What?"

"Well . . ." He rubbed the back of his neck. "Zoey warned me you'd say something like this."

My heart dropped. "*What?*"

"Yeah." Dylan shifted uncomfortably. "It was after you snapped at her in chemistry class the other week. She was all upset, and I asked her what was going on." The thought of her confiding in him made jealousy slice through me. "She said lately you blamed her for everything that went wrong, even if she had nothing to do with it. That you were mentally unwell—paranoid."

My mouth dropped open, and my cheeks flamed. How *dare* she! I'd never told her about my panic attacks, thinking she wouldn't understand; not like Akira would. But maybe she knew. And now I knew exactly what she was doing. She was gaslighting me—trying to discredit me if I ever told anyone she cheated. But to lie or exaggerate about someone's mental health, to imply it made them untrustworthy, to use it as a shield for their own misdeeds—that was utterly repugnant.

"I . . . I'm not . . ." The fury in my gut seemed to scorch any words I tried forming. I remembered when Dylan caught me glaring after Zoey this morning as she raced back to her house instead of climbing into Matty's car. "Is that why you called me paranoid earlier?"

He let out a sigh. "I mean, maybe. But now I know it's not true."

I bit my lip. "You believe me?"

"Obviously."

"*Is* it obvious?" I asked, incredulous.

He smiled slightly. "I don't think you'd admit you broke into Zoey's bedroom if you didn't actually find proof." Relief simmered down my anger a bit. "But why didn't you tell us Zoey was cheating?"

I cringed. As much as Zoey had lied to our friends, I'd lied by omission. But I couldn't tell him about her blackmail, or Brady. "She promised she wouldn't do it again. If I told, she would've been banned from MortalDusk."

"Rightfully so!"

I avoided his gaze, staring out the window at Zoey's.

"You're hiding something, aren't you?"

I picked at a strand of white thread dangling from my sweater. "No." Yes.

"You are." He rubbed his chin, thinking. "There was that thing at the hospital earlier . . . You were all beating around the bush about something. Does it have to do with that?"

I tensed, and my eyes flicked up to his. How much did we reveal?

When I said nothing, Dylan snapped his fingers. "Yep, that's it, isn't it? Akira said something about someone waiting five years." *Dammit, Kiki.* "What was that all about?"

I hugged my knees to my chest, truly light-headed now. "Nothing."

"Didn't seem like nothing." Dylan's eyes searched mine, like if he looked hard enough, he could see the truth play out like a movie in my retinas. But if he knew what we did, he'd never look at me the same way again.

"I . . . I can't . . ." The words caught in my throat, and I let out a small cough. I was so thirsty—I'd barely had a chance to be a functioning human today—but the thought of going down to the kitchen for water seemed a gargantuan task. I swallowed hard. "Listen, I'm pretty sure whoever framed you with that test is behind all this, and you weren't here for that. So it . . . it doesn't matter . . ."

Ugh, it was so late, and I was utterly drained and dehydrated. I wished I could just go to sleep, to wake up and

have everything be right again, like some sort of reset button. I covered my eyes, apparently making Dylan think I was
crying.

"Aw, Crys, I'm sorry. I shouldn't have pushed you . . . C'mere."
He pulled me close, and suddenly we were snuggling, my head
resting against his chest. "I still don't think Zoey would do this.
Cheating's one thing, but this? Nah. I think it's Jeremy. We've
destroyed his standings, humiliated him . . . and not just on his
livestreams but that date of his, too. It's *gotta* be him. It's the only
thing that makes sense."

Of course he'd defend Zoey—*something* happened between
them. Still, he was probably right.

The steady *thud, thud, thud* of his heart, the musky sandal-
wood scent of his soap, the feel of his arms around me were
more soothing than I could have imagined. Nobody had ever
held me like this before. I let out a deep sigh. Exhaustion crept
in from all angles, and my eyelids were heavy. So heavy. After
everything that happened today, all my body and mind wanted
to do was shut down, to escape into the cloudy void of uncon-
sciousness. But I couldn't fall asleep. I had to find Jeremy Fischer's address. I forced my eyes back open.

"You know, I've been wanting to tell you something . . ."
Dylan muttered, his breath warm on my ear.

"Hmm?" I looked up at him.

He hesitated a moment. "What happened at Lucia's party . . .
I didn't want that to happen."

Zoey's kiss? Is that what he meant? His lips were so close to
mine now. It would take the smallest movement to bring them

together. He was only a breath away. But now . . . I couldn't . . .
not after Matty. *Matty.*

Dylan pulled me closer and kissed my forehead instead. He
knew now was the wrong time. I struggled to blink as thousand-
pound weights closed my eyelids. He stroked my hair, and I shivered . . . Could he feel that? Would we ever kiss . . . or have this
moment again . . . Would tomorrow ruin everything . . . Tomorrow . . . What would happen . . . My thoughts were getting
jumbled as I slipped in and out of consciousness. Dylan said
something else . . . something in a soothing voice . . . but his
voice merged with those in my dreams . . .

Fishman's voice, calling me a traitor.

Matty's voice, saying he couldn't breathe.

Caelyn's voice, begging for help.

And another voice, low and robotic, telling me I'd never see
my sister again.

CHAPTER 25

*B*uzz. Buzz.

My eyelids still weighed a gazillion pounds as I peered through my lashes. A wall was so close to my nose I could see the paint's rippled texture. Where was I?

Buzz. Buzz.

Was that my phone? My alarm was usually a pleasant twinkling sound—

Memories from the previous day flooded me like a tsunami, and I jolted upright, nearly yelling out in surprise at the figure curled up beside me. Someone else was in my bed.

Dylan.

He was still here, his phone lying next to his face like he'd fallen asleep reading it, his lips gently puffing out with each exhale. Mom probably would've been fine with him spending the night under the circumstances, but she'd murder me on the spot if she knew he'd spent it *in my bed*. I had to get him out of here. Neither my sudden movement nor his buzzing phone had woken him. Maybe he was a heavy sleeper, like Akira. *Akira.* Oh, God. I had to check on her.

I spidered down to the foot of the bed and darted to my desk, then hesitated—my phone was dead, and it wasn't safe to use it or my laptop. How was I supposed to get in touch with her? Ugh, my head felt like a boulder, my tongue like a mound of sand. Was this some sort of panic hangover?

Buzz. Buzz.

My phone. Not Dylan's. Resting on its charging pad, the one place it absolutely wasn't supposed to be. *No.* I gingerly reached for it—like it might spring legs, race up my arm, and claw at my face—and flipped it over.

A video started auto-playing, the volume on. It was Caelyn—the black gag had been removed from her mouth, and her eyes looked weary and hazy. Her glasses were still missing. My heart lodged in my throat, choking off my air supply. "It's eight in the morning on Saturday. And it's time for the next game." Her eyes flicked from side to side, almost like she was reading a cue card. "If you don't play, they'll kill me. Are you ready?"

"Shit!"

Dylan snorted and burrowed deeper into my pillow.

My lungs seemed to fill with gravel. I could've sworn I'd left the phone off its charging pad after the battery drained. Was I absolutely losing my mind? Maybe Dylan put it there, thinking he was doing me a favor. How long had it been on? What might An0nym0us1 have heard? I rushed over and shook his shoulder. "Dylan. Dylan, wake up."

"Huh?" He made some incoherent grumbling noises, then

squinted up at me, like he was confused where he was. He sat up and pawed sleep from his eyes. "Oof. I passed out."

"Obviously. Did you turn on my phone?"

"What?" He fumbled for his glasses on my dresser behind his head.

"My phone," I prodded, breathless, "did you turn it on?"

"Uh . . ." He scrunched his nose. "Why would I?"

Dammit. After checking to make sure the phone was off, I must've absentmindedly dropped it on its charging pad out of habit, distracted by Dylan's questions about my suspect list. I hadn't been vigilant enough.

Negligent.

Careless.

That meant An0nym0us1 might've heard our entire conversation. Now what would they make me do? Would they try to make me hurt Dylan? Had they realized Akira was okay by now? *Was* Akira okay?

"Are you alright?" asked Dylan, concerned by my panic. "What's going on?"

Oh, God. I had to check on Akira. And I still had to find Fishman. How the hell was I going to do that now? Either way, I had to get Dylan out of here. He wasn't safe with me. "C'mon, I need you to leave. If Mom sees you spent the night, she'll *kill* me."

He stood, stretching his arms overhead. "What time is it?"

I glanced at my alarm clock. "Almost eight." That meant Mom had already left for her nursing shift. She must not have checked on me before she left, wanting to let me sleep.

But Dylan didn't need to know she wasn't here.

"Please. I need you to *go*." I motioned to the window.

He pulled his fingers through his mussed hair, then collected his thermos, checking that his cup was empty before twisting it on. "Should I wait for you? My Jeep's parked down the—"

"No. I'll text you later, after my mom goes to work."

He stilled, and his nostrils flared. "You won't go anywhere until then?"

"What makes you think I'm gonna go somewhere?"

He picked up my notepad and tapped the address scrawled next to Jeremy's name. Crap. That wasn't even the right address, though. I tried to yank the notebook back, but he wouldn't let go. "Don't, Crystal. It's too dangerous." No. What was too dangerous was involving him. What was too dangerous was continuing this conversation any longer.

"Now *you're* being paranoid. Just because I wrote that down doesn't mean I'm planning to *go* there."

"Well, I'm not leaving until you promise me you won't go stalking him. If it *is* him, and that asshole hurts you—"

"I won't, okay?" I huffed, cutting him off, and clutched my phone to my sweater to try muffling our voices. "Now, please, just go." I slid the window open and nudged him toward it. "I don't want to get grounded for the rest of my life."

"*Promise* me."

I winced. I hated making promises I had no intention of keeping. When he saw me hesitate, something like fear crossed his face. "At least let me come with you."

But teaming up with Dylan would mean revealing my plan and telling him about An0nym0us1, which would explicitly

break their rules. They'd kill Caelyn. They'd make me kill *him*.
"I'm not going *anywhere*."

"You'd better be telling me the truth," he said, his voice low
and raspy.

"I—" But before I could say anything else, he was kissing
me, pressing me back against the wall next to my window. My
heart seemed to trip over itself as his lips moved against mine,
but then I cupped his face and kissed him back. He let out a soft
moan. Warmth like heated honey oozed through me, and I tried
pulling him closer even though he was already crushed against
me. I was desperate to feel safe, even if only for a moment. His
kisses felt urgent, hungry, like he was afraid to lose me before
he ever even had me.

The moment our lips parted, he whispered, "Promise me."

"I promise." A lie. Obviously.

"Okay. Thank you. Text me when the coast is clear. I'll come
pick you up, and we'll figure this out together."

"Alright."

He grabbed his thermos and climbed out the window, and
my heart thrashed against my rib cage as I watched him descend
the hill. My God. What the hell just happened?

I couldn't let kisses and my mushy insides distract me right
now. I shut my blinds and brightened my phone screen, and the
video of Caelyn started again, playing on a loop.

Anger burned my lungs. I couldn't let An0nym0us1 control
me. I couldn't let them try to hurt any more people I loved. What
if they made me go after Akira again? Or Randall? Or *Dylan*?
I touched my lips. *No.* This deck was stacked against me, with
every advantage in their court.

I couldn't win this game if I played strictly by their rules.

Now it was time to bend them.

I let the phone fall from my grip and gasped like it was an accident. It clattered on the edge of my desk, then fell to the floor. I threw myself over it, covering the front-facing camera as I held down the power button for ten . . . nine . . . eight . . . seven . . . six. . . .

If you don't play, they'll kill me.

Three . . . two . . . one.

I had to move fast.

I had Mom's laptop now—I'd surreptitiously watched her type her password enough times to know it was *Crystal-Caelyn123.* Now I was free to search for Jeremy's address faster than on my slow Kindle, but all I could find was that listing with his parents' address. It displayed lots of useless information about them—their ages, occupations, education levels, phone number—

Huh. Phone number.

If An0nym0us1 could make me pretend to be some Lance Burdly dude, I could pretend to be someone else.

But I couldn't turn my phone back on. We did have a land-line in the kitchen, one we never used . . . but what if An0nym0us1 was monitoring that as well?

If you think I didn't think of everything, your sister won't survive.

I squeezed the bridge of my nose. They couldn't have thought of *everything.* There had to be some way to outsmart them. I needed to get creative.

I pulled up an incognito window, set up a burner Gmail account, and logged in to Google Voice. Dammit—I had to create a new number before placing any calls, and I'd have to verify an existing phone number first. But there was an option for them to call me with a four-digit code. I could use the landline for that.

Risky. So risky.

But it was this or play some sick game and hurt someone else. I couldn't waffle. I had to do this.

I hurried down to the kitchen, entered our landline number in the verification field, and waited for the call. A few moments later, I was all set up with a shiny new Google Voice number. Okay. I got this.

I dialed Jeremy's parents' number. *Ring. Ring. Ring*—

"Hello?" A woman's voice.

"Good morning, ma'am." Oh, God. I was totally riffing here. "This is Jeanne with Citibank customer service. Can I please speak with Jeremy Fischer?" For some reason, I reflexively faked a Southern twang, trying to sound as official as possible.

"Uh . . . sorry, you have the wrong number."

I grimaced, and my stomach wobbled. Had Jeremy's parents moved as well? I'd assumed he'd moved out and gotten his own place, but maybe his whole family moved.

"Jeremy moved out a few months ago," she went on, filling the awkward silence. Ah. This must've been Jeremy's mom. "Who did you say this was?"

"This is Jeanne, ma'am, with Citibank customer service. We tried mailing his credit card to an address in—let's see here—ah, here we go, in Lakecrest, and it was returned to sender. Now, if I could just confirm his new mailing address—"

"He's at 2672 Bridgeport Terrace."

Jesus, lady. Talk about trusting.

I typed the address into a new compose window so I wouldn't forget it. "Ah, that explains it—the address he gave us was 7226."

She chuckled. "He's dyslexic—sometimes he still mixes things up. Do you need his phone number, too?"

"That'd be great—I'll update our records, and I won't bother you again."

"Not a bother at all, dear." She rattled that off as well. But I already had exactly what I needed.

Two could play at this game. And I never wanted to win more.

CHAPTER 26

Thought I wouldn't check for tracking devices, didn't you?" I muttered as I peeled the device from the rear bumper of my car and dropped it onto the gravel lining the driveway next to Matty's car, which his mothers hadn't picked up yet. The gratification of finding the tracker outweighed any shock that An0nym0us1 had bothered, or that they'd stood in this very spot. At this point, it would take a hell of a lot more than being tracked or stalked to rattle me.

Fuck this anonymous asshole.

Hopefully they wouldn't be anonymous much longer.

By the time I reached Jeremy's street—sans GPS, using directions I'd hurriedly scrawled in my notebook—my palms were slick with sweat. It'd been thirty minutes since I turned my phone off. Thirty minutes of being invisible. I tried not to think about the horrible things An0nym0us1 might be doing to Caelyn in their fury. I had to do this. It was the fastest way I

could think to catch Jeremy in the act . . . or to rule him out as
a suspect.

My plan was this: Spy on Jeremy, turn on my phone, and reply
to An0nym0us1's message. If Jeremy looked at his phone exactly
then—better yet, if he *replied,* and that timing also matched—I'd
know he was An0nym0us1. If not, it was someone else.

Yeah, I never said it was a *good* plan.

I set off down the street, phone in hand, leaving my car in
the bramble alongside the narrow rural street. Silver clouds hung
low in the sky, threatening rain that would leave an icy sheen on
the frigid pavement. I shivered from the wind that whipped by,
rustling the branches overhead.

Jeremy's house was a dated one-story ranch that sorely needed
painting. The yard was unkempt, dotted with overgrown shrubberies and weeds peeking out between the stones of his front
walkway. Mounds of blackened snow lined the driveway, the
asphalt cracked and pitted. You'd think with his millions of subscribers, he'd be raking in enough dough from ads and sponsor-
ships to fix up this place. Maybe he couldn't be bothered. Or
maybe he didn't earn as much as I'd thought, especially if his
revenue had taken a hit thanks to us, or he was using the money
for something else—debt or medical bills—who knows? I knew
nothing about his life. Maybe he really *was* desperate for the
tourney prize money.

Someone shrieked nearby, and I startled, the jolt sending
sparks over my skin. Across the street, a pair of sisters, maybe
five or six years old and wearing matching bright blue puffer
jackets, chased each other across the lawn as their mother sat on

the front stoop, scrolling through her phone. The sight made my heart clench. I had to get Caelyn back. I had to do this.

As I crept onto Jeremy's yard, something like vertigo tingled the pads of my feet. At least when I'd broken into Akira's house, the night's darkness had shielded me. Now, in broad daylight, I was exposed. Vulnerable. This wasn't like MortalDusk—I couldn't dart from shrubbery to shrubbery to stay concealed. If the woman across the street merely glanced my way, I was toast.

Good thing people rarely looked up these days.

I flipped up my hood, loped around the side of the house, and prowled to the closest window. Kitchen. Jeremy was clearly a slob. Dishes were piled high in and around the sink, and open bags of chips cluttered the stone-slab countertops. Pots and pans hung over the stove, and a knife block sat next to it. The slit for the chef's knife was empty.

It could mean nothing. The knife could be in the sink or something.

Or it could mean everything.

The next window's blinds were drawn (dammit), so I passed it, rustling through dead leaves and bramble to stoop next to a tiny window nestled near the ground. Basement. I got on my knees and cupped a visor around my eyes to cut the glare. Since the lights were off, I couldn't see far into the room, but it seemed unfinished. Empty metal shelves lined faux-brick concrete walls, and cardboard boxes were stacked under the window.

An image flashed through my mind: a gloved hand brandishing a knife over Caelyn, the wall behind her faux-brick concrete.

My pulse quickened. I tried sliding the window open, but

it was locked, because of course it was. Breaking it wouldn't help—it was so small, I didn't think my hips would fit through. I had to move on.

I sidled past the back stoop—and that's when I heard it. A muffled voice coming from the next room. I pressed my back against the wall, heart racing, and craned my neck to peek inside. The lights were on, blinds wide open.

There he was.

Fishman.

And he was playing MortalDusk, facing his massive monitor against the right-hand wall, wearing huge black headphones as he spoke to an empty room. I couldn't make out what he was saying, but he was clearly streaming.

I bit my lip, considering this. He hadn't gone live yet when I checked his channels earlier on Mom's laptop. If he was really holding a thirteen-year-old girl hostage in the basement, would he stream? Maybe he thought it could be an alibi, however shaky. I slid my phone from my pocket. The moment I turned it on, my GPS coordinates would be traceable, my cameras functional. This was an incredibly stupid idea, wasn't it? If Jeremy was An0nym0us1, and he caught me, he'd kill me. Not to mention Caelyn.

Dammit. I wished Dylan were here—and not because I needed a knight in shining armor or some crap. When I left my house, so much rage bubbled in my belly it felt like I could Hulk-smash Jeremy's face in if I needed to. But realistically, it'd be nice to have backup in case shit hit the fan. How well could I defend myself, unarmed and alone, against a sadistic twenty-one-year-old dude?

But it was too late to turn back. I was right here. I *had* to know.

Pressing the power button felt like touching a flame to a dynamite fuse. After a few moments, the screen brightened. I'd missed several alerts, but ignored them and navigated to An0nym0us1's app. I wasn't sure how many of their messages I'd missed, since I could only see their most recent one.

Why is your phone off? You're playing with fire.

Glancing up at Jeremy, I gnawed at the inside of my cheek. His phone was on the desk next to his mouse. I couldn't tell if it was faceup or not.

With trembling fingers, I typed. Sorry, ran out of battery. Full charge now.

Sent.

Time seemed to slow as I watched Jeremy, and my heart thundered in my ears. Did the screen brighten? I couldn't tell from this angle. I breathed hard, puffs of white condensation escaping my lips like homing beacons.

No reply from An0nym0us1.

Jeremy was in the middle of a sword fight, leaning forward, hammering on his space bar. Maybe he'd missed the notification. Finally, he threw his hands in the air. "Ohhhhh!"

Someone killed him. Or he'd won. Either way, the round seemed to be over.

Maybe I should try again. Jeremy was still talking to his audience, muffled just enough so I couldn't make out the words, probably giving his usual postmortem; whenever he won, he'd belittle his opponent, and when he lost, he'd run through some other tactic he should have tried. I shot off another message.

Well? What's next?

At that exact moment, Jeremy picked up his phone.

It had been facedown. He stopped talking. I couldn't see his expression. Was he tightening his jaw? Was he *angry*? My heart went still.

It was him. It was *him*.

He seemed to shake away some thought and spoke again, setting down his phone. Still no reply from An0nym0us1. Was that enough of a confirmation? What should I do? I hadn't thought this far ahead. I could call the cops. They could free Caelyn from the basement. We weren't close to a police station—it would take them a while to get here. Once Jeremy realized where I was, would he kill Caelyn in a last-ditch effort to win his sadistic game?

Caelyn.

I had to check for another basement window. I had to—

My phone buzzed. A message from An0nym0us1.

I know where you are.

No. *No.*

Jeremy hadn't picked up his phone again or touched his keyboard. His fingers were clasped behind his head as he continued his recap. Had he somehow dictated the message without his audience knowing?

No. My gut sank. Checking his phone had been a coincidence. He wasn't An0nym0us1.

That meant it was either Lucia or Zoey . . . or someone I hadn't thought of yet. It also meant I'd broken An0nym0us1's rules for absolutely nothing. I gritted my teeth, choking back a frustrated scream, when a new message appeared.

Have you given up? If you forfeit, I'll keep playing without you. Then she dies.

Wait, *what*? They'll keep playing? What did that mean? Before I could make sense of it, Jeremy glanced out the window and spotted me.

5 Years Ago

The screaming jolted me awake.

"Brady!" A woman's voice pierced the silence of Zoey's den as footsteps thundered down the stairs. "We're going to be late to church—" The lights flicked on. My head swirled after what must've been only a few measly hours of sleep. Matty groaned somewhere nearby. "They're still asleep? It's nearly seven thirty."

Even Zoey's mom, who stood at the foot of the stairs in a bright blue robe, looked baffled. "Well, I let them stay up late. And it is Sunday . . ."

Mrs. Cullen gave an annoyed huff. "I told him we were going to the early service today. Brady?" She nudged Brady's BB8-themed sleeping bag with the tip of her shoe. But only his pillow peeked out.

"Maybe he's in the bathroom," suggested Mrs. Bloom.

The five of us exchanged bleary-eyed, worried looks.

I tried propping myself on my elbows, but my right arm had fallen asleep while squished against the hard floor and was now a useless flopping appendage. "He wasn't in his room?"

"No." *Mrs. Cullen gave me a confused look.* "He came back here with you." *Oh no. If he wasn't in his room, where on Earth could he be?*

Zoey looked panic-stricken. If her mom found out we'd snuck out to play Manhunt, she was a dead girl walking. And it would all be my fault. She'd hate me forever, wouldn't she? What if she sidled me out of our trio for good? I couldn't lose my best friends over this.

"He left again later," *I said, surprised by how easily the lie came to me.* "He wanted to sleep in his own bed. The floor's hard as a rock." *I shook out my lifeless arm, demonstrating. Pins and needles prickled my fingertips as blood flow returned. Everyone nodded along with my lie.*

"Oh," *said Mrs. Cullen.* "You know, I didn't even think to check his room. I just assumed he was here!" *She laughed, shaking her head at herself.* "I'll take his things, I guess. Weird that he left them . . ." *Matty rolled up Brady's sleeping bag and cinched the straps as she gathered the rest of his stuff.* "Even his phone . . ." *she muttered, tossing it into his bag with the rest. Once the moms went back upstairs, we all stared at the empty spot.*

"That's why he didn't pick up his cell," *said Matty.*

"You guys, what if Brady isn't in his room?" *Zoey's voice was laced with hysteria.*

"He is," *said Randall.* "You heard his mom. She didn't check."

"But what if he isn't?"

I bit my lip, and different sorts of pins and needles prickled my spine. "He couldn't still be hiding in the woods . . ."

"No way." Matty checked his watch. "He'd've been hiding for, like, seven hours."

"Maybe he fell asleep," said Akira.

"Outside?" said Zoey. "It's freezing."

"Guys, stop." Randall covered his face with his pillow. "I bet he watched us out his window, laughing his shrimpy little butt off."

But I couldn't shake the pinpricks of fear as I fished my toiletries bag from my backpack. My mouth tasted rancid. After getting all minty fresh upstairs, I headed back for the basement as someone rang the doorbell. Not a moment later, a frantic knock. Mrs. Bloom rushed over. "What on earth?" This time, she let in Mrs. Cullen along with her husband and eldest son, Andrew, dressed for church in a striped button-down and navy slacks.

"Brady's not home." Mrs. Cullen bristled. "He must be here." Andrew spotted me and rolled his eyes, like he thought his mother was overreacting. But my stomach sank. Was she?

"He's probably trying to get out of church." Mr. Cullen chuckled and pushed his wire-rimmed glasses farther up his nose. His eyes sparkled like he'd be proud of Brady if that were true.

I raced back downstairs. "Brady's not home. His whole family's here."

Zoey gasped.

"Ohhh, farts," said Matty.

"D'you think he got kidnapped or something?" said Akira.

"Maybe the bears got him!" said Randall.

"Should we tell them what happened?" asked Akira. Zoey's eyes widened, and my heart jolted. I'd already lied to her mother, and Zoey had gone along with me. Telling the truth now would get her into even more trouble.

Quick footsteps started down the stairs.

"What do we do?" Akira squeaked.

Zoey scowled at me. "This is all your fault."

Panic buzzed in my chest. She was right. I couldn't let Zoey get in trouble over this. "Stick with the story," I hissed.

Before anyone could argue, Mrs. Cullen reached the bottom of the stairs. "Brady? This isn't funny." She searched the room, like he might be hiding in the shadows. Andrew watched, hovering at the foot of the stairs as she opened the creepy storage room door. "We talked about this. It's just an hour a week."

"He's really not here." I struggled to keep my voice steady. Mrs. Cullen stared me down, waiting for me to say something else— for anyone to say something else—but nobody did. The fewer lies the better.

Her eyes darted among us, her red curls more frazzled than earlier, like a measure of her rising panic. "But where could he be?"

We all shook our heads, dumbfounded.

That, we truly didn't know. He had to be somewhere out there, out in the woods. But if we told her that now, she'd know we lied.

We'd only spun a thread of a lie, but it was enough to strangle us.

CHAPTER 27

Hey!" Jeremy shouted.

I had to move. I had to *run*. But it was like my legs were rebelling against my brain's neurons, frozen in place. Jeremy said something else, reached for something on his desk, then threw off his headphones and darted to the window. Recognizing me, anger washed over his face. "You!"

Craaaaaap.

He hurtled into the hall, and I bolted past his front stoop, shoving my phone into my pocket as I rounded the corner toward the front lawn. Did he go out the back door? Was he right behind me? As I glanced over my shoulder, I tripped over something, and my arms reflexively shot out before I bit it. My left palm smashed into a tree root protruding from the ground, and searing pain flamed up my wrist. I cried out, but there was no time to writhe in agony. I scrambled to my feet and dashed into the front yard, clutching my wrist as Jeremy burst out the front door in nothing but a black T-shirt and red plaid pajama pants.

"Hey!" he screamed again. I raced toward my car, but even though he ran barefoot, he was faster—his fingers hooked the edge of my hood, and he yanked me back.

"Argh!" I whipped around to face him, breathing hard. My eyes watered from my throbbing palm and wrist.

"What the ever-loving fuck are you doing here?"

"I . . . I . . ." My phone buzzed. Probably An0nym0us1. Surely they'd punish me now—and the worst way to hurt me was to hurt my sister.

"What, were you gonna break in?" Jeremy asked. "Hack into my MD account?"

"No! I—"

"Lemme see what's in your pockets. You got a USB? Were you gonna install something?"

I cringed as a spasm of pain radiated up my arm. "No—"

"Turn out your pockets!"

Wow. I mean sure, it probably seemed sketchy as hell to be spying on him, but talk about paranoid. "I wasn't going to hack anything." I turned out my pockets with my good hand, taking out my cell and mini-charger I'd grabbed from my desk in case my phone ran out of batteries today.

"Aha!" He pointed at the charger. "I knew it!"

"It's a—"

"What were you gonna install, huh? A keystroke recorder? Ransomware? Were you gonna fucking blackmail me?"

"No—"

"Oh, man. That's why you invited me to the park yesterday. You followed me home, didn't you? That's how you found out where I live."

"I didn't—"

"You know, I could get you banned from MortalDusk for life for this. I could call the cops—"

"Will you slow down a minute and let me talk?" I shrieked.

He finally shut up, hands on his hips. "So? Talk."

"This"—I brandished the charger—"is a cell phone charger." I pulled out the inner lining of my jacket pockets. "I have no USB or anything with any viruses on them. I wasn't going to install anything on your computer, or even *touch* your computer."

"You could have done it remotely." He pointed at my phone. "You could have—"

"Jeremy," I said, exasperated, "I don't even know how to do something like that." Zoey, maybe. But me? Not a chance. I stuck the charger back in my pocket and brushed dirt off my injured palm. The pain was slowly subsiding. Or maybe it was just going numb.

He crossed his arms. "So what the hell are you doing here?"

I racked my brain for an excuse. How the hell was I going to explain this? My phone buzzed again, and I glanced at the screen.

Leave NOW, or she dies.

The ground seemed to wobble under my feet. "I'm sorry, I have to go—"

But Jeremy stepped between me and my car, raising his arms like a barrier. "No way. I need some answers here. Why the hell were you spying on me?"

I bit my lip. Just because he wasn't sending An0nym0us1's

messages didn't mean he was innocent. What if he was working with someone else?

But Jeremy seemed genuinely baffled by my presence.

I remembered Dylan's theory at the hospital that it could be one of Jeremy's teammates or fanboys or something. Maybe he'd have some idea who it was. This was completely, utterly reckless. But I was desperate. Clutching my phone to my jacket to mute the mic, I spoke softly. "After we ran into each other at the park"—he scoffed, but let me go on—"my friend Matty . . ." His cheeks had gone purple, his honey-brown eyes wide with terror, and—*no.* I shoved the memory from my skull. I couldn't think of that now, because if I thought of it, I'd feel it, and if I felt it my legs would give out beneath me, and the earth would swallow me whole. And right now, I had to keep my shit together. I had to focus on finding Caelyn. "He died."

Jeremy's expression softened. "Oh, shit, yeah."

Suspicion flared in my mind. "Wait, you *knew*? How?"

"Er . . . you know he was livestreaming when his coughing fit started, right? The video's still up on your channel. And once people heard what happened—well, people are morbid shits." Oh, God. Randall must've forgotten all about it in the chaos of everything else. No wonder so many people sent me messages. "I, uh . . . I'm real sorry about that. But that doesn't explain why you're *here.*"

I hesitated a moment. "Well, the thing is, we're not sure it was just an allergic reaction. It might've been . . . intentional."

Jeremy looked stunned. "What, like someone poisoned him?"

"More like tampered with his food to add nuts—but yeah,

essentially. And it's not just that. My other friend Randall got swatted last night."

"You're *kidding.*" Jeremy gaped at me, eyes wide. I guessed that hadn't made the news. Maybe Chief Sanchez managed to keep it hush-hush as he investigated. "Is he okay?"

"Yeah. Actually, he was at my house when it happened—there was a last-minute change in plans—but his dad had a heart attack when the SWAT team busted in."

"Holy . . ." Jeremy clasped his hands behind his head.

My phone buzzed against my chest, sending a current of fear through me. "Anyway, the cops are trying to find whoever called in the fake tip. And I thought maybe—"

Jeremy's face went stony. "You thought maybe it was *me.*"

My stomach dropped. "No!" Well, yes. "I . . . I thought maybe you'd know who might've done it—"

My phone buzzed again. This time I dared a glance, and my knees nearly buckled. A gloved hand gripped Caelyn's pale, slender wrist, and a long gash ran down her forearm, blood streaking from the wound. They'd cut her. They'd cut Caelyn. Bile leaped into my throat, and I clasped a hand over my mouth. "Oh my God."

"What is it?" Jeremy tried edging over to see my screen.

"I can't . . ." I stumbled past him toward my car.

"Hey, wait a minute!"

Where should I even go? Lucia's house? Zoey's? Even if they each had a legit motive, I couldn't imagine either of them dragging a blade down Caelyn's arm. But who else could it *be*? I felt so damn helpless. My baby sister was in pain, terrible pain, and I couldn't stop it. Could she bleed out from that wound? She needed an ambulance, *now*. But I didn't even know where she was!

Desperate, I turned back to Jeremy. "Do any of your teammates live nearby?"

"Which—"

"The ones playing with you in the tourney tomorrow."

He wiped his nose and folded his arms, shivering. "Not super close? Two are just north of Burlington, and the other two are by the border." That's what I thought.

"What about your fans? Like, superfans. The ones who egg you on when you bully us."

Jeremy flinched at this, like maybe that wasn't how he saw it. He shook his head. "I dunno. Maybe . . ."

"Would any of them try to pick us off?"

"Oh, shit, man . . ."

"I know it sounds completely off the wall. But if it's true, can you think of *anyone* who'd want to hurt us?"

"No!"

Ugh, he was useless. I spun and dashed to my car, and this time, Jeremy didn't try to stop me. Once inside, I let out a sob and held up my phone so An0nym0us1 could see me. "Please, stop it. Please don't hurt her anymore. What should I do? Tell me what to do."

You play by MY RULES, or she dies.

Did that mean the wound on her arm wasn't fatal? Oh, God. Whoever was doing this was willing to torture and lacerate a thirteen-year-old girl. I was a fool to think I could outplay this person. The power imbalance was too great. I had nothing on them, and they had what mattered to me most. I thought of their threat to keep playing the game without me. That meant terrible things would happen either way, but doing them myself could save Caelyn.

"Fine," I said in my panic, wiping tears from my cheeks. Jeremy was watching with the most bizarre, aghast look on his face. I had to get out of here. "Fine, I'll play. I'll do whatever. Just tell me what to do."

Good. It's time for a scavenger hunt.

CHAPTER 28

Built with ancient stones piled high
My towers stretch into the sky
And though no royals live nearby
If you run late, then she will die

The clue couldn't be any more obvious. At this point, I was almost impressed An0nym0us1 was bothering to keep up the pretense of a game.

Because I knew now. I knew it'd be worse than it seemed.

I mean, come on, they wanted me to post a picture of Hanover Castle to Instagram—for what? To flex my nonexistent photography skills? Hardly.

Something else would come of this. Something terrible. But I had twenty minutes to do it, *or else*. What choice did I have?

The picturesque early-twentieth-century structure stood on the bluffs of Mount Morgan, one of southern Vermont's most popular wedding venues. Mom and Dad's marriage started here and ended farther up the mountain. Life was full of those little ironies.

As mountain air whipped through my curls, I lined up my shot of the small castle, giving zero fucks about composition or lighting. My left wrist throbbed from the fall in Jeremy's yard, and I vaguely wondered if I'd sprained it, but then thought of Caelyn, her gouged arm, the scream I couldn't hear through a picture. Determinedly, I snapped the pic and posted it to Instagram, sans caption. Remembering how Jeremy had mentioned stalking me on here yesterday, I scrolled to my profile page. Yep, public now. There was no point setting it to private again—AnOnymOus1 would just switch it back.

"Alright, that's done," I said to my phone.

> Not quite a recluse
> And less like a crab
> Come to my dwelling
> Or else she'll get stabbed

They gave me ten minutes this time. But this one threw me for a loop. Was there another building on Mount Morgan? I didn't think so, but this landmark had to be close with so little time allotted. Yet no matter how many times I reread the clue, the recluse and crab bits made zero sense.

"You never said I couldn't google things," I said aloud as I typed *mount morgan vermont landmarks* into my search bar. "So this isn't cheating."

The search results came up.

Ah, of course.

The lookout point on Mount Morgan. I didn't know the official name was Hermit Thrush's Nest, apparently named for Vermont's state bird and the lookout's U-shaped stone barrier. *Not quite a recluse.* A hermit was similar to a recluse. *And less like a crab.* A bird, not a crab. *Come to my dwelling.* Its nest. Wow. How long had they been planning this sadistic mindfuck?

I could only reach the lookout point on foot, so I ditched my car in the castle's parking lot and headed for the familiar trail Dad and I used to hike all the time.

Something deep in my heart twisted, the part of me that missed him . . . at least, the old him. I missed how he'd point out the castle where he and Mom got hitched, like he was still giddy she'd said, "I do." How he'd grin so widely, layers of dimples creased his cheeks. How he'd cover my scraped knees with Mickey Mouse Band-Aids, and when I complained they were babyish, he'd slap one on his arm and say, "No one's too old for the mouse."

It was all uphill to the lookout point, and I sucked wind as I jogged the dirt path. Taking my time was a luxury I couldn't afford. It was starting to drizzle, the frigid droplets like tiny pellets of ice on my scalp. I flipped up my hood. The silver clouds had darkened, threatening to break open. I only passed one hiker, a middle-aged woman walking her golden retriever. She gave my outfit a funny look—who goes for a run in jeans?—but I couldn't care less.

A stitch formed under my rib cage, and I dug my fingers into my abdomen through Mom's puffer coat, trying to relieve the stabbing pain. Nothing worked, so I hunched over, running through it. Mind over matter.

Finally, there it was. Hermit Thrush's Nest—the scenic overlook point past a break in the trees, where a waist-high stone barrier stretched in an arc across the cliffside. On one side of the structure, a huge, flattened boulder jutted from the ridge, where daring selfie-aficionados could capture the perfect shot with a backdrop of Hanover Lake snaking through Newboro's rolling hills, littered with pine trees. The lake was a dull, murky brown under a clouded sky, and the sight of the water below flooded my mind with memories.

I won a game here once.

One I wished I'd never had to play.

After Mom refused to go the police about Dad, I'd decided to take matters into my own hands. I couldn't let him hurt Caelyn. Mom's biggest hesitation was that the cops wouldn't believe her, so I figured I needed to collect evidence. Evidence Dad couldn't refute. After all, seeing was believing.

So I did what I did best.

I turned it into a game.

Ten points for the pic of Mom's collarbone bruise (snapped as she napped on the sofa). Five points for the shot of a suspicious dent in the wall (under the missing picture frame). Fifteen points for the audio of a screaming match culminating in a crisp slap (snagged outside their bedroom door). Twenty points for the video of him yanking her from the sink as she drained his whiskey (recorded via a webcam on the fridge). Bonus ten points for the photo of the resulting welt (taken during a pretend selfie).

A hundred points, I'd decided. I'd get that many, then go to the police.

But one Sunday morning, around the seventy-point mark, Dad stopped me on my way out the door after Mom kissed me goodbye on the cheek. "Where are you going?"

"To Matty's. We're going to play MortalDusk." I'd avoided having my friends over since that time Matty and Akira overheard one of Dad's outbursts. They'd both hugged me extra long before leaving. It should've felt comforting, but I was mortified.

"Well, hey, what about our Sunday morning hike?"

I gripped the backpack strap digging into my shoulder. "We haven't done that in months."

"All the more reason to go."

Mom piped up, "She has plans, Danny—"

"She can break them. C'mon, spending one morning with your old man won't kill you."

Mom and I exchanged a look, like we weren't so sure. That alone killed me.

I kept quiet most of our hike. I could tell my silence bugged Dad—he'd remark on the chipmunks darting past, or the dewy smell foretelling rain, then glance at me expectantly. But I kept my mouth shut, thinking about that look Mom and I exchanged. No girl should wonder whether she was safe with her father. And if he'd brought Caelyn instead, I'd be going berserk with worry.

"What's the matter with you?" Dad finally asked as we reached the lookout point.

Right then, I knew it was time. I had enough points to face the final boss.

"I want you to leave," I said so quietly Dad had to ask, "Say that again?" Or maybe he'd heard but couldn't believe it. "I want you to *leave,*" I repeated. "Leave us. Leave Mom."

He looked genuinely shocked. "*What?* Why would you say that?"

"Why do you think? You've been hurting her. *Hitting* her. And I'm not so sure you won't hurt me or Cae. All you do now is drink and gamble, and you won't get help. So I want you to *leave.*"

Dad's face went beet red so fast I took a few steps back. Maybe it wasn't such a good idea to bring this up on a steep cliff. As my eyes darted between him and the stone wall, he seemed to realize what I was wondering. Whether he would hurt me. His face crumpled, shock morphing to pain. "Crystal, I would never . . ." He seemed lost for words. "I'll get help, okay? I'll stop drinking. I'll go to one of those rehab facilities." His eyes filled with remorse.

"It's too late." I screwed up my face, tears streaming in full force, though I didn't remember starting to cry. "You already told Mom you'd get help, but you didn't. You never do."

"But I *will,* this time. I promise." Then he shook his head. "What do you mean, 'it's too late'?"

"I . . . I've been collecting evidence." I whipped out my phone, navigated to a folder in my photo gallery, and showed him one of the pics of Mom's bruises. "I have photos. Recordings. Of what you've been doing to Mom. Of your fights."

His eyes widened, and he stepped closer. "Let me see—"

"No!" I leaped back again in case he wanted to chuck my phone over the ridge or something. "I have it all saved on my computer, and on Dropbox. And if you don't leave Mom, I'll show all of it to the police."

There it was. Me, blackmailing my own father. I thought he'd spit with rage. But instead he stared with this dazed, defeated look. Like this was something he never expected, and the shock was too much.

He left a week later. I'd won. It was the worst game I'd ever played.

Until now.

I took my phone from my back pocket, about to snap a pic of the overlook point for Instagram, when I noticed a girl with a short black ponytail, black leggings, and a formfitting purple coat sitting cross-legged on the boulder, admiring the view. Was that—

"*Kiki?*"

CHAPTER 29

Akira twisted to look at me. It *was* her! Her eyes were red and puffy like she'd been crying, but she was here. Safe. *Alive.* She scrambled to her feet. "Well, halle-freakin'-lujah." Before I could ask what she meant, her face scrunched up, and she practically barreled into me. We clung to each other for a long while, her having no clue I hugged her back so hard from sheer, overwhelming relief. "I still can't believe . . ." She trailed off.

"I know." Matty's face flashed through my mind. Gone forever.

As she sobbed softly, my relief turned to wariness. What was she doing here? This couldn't be a coincidence.

"Sorry." Akira finally pulled away and wiped at my shoulder. "I got snot all over your jacket." The last word came out garbled as a fresh wave of tears consumed her.

"It's fine. Sorry you didn't get to have your sex romp with Randall," I said, trying to make her laugh. It worked.

"Ugh, I know." She used her sleeve to mop her face. "Instead I vommed all over him."

"Eh, it mostly landed on you. I don't think he even noticed, anyway . . ." Due to the fact that he'd basically gone into zombie mode.

"How is he now?" She rubbed her hands together, her fuzzy purple gloves with cutoff fingertips clearly not warm enough. "He seemed okay on FaceTime earlier—thank God his dad's okay, right?—but . . . how was he *really*? Fuck you, by the way. I totally would've gone with you to the hospital." Her teeth chattered, making each rushed word seem to vibrate. I was too confused to appreciate the good news about Randall's dad.

"I . . . I haven't gone to the hospital. I haven't seen him yet."

Akira wrinkled her nose. "Dude, why'd you make me wait here for an hour, then? It's *freezing*—I was about to give up."

My spine prickled. "I don't . . ." I swallowed hard. She'd expected to meet me here. Same as Jeremy yesterday.

"You literally said you were just at the hospital."

"No, I didn't."

"Um, yes, you did." She tapped on her phone and showed me a text. From me.

Sorry I'm late. Dropped by the hospital super quick to check on Randall. Be there in a few!

My fingers went numb. I never sent that.

Akira went on, "You're the one who wanted to go for a hike. You wanted to tell me something important, remember? Why couldn't you tell me, like, in an indoor venue?"

"I . . . uh . . ." My mind reeled. An0nym0us1 had to be behind this. But knowing didn't make it any less disorienting. "Did that text come from my number?"

"Obvi."

"Can I see?"

"See what?"

"The text thread."

Akira squinched her face again but showed me the screen. My name was at the top. I tapped it, pulling up the contact. It was me. My number. An0nym0us1 was sending texts *as me.* This wasn't just spoofing.

Wait . . .

"What's wrong?" Akira asked.

On my own phone, I opened the email app and scrolled to the sent folder. My blood ran cold. There were messages I didn't recognize—one to Fishman, one to the school principal. Holy hell. Mr. Chen thought *I* was the one who ratted out Dylan. I remembered the way he nodded at me in the hall. *Shiiiiit.*

"What *is* it?" Akira prodded.

"Listen," I whispered. "I know this is going to sound batshit, but I didn't send that text. I never asked you to come here."

"But, Crys . . . you *called* me." She spoke slow and loudly, like she was talking to a petulant three-year-old. "You literally *begged* me to meet you here."

Her words coiled around my lungs, suffocating me. I didn't talk to Akira this morning. I shook my head feebly. "No, I didn't."

Akira puckered her lips for a moment, considering me. Then she laughed. "You're messing with me, aren't you? Like, to make me feel better?" She tilted her head. "It's not really funny, though—"

"I'm *not*. I'm being serious."

"But you left a voicemail—which, weird," she threw me a judgy look, "and then I called you back, and we talked."

"Wait, there's a voicemail?"

Her expression fell, perturbed. "Here, I didn't delete it yet." She tapped her screen again, then thrust her phone at me. I never left voicemails, like, as a personal policy. My own inbox had been full for years since I refused to check it. But there it was. A voicemail from me. My contact. My number. Placed at 6:30 a.m., before I'd woken up.

At least, I didn't *think* I'd woken up yet.

Akira leaned against the wide stone barrier, fiddling with a twig she picked up and watching as I pressed Play and held the phone to my ear.

Hey, Kiki. I'm so sorry to call you this early, but I . . . I really need to talk to you. It's really, really important. Can you please call me back before you talk to anyone else? Love you.

It felt like I'd plunged into the icy waters of Hanover Lake. I'd always hated the sound of my own voice on our streaming videos—it sounded alien, somehow. And this was my voice. My intonations and inflections. Even down to calling Akira *Kiki*. Zoey and I were the only ones who called her *Kiki*.

That was the most unsettling thing of all.

"So, then . . . you called me back?" I asked.

Akira chuckled nervously. "Yeah . . . you really don't remember? We made plans to meet. You said you had an errand to run first across town, so you wanted to meet here instead of driving over together." She picked some bark off the twig. "I wonder if it's some sort of PTSD thing. Did you black out or something?"

Was she right? Had I wanted to tell Akira about Zoey's cheating and blackmail, since I'd already told Dylan most of the story . . . and then my brain short-circuited?

No. No way. Dylan had been lying in bed next to me—I would have remembered edging around him to get to my phone without waking him, and then climbing back into bed.

This had to be An0nym0us1's doing. I thought of the voice changer I'd used yesterday to call in the fake tip, now in a nylon bag somewhere at the bottom of the lake. They could have used a voice changer, too; a more convincing one than the one I'd used. But they hadn't just gotten the tone and pitch right—they'd used my inflections, my vocal mannerisms, even my nickname for Akira. They had to know me really freaking well—

"What's going on?" said Akira. "Something's clearly very wrong."

"I . . . I can't tell you."

It started drizzling again, but we both ignored it. "Why not?" My heart broke at her pained expression. "I thought we agreed. No secrets between us. Ever. But you've been hiding something for *weeks*."

"What do you mean?"

"What's been going on between you and Zoey?" she asked. Of course. She hated that neither of us would tell. I wiped a hand down my face. It was such a long story, and I was still trying to work out why An0nym0us1 summoned Akira here. Was she a distraction, like Jeremy? Why make us meet here, of all places—

The realization hit me like a meteor. I knew what the next game would be. *No.* I couldn't let that happen. I scurried back toward the trail, distancing myself from Akira and the stone barrier.

"What is it—"

"Mountain lion!" I cried. "Run!"

Akira's eyes widened as she scanned the woods. "Where?"

"Run! Get out of here!" I thought I'd saved her last night. I thought I'd outsmarted An0nym0us1. But they wouldn't give up that easily. Of course they wouldn't.

My phone buzzed in my pocket, right on time.

"What about you—"

"Dammit, Kiki. *Go!*" If only it were Dylan, checking in. If only it were literally anyone else. But I had all my alerts turned off save one.

What if I ignored it? What would An0nym0us1 do to Caelyn? She was already cut. Already bleeding. But they said they'd kill her if I broke their rules, and I already had once today.

So I looked.

A knife was pressed against Caelyn's pale throat as she squeezed her eyes shut. Blood drained from my face in a rush, and my vision went hazy and slow, giving everything jagged edges, making the text overlay hard to read.

Let's play *The Pushing Game.* Push Akira off the cliff, or your sister dies. You have 2 minutes. Ready? GO!

How could I possibly choose? Akira or Caelyn. Caelyn or Akira. There are some choices a person should never have to make. It's one thing for an ER doctor to decide which patient gets the ventilator. For a firefighter to pick who to carry from a smoldering building. For a search and rescue responder to prioritize airlift pickups from a swift-water flood. Their choice would let a stranger survive when they would've died otherwise.

But this was something else. My choice would needlessly rip a person I loved from the world. It would tear my soul in half. There was no coming back from this.

"What's going on?" Akira was screaming at me now, glancing between me and my phone. Oh, God. After everything Akira endured over the past few years—the battles with her own mind she'd fought and *won*—it couldn't end like this. It wasn't right. It wasn't *fair*. Now she refused to run, refused to leave me in danger. We always looked out for each other. Always. Or maybe she knew I was lying about the damn mountain lion. She could always read me like a book. How could I kill her? How could I kill my best friend?

Well, technically, the *how* was clear. I could beckon her to look at something near the edge, and all it would take was one small, unexpected shove. She'd tumble over to the rocks below, hitting her head, breaking her neck, or shattering her spine. It wouldn't be the first time it happened—every few years, an overzealous photographer or careless selfie-taker slipped off the boulder, plummeting to their death.

I squeezed my eyes shut. Just imagining it was unbearable. But if I didn't push Akira, An0nym0us1 would slice Caelyn's neck, and my baby sister would be gone forever, and all I'd done to save her would've been for nothing. Matty would've died for nothing. Randall's dad would've had a heart attack for nothing.

I'd tried so hard to protect Caelyn—playing this sadistic game, vying for the tourney prize money, driving our father away. And now, after everything, I was failing her.

How would I survive knowing I didn't do all I could to save her?

How would Mom forgive me if I let her die?

How would I forgive myself?

But Akira was also my sister, if not by blood. Even if she wasn't, she didn't deserve to die. What made Caelyn's life worth more than Akira's? How could anyone make this choice?

"Crystal!" Akira's sneakers crunched on gravel, and suddenly she was right in front of me, gripping my shoulders, shaking me gently. "*Please* tell me what's happening."

My phone vibrated again. My eyes snapped open, and I instinctively scrambled away from her, closer to the edge. "I can't." There was a new picture of Caelyn. No text this time. The knife was still at her throat, but now a thin red slice stretched across her neck. And this time, she was screaming.

Or I was screaming.

I had no idea.

Before I could react, Akira lunged at me and grabbed my phone, leaving hers still clenched in my other fist.

"*No!*" I cried.

But it was too late. She looked at the picture and gasped. "What the hell?" I grabbed for the phone, and pain shot up my left wrist from the sudden movement. Akira sidestepped me and raised it out of reach. "Is this *Caelyn*?" She rushed to the other end of the stone wall, trying to swipe to another photo, but there were none. You could only see one photo at a time.

I reached for the phone again. "Give it back—"

"Stop it!" Akira cried, squinting against the frigid drizzle. "Tell me what's happening."

I extended my hand, palm outstretched. "Please, give it back."

"Why won't you let me *help* you?" Her lower lip quivered, and she stepped back onto the boulder protruding from the cliff, speckled with dark dots that merged as the rain picked up. We both flipped up our hoods. I eyed the boulder warily, legs wobbling with vertigo. She knew I was afraid of heights. She knew I wouldn't follow.

"Kiki, *please,*" I said in a hissed whisper. I couldn't push her off this rock. "Let's get out of here." *I can't, I can't, I can't.*

She took another step back. "Not until you tell me what the hell's going on . . ." Realization dawned on her face, like she was putting together the pieces, constructing the truth for herself. "We were right, weren't we? Someone's after us. And this has to do with all that. They've got Caelyn. Oh my God, did they threaten you to keep quiet?" Fear gripped my heart. *If you tell your parents or anyone else, she dies.* But what if someone else figured it out for themselves?

I couldn't take that risk. I couldn't let her see whatever the next message would be.

I edged onto the boulder, shuffling my feet, glancing toward the pine tree tops underneath us, below the boulder. A rush of vertigo surged through me, making my whole body shudder. The freezing rain wasn't helping. "Just give me my phone, okay?" I held hers out like a peace offering.

"Oh my God," she said again, my lack of abject denial confirming the truth. Suddenly, she looked at the screen. It must've buzzed. Shock filled her eyes, and her mouth dropped open.

My heart plummeted, and panic flooded every capillary in my body. *Caelyn.* Were my two minutes up? "Oh, God. What is it?" I rushed forward, my terror for Caelyn momentarily outweighing my fear of heights.

Akira screwed up her face and clutched the screen to her chest. "No, don't look." What was she protecting me from seeing?

"Give it to me!" I tried to pry my phone from her grip and dropped Akira's phone in the scuffle. She instinctively shot out her other hand to catch it.

That's when she lost her balance.

The boulder sloped down behind her and was slick with frozen rain, and she couldn't regain her footing. Her arms shot forward, and I tried grabbing one of them, but it all happened so fast I caught nothing but air. Still clinging to my phone, eyes frenzied, mouth set in an open, horrified grimace, she tumbled backward. We both shrieked. I crouched, pressing my palms to my ears and squeezing my eyes shut as her scream continued the whole way down.

CHAPTER 30

Akira's fall seemed to last an eternity, until a cluster of pine trees crackled, and her cry suddenly cut off.

"Kiki!" I dropped onto my hands and knees and considered peering over the edge, but I couldn't, I *couldn't,* there was no edge—the boulder gradually sloped until it was too steep. I couldn't move, couldn't breathe, shock penetrating every fiber of my being. My chest heaved like I was about to be sick, and my whole body trembled so hard I feared I'd involuntarily pitch forward and fall, too. My fingers groped at the boulder for something to cling to, but there was nothing, *nothing,* and Akira couldn't have survived that fall, and I let out a terrible shriek, hot tears and frigid rain mingling on my face.

This couldn't be happening.

Akira was supposed to get into Cornell, become an architect, bring more beauty into this world. And now everything about her—her plans, her dreams, her life—was gone, just like that. Because I killed her. I killed my best friend. I may not have pushed her, but I wrestled her for my phone despite our precarious position.

Reckless.

Careless.

My fault. I might as well have shoved her, just like An0nym0us1 wanted.

An0nym0us1. Shit. My phone had sailed down the cliff with Akira, severing our connection. I only had a few hours left to win the game. But how could I play without a new set of rules to follow? Would this force a forfeit?

If you forfeit, I'll keep playing without you. Oh, God. I had to warn the others. I had to get it together. Breathe in. Breathe out. Just me and the air.

In.

Out.

Once I managed to slow my breathing, I got my bearings. I was too shaky to attempt standing on this uneven surface, but could sidle back to safety. Akira's phone lay facedown a few feet away in its purple case. Maybe she did survive the fall. If so, I had to call for help. I stretched my arm, reaching, reaching, and my trembling fingertips grazed the edge of the purple case, scooting it farther away. Vertigo zipped down my spine.

Oh, God. No. Deep breaths. I could do this. I *had* to do this.

I leaned over as much as I dared and grabbed the phone, then spidered backward on my hands and knees, ignoring the agony in my wrist, as though an enormous, monstrous hand might reach up from the trees below and rip me from the boulder. By the time I hurled myself back onto the dirt trail, the cuts on my left palm were bleeding again. I scrambled to my feet and leaned against the waist-high stone barrier, peering over the edge.

I could only make out a smidge of Akira's purple jacket through the branches below from this angle. Was that . . . movement? Or just the branches between us rustling in the breeze? "Kiki!" I called to her again and again, hoping she'd regain consciousness and call back. It was such a steep drop; I'd have to go around to the lake and hike alongside it to reach her.

I brightened Akira's phone screen—even though it was locked, and I didn't know the passcode, I could access the emergency screen. I hovered my thumb over the emergency call button. *If you call the police, she dies,* I remembered.

"Dammit!" Would An0nym0us1 even know? Even if they weren't tracking Akira's phone, they might be monitoring the police scanner. At this point, I couldn't tell the difference between feasibility and paranoia. Either way, I couldn't waste an opportunity to save Akira's life—if there was still a life to save—on the off chance some sadist knew I took it.

So I called 911. Held the phone to my ear. Waited for a ringtone that never came.

The call wouldn't go through. Naturally.

"You've *got* to be kidding me." The phone only detected a smidge of a signal—enough for texts to get through, apparently, but not to place calls. The universe refused to stop punching me in the face.

Or maybe An0nym0us1 blocked the call. Just like I suspected when I'd tried calling 911 as Matty gasped for his last breath.

Paranoia? Or was it possible?

No matter. I had to get help, warn my friends, and find

Caelyn—before she bled out from either of her stab wounds. The one on her neck didn't look deep in that picture, but I couldn't be sure. I bolted back down the trail toward the parking lot at the castle, hoping I'd run into that woman and her dog again. But the trails were empty now that the rain had picked up.

As I hurtled into the parking lot, a couple were getting into a black SUV, closing their umbrellas before ducking in. "Wait!" I cried. "Help!" The driver twisted around to look, and I recognized him. "Mr. Ferguson!" Our chemistry teacher. I couldn't see much of the woman already in the passenger seat. I knew he was engaged; maybe this was his fiancée, and they were checking out the castle as a wedding venue or something. Welp, I was about to ruin the vibe of this prospect.

"Crystal! What's—"

"Please . . ." I said, out of breath. "Call 911 . . . Akira . . . the lookout point . . . Hermit Thrush's Nest . . . She fell off the boulder. She might be dead . . . I don't know . . . Phone isn't working."

"Oh my God," Mr. Ferguson's fiancée gasped.

I glanced at Akira's phone screen. There was more of a signal now, but Mr. Ferguson was already dialing on his phone. As he held it to his ear, he asked, "What were you doing there?"

I shook my head. "Just . . . talking. We'd gone for a hike. Is the call going through?"

Mr. Ferguson held up a finger. "Hi, yeah, there's an emergency at Newboro State Park—"

Now that I knew help would be on the way, I raced to my car at the other end of the parking lot.

"Wait, Crystal!" Mr. Ferguson called after me.

But I couldn't stick around. I launched myself into my car and peeled from the lot. Oh, God. Where should I go first? Akira had mentioned that Randall was back at the hospital.

And I had to get to him before An0nym0us1 did.

5 Years Ago

The police didn't question us for long.

We told them we'd fallen asleep watching Frozen. Brady wanted to sleep in his own bed. We weren't sure what time he left—maybe around 1:00 a.m. I thought at some point the truth would slip out in a frenzy of tears, but we were all too afraid to say anything else. Even Zoey stayed on script, though I thought the way she clamped her lips like she was sucking in a secret was a dead giveaway. Apparently not.

Zoey's parents and grandmother had slept through the night. They hadn't heard us slip out and back in. And the police had no reason to suspect us.

As our parents came over, they hugged us fiercely, as though some creature had descended from the sky and snatched Brady from the space between his and Zoey's houses, sparing the rest of us. Mom and Dad nearly suffocated me in their embrace, and Caelyn clung to me, even when the other siblings her age sprawled on the living room carpet to play with Zoey's LEGO set. Andrew sat *in the corner, looking so helpless and pitiful as he zoned out at the kids playing, eyes red-rimmed like he'd been holding back tears all morning.*

"D'you have security cameras?" *I heard Chief Sanchez ask in the kitchen, where the parents were gathered. I knew him from school—he ran the DARE program, told us how drugs would turn our brains to mush.*

"Yeah," *said Mrs. Bloom. I gave Zoey a wide-eyed look over Caelyn's head. She sat between us, grasping my arm.*

Only at the front door, *Zoey mouthed.* We'd snuck out the side one.

"We don't," *Dad chimed in.* "We thought about it, but the crime rate's so low and we've never gotten our packages stolen, I figured it'd be a sunk cost." *The other parents murmured similar excuses.*

"We'll check the neighborhood," *said Sanchez,* "see if there's any footage to look at." *My stomach sank. Was there a recording out there of us running around someone's backyard? It never occurred to me the houses might be* watching.

Zoey beckoned the four of us out into the foyer. I managed to disentangle myself from Caelyn's grip, promising to be back soon, and slinked past Andrew to the front door, where my friends huddled.

"We have to say something," *Zoey whispered.*

"But we'll get in so much trouble," *I said, looking to Akira for backup, but she remained quiet.*

"We'll get in even* more *trouble if we got caught on camera," said Zoey. "They'll know we were lying this whole time."*

"But maybe we didn't," *I said.*

"It's too late anyway, though, right?" said Matty. "Even if we say something now, they'll know we've *been lying.*"

"Right." Randall nodded. "I say we wait and see. What difference will a few hours make?"

From our strained expressions, you could tell we were all thinking it.

It'd make a difference to Brady.

CHAPTER 31

Halfway to the hospital, Akira's phone jangled in the passenger seat. My heart twisted at the peaceful ringtone—the theme from Minecraft, her favorite video game. I groped for it without slowing and dared a quick glance at the screen.

FaceTime call from Randall.

I cut the wheel and pulled onto the shoulder of the one-lane highway. The car behind me blared its horn and swerved, and the driver, some hulking dude with a buzz cut, gave me the finger.

"Get over yourself!" I yelled before answering the call. I half expected to see Randall facedown in a ditch or something as a shadowy figure gloated nearby, but instead, Randall's perfectly alive face filled the screen. "Oh, thank God," I said. "Are you okay?"

"Crystal?" Randall scrunched his brow, confused. Even on video, I could see his eyes were bloodshot and bleary. I bet he hadn't slept a wink. "Where's Akira?" Of course he was calling—he was probably wondering why she hadn't come to the hospital yet.

"She . . . uh . . ." The words stuck in my throat. Was she alive or dead? And what if he didn't believe Akira's fall was an accident? Zoey had been quick to blame me for the brownies yesterday. Would Randall do the math here and come up with the wrong solution? "She forgot her phone in my car," I said, skirting around the question. "You still at the hospital? How's your dad?"

"He's okay." He still looked confused. "We went home to crash for a few hours, but my mom dragged us back here around six. Dad's out of the ICU, sleeping now." Randall suddenly held his phone so close I could see the pores on his nose. "Geez, it looks like a bomb went off in your face."

I shot back, "You're one to talk," as another voice chimed in, "How rude!"

Wait, I knew that voice . . .

Randall got smaller as he lowered the phone. "She knows I'm kidding." But he mock-pouted at me and shook his head, like, *not kidding.*

Another face edged on-screen, trying to get a better look at me. My heart went cold.

"*Lucia?*"

No. Panic clawed at my throat. She was An0nym0us1. She was desperate to keep us from spilling the truth about her and destroying her future. She'd beaten me to the hospital. She'd gotten to Randall first. I was too late. *No, no, no.*

"Hi, Crystal." She gave a little wave, wiggling her fingers. Gloating.

"Get away from him." My heart beat wildly as Lucia's smile slid off her face. How could she have stabbed my sister? How could she leave her alone and bleeding? *How?*

"Whoa, chill." Randall centered himself on the screen. "She texted last night, and I told her about my dad." A blur of yellow, pink, and green filled the screen. "So she brought flowers for my mom. See?" Lucia must've sent sympathy texts to all of us. Fake sympathy. Randall was so freaking gullible.

"I'm so, so sorry about Matty," said Lucia. Randall tilted the camera toward her, and I searched for traces of blood, but she was wearing all black. Besides, she would've changed out of anything incriminating before heading to the hospital. "I'm sorry about *everything.* I can't even imagine what you guys are going through." Just like her text last night, those weren't the words of a psychopath. But An0nym0us1 was clever. They'd know how to throw us off.

I took a shaky breath and plastered on a smile as fake as hers. "Randall?" I said through gritted teeth. "Can I talk to you alone for a sec?"

Lucia frowned, but leaned back in her seat, out of view. "What's up?" said Randall.

"*Alone,* Randall."

"Alright, alright." To Lucia, he said, "Be right back." The screen went all jagged and pixelated, and then he reappeared in front of a white-and-green-tiled backdrop. "Why've you been ignoring my texts, anyway?"

"Oh . . . uh . . . I didn't see them."

He gave an annoyed huff. "Well, listen . . . we're gonna take a break from the hospital and pick up some food for Matty's moms and, you know, visit with them for a bit—"

"No!" I shouted. Lucia was trying to lure him from the hospital. How could he be so oblivious? I had to stop this. "Don't you dare leave that hospital with her."

"Dude, you need to chillax. Paying our respects isn't exactly anyone's idea of a hot date."

I almost laughed. If only my concern were Lucia encroaching on Akira's turf. "That's not—"

"And I was literally just calling to ask Akira to meet us there. Where *is* she, anyway?"

I ignored his question. "Why are you even talking to Lucia? How can you trust her, after everything she did?"

"She apologized for that. Just now."

My breath caught. "She admitted to trolling us?" When Zoey confronted her, she'd denied everything.

"Yeah. And to lying to you and Zoey. She really wants to apologize to Akira—she knows that matters most. And she feels terrible she never got to apologize to Matty. She wants to make up for it. She even offered to take Matty's place at the tourney tomorrow, so we could all play."

My heart dropped. So this *was* about MortalDusk. She must've leveled up her skills and wanted in on a tourney team. "Oh, *big* sacrifice. Come *on,* Randall, that's fishy as fuck! How do you not see that?"

"It's not. She thought we still needed six players."

Oh, God. He had no idea we were down to four. There was room for one more. "Randall, you need to get with the program, right now." My voice shook, frantic. "Someone is after us. Someone *swatted* you. And I think she did it. You *cannot* trust her. You can't leave that hospital with her. You need to stay in a public place. *Please.*"

Randall clenched his jaw, for once in his life looking genuinely angry. It took me aback. "Crystal, stop it. Stop always assuming the worst in everyone. You're so . . . so . . . *paranoid.*"

My heart jolted. There was that word again. *Paranoid.* He'd spat it like he'd tried to find another, but nothing else fit. Zoey had told Dylan I was paranoid, feeding him lies to make him think he couldn't trust me. Had she implanted the idea in our other friends' minds, too?

"Lucia's being nice," Randall went on. "She went out of her way to come here and be *nice.*"

"Why, though?"

"Maybe because she's a *nice person.* Maybe she made a mistake once, and that's not really who she is. Just because we're awful doesn't mean everyone else is."

A rock lodged in my throat. I knew he meant what we'd done to Brady. And I wondered, then, if maybe I *was* a bit paranoid—quick to suspect people, to assume the worst of people—because I didn't even trust myself.

I was the biggest liar I knew.

"Trust me," he went on, "it wasn't Lucia. We had this whole long talk just now. She didn't, like . . . *like* me or anything. I know that's what you girls thought. She started watching our YouTube over the summer and thought I was funny. She liked my vids the most. That's it." Randall's livestreams did get the most views on our channels, followed closely by Matty's, much to Zoey's chagrin—but it was no big surprise, since they were the funniest. I remembered how Lucia ogled Randall at try-outs. Starstruck, not crushing. He was her Fishman. I'd just assumed she liked him and would try to steamroll Akira. "But we humiliated her at tryouts, so she wanted to throw back some shade. One comment turned into two, and . . . well, she got carried away—"

"Wait a minute," I cut him off. "How long have you two been talking? How long has she been there?"

"I dunno, about an hour, I guess?"

My breath caught. "Are you *sure*?"

"Yeah. Maybe a little longer, actually. Why?"

"And has she been on her phone a lot?"

He tilted his head. "Uh . . . I don't think so? No, not at all, actually."

If Lucia had been at the hospital talking to Randall for over an hour, there was no way she could have sent me those messages or gotten the timing right. There was no way she could've stabbed Caelyn while I was at Hermit Thrush's Nest. There was no way she was An0nym0us1. It was physically impossible.

But that left only one suspect.

"Uh . . . have you heard from Zoey at all?" I asked.

"Nah," said Randall, "she hasn't answered my texts either . . ."

Well, damn. A sour taste filled my mouth, and I checked the time on my dashboard. Almost noon. If I weren't in this har-rowing predicament, I would've checked in with Randall first thing to make sure his dad was okay. But Zoey had been MIA all morning, like most of yesterday. She'd be on her own today; her parents worked at their dental practice Tuesday through

Saturday. And there was that creepy room in her soundproofed basement . . .

My God. I hadn't thought Zoey was capable of something like this. But she'd already proven herself to be a liar and a cheat, a backstabber and blackmailer. Once was a mistake. Twice was bad judgment. Three times was depravity. And that wasn't paranoia talking—it was real, proven behavior. Sometimes people took extreme measures to escape from abusive situations. I knew that only too well. Her desperation to escape from her domineering, perfection-seeking parents and win that prize money had turned her into a kidnapper and a murderer. To top it off, she was trying to make everyone distrust me, setting the stage for her game so she could frame me, and nobody would believe my side of the story.

But why *torture* me like this? Did she really hate me that much?

Our competitive streak *had* become toxic. She'd been jealous of my and Akira's bond for ages, and now she had something else to be jealous over: Dylan choosing me. And she clearly blamed me for what happened to Brady all those years ago, resented me for the guilt that tormented her, a fact that bubbled over when I foiled her plans to cheat her way into the tourney.

Now I needed to foil her plans once more.

I snapped Akira's phone into my dashboard holster and swerved back onto the highway, toward home. "You're right, Randall. It's not Lucia."

"No shit, Sherlock." I couldn't watch his expression change with my eyes on the road, but his tone softened.

"Actually, can I talk to her for a sec?"

He eyed me skeptically. "Why?"

"I need to tell her something."

"Tell her in person. Come with us to Matty's—"

"*Please,* Randall? It'll just take a sec."

The screen went all garbled again, and he passed me off to Lucia. "She knows," I heard him say. "I told her what you said. She wants to talk to you."

A moment later, her face filled the screen. "Crystal. I am *so* sorry. I'm an asshat of epic proportions. It's just . . . what you said at tryouts really hurt my feelings, and I was angry, and I got carried away. And I didn't realize how bad that last comment sounded until after I posted it—I didn't mean it like that—but by the time I went back to delete it, it was already gone. And I know how it looked. I know it doesn't matter whether I meant it or not. I totally fucked up—"

"Lucia, stop," I tried, but she was talking so fast, I could barely get a word in.

"—and I was so mortified. I know I should've owned it right away. Oh, and also, I really wasn't making fun of your sweater at my party. I really did like it! And yesterday, I came to check on you in the bathroom—"

"*Lucia!*"

"Sorry."

I exhaled deeply. "I'm sorry, too. For everything. I've been an asshat right back." Everyone makes mistakes. I of all people should've known that. She'd made a pretty bad one, and like Randall said, she owed Akira the biggest apology. Knowing she might never get to sucked the air right out of my chest. Zoey and I had handled the situation poorly—if Lucia hadn't felt threatened, this conversation might've happened ages ago. Either way, she'd clearly learned from her mistake, admitted to it, and was trying to make amends. But now I needed her help to make sure An0nym0us1 couldn't hurt Randall. That *I* couldn't hurt him. "But Akira and Randall never did anything to hurt you," I said. "That terrible thing you said . . . whatever your intent, they didn't deserve that. *She* didn't deserve that."

"I know. You're absolutely right." I wasn't watching her expression while driving, but her voice shook, and I imagined her eyes welling with tears.

"Well, I need you to do something to make it up to them." I'd already lost Matty, and possibly Akira. I couldn't lose Randall, too.

"Anything."

"Can you stay with Randall today? Keep him company?" I didn't know if making sure Randall wasn't alone was enough to protect him from An0nym0us1's wrath. I wasn't even sure whether this would put Lucia in danger. But it was the best thing I could think of. The *only* thing.

She paused for a moment, taken aback by my request. "I will," she said earnestly.

"Thanks." Unprompted, an image of Akira tumbling backward, eyes wide, flashed into my mind. I screwed up my face and covered my mouth.

"Are *you* okay?" Lucia asked.

Tears blurred my vision. I couldn't let them blind me while driving. "I gotta go—"

"Crystal, I'm so sorry."

"I'm sorry, too," I managed to whisper before hanging up. I had so many things to be sorry for.

But I couldn't let my sister's death be one of them.

CHAPTER 32

The thing about toxic friendships is eventually, they'll poison you.

Zoey's, it seemed, was the torturous kind of poison that shuts down your nervous system, so you die in extreme agony. Now I had to cut off a limb to stop it from spreading.

I pounded on her front door so hard I thought my fist might bruise. "Zoey! Open the door! I know you're home." As I kept going over it in my mind on the drive, it made sense why the games paused last night—Zoey had to wait until her parents were asleep to keep playing. And once they'd left for work this morning, the games resumed.

Finally, I heard shuffling, and a moment later, Zoey cracked the door open a sliver. Her hair was disheveled and matted at the roots, like maybe she hadn't washed it in a while. The long black sweater she wore over burgundy leggings matched AnOn-ym0us1's black sleeves in those photos pressing a knife to Cae-lyn's throat. I probably should've grabbed something to defend myself with before storming over, but with one hand on the doorknob and another gripping the doorframe, she seemed unarmed. "Chill." Her voice cracked as she peered at me. "I was in the bathroom—"

"Bullshit." I shoved the door open wider and barreled in, on a warpath to the basement stairs next to the kitchen.

She gasped and retreated against the wall, cowering. I stilled, thrown by her reaction, unsure what unnerved me more—that I thought she'd hurt me, or that she seemed to think I'd hurt *her.* I shook off the thought and dashed past her, hurtling downstairs.

"Hey!" she cried, following.

The den was different from the last time I was down here—we'd avoided gathering here ever since what happened to Brady. The pool table had been reupholstered with red felt instead of green, and Zoey's violin and music stand had moved to the other side of a larger flat-screen than the one on which we'd watched *Frozen.* But that creepy, wood-paneled door in the back corner was the same.

I threw it open and flicked the light switch, my heart pumping so fast I thought it might burst.

The room was empty.

Well, there was *stuff* in here. A refrigerator, humming gently. An ancient-looking oak rocking chair shoved in the corner. Shelves stocked with tools and gardening supplies, paper goods, boxes and cans of food. Rows of plastic bins labeled things like BABY CLOTHES, SCARVES/GLOVES/HATS, ZOEY'S TOYS, GAMES/PUZZLES.

It was a perfectly normal storage room, sans hostage.

"What are you *doing*?" Zoey cried.

I let out a frustrated cry and pushed past her into the den. A fresh wave of pain rippled up my left arm, and I clutched it, grimacing. I couldn't let pain distract me. Mind over matter. Maybe Zoey was keeping Caelyn somewhere else. That had to be it. Otherwise, Zoey's parents might've discovered Caelyn struggling down here when getting some toilet paper or something.

Zoey spotted my raw, red palm, streaked with dried blood. "What happened to—"

"Where are you keeping her?"

Her mouth went agape for a moment. "Who?"

I clenched my fists to stop myself from trembling. "Don't play dumb. Where *is* she?"

"I have no clue what you're talking about." She rubbed her eyes. "I literally just woke up." I scoffed. A likely excuse. "What? It's true! I couldn't fall asleep until like three in the morning. Every time I finally started to drift off, I heard *your* window slam shut." She *had* been watching me. I knew it. "What the hell were you doing, anyway?"

"Oh, you know exactly what I was doing. You made me do it."

"Um, no, I did *not* make you let Dylan sneak into your room," she said bitterly. Dylan was yet another competition she'd lost. I wished he were here—I'd considered texting him from my laptop first, but couldn't wait. I had to get to Caelyn. Where *was* she?

"That's not what I mean, and you know it," I said. "I'm talking about the games. About breaking into Kiki's to start her mom's car." Zoey looked at me like my face had morphed into an eggplant. Doubt prickled my mind, but I shook it away. "And what you had me do to Matty, and to Randall's dad—"

"Whoa, *what*?" Her eyes widened, realization dawning on her. "I *knew* it. You *did* poison those brownies on purpose. And *you're* the one who swatted Randall!"

"No! You made me! You made me do all of it!"

She flailed her arms. "I didn't make you do anything!"

"Yes, you did. You sent me all those instructions, and now you're trying to frame me—"

"Holy shit, you're out of your mind."

"Yeah, that's what you want everyone to think. That I'm paranoid, right? Mentally unwell—that's what you told Dylan, right?"

"No—"

"*Liar*. You're a liar, and a cheat, and—"

"Oh my God. Why would you even think I'd want to kill Matty? Over what, *MortalDusk*?" I opened my mouth to retort, then paused. *Matty*. Just Matty. Like she didn't even know about Akira.

"Not just MortalDusk . . ." I started breathing faster, losing my nerve. "The prize money. You said it yourself . . . You want that money to get out of this hellhole, to get out of going to dental school."

"Well, yeah, but I wouldn't *kill* anyone over it. I mean, come on, I can code like a beast. I bet I could get a dozen offers from tech start-ups without ever setting foot on a college campus."

Panic permeated my veins. If Zoey wasn't An0nym0us1 . . . they were still out there. It could be *anyone*. No. *No*. It had to be Zoey. I had no way to get in touch with An0nym0us1. No way to reach my sister. No way to get more clues. This was the last thread. If it unspooled, I'd have nothing.

"But you said you needed that money," I said, clinging to my logic. "You *said* that's why you cheated."

She cringed, hesitating. "I . . . Yeah, the money would help, but . . ." Her lower lip trembled. "I thought you'd throw me off the team if you knew the real reason."

"What *was* the real reason?"

"Oh, please," Zoey spat. "Like you even actually care. You didn't care then, and you don't care now. You'll just twist it around for whatever fucked-up narrative you're trying to spin here. All you care about is your spot at the tourney. Playing games is all that's *ever* mattered to you." My stomach tied in knots. Her words echoed Caelyn's accusation yesterday morning. *All you can think about is your stupid video game . . . Do you even care about anything in the real world?* What if they were both right? She went on, "This isn't the first time you hurt someone over a game. My God, Crystal, what have you done—"

"That is *not* fair. What happened to Brady was an accident."

"But it never would've happened if you didn't make us play that stupid game."

"It never would've happened if *you* didn't make such a stink about being Brady's partner in that board game."

"You always got to be partners with Kiki. *That* wasn't fair."

Regret stabbed my heart at that. Akira and I had always clicked like two L-block Tetris pieces, while Zoey was more like a Z-block; she took some finagling to fit. And once we got older, it was easier for Akira and me to confide in each other about the tough stuff—her with her eating disorder, me with my panic attacks. There was no shame between us. Afraid to burden Zoey—afraid she wouldn't understand—we'd left her out of those conversations. Still, I skirted around her comment. "Dammit, we could throw accusations back and forth forever. It was both of our faults, and it was neither of our faults. It was an accident. A terrible accident."

"Then why couldn't we just tell the truth? Why'd you make us *lie*?"

"I didn't make anyone do anything. We were all scared we'd get in trouble—you especially! I was trying to protect *you*." I wiped a hand down my face. "If you wanted to tell the truth so badly, why didn't you?"

Her expression twisted, pained. "You all insisted we keep it a secret. And I thought . . . if I told . . . or if I pushed you to tell . . . that you . . . you . . ." She crossed her arms, her chin quivering.

"That I'd *what*?"

"That you'd all turn against me!" she cried. A tear streaked down her cheek, and she flicked it away like she was mad she'd let it slip. "I thought I'd wind up all alone . . . just like him."

Oh my God. Suddenly, it all made sense. Everything Zoey had done was out of fear of being ostracized. She'd already been sensitive to how Akira and I were extra close, but something in her must've broken after what happened to Brady. That was the real reason she'd cheated. For years, the five of us clung together, almost like we'd built a wall around ourselves to shield us from our guilt—and to hold our secret captive. The tourney was the first time we'd need to intentionally exclude one of us. And she was afraid she would be the one left out. It had nothing to do with the prize money. And then she was so scared to be booted from our team, she blackmailed me. All because she was terrified to be abandoned, just like *him*. She was dealing with some serious PTSD, and I'd had no idea.

But that meant she'd never kill us off. Nothing would make her more alone.

So who the hell was making me play this terrible game?

"Game? What game?" Zoey asked, making me realize I'd asked the question aloud. "God, why does everything have to be a *game* with you?"

"No, you don't understand. If it's not you . . ." Who could it be? I clutched my throat—I couldn't breathe in this stuffy basement. I couldn't *think*. I had to go. I had to keep searching. Maybe Lance Burdly was a legitimate clue after all—one last dangling thread. I started for the stairs, but Zoey grabbed my bad wrist and tugged me back, making me cry out in pain.

"No!" she said. "You're not going anywhere until you tell me what the hell happened to Kiki. What did you mean about her mom's car?"

I shook my head. "That's not what killed her—" Cringing, I clapped a hand over my lips. Akira couldn't be dead. She *couldn't* be.

Zoey gasped. "What the fuck?"

"No, you don't understand . . ." Oh, God. I didn't have time for this. "We were at the lookout point on Mount Morgan this morning, and, well, at one point, we were wrestling over my phone, and she fell." Zoey's eyes were amber saucers, her mouth agape. "I . . . I don't know, maybe she survived the fall. But it was an accident, I swear it."

Her expression hardened. "Oh, sure. And you just *happened*

to grab the wrong bottle of extract. And oops, you slipped and called in a fake tip to the police—"

"No!" Panic rose in my throat. "Listen . . . someone *made* me do all those things."

"How?"

I considered her, biting my inner cheek. After everything, could I trust her? Maybe she never should've left my bubble of trust to begin with. I'd been a terrible friend, but if I was ever going to make it up to her, I needed her to survive this. I needed to keep An0nym0us1 from getting to her. Maybe she could even help me figure this out.

I took a deep breath. "Alright, listen . . . someone kidnapped Caelyn yesterday. They've been—"

"*What?*"

"Let me explain, okay?"

"Isn't she supposed to be in Frost Valley?"

"Yeah, but they took her before she could get on the bus."

"Aren't *you* the one who dropped her off?" This was the exact opposite of letting me explain.

"Yes, but . . ." I raked back my curls, frustrated. "Just *listen.* Her kidnapper's been sending me anonymous messages through some app they hacked onto my phone, and they've been threatening to kill her if I don't do whatever they tell me to. They've turned it into some sick, twisted game."

Zoey extended her hand. "Lemme see your phone."

I swallowed hard. "I . . . I don't have it. It went over the cliff with Kiki."

"My God." She rubbed her eyes, thinking for a moment. Then she headed for the stairs.

"Where are you going?"

"To call the police." She must've left her cell upstairs.

A boulder lodged in my throat. An0nym0us1 was surely monitoring the local police scanner. If Zoey called the police, she'd get Caelyn killed. I scrambled to block her path. "No, you can't. When this . . . *game* . . . first started, the kidnapper told me I couldn't call the police, or tell anyone what was happening, or they'd kill Caelyn."

"Well, *I* could call the police."

"But you knowing about this means I told you. That'd be significant rule breakage."

"Screw that." She tried skirting around me.

"*No!*" I screamed. Zoey sprang back, stumbling into the couch and throwing her hands up defensively. Like she was *scared* of me. My heart sank. "Zoey, I'm not going to hurt you."

Her eyes were wide with fright. "You just told me you killed our friends. You pushed Kiki off a *cliff*."

"I didn't. I told you, it was an accident. She *fell*."

"Prove it."

I felt the blood drain from my face. "You . . . you think I made all of that up? But why?" She shook her head, like she was afraid to explain. "*Why?*"

She flinched. "You're the one who's been desperate to play in the tourney. To save your house or whatever. And you've always been so desperate to keep the secret about Brady. The way you snapped at the hospital . . . I had a feeling, right then." Holy hell. As much as I'd suspected her, she'd suspected me right back. "It's my fault," she went on. "I shouldn't have brought it up again. I shouldn't have threatened to go public. It made you snap, didn't it? You'd do anything to protect that secret. Even if it means killing the rest of us."

"That doesn't even make sense!" I cried. "Killing more people would just, like, exponentially compound my secret."

"*Well, then, why are you doing this?*"

"I'm not!"

But she clearly didn't believe me. Suddenly, she sprinted past me and yanked the coat stand so it toppled with a crash and blocked my path as she raced upstairs.

"Wait! Zoey, please!" I screamed, leaping over the heap of jackets and sweaters, but she was fast—by the time I reached the kitchen, she'd already dialed and held her cell to her ear. "No, don't!"

I lunged and grabbed her wrist, managing to yank her hand down enough to hit the End Call icon. She twisted from my grasp with a strangled cry and ran around the kitchen island, navigating to the dial pad again. Blood roared in my ears. I couldn't let her do this. Calling the police was a death sentence for Caelyn. Matty's death—and possibly Akira's death—would be for nothing. The thought threatened to make my knees buckle, but sheer panic and desperation kept me upright.

"Stop!" Before I could think twice, I spotted the butcher block on the kitchen counter and grabbed a knife, tugged it free, and raised it over my head. "Don't move!"

CHAPTER 33

I didn't want to kill Zoey.

Dread churned in my belly as I inched toward her. She looked horrified, staring open-mouthed at the knife in my grip. Backed into the corner next to the fridge, there was nothing within reach she could use to fight back.

Now was my chance to grab her phone.

My fingertips tingled as I edged closer, determination flooding my veins. How should I do it? I could try swatting the phone from her clenched fist, or wrestling it away, but she might not let go. She'd already dialed 911—all she had to do was tap the call icon. The thought of piercing her skin was unbearable. But you never know the lengths you'll be willing to go to, to protect the people you love—even if it means sacrificing your own humanity.

Was I sacrificing mine? Was I really willing to plunge a blade into another human being if it meant keeping my sister alive?

I hadn't shoved Akira off that cliff. I never meant for her to fall. I hadn't given up my humanity then. And I wouldn't now. I could never stab Zoey.

But she didn't need to know that.

"Just give me the phone, okay?" I extended one hand toward her, raising the knife higher.

Her eyes widened, and her thumb moved over the screen.

"Don't!" I lunged, feigning a strike, and she shrieked and dropped the phone. It clattered on the tile floor.

Zoey crouched and covered her head with shaking hands. "No!" She must've really thought I'd do it.

"Jesus," I muttered, picking up the phone. She hadn't placed the call. I powered off the phone and slipped it into my back pocket, under my coat.

"Please. *Please* don't kill me." Zoey's voice was strained. "I won't tell anyone what you did. I promise. I *promise.*"

I gaped as she knelt there, trembling and helpless, cheeks streaked with tears. "You really don't believe me. You really think I killed our friends on purpose."

"You're literally waving a knife at me!" Zoey cried. "And I don't see anyone with a gun to your head."

Fair point. Before, when An0nym0us1 had eyes on me, I had to follow their instructions within their time limits. But now I was calling the shots. My stomach twisted. "I had to stop you from calling the police . . ."

This was exactly what An0nym0us1 wanted, wasn't it? To turn me into a monster. To frame me for killing my friends. But Caelyn was out there somewhere, and she knew the truth. She'd tell the police how someone was holding her hostage. She'd clear my name.

"Do you know anyone called Lance Burdly?" I asked.

Zoey screwed up her face. "No—"

"Think harder!" I shouted. "You've *never* heard that name before?"

She flinched, then she hesitated. "Why *does* that name sound familiar?"

I let out a frustrated huff. "Sanchez mentioned him at the hospital. When Caelyn's kidnapper made me call in the fake tip, they sent me a script, and I had to use a voice changer and pretend to be some dude named Lance Burdly." Zoey looked skeptical, but I went on, "I couldn't find anything about him online. I thought, I dunno, maybe his name was a clue or something."

"Can't the police look it up in their database or whatever?"

"I *told* you, I can't call the police." Zoey didn't get it—the constant fear of keeping this secret, *or else.*

Or maybe she did. Maybe this was akin to keeping our secret about Brady, tortured by it all these years. Gah, I couldn't think about that now—

Taking advantage of my momentary distraction, Zoey scrambled to her feet and dashed around the corner into the dining room. "Stop!" I chased her into the foyer, and as she started opening the front door, I hurled into it, slamming it shut, making pain flame in my wrist. I was blocking her path to the main staircase, so she dodged past me and down the basement stairs, pulling the door closed behind her.

"Zoey!" I banged on the door. There were no exits down there, but was there a landline? "Don't call the police!" But I didn't have time to beg. It would take seconds for her to reach a phone and call the cops. Even if I made her hang up before she could explain, they'd hear the distress in her voice and easily locate us. An0nym0us1 would hear the dispatcher send a cop over on the police scanner.

Zoey was going to kill my sister.

Knowing my luck, trying to kick down the door would break my ankle instead. Desperate, I twisted the knob—oh, and it opened. There was no lock. D'oh. Zoey yelped at the bottom of the stairs.

As I plunged downstairs, she raced toward the creepy storage room, and I wound back my arm as though poised to throw the knife at her, just like I would in MortalDusk. "Stop!"

She froze, eyes bugging as she took in my stance, and raised her hands. "Please! Don't!"

I scanned the walls for a phone, then nodded toward the storage closet. "Is there a phone in there?"

"N-no!"

"Oh." She came down here to hide from me. That's all. I lowered the knife and let out a shaky sigh. "I . . . I know this looks bad—"

"It looks horrific!" she screamed.

I winced. "Well, I don't know how to convince you I'm telling the truth!" I needed to find An0nym0us1, or at least some way to reach them, without Zoey calling the cops. What the hell should I do about her? She'd call them as soon as I left. I couldn't bring her with me; she'd bolt down the street and cry for help the moment we stepped outside. And the basement door had no lock.

An image of Caelyn tied and bound flashed through my mind. I had to save her. I had to do whatever it took.

I swung open the creepy door. "Get in."

"*What?*"

I brandished the knife at her. "*Get in.*"

She scrambled into the storage room, and I pointed to the old rocking chair. "Sit." She sat gingerly, without taking her eyes from the knife. The door didn't have a lock. I'd have to tie her up somehow. But with what? I scanned the shelves lined with tools and boxes of household and gardening supplies. Was there rope anywhere?

Then I spotted the plastic bin labeled SCARVES/GLOVES/HATS. I tugged it from the shelf, chucked the lid aside, and dug through the fabrics for scarves. "What're you doing?" Zoey asked, but I ignored her. I couldn't believe I was doing this. But she'd left me no choice. No choice.

Once I had four scarves, I knelt beside her.

She shifted forward. "No way—"

Out of patience, I raised the knife again, and she whined as she sat back. "Sit still." I'd wasted so much time here already.

Should I tie her wrists together, or each one separately to the armrests? I couldn't exactly google "how to tie someone to a chair" right now. And should I secure her ankles or hands first? If I bound her hands first, she could kick me. If I bound her ankles first, she could grab my hair or punch me. How did kidnappers *do* this?

She was already clutching the armrests so hard the tendons on her hands bulged, so I started there, keeping my grip on the knife. I stretched a scarf over her wrist and looped it around the armrest several times, ignoring the pain in my own wrist and trying not to nick Zoey with the knife. As I tied a knot beneath the armrest so she couldn't lean forward and gnaw at it or anything, she grunted and tugged at the fabric with her free hand. "You're cutting off my circulation." Frustrated, I swatted her away, accidentally swiping her arm with the knife. Both of us gasped. "Ow!"

A thin red line appeared on her wrist; I'd broken the skin, but barely. My heart plunged. "Dammit, stay still, or you'll make me cut off more than your circulation."

Zoey blanched, and a new sort of fear filled her eyes.

"Oh my God, I . . . I didn't mean it like a threat, I only meant . . ." I stuttered, choking back a sob. "Just . . . hold still. Please."

She started crying as I looped a scarf around her other wrist, covering the tiny red droplets oozing from the cut, trying to ignore what I'd done. I hadn't meant to do it. I never wanted to hurt her.

But that didn't really matter now, did it?

I repeated the process with her ankles, binding them to the frame of the rocking chair. As I stepped back to examine my handiwork, Zoey glared at me. "How could you do this?"

"To save my sister's life," I said, digging a fifth scarf from the bin. "I'm telling the truth, whether you believe me or not." I didn't want to gag her, but what if AnOnymOus1 came hunting for her and opened the basement door? This was for her own good. "Listen . . . it's safer for you here than anywhere else. If this psycho tries sending me after you, I'll say I don't know where you are. But if you hear someone come in . . . well, you won't want them to find you."

She visibly swallowed. "But . . . what if I have to pee?"

I cringed. I hadn't thought of that. "You'll have to hold it, I guess." I raised the scarf to her face.

"No, wait!" she cried. "I won't scream, I swear."

"You're literally screaming right now." Instead of trying to get the scarf between her teeth—that seemed too uncomfortable—I looped the scarf over her mouth and tied it behind her head, careful to leave her nostrils exposed. She let out one last muffled cry before I picked up the knife and backed away, giving her a forlorn look.

I wished I could trust her. I wished *she* trusted *me*. But she thought I was capable of killing our friends. Heck, at this point, I didn't blame her. "I hope you'll forgive me for this. I swear I'm telling the truth. I swear you're safest this way."

Then I left and shut the door, leaving her bound and helpless.

Somehow this felt worse than all the rest of it.

CHAPTER 34

Back in my room, you'd think everything was fine.

My fluffy purple quilt beckoned, offering comforting solace. Whiskers curled up on my pillow, slow-blinking at me, wanting pets. Video game posters lined the walls—Zelda, Skyrim, Assassin's Creed, and of course, MortalDusk—promising memories of adventure. Friendly faces grinned at me from photos pinned to the corkboard above my desk—our family selfie at the lake, my friends at ten years old from the time Matty brought a retro Polaroid camera to school. The cosplay costume Caelyn made for me to wear at the tourney hung on my closet door.

Here, I could almost believe the world outside wasn't burning to the ground. That I'd somehow reloaded an earlier save.

But Zoey's kitchen knife in my grip was a stark reminder that I hadn't. My throbbing headache, torn-up palm, and pulsating wrist were all more proof that the past twenty-four hours had happened.

I set the knife next to my laptop and booted it up. If An0n-ym0us1 had hacked it, too, here I was. Exposed. Vulnerable. But that was the point—I needed to reach them. If they weren't monitoring my webcam, I could send an email to myself so they'd see—

The red dot over my messenger app caught my eye, and I re-flexively clicked on it. Our group text chain was at the top, the most recent message from Randall.

CRYSTAL WHY DID YOU STALK FISHMAN???

The floor seemed to drop out from under my chair. I quickly scanned the other messages I'd missed this morning.

Randall: Back in the hospital. Dad's out of ICU in a recovery room.
Akira: YAYAYAY ILUUUUU

I let out a soft sob. Was this the last text she ever sent?

If I let my thoughts linger there, I'd fall apart. But I felt my anguish swelling like a tidal wave cresting near the coast. *Akira. Matty.* At some point, that wave of grief was going to crash over me. But I couldn't let myself drown. Not when Caelyn was still in danger. I had to shut down that part of my mind—at least, for now.

Taking a deep breath, I focused on the text chain again.

Dylan: That's a relief! I'll swing by in a bit. Gotta head to the train
    station first.
Randall: Thanks dude.

Randall: You all okay?

Dylan: Yup. Sorry, train's delayed. Be there soon.

Randall: No it's cool.

Randall: Where's everyone else?

That was when Randall FaceTimed Akira, and I picked up.

Randall: Heading to Food Xpress with Lucia to pick up food and
flowers for Matty's moms. Anyone wanna join? Where ARE
you guys?

Dylan was probably still waiting for his dad at the train station or driving him home—I'd forgotten he had to do that this morning. Zoey was obviously preoccupied at the moment. And Akira—

I swallowed hard. Yeah.

Then a few minutes ago:

Randall: CRYSTAL WHY DID YOU STALK FISHMAN???

Three dots appeared next to Randall's name—he was typing right now.

HOW DID YOU NOT MENTION THIS BEFORE?

Then he sent a row of scream emojis.

My fingers shook as I navigated to Jeremy's Twitch channel—that asshat must've blabbed on his stream that I'd spied on him. This was bad. Really bad. He was livestreaming now, playing

MortalDusk. The chat pane whizzed by in a flurry of chatter. As I skimmed, my heart jolted—people were buzzing about some stalker. I scrolled up until I spotted a Reddit link, and a panicked nausea surged up my throat.

Atop the thread titled *FIND FISHMAN'S STALKER* was a ten-second video. I clicked Play. "Shit, you guys, someone's *spying* on me," Jeremy said, and the screen blurred as he swiveled his camera to face the window. It took a few moments for the lens to focus and adjust to the brightness, even though it was overcast outside. But for a split second after Jeremy yelled, "Hey!" you could see me dart from view.

Apparently, that split second was enough.

Jeremy never said who it was, but the Reddit thread blew up as people posted screenshots of the still frames and enhanced the images, trying to figure it out for themselves. Fuuuuuuuck. Had Randall recognized me in the shot, or had they found me out?

If they had, the whole world would think I was a complete maniac.

I glanced at Zoey's kitchen knife, thinking of how I'd tied her up. Maybe I *was* a complete maniac. I rubbed my forehead, trying to relieve the pressure in my temples, to scrub out the creeping doubt. I had zero evidence An0nym0us1 existed. Was I so desperate to win that prize money that I wanted to take my friends out of the running? Had I snapped after Zoey dredged up our past with Brady? Was she right about me?

No, no, no. This was exactly what An0nym0us1 wanted. They wanted me to doubt myself. They were real. Those videos of Caelyn were real. Those messages were real. If the cops swept

Hanover Lake, they'd find a nylon bag filled with gravel and the burner phone and voice changer someone had left in that locker for me—that I definitely hadn't purchased myself.

Prove it.

No, no, no. I knew myself better than that. And I didn't have blackouts. There weren't blank spots in my memory. Though, if I did, how would I know it?

I kept scrolling through the Reddit thread, hoping nobody would connect the dots. There were hundreds of messages over the past two hours. I scrolled to the bottom of the page, but that showed the lowest ranked, irrelevant comments. Impatient, I searched the thread for my name.

Oh.

Oh, God.

There was a message from An0nym0us1.

Hey that looks like Crystal Donovan. She's ShardsOfGlass. They'd pasted in a side-by-side comparison of one of my recent Instagram posts alongside one of the enhanced screenshots, linking to my now-public Instagram.

A mix of horror and vindication swelled in my chest, and I jabbed the screen. "You *are* real, you piece of shit!" They were real. They were *real*.

And they'd doxxed me. This sadist was out to ruin literally every aspect of my life. Below An0nym0us1's post, people unanimously agreed I was Jeremy's stalker. And they were pissed Jeremy wouldn't confirm it on his stream.

So it wasn't Jeremy's fault I'd been doxxed. He wasn't *completely* terrible.

But An0nym0us1 was.

They were vile, malicious, evil in every way.

I hovered over An0nym0us1's username on Reddit; they were offline. But now I technically had a way to contact them directly.

This seemed like a reckless move on their part. Couldn't the police get a warrant for the IP address from Reddit? Then they could trace wherever this message originated. Unless, of course, An0nym0us1 was using a VPN to spoof their IP address. Still, if I were them, I'd have used a different username to dox me. This was proof that they existed.

Unless . . . oh no. My lips went numb. Everything they did served a purpose, always one step ahead. Whether or not they wanted me to doubt my own sanity, they definitely wanted to frame me. Were they just doxxing me? Or were they making it look like I was planting evidence a blackmailer existed? My web browser now had this exact page in its search history—good luck proving I hadn't posted this message using a VPN.

Dammit.

But if everything they did served a purpose, the name Lance Burdly must've meant *something*. There were no false leads in An0nym0us1's playbook. No useless moves.

Desperate, I googled the name again, but it was still a dead end—not even a single result to dig through. Usually there were at least some incorrect results; other people who shared the name, or misspellings.

I glowered at the message underneath: *Including results for lance bradley.*

Maybe I had the spelling wrong. I'd only seen the script for a moment before reading it aloud—

Wait a minute. I leaned forward, gawking at Google's

suggestion "bradley." So close to Brady. I drew a sharp breath. No way. It couldn't be that simple.

Well, *was* it simple if it took me a whole day to figure out?

I frantically flipped to the page in my notebook where I'd scrawled his name.

LANCE BURDLY

I rearranged the letters, crossing out each one as I spelled a new name underneath.

BRADY CULLEN

That was no coincidence. That was a fucking anagram.

My chair seemed to disappear beneath me, and it felt like I was falling into an infinite abyss. I gripped the cushion to steady myself, to confirm it was still even there. Zoey was right. This *was* about Brady. Was I meant to unscramble this clue? Or had An0nym0us1's game glitched, and I finally spotted it?

Either way, now I knew. This wasn't about MortalDusk at all.

It was about revenge.

5 Years Ago

It seemed half the town had joined the search party in the woods by the late afternoon. Our little game had become a real-life, terrifying manhunt.

I begged Dad to let me search with him, to help find my friend. Warm, guilty tears slid down my cheeks, and he couldn't help but agree. He kept a firm grip on my hand the whole time, as though some unseen presence might whisk me away, just like it had Brady.

The police had already searched Zoey's and Brady's properties with a fine-tooth comb, but there was no indication of a kidnapping—no tire tracks, weird footprints, dropped belongings, or signs of a struggle. A couple of the houses on the other side of the woods had security cameras, but only facing the front doors to dissuade thieves from stealing packages, like Zoey's parents had. We hadn't gone close enough to the front doors to appear on the recordings.

Zoey's footage showed Brady leaving, me following soon after, *then both of us returning together. But nobody passed through the front door again until Brady's mom came over in the morning.*

The police assumed Brady went out the side door, and then . . .

Well, that was the mystery.

He'd simply vanished.

By now, we'd sunk so deep into our lie there was no clawing back out. Besides, as Randall reminded us, we were sweeping the woods anyway. There was no point fessing up now.

Rumors and theories rumbled through the search party—of kidnapping, of bears, of Brady running away. But I kept dragging Dad to all the possible hiding places we hadn't checked last night, and even some we had: shrubberies with enough space underneath, sheds, under gardening tables, underneath people's back decks. I even dragged him to the Nelsons' backyard—it had been out of bounds, but maybe Brady had been determined to outplay us.

I was the one who spotted it—the bright red fabric peeking out from a slim, metal storage unit leaning against the Nelsons' detached garage. Much of it was rusted orange, and the parts that weren't matched the forest-green trim of the Nelsons' house looming nearby under an awning of pine trees.

"It's his sweatshirt!" I cried. Matty's sweatshirt. The one Brady had borrowed. Relief washed over me. No wonder we hadn't been able to find him all the way over here.

Dad tried the rusted handle, but it was stuck. "Are you sure?"

"Yes!" I pounded on the metal door. "Brady? Brady, can you hear me?" I pressed an ear to it, but jerked back—the door was frigid. "Brady!"

Dad jiggled the handle so hard I thought the locker might pitch forward, but it stood firm against the garage. Then he tugged at the fabric. "This is making the door stick. Hey," he called to a nearby crowd at the edge of the woods. "Hey, over here!"

Chief Sanchez was in the crowd, and he dashed over. "What is it?"

Dad motioned to the fabric. "My daughter thinks that's his."

Sanchez gave the handle a fruitless jiggle. "Locked?"

"Or stuck, from the fabric," said Dad.

Sanchez radioed in, "Sanchez here, I need a crowbar at 65 Chester Street."

"Ten-four, Chief," a voice called back. "I got one, heading your way."

The elderly Nelson couple had noticed the kerfuffle and trudged the wide length of their backyard to reach us, clutching peacoats closed over matching plaid bathrobes. As Dad explained what was happening, I brainstormed how to convince Brady to go along with our lie—that we hadn't snuck out last night to play Manhunt. He could say he'd been sleepwalking! Yes, that was it. He sleepwalked out here to the Nelsons' yard, and somehow ended up in their storage locker.

Another police officer arrived a few minutes later, gripping a crowbar with Brady's family in tow. His mother's eyes were wild with worry, and his father and brother looked drawn and ashen. But they should be relieved! We'd found him! "He's not responsive?" asked the cop.

"Nope." Sanchez took the crowbar. "If it is Brady."

"It is!" I said. It had to be. Dad put his arm around me.

Sanchez gently knocked on the door. "Brady? Try to lean away from the door, son." A chill had settled over the group—one that had nothing to do with the cold breeze whipping through my curls.

Why wasn't Brady answering? Surely all the noise and commotion would have woken him.

Dad clutched me even tighter as Sanchez wedged the edge of the crowbar into the doorframe, putting all his weight into it. After a few moments of him grunting and straining, the door burst open, and Brady flopped out. Sanchez caught him before he hit the ground.

Wow, he must have been exhausted from being in there all night.

"Brady!" I cried, lunging toward him, wanting to be the first to talk to him, to keep him from telling the truth. That's when I saw Brady's face.

Dad yanked me back and buried my face in his chest.

But it was too late.

Brady's skin was purple, and his eyes were open, wide and glassy, staring blankly at the sky. I'd never seen a dead body before—not in real life, anyway. But I knew. And the anguished howl that tore from his mother confirmed it.

He was dead.

I shrieked into Dad's chest. This couldn't be real. This couldn't be happening. This was my fault. My fault, my fault, my fault. I was the one who'd dragged Brady away from his jigsaw puzzle. I was the one who'd wanted to play Manhunt. I'd given up looking for him. And I'd lied.

I peeked back at Brady's family. His mother had collapsed into her husband's arms, and Andrew knelt next to Brady, his face screwed up in denial. He reached out to touch Brady's hair, but Sanchez blocked him with his arm. He flinched back, covering his mouth instead and shaking his head, lost, helpless, like there was *no way this was happening. No way it was real. But it was. It was. For a moment, Andrew glanced up at me, and the tortured look on his face made a fresh wave of agony consume me.*

"It was just an accident," Dad said in a soothing voice. "A horrible accident."

But he didn't know. He didn't know. And I could never tell.

Dad hadn't carried me in years, but he picked me up then, carrying me away from the boy I'd killed.

CHAPTER 35

Sometimes when you bury a secret, it claws at your heart like bloodied fingernails scraping against a coffin lid as you suffocate under the weight of all that compacted dirt.

But now, after all this time, someone had dug up our secret—and they were trying to whack us with the shovel, one by one.

Who the hell could it be?

My first thought was Brady himself, like some bizarro soap opera twist. But that was impossible.

I'd seen his body.

I'd been to his funeral.

I'd watched his brother, Andrew, give a monotone eulogy, eyes like hollow pits of despair. I'd noticed his father glaring at mine, as though finding Brady in that locker was what killed him, à la Schrödinger's cat. I'd seen his mother lose it as his coffin lowered into the ground, her flaming hair masking the snot dribbling down her chin.

You can't fake that shit.

Plus, there'd been an autopsy and everything. The temperature that night had dropped low enough for Brady to succumb to hypothermia, but he'd suffocated before he could freeze to death. When he shut himself in that storage unit, a piece of fabric from Matty's sweatshirt had wedged into the lock, jamming it. In such a confined space—barely enough to move—it didn't take long for him to run out of air and start inhaling his own carbon dioxide.

He might've screamed for help, but we'd been too far to hear. The Nelsons' yard was out of bounds, and we hadn't wanted to venture so deep into the dark woods. The Nelsons hadn't heard him, either—Tom had hearing loss, and Cheryl had taken a sleeping pill. Both slept through the night, unaware.

Entrenched in our lie, we vowed to stay silent. Nothing we did would change Brady's fate. Nothing we did could save him. No good would come from telling the truth.

I figured the guilt gnawing at our insides was punishment enough.

Apparently, someone disagreed.

But it was an accident. An *accident.* As I stared at the solved anagram, another pattern occurred to me. An allergic reaction. A car left idle in a garage. Falling from an infamous cliff. A prank call gone awry. Even a poorly timed locker inspection. All of them could seem like accidents.

Fucking hell.

Who else knew we'd played Manhunt that night? I'd never told a soul. Zoey clearly hadn't, or else she wouldn't have used it as blackmail fodder. I obviously couldn't ask Matty or Akira if they'd blabbed, and I doubted Randall had. Honestly, I doubted anyone else in this sleepy town even cared enough to remember. Brady's family had moved to California only a month or so after his death.

Out of sight, out of mind.

My mind snapped to Brady's brother, Andrew, friendly yet reclusive. He'd snipped at me when I came to bring Brady back to Zoey's. But he didn't know all the rest of it. Besides, he'd been in California all these years. Whoever was doing this *knew* us. Matty didn't exactly advertise his nut allergy to the world, and they'd known Akira's family would be out of town, that Randall's parents were website designers, and about our rivalry with Fishman. It had to be someone local. *Right?*

I pulled up Facebook. I'd always avoided stalking Brady's family on social media, unable to swallow the thought of his family grieving somewhere out there, in pain because of me. Because I'd wanted to play a game. It was bad enough whenever I babysat the Rao kids in Brady's old house; the walls seemed to stare accusingly at me, for killing the boy who was supposed to finish growing up within them.

Sometimes I'd find myself wondering what Brady would've been like when he got older. Would he have busted out of his shell? Or would he have remained a quiet, creative soul? It was torturous, knowing I'd never know, knowing it was my fault. So I distracted myself with video games, slipping into virtual worlds for hours at a time, eventually discovering MortalDusk, a fantasy realm where you could level up indefinitely, regenerate infinitely. You could never really win, but you could never really die. Nothing was permanent.

Not like what I'd done. That was as permanent as it gets.

On Facebook there was a slew of results for Andrew Cullen, but none were a match—everyone was either too old or too young. I reached for my phone to look him up on Instagram, then remembered it was lying next to Akira's broken body. I shuddered. Had she been rescued by now? Or . . . recovered? I choked back a sob, refusing to let myself drown in sorrow. I had to focus.

What about their mother, Marcia Cullen? I searched—no results. But she'd had a Facebook profile at some point. I remembered Mom telling Dad she started posting on Facebook again about a year after Brady died, and she felt awkward commenting after losing touch. Maybe it was a private profile. If so, Mom might still be friends with her, though she rarely checked that hellsite after Dad left. Her laptop, still on my bed from earlier, caught my eye. I lunged for it and navigated to Facebook, and voilà—she was already logged in.

Mrs. Cullen's profile came right up; they were still friends after all. There was no mistaking her flaming red hair in her profile picture, though her curls had been cut and blow-dried into a sleek mom-bob. She grinned at the camera, though her eyes had this mournful, faraway look. The most recent post was some silly meme—

"Oh *no*." The comments were all condolences, like, *Rest in Peace, Marcia and Nate.* My heart clenched as I scrolled through them, piecing together what happened: a car accident about eight months ago. A few of the messages were well-wishes for Andrew—either he wasn't in the car or had survived the crash— but none linked to another profile, since he didn't have one.

Wow. That meant Andrew was all alone now. Did he have any

grandparents? Aunts or uncles? He was about two years older than we were—that'd make him eighteen or nineteen now. He would have graduated high school last spring, so he'd be in college, if he'd gone.

I clicked on Marcia's recent photos. Her last was with her husband, Nate, about a month before they died. His hairline had receded, and his wire-rimmed glasses had been swapped out for tortoiseshell frames. The previous picture was from Andrew's high school graduation. His parents stood next to him in his cap and gown near bleachers where they'd clearly just had the ceremony—

What. The. Fuck.

I squinted at Andrew. Scraggly chestnut hair came to his chin, and he didn't wear glasses, but . . . the sharp angle of his jaw. The slight curve of his lip. Those eyes, piercing mine through the screen. Such a strong chill coursed through me it felt like someone pumped liquid nitrogen into my bloodstream.

He looked a hell of a lot like Dylan.

No. That was *impossible.*

My heart jammed itself into my throat as I scrolled back through time. Marcia didn't post frequently, and when she did, they were usually memes, but the few pictures of Andrew showed how he'd slimmed over time. Losing his baby fat had revealed prominent cheekbones and a sharp jawline. Even his nose seemed to elongate and thin out.

And those *eyes* . . .

I zoomed in as far as the browser would let me. Brown eyes. Not gray. But the contrast could be from the lighting or a filter or whatever. Their intensity, the way they crinkled in the corners, the tiny mole next to his left eye—the resemblance was more than uncanny. It was *spot-on.* I grabbed a fistful of my comforter, feeling like my room had flipped upside down.

No.

No.

Dylan was Dylan. Not Andrew. He was a sixteen-year-old high school junior who was snarky and clever and wanted to go to MIT and lived with his father near . . .

Actually, I didn't know where they lived. We always met up at my place or Matty's. And I'd never met his dad . . . He worked long hours and frequently went to book festivals in other states and abroad. At least, that's what Dylan told us. And his mother had died in a—

"Car accident," I breathed. My God. He did tell me that last night.

Maybe *both* of his parents really died in a car accident—five years after his little brother died in a different sort of freak accident—leaving him all alone.

Maybe he'd cut his lanky hair into a tousled short shag, bought preppy clothes, got those tortoiseshell-rimmed glasses—like Mr. Cullen's. The same ones? Maybe he was a hacker—a hacker like Zoey—but kept it on the DL. Maybe he'd moved back here pretending to be two years younger, enrolled in our school, joined our team, learned about our allergies, our families, our fears, got us to trust him.

And then.

"No. Nope. Absolutely not," I said, scrolling farther back through Mrs. Cullen's feed, wiping my clammy forehead. I never would have let myself crush on such a charlatan. I would've recognized him. Some instinct would've kicked in, warning me off.

I always had trouble reading him. Or so I thought. Maybe my instincts had been right; I had trouble reading him because he wasn't *him.*

Marcia's post from right before Brady died was of him and Andrew solving a jigsaw puzzle at the coffee table. My heart squeezed like a vise; I hadn't seen Brady's face since that awful, awful day. White-trimmed ruby socks dangled from the fireplace, and a Christmas tree nestled in the corner. The caption read, *Best of brothers and best of friends.*

I stared at Andrew. This made no sense. The helpless misery I'd seen on his face after Brady died had burned into my mind, making Caelyn's safety and happiness my top priority, turning me into an overprotective big sister. How had I not spotted even a slight resemblance before, when I thought of that image so often? Maybe my memory had warped his features over time, making them fuzzy and unrecognizable.

I zoomed in on the graduation picture again. No. It couldn't be. Dylan and Andrew were lookalikes, that's all. Lots of people had doppelgängers. Lots of boys had eyes that crinkled in the corners, with a mole in that exact spot. I was sure if you took inventory of everyone in the world who fit those criteria, there'd be at least a thousand of them. Maybe more. There were almost eight billion people in the world. Statistically speaking, it was a coincidence.

Besides, I'd gotten a message from An0nym0us1 when Dylan was standing right in front of me, and he wasn't using his phone at the time. And lots of people die in car accidents. Wasn't it one of the leading causes of death in the United States? Just because Andrew's parents and Dylan's mom died in car accidents didn't make them the same people.

Dammit, I didn't trust my own judgment anymore. I'd jumped to so many conclusions over the past day, chased false leads, wasted time. I'd tied up Zoey like some maniac because we'd both jumped to conclusions.

This time, I needed proof.

My own laptop was still open to An0nym0us1's profile on Reddit. At this point, I had to guess they hadn't hacked my laptop; otherwise, they would have contacted me by now. I tapped on the Chat button, and a chat box appeared. I could send a message to An0nym0us1 and Dylan at the same time—

Oh! Zoey's IP matching widget! The one she created to find our troll. I'd bookmarked it, right?

Yep, there it was. I jogged my memory for the steps. I had to upload two images, then send one to An0nym0us1 and one to Dylan. The tool would log the viewers' IP addresses, and if they matched, I'd know they were the same person. So simple. So clever. Dammit, I should have thought of this sooner. Regret overwhelmed me as I marveled at Zoey's cunning. I remembered how we used to wordlessly communicate with the colors of our lights. With some cleverness, I could've found a way to confide in her. I could have gotten my teammate's help. My *friend's* help. Instead, I let suspicion and fear get the best of me.

Paranoid.

Zoey had denied telling Dylan I was paranoid and mentally unwell, but I hadn't let her finish speaking. What if it was really the other way around? Had Dylan been sowing seeds of distrust, gaslighting me all along?

I'd know soon enough.

What image should I send Dylan? Some random pic of puppies or something would be too obvious, so I took a screenshot of the Reddit page, uploaded it to Zoey's widget, and copied the URL it spit back out. Then I typed—Please don't get mad. I can explain.—and pasted the URL. Sent. I twirled my pen as I stared at the blank spot where the IP address would appear.

Within a minute, a series of numbers popped up. Dylan had clicked the link. A moment later:

WHAT? YOU PROMISED ME.

A sob tried clawing its way up my throat as I imagined his lips on mine. *Promise me,* he'd said. *Promise me you won't go stalking him.*

He sent another message: Where are you now? Are you okay???

Panicked. Concerned. Could be an act. Ignoring his text, I uploaded a recent selfie to Zoey's widget, then quickly created a throwaway Reddit account and clicked to An0nym0us1's chat pane. My fingers shook as I typed, Are you sure this is her?, pasted the URL, and sent the message.

Back on Zoey's app, I waited, twirling, twirling, twirling my pen, the events of the past day flickering through my mind like a movie reel.

Yesterday morning, Dylan left our MortalDusk practice in his Jeep. I never saw him follow Matty's car, never asked if he went to Starbucks with everyone else. He could've followed me to Caelyn's school, kidnapped her, tied her up, and taken the videos and pictures of her to send later. I hadn't seen him until fourth period.

What about the exam in his locker?

He could have made himself his own first victim so I wouldn't suspect him. If he'd already graduated high school, getting suspended wouldn't matter. Cutting class wouldn't matter. He'd been using his Chromebook in history class—he could've sent those messages through an app, discreetly from his seat in the back row. He could've emailed Mr. Chen through my account. He could've sent me the correct locker combination the instant Mr. Chen asked him out into the hall. That'd explain the perfect timing.

Then, after I got home, I had to wait for An0nym0us1's next set of instructions—probably because Dylan was stuck in Mr. Chen's office as he tried to contact Dylan's father. Tried, and failed.

Because Dylan's father was dead.

Dylan was the first to come over after I'd saved the brownies from the oven. He'd eaten one right away—perhaps to demonstrate how "safe" they were. Icy tendrils wrapped around my heart. God, I'd been so gullible.

And last night, he could've left Caelyn on her own as we all slept. He could have scheduled that message to come from An0nym0us1 right after he slipped through my window. He could've been the one who set my phone on its charger. Not me. And when my phone buzzed this morning, awakening me, Dylan's phone had been next to his face. I'd assumed he'd fallen asleep reading it, but maybe he'd sent Akira a text through some app that let him spoof me, sent me a message as An0nym0us1, then pretended to be asleep. Then, after he left, he could've left Akira a voicemail, spoken to her, pretending to be me. The more I thought it through, the more it made sense. Yet it made absolutely no sense at all—

An IP address appeared under An0nym0us1's picture.

They matched. The numbers matched.

An0nym0us1 was Dylan.

Not paranoia. Confirmation. Fact.

My heart shattered into a million pieces, and I leaped from my chair, howling as a raging fury thawed the ice in my chest. The sound startled Whiskers, who darted from the room. We'd let this boy into our lives. We'd welcomed him onto our team, befriended him, trusted him. I'd started to *fall* for him. And then he took my sister. He tortured me. He killed two of my friends—

Someone pounded on the front door. I gasped. Was that the police? Had someone found Zoey tied up? Whoever it was barely waited a moment before knocking again. Persistent. Loud. Angry.

I instinctively grabbed the knife and slinked across the hall to Caelyn's room to peer out the window. I couldn't see the front stoop from this angle.

But Dylan's Jeep was in the driveway, parked behind Matty's car.

My stomach twisted. How had he gotten here so fast? Had he already been sitting in the driveway? When I sent him the screenshot, he must've realized I was home, using my laptop. He must've realized I'd figured it out. He was there when we busted Lucia. He must've clicked the link on Reddit as An0ny-m0us1 and realized what he'd done.

Yeah, that's right, bitch. I figured it out.

Hatred, hot and thick, permeated my veins as he shouted, "Crystal!" He bashed on the door again, each pound reverberating in my ears. A minute later, the shrubberies under Caelyn's window rustled. He must've been edging behind them to peer through the living room window. The hairs on the back of my neck stood on end. I hoped all the windows and doors were locked—I always forgot to lock things. I tightened my grip on the knife as Dylan backed away from the window, lifting his eyes to the second floor.

I ducked, my pulse racing. Did he see me?

"Crystal!"

I held my breath as the sound of rustling foliage moved around the corner of the house. He was checking every window. I crawled into the corner next to Caelyn's bed and hugged my knees to my chest, gripping the knife hilt so hard my fingernails cut half-moons into my palm.

I'd let him *kiss* me.

He called my name on the other side of my house. My blinds were drawn now, so he wouldn't be able to see into my bedroom. Several minutes of silence passed that felt like a lifetime—more minutes that Caelyn was hurt and bleeding. Had Dylan stanched her wounds before leaving her alone to come after me?

My breath caught in my throat. He'd eventually give up here. Then I could follow him back to Caelyn. *Yes.* He'd lead me right to her. I scrambled to my feet and peered out the window. His Jeep was still in the driveway. I could do this.

I slinked back to my room to grab my car keys, then inched down the hall, heart galloping like a wild stallion as I peeked down the stairs to the front door. There was a shadow behind the opaque stained glass, and I could see Dylan's blue-and-white-plaid jacket through the narrow translucent swirls in the design. I yanked myself back. If he spotted me, he'd never leave. I knelt and peeked around the banister. He was pacing, waffling, unsure. My car was in the driveway, but since I kept my bike in the garage, he wouldn't be able to tell if I'd ridden it somewhere. Without my phone, he couldn't track me.

Good.

Let him be confused. I'd spent the last day out of my mind.

Finally, he stilled, then disappeared, perhaps convinced I wasn't home after all.

I crept downstairs and leaned against the door to peer out one of the tiny swirls of translucent glass. Oh God, he was still there. Sitting on the front stoop. Hunched over like he was scrolling through his phone. I stooped, covering my mouth, praying he hadn't heard me.

The wooden steps creaked. If I could hear that, surely he could hear my heart thrumming against my rib cage.

"Crystal?"

I squeezed my eyes shut, like that would somehow make me invisible, and held my breath, cowering against the door. If he looked straight down, would he see me at this angle?

Whiskers meowed, and my eyes snapped to her, standing in the doorway of the kitchen, looking right at me. I shook my head, hoping she'd somehow understand the frantic look in my eyes and know to go away, to pretend I wasn't here. Instead she trotted right over, thinking I'd gotten down to her level to play. She rubbed her fuzzy body against mine, giving me a cat-hug as I remained frozen, terrified, my ankles cramping up from kneeling like this, holding my breath.

Something squeaked overhead. I held in a gasp and looked up, and watched helplessly as the doorknob turned.

CHAPTER 36

I'd forgotten to lock the door, hadn't I? I always forgot. *Dammit.*
Dylan turned the knob all the way and pushed. But the door didn't budge. I'd remembered to lock the dead bolt after all.

Still, if he really wanted to get in, he could. He could throw a rock into the living room window or—

Bam. He pounded low on the door, hard, like he suspected I was crouching beneath his line of sight. I swallowed back a scream, clasping my mouth. He was trying to get me to cry out. He was trying to get me to reveal myself. Instead, Whiskers skittered away from the door, her back paw nails loudly skidding on the hardwood as she rounded the corner into the living room.

I heard Dylan grunt, and then his shadow disappeared as footsteps stormed down the front stoop's steps. He must've thought the cat was making all the noise.

That little fuzzball saved me.

Legs shaking, I peeked outside. Instead of heading toward his Jeep in the driveway, he veered left.

Toward Zoey's house.

I'll keep playing without you.

No.

No.

I hadn't been able to lock her front door behind me. He could easily let himself in and find Zoey in the basement. If he were clever—which, clearly, he was—he'd kill her without touching anything, and it would be *my* fingerprints all over the crime scene, and mine alone. Fury swelled in my chest like pressurized lava. Brady's death was an accident. How *dare* he snatch our lives away like this!

I dashed into the dining room to get a clearer view of Zoey's house. If he killed her, I'd never get to apologize. Just like I never got to tell Matty how I felt. More unspoken words. More death. I couldn't let it happen. But if I confronted Dylan now, I wouldn't be able to follow him to Caelyn. She'd be trapped for God knew how long, or worse, bleed out—if she hadn't already.

No. I *had* to assume she was still alive. She was alive and needed to get to a hospital.

All I could see of Dylan was his blue plaid coat sleeve as he rang Zoey's doorbell, the chimes faint through the window. Had he tried the doorknob? He shouted Zoey's name, but she wouldn't hear him in the soundproofed basement. Was he tracking her phone? I'd chucked it onto her kitchen table on the way out, having no need for another locked phone. I braced to run over if he went inside. I couldn't let him hurt her.

But after a few moments, he dashed back down the stairs. As far as he knew, she had no reason to avoid him, so he must've thought she wasn't home. "Oh, thank God," I whispered, getting my first clear view of his face as he crossed my yard—jaw clenched, mouth set in a grim line, brow furrowed. Frustrated. Maybe a little worried. His plan had gone awry after all.

As Dylan climbed into his Jeep and backed down the driveway, I huddled at the front door and slid the knife into my coat pocket, hoping it wouldn't tear through the fabric. Once he turned down the street, I'd have to move fast. Hope and fear mingled in my chest—this might lead me to Caelyn, but how the hell would I rescue her?

Dylan waited for a car to pass, then backed into the street. As soon as he accelerated, disappearing down the street, I whipped the door open and sprinted toward my car. It'd stopped raining, but the walkway was slick with patches of black ice, and I almost fell. By the time I teetered the rest of the way to my Prius and turned onto the road, he was gone.

"Dammit!" I smacked the steering wheel. But when the road curved, I spotted him up ahead, stopped at a red light. I slowed a few car lengths behind him. If he glanced at his rearview mirror, he'd spot me. But the light turned green, and Dylan made a right turn without indicating.

I followed, palms slick with sweat, keeping some distance between us. The light up ahead turned yellow. There'd only be time for Dylan to whiz through. It was a long light, too—Caelyn and I had gotten stuck there yesterday morning. This was no action movie; I couldn't blast through the red light once traffic started in the other direction, swerving around cars screeching out of the way—

But Dylan slowed before reaching the traffic light and turned onto a long driveway.

Um? Where was he going? You couldn't see the house from the street, but this was the Nelsons' old property.

After we'd found Brady in their storage locker, the Nelsons put their house up for sale, just like the Cullens had. But their house was more of a fixer-upper, and whispers of the boy who'd died in the backyard reached any prospective buyers. Unlike the Cullens with their cookie-cutter modern home, they had a tough time getting offers.

And then Mr. Nelson passed away—cancer, I'd heard—and Mrs. Nelson followed soon after. The house had stood empty ever since, now belonging to their only child, who lived in France with her husband. I'd overheard Mom and Chantel gabbing about her once, speculating she was saving it to move back here if she ever had children of her own.

Going down the driveway wouldn't exactly be subtle, so I pulled off onto the shoulder and headed toward the house on foot, sticking to the shadows under the pine trees lining the driveway. Spotting Dylan, I scrambled behind a wide tree trunk. He'd parked in the old detached garage and was jogging to the front door.

What on earth?

Had Dylan been squatting here all this time? He always drove to my house . . . but this was walking distance. He'd made it seem like he lived across town, when really, he'd been right around the corner.

Once he was inside, I crept to the wraparound porch. All
the window shades were drawn, but one room's shades had torn
reams, and I could see movement inside. As I climbed the porch
stairs, the middle step creaked under my boot, and I froze. But
the space between the torn shades went light and dark, light and
dark. There he was. Pacing. He hadn't heard me.

Slow as a sloth, I reached the window and stooped to peek
inside. Dylan's laptop was propped open on a faded blue floral couch, and he wore a stony expression, fists clenched at
his sides. Nobody else was there. Caelyn must've been in the
basement. His headphones flattened his tousled hair—was he
blasting hip-hop, stressed out of his mind?—and without his
tortoiseshell-rimmed glasses, he looked like the sullen boy
I remembered from my childhood. Now that I knew he was
Andrew, I couldn't believe I'd never spotted the resemblance
before—that *none* of us had.

But why would we have? It was like when you ran into a
teacher at the grocery store. Out of context, you didn't recognize them at first.

Dylan was utterly out of context. We never imagined Andrew
would move back to town, let alone change his name and appearance, claim to be two years younger, wheedle his way onto
our esports team, and plan a deadly game of vengeance. I'd almost let this boy steal a piece of my heart while he tried to steal
everything else from me. Had he ever liked me at *all*? Obviously
not. What I'd thought was flirty snark was actual resentment.

He paused at his laptop and scratched his temple. Classic
brainstorming move. He was trying to think how to find me.

But I'd found him first.

If Caelyn were in the basement, could I free her out from under his nose? The pain in my wrist pulsated as though in response, evidence of my clumsiness so far today. I considered my other options.

Option one, confront him—try to reason with him and talk him out of this madness.

Option two, call the police. Akira's phone was still in my car. But if he heard their sirens—

A breeze rustled the wind chimes next to the front door, brushing my curls back from my face. That's when I noticed the smell. Rotten eggs. I cringed. What the hell *was* that?

The sulfuric odor triggered a memory from chemistry class— the same gas safety unit in which we'd learned about carbon monoxide. "Natural gas is colorless and odorless," Mr. Ferguson had told us, passing around a jar of diluted hydrogen sulfide. "So gas companies make the stuff smell like rotten eggs so in case there's a leak, you'll know."

Matty had winced when he took a whiff. "Ugh, it smells like a million farts."

Mr. Ferguson chuckled. "Well, if your house ever smells like a million farts, tell your parents right away, or call 911. And do not, under any circumstances, light a fire."

That's what it smelled like now. A million farts.

Had Dylan somehow filled the house with natural gas? If I called the cops, all he had to do was strike a match . . .

Oh, God. I had to get Caelyn out of there. Now.

I slinked off the porch to seek out basement windows, getting déjà vu from Jeremy Fischer's house as I crunched over dead leaves and overgrown weeds, hoping Dylan didn't hear. Behind the house were two windows into the basement. Bingo. I wiped a layer of grime from one of them with my fist and peered inside. It was dark—I couldn't see much. The entire window frame was big enough for me to crawl through, but even if I could magically turn the lock inside, the window pushed in from the bottom, and I wouldn't be able to fit through half the space.

I had to break the glass. I scanned the backyard for some sort of blunt object, then jogged to the garage. Dylan's Jeep was parked inside, and some folded cardboard boxes were stacked against the back wall. Other than that, it was empty.

What about the storage locker? The one behind the garage, where we'd found Brady? Was it still even there?

My fingertips went numb, and I swallowed hard. Well, it was worth a look.

I dashed around the garage and found it standing there, same as ever. The storage locker, the door from my nightmares— always running toward it, always trying to save Brady from the monster trying to snatch us both as the distance elongates between us and I can't move fast enough. Why the hell didn't the Nelsons get rid of it? I touched the handle; the cold metal made me shudder. Unwilling to hesitate lest I chicken out, I threw open the door, half expecting a body to tumble out.

Of course, none did. And inside was exactly what I needed.

I grabbed the rake and hurried back to the basement window. There was no way to do this quietly. Hopefully Dylan wouldn't hear it over whatever he was listening to. I flipped the rake in my grip, wound back, and drove its handle at the window, biting back pain in my wrist as the old glass cracked and shattered after a few more well-placed pummels. I froze, clutching my wrist and listening for footsteps rounding the house.

But all remained still and silent.

I used the rake to clear the window's edges of any lingering glass shards. The pungent, rotten egg smell wafted from the window, making me crinkle my nose. I squatted and scream-whispered, "Caelyn?"

No response. A wooden desk stood next to the window. I slid in legs-first, careful not to press my palms into any broken glass, lowered myself onto the desk, and hopped to the floor. The room was carpeted and vaguely damp, like there'd been flooding at some point and the room hadn't properly dried, and the sulfuric smell mingled with must and mildew. Old-fashioned metal filing cabinets and bookshelves lined the walls, stacked with ancient books and magazines. Stairs led up straight ahead, and to the left, a door.

I opened it and nearly gagged. The odor was stronger in here. I edged into the windowless room. The light was already on. "Caelyn?" This room was unfinished—boxes and bins were stacked against the faux-brick concrete walls, like the one behind Caelyn in the pictures and videos, and like Jeremy's basement—walls like these must've been common in unfinished basements. In one corner stood a cat tree that long since homed any feline residents and a wooden dollhouse almost as tall as I was. There was a chair next to the door, but there were no tied-and-bound thirteen-year-olds.

Desperation clawed at my throat. Where *was* she?

Another door across the room stood wide open. I raced over,

disappointment instantly flooding my chest. It was a tiny utility room containing just the furnace and water tank. There was a low hissing, and I noticed a pipe bent at a weird angle. That's where the gas was coming from. Ugh.

"Caelyn," I whispered one last time. But she wasn't here. Dylan must've been keeping her upstairs.

I'd have to creep past the living room after all.

I tiptoed up the stairs and pressed my ear against the door. I couldn't hear any footsteps. Had Dylan stopped pacing? What was he doing now? Maybe he'd left. There was only one way to find out.

Practically vibrating with nerves, I inched the door open, holding my breath, careful not to let the hinges creak, and edged toward the foyer. The main staircase was by the front door. I'd have to go directly past the living room. I stilled, listening.

Tic-a-tic-tap.

He was typing.

Frustration pulsed through me. No matter how stealthy I'd been so far, there was no way I could pass the living room without him spotting me. All he had to do to stop me was strike a match, and the whole house would spontaneously combust or something. I hated confrontation, but I had to reason with him. I had to try to convince him to let my sister go.

I crept toward the living room. He sat on the couch, laptop on his lap. With one last deep breath, I held my chin high and strode into the room.

This, he wasn't expecting.

His mouth dropped open. "Crystal? How . . ." He threw off

his headphones and, squinting, felt around for his glasses, found them on the coffee table, and slid them on. But of course, he didn't need them. He never did. "You know where I live."

"Obviously."

He shook his head, befuddled. Then his posture relaxed, like he was relieved. "Thank God you're okay." He set his laptop on the coffee table and scrambled to his feet. "Why haven't you been answering your texts—"

I cut him off. "Where's Caelyn?"

He tilted his head, frowning. "Uh . . . I have no idea. You said she was on a field trip, right?" He started toward me. "I can't believe you went after Fishman anyway—"

"Enough!" I sidestepped him, maintaining our distance. "Just drop the act, okay?"

"What *act*?" His gray eyes were wide, pleading. "Crystal, I've been looking everywhere for you. Did you hear about Akira?"

Akira. My heart clenched. Akira was dead, wasn't she? This sadistic sociopath had killed her. "They found her at the bottom of—"

"Stop it!" Seeds of doubt needled my mind, but I refused to let them sprout. I was wrong about Zoey, but this time, I knew the truth. I'd seen evidence. I wouldn't let him fool me any longer. "I know you took her."

"Took who? Akira?"

"No, Caelyn! Just give her back, okay? I won't tell anyone what you did. I'll take the fall for everything. You can even kill me if you want, just, please, let my sister go. She has nothing to do with—"

"Whoa!" Dylan's eyes went wide as silver dollars. "Why

would I kill you? What the *hell* are you talking about? You think I took your sister? As in . . . you think I *kidnapped* her?" He wiped a hand down his face. "How could you think that? Crystal, you *know* me. You know I'd never do something like that."

"I *do* know you." My entire body trembled—not from fear but rage. "I know exactly who you are, *Andrew*."

Hearing the name made him go as still as a statue except for the subtle rise and fall of his chest.

"So, where is she?" I pressed. "Where are you keeping her?"

There was a long pause as he studied me, like I was a Rubik's Cube and he was searching for the sequence to solving me. His eyes widened for a nanosecond as he realized there was no solution.

Then his jaw clenched. "Why do you think I'd tell you? You haven't won yet."

CHAPTER 37

My first impulse was to punch Dylan in the face. How hard would I have to throw my fist to dislocate that sharp jaw? I didn't, though—instead I balled my fingers and said, "If you think I'm going to keep playing this psychotic game, you're out of your mind."

He chuckled. "You know what? I'm kind of impressed. How'd you find me, anyway?"

"How about *I* ask the questions? Where the hell is my sister?" So much for reasoning with him.

"Calm down, alright? She's fine." Relief spread through me like a cool stream over dried grass—until someone bent the hose. How could I believe a single word he said? "Well?" he prodded. "How'd you figure it out?"

Now it was my turn to laugh. "You made Brady's name an anagram. I mean, come on. Lance Burdly? *Really?*" Dylan's cheek muscles twitched, and he muttered a curse. "Did you not think I'd catch that?"

"Not so quickly." He rubbed the back of his neck. "I thought maybe someday, sitting in jail, you'd piece it together, but . . ." So he did mean to frame me. "Still, how'd you know it was *me*?"

"You left your mother's Facebook page active." I had to stop myself from adding *dumbass*. "There were pictures."

His eyebrows shot up, and he whipped out his phone.

"I don't get it," I went on. "How could you plan all this so perfectly, and forget to take down her Facebook profile?"

"If you think this has gone perfectly, *you're* the one out of your mind," he muttered without looking at me, focused on his phone, gritting his teeth. I reached into my front pocket and gripped the knife's hilt.

I could stab him right now.

But if he was keeping Caelyn somewhere else, I needed him to tell me where.

Plus, I still wasn't sure I could plunge a knife into another person, no matter how evil they were. Thinking of feeling the blade meet resistance—skin, then muscle, then bone—made bile leap into my throat.

"I don't see it," he snarled.

"It's a private profile. My mom's still Facebook friends with her." I snickered. "Foiled by social media, huh? You always did say it ruined everything. Guess you were right."

His face went all stony, and after a few moments, he kicked the couch. "Dammit!"

I scrambled back toward the door. How the hell had I fallen for this maniac? I'd *trusted* him. I'd reassured him about getting suspended as he ate that first brownie, acting all vulnerable. I'd told him Zoey had cheated when I hadn't even told the others—my *real* friends. I'd let him hold me as I fell asleep—

"Oh." The realization hit me like a bucket of ice. "The hot chocolate." The stuff he'd brought over in a thermos. That's why I'd felt so parched, why my eyelids had felt like lead weights. He'd drugged me. That way, I couldn't stay up to investigate or strategize. Whenever he'd placed my phone on its charger while I slept, he must've also dumped his own hot chocolate back in the thermos.

He tossed his phone next to his laptop. "Oh, for Christ's sake. You're going to want a play-by-play, now, aren't you?"

I started at his blasé tone. "No. I can guess at enough. I just want to know where Caelyn is."

He roughly wiped his forehead with the back of his hand, exasperated. "You think I'm going to let you have a happy reunion that easily? You killed my brother."

I grimaced. "No, it was an accident. A freak accident." That's what the police had determined. They'd swept the storage locker for fingerprints, but the only recent ones were Brady's. Nobody had stuffed him into that locker. At the time, I thought they'd at least trace Zoey's flashlight back to her—Sanchez found it at the bottom of the locker, switched on, batteries drained—but they didn't. Zoey had been wearing gloves when she passed out the flashlights. The police assumed it was the Nelsons', that Brady found it in the locker.

What had driven Brady into the Nelsons' backyard remained a mystery to everyone but us. At first, we were sure at least *one* person in the entire neighborhood must've spotted us playing in their backyard so late at night or had security cameras pointed at their backyard. We kept waiting for the other shoe to drop.

But it never did. Until now.

"It wasn't, though. I *saw* you," said Dylan. Andrew. Whoever he was.

My stomach sank. "What?"

"I saw you all outside, in Zoey's backyard, after midnight. I know you went out to play hide-and-seek."

"Manhunt," I automatically corrected.

"Whatever," he spat. "And I know it was *your* idea. Brady told me what happened, you know, when he came back for a few minutes. That you convinced everyone to play a game, but none of you wanted him on your team. And then later, as I was drifting off, I heard something outside . . . It was you all, huddled in the backyard. I opened my window to listen. Zoey tried talking you out of it. Brady complained how cold it was. But you pushed everyone to play your stupid game."

Shards of ice stabbed my heart. That's why he'd chosen *me* to play these deadly games.

Andrew shook his head. "I watched you all split up to find your hiding places. But when it was his turn, you couldn't find him, could you? And you just *gave up* on him. You'd always made him feel like a wad of gum stuck on your shoe, like you had no choice but to drag him along. You didn't give a shit about him."

I flinched. I'd always tried to include Brady, even though he didn't fit in. I'd genuinely liked him. But maybe I hadn't defended him enough when Randall teased him, when Zoey rejected him, when Matty laughed at him, when Akira swatted him away from her LEGO bricks. Maybe that was my fault. Should I blame my eleven-year-old self for that? How far should you go to force a friendship?

"We thought he went home," I said. "He said he wanted to keep us out looking all night, so we thought he was trying to trick us. How were we supposed to know?"

"You could have checked! You could have asked an adult to help find him."

"It was one in the morning!"

"Yeah, it *was,* and it was freezing! And you left him out there all alone to die. And then you *lied* about it." I cringed, swallowing hard. He was right about that. "You know, that's what really got me. None of you broke. Even after it was clear he was missing, none of you panicked. You were so convincing, *I* almost believed you. I started to doubt myself. I figured, you know what? Brady never would've snuck out like that; he was scared of the dark. I figured I'd been dreaming or something. I thought, if you really had all been out there, surely you would've said something once the search started. But then after . . . after . . ." He recoiled, and I knew we were both picturing Brady, dead. "I knew what I saw. I saw you all out there with my own eyes. How could you lie like that? *How?*" He screamed the last word, making me jump.

"I . . . I don't know. It was impulsive. Zoey's parents were so strict, she would have been grounded forever if they knew we snuck out. So I covered for her. I said Brady went home in the middle of the night, thinking it was only a white lie. And then once we realized . . . once we'd already lied . . ." I trailed off.

He pursed his lips and shook his head. "But when you knew he was dead—when you knew what you really *did*—"

"We were *kids*. We were terrified. We didn't know how much trouble we could get in. And he was already dead. We couldn't help him anymore."

He scoffed bitterly. "So you thought, hell, might as well get away with it."

Wait—something wasn't adding up. "I don't get it," I said. "The next morning, when you realized he was missing . . . why didn't *you* say anything?"

His face reddened, and a cord in his neck bulged as he stepped forward, fists clenched. "His death wasn't *my* fault," he practically barked.

I backed away again and fumbled my footing, tripping into a china cabinet. The delicate glasses and trinkets inside rattled. "I never said it was!" As I took in Andrew's tortured, haunted expression, I realized he blamed himself, too. He knew we'd snuck out. He could've kept an eye on us. He could've made sure his little brother made it back to Zoey's. He could've told his parents the truth right away. But he didn't. He fell asleep, and the next morning we'd confused him with our lie—so much that he'd rationalized away what he'd seen. And he'd always been so soft-spoken; in the moment, he'd probably been wary of refuting our lie. It'd have been five against one. And by the time he watched Brady tumble from that locker, it was too late.

He was as wrapped up in our secret as we were.

And the guilt had tortured him, maybe even more than it had tortured us, because they were brothers. If our positions were reversed, and it happened to Caelyn, I'd never forgive myself. I would've hated myself for not doing everything I could to protect her.

Which was exactly what he was doing, turning the table on me.

"D—Andrew . . . it *wasn't* your fault."

"I know that!" he shouted. But did he? "It was *yours*. But then you all went on with your happy little lives like nothing happened."

"No, we didn't . . ." Or did we? Zoey and I dwelled on it, for sure, but the others had bounced back pretty quickly. To be fair, they hadn't been Brady's neighbor. They'd barely known him. Did that matter? A boy had lost his life over our negligence.

"Yes, you did. I followed you on Instagram for years, you know—you and Akira both followed my sock puppet account back." He snorted. "Amateurs. And once you started streaming, I watched that, too. You all just played your stupid games, excited for your stupid tourneys, acting like everything was fine." So that's how he'd hatched a plan to finagle his way onto our esports team.

I nearly gasped. "Were *you* the one who started the rumor on Discord about teams of six at the tourney?"

He sneered, basically confirming it. "I knew you'd want a play-by-play—"

"And *that's* why you chose this weekend." I'd figured it was so we'd suspect someone like Jeremy Fischer, or someone connected to MortalDusk. Instead, it was so we'd never get to play in the tourney. So close yet so far.

"Is that really all you can think about?" he shouted, and I winced. "You know, all these months, I waited for one of you to mention Brady, *once*. But none of you ever did. Not until last night. When Zoey brought it up, I thought, *finally*. Some acknowledgment! But then you fucking laughed it off." He jabbed a finger at me. "You literally said it was *no big deal.*"

I gripped my throat, seeing now how that must have sounded. "Of course it was a big deal. I was just trying to change the topic . . . to keep *you* from finding out. You have to understand, we didn't just keep our secret to get away with it. We were disgusted with ourselves. We thought anyone who found out would be disgusted with us, too."

"Bullshit. You all did plenty of other cringeworthy things. Randall ragged on anything that breathed. Matty led on girl after girl, never giving a crap about any of them. Zoey cheated right under all your noses for weeks. I love how long it took you to figure that out, by the way. Akira—well, she was also complicit, but she was the best of all of you."

"Then why did you want to *kill* her?"

"*You* killed her."

"No—" Grief constricted my throat, making the word stick. Did he *know* she was dead? "I didn't. She fell . . . It was an accident."

"Just like Brady was an accident, right?" He shook his head. "You dragged Brady from our house, made him play that stupid game."

"I never *forced* him—"

"And then you felt no remorse for leaving him out there. That's why Akira had to go. So it'd *hurt.* So you'd finally feel an ounce of *something.*"

His words knocked the air out of me, like he'd punched me in the gut. "Of course I felt remorse. It . . . it's *tortured* me. For *years.*"

"Not like it tortured my family. My mom never got over it. She was so depressed, asking herself over and over why he ended up in that locker. Was some pedophile chasing him? Or a bear? Had he been terrified out of his mind? She even wondered if maybe he was running away from home, to get out of going to church, even though that made no sense. One time, I *did* tell her the truth, just so she'd *stop*. But she didn't believe me. She figured I was trying to make her think he'd died doing something fun—playing a game. She always assumed the worst. She died thinking the worst."

So that's what set him off. I'd figured it would take a sociopath—someone who experienced no emotion or empathy—to make me play this sadistic game. But Andrew felt emotions. His brother's death had been traumatic, and on top of his guilt, the unfairness of us getting away with everything tormented him, embittered him, provoked him to seek revenge. He'd dwelled on it for years, and his parents' deaths—dying without closure, leaving him all alone—triggered him to enact his plans.

"But how could you kidnap Caelyn?" I asked. "She had nothing to do with any of this. Nothing!"

He jabbed a finger at me. "But now *you* feel just as helpless as I did, don't you?"

"I didn't hurt Brady on purpose!" I cried. "But you've been hurting—*torturing*—an innocent thirteen-year-old girl. And you're going to *kill* her—"

"*No.* I'm not a complete monster!"

What? "You stabbed my sister! And, sorry to break it to you, but killing *two people* is definitely monster territory."

"I didn't kill anyone. *You* did."

My heart jerked. "Following *your* instructions. And you tampered with those brownies, and stole the EpiPens . . ."

He raised his eyebrows. "You sure about that?"

There he went again, trying to make me doubt myself. But I wasn't going to let him fool me anymore. He wanted to make me feel the crushing guilt he'd felt for years, but I wouldn't let him pile any more stones on my chest.

His eyes bored into mine—eyes that made my heart flutter just this morning. Now they were like silver daggers piercing my soul. There was so much anger in them, so much hatred. He'd hidden it so well. He glanced at his watch. "You're almost out of time. And you know what happens if you don't win."

My stomach lurched. "No way. Your game is *over.*"

"It wouldn't be fair to call it now, would it?" He took something from the coffee table and handed it over. A burner phone. Just like the one now at the bottom of Hanover Lake. "We still have two games left." *Two.* Zoey and Randall.

"But Randall's game was yesterday . . ."

"No, it wasn't," said Andrew. "I just wanted to scare him with the SWAT team. I didn't think his parents would make it home so fast. And his dad having a heart attack? Yeah, didn't expect *that* either," he muttered, raking his hair back, like accidentally giving a man a heart attack was more obnoxious than anything else.

"Not a very good game designer, are you?"

"Well, a good designer needs to be flexible. I had Akira's game planned for weeks, after she mentioned her parents' trip to California. But when you screwed that up, I had a work-around ready to go." He considered me saving Akira's life a screwup. And suddenly I realized he'd never let Caelyn go. That would ruin his plans to frame me. She'd tell the police someone kidnapped her, that someone was forcing my hand. None of his plans worked if he let her go. He *had* to kill her.

I'd been playing an unwinnable game all along.

"You'll never get away with this." I clutched the phone so hard I thought I might crush it. "I'll tell the police what you've done, who you really are."

He shrugged. "They won't believe you. Once you tell them your 'theory' about me"—he made air quotes—"you'd have to tell them what you did to Brady. Then they'll know you're a liar. Even if they dig into it, there's no physical evidence I'm Andrew. None of his things are left in California. There's nothing to DNA match. And he used his passport to go to Europe. He's going backpacking for a year, you know—there's no telling where he might end up." The way he talked about himself in the third person, like he'd completely dissociated from himself, sent tremors down my spine.

"You . . . you went to Europe first? Before coming here?"

"No. The dude who bought Andrew's passport did, though." My God, he'd thought everything through. "Nah, the police won't be able to prove anything. But you? All the things you did? They'll be able to prove all of that."

"People will believe me over some kid who just moved to town."

"You think I plan to stick around to convince them?" His eyes sparkled mischievously. "It's not as hard as you'd think to become someone else."

"If you disappear, that's even more reason for everyone to believe me."

"Not if people think you killed me, too." Andrew whiffed the air. Then it dawned on me. The natural gas. My nose had quickly gotten used to the smell. He planned to blow up the house, to fake his own death. But wouldn't the police think it odd they couldn't find his body? I thought they usually found some remains in fires—bones, at least. Maybe I was wrong. Could they DNA-match ash? I didn't know much about that sort of thing.

"How will you explain the fact that your father doesn't exist?" I asked, desperate to poke holes in his plan.

"Because nobody but you and your friends think my father exists. I've been renting this place myself. I enrolled in school as an emancipated minor. Mr. Chen, the teachers, everyone thinks I'm an orphan whose parents left me enough money to take care of myself. Which is entirely true. They just think I'm two years younger than I am. I was in eighth grade when we moved, so none of our teachers would've recognized me." That meant once he "died," nobody would come home to bury him, or look for him if the police never found his remains.

He had absolutely nothing to lose, no tracks to clear behind him.

"Anyway," Andrew said, glancing at his watch again, "it's time to keep playing."

"No. No way. I'm not killing anyone else."

He pulled something from his pocket—a bright blue Zippo lighter—and flicked it open, pressing his thumb threateningly on the spark wheel. "If you don't, she dies. And then, I guess, so do we."

All the air squeezed from my lungs. Caelyn was upstairs after all.

But Andrew had already shown his hand. He meant to run away. To start a new existence. He'd never blow up the house with himself still inside. He didn't want to kill me, either—he wanted me to live with the guilt, to be in pain just like he was.

It was time to call his bluff.

Before he could stop me, I chucked the burner phone at his head as hard as I could and darted from the room.

CHAPTER 38

It took ten seconds to climb those stairs. Ten seconds, max, to put one foot in front of the other, taking them two at a time. But it felt like an eternity, time stretching and slowing like in one of my recurring nightmares, the distance between me and my destination elongating infinitely as a monster chased me down.

As it turned out, reality could be just as horrific—monsters and all.

"Caelyn!" I shouted as Andrew followed like a shadow. Before I could swing open the nearest door, he grabbed my left arm above my injured wrist and shoved me against the wall, making my arm sear with agony. It took all my restraint to keep from crying out. I couldn't let him see my weakness. Not when I was this close to getting Caelyn back. I could almost sense her presence. I was so close. "Cael—"

Andrew covered my mouth, bracing me against the wall with his forearm. I tried shoving him back, but when he pressed the metallic tip of the cigarette lighter into my cheek, I froze. "Don't move, or we're all dead."

I flinched as the metal pricked my cheek and involuntarily cringed against the wall as though bracing for an explosion. But I knew he was bluffing. He wouldn't end his own life to keep me from getting to my sister. That wasn't his endgame. I straightened and said into his palm, "Bullshit." Even muffled, the word was clear. I held his gaze and hoped mine was filled with fire.

He gnashed his teeth as a battle raged in his mind. With his face this close, gray eyes inches from mine, I could see a subtle ring around his irises. Contacts. Colored contacts. So it wasn't just a filter or trick of the light that made his eyes brown in those Facebook pictures. I already knew the glasses were just for show, but this one last deception made the fury in my chest spew up my throat like a dragon.

He lied about everything.

He took everything.

He destroyed *everything.*

Before he could react, in one fluid motion I yanked the knife from my pocket and drove it upward toward his forearm bracing me to the wall, aiming for the exposed skin his plaid coat sleeve didn't reach. I could have plunged it into his belly, but didn't want to kill him—I just wanted him to release me and drop the lighter. The blade easily tore through skin and sinew.

"Aaah!" He reflexively backed away, and when I tugged out the knife, blood sprayed all over me. We both screamed—him in pain, me in surprise at how much blood there was.

Andrew clutched his arm and dropped the lighter, and we

gasped as it fell to the carpet. With all that gas in the air, all it would take was a spark to make the house blow.

But nothing happened.

We stared at it, breathing hard.

Our eyes flicked up to each other.

And then we lunged for it. I was closer, so I snatched it and leaped out of reach, brandishing the knife at him. He recoiled. Blood gushed down his arm, and he'd already left a trail of red on the beige carpet. I must've hit an artery or something. He followed my gaze and let out a hiss as he took in the steady stream of blood running down his middle finger, down to the floor, like he hadn't quite realized the depth of his wound. Maybe his brain was releasing chemicals to block the pain. He clasped his arm again. "Jesus."

I took advantage of this distraction and dashed to the next room. "Caelyn?"

She wasn't there.

"Stop it—" Andrew lunged at me, but I raised the knife in a silent threat. He curled his lip in frustration, keeping his distance, believing me. Believing I would do it.

And he was right.

I checked all the rooms and closets upstairs in a sort of grotesque dance with Andrew, warding him off with my knife each time he got too close. I even tugged down the ladder into the attic at the end of the hall, climbing just enough to poke my head up there and check. But Caelyn wasn't anywhere. This reminded me of how my friends and I couldn't find Brady—he'd seemed so close, yet nowhere at all, like he'd slipped through a crevice between dimensions as we'd counted to one hundred.

I stilled and gripped a doorframe, starting to feel light-headed from all that gas in the air, and strained to hear shuffling, movement, any sign of life besides us. But there was nothing. Caelyn wasn't here.

And that was all I needed to know.

I turned back to Andrew and raised the lighter, flicking it open again and hovering my thumb over the spark wheel. "Game over, you son of a bitch." If Caelyn wasn't here, I could end this game now. Randall and Zoey would be safe. Caelyn would be safe—still lost, but *alive.*

Andrew raised his hands like I was about to launch a shock bolt at his face, eyes wide as silver dollars. Blood streamed freely from the gash in his arm, and he gripped it again, grimacing. "You don't want to die, either."

"*Obviously.* But I would. I'd do it to save my sister. You don't think I'd sacrifice myself to save her? To save my friends? Then you wasted all these months, because you don't know me at all."

He clenched his jaw, obviously trying to think of some way out of this.

"Let's play a game." I tried for a mocking tone, but my voice shook so hard I could barely pull it off. "It's called *Exploding Murderers.* Call the police and tell them everything that's happened, and exactly where Caelyn is, or else we both go up in flames. You have one minute."

His chest puffed out like he was holding his breath. If he confessed, he'd never get to finish his game. All his diligent plans would crash like a blue screen of death.

"Ticktock!" I shouted, tightening my grip on the lighter. "Fifty-five. Fifty-four. Better get to your phone."

"If you think I'm turning myself in, you're nuts."

"If you think I'm letting you get away with this, you're nuts. Thirty-five, thirty-four—"

"It hasn't been twenty seconds—"

"*I'm setting the rules now!*" I shrieked. My whole body trembled, but I was absolutely ready to burn it all down.

He knitted his brow and glanced down the stairs. Then at the blood streaming through his fingers as he clutched his arm. Then back at me. Calculating. Always calculating. "Fine. I'm going."

I followed him down the stairs, training the knife on him in case he tried any funny business. When we reached the foyer, I could see his phone sitting on the couch next to his laptop in the living room. All he had to do was call the police, and this game would end. I wouldn't have won, exactly. There was no winning—not after losing Matty and Akira, and hurting Randall's dad. Not after Caelyn and Zoey were traumatized, probably for life. But at least it would be *over*.

But Andrew's knees buckled, and he collapsed in the middle of the foyer.

I leaped back, and my heart shot into my throat. What the hell was he trying to pull? Was he going to grab my ankles? Pull me to the ground? Wrestle the lighter away from me? "Get up!" I screamed.

He raised a bloodied hand at me and shook his head as though trying to clear it. "I-I can't." Blood dripped from his arm, pooling onto the wooden floor. How the hell was there so much blood? His eyes were unfocused. Wide. Scared.

I regretted stabbing him so aggressively. A small slice would have gotten him to drop the lighter. But adrenaline and anger had raged through my veins, and I was so scared he'd keep me from Caelyn—I'd driven the knife upward with all my strength.

Could that wound really kill him?

I didn't want him to die—not even after everything he'd done. Because I wasn't *him*. Death never justified more death. And true justice would be living with the guilt of what he'd done.

I knelt next to him. "Take off your belt."

"What?"

"You need a tourniquet. Take off your jacket, too."

His eyes darted between mine, his expression softer than before. More like the Dylan I thought I knew. "You . . . you want to help me?"

"I'm not a complete monster," I snapped, inadvertently repeating his own words. He stared, astonished. Not wanting him to get the idea he deserved my compassion, I changed tack. "And you can't tell the police the truth if you're dead." I tried sounding tough, but my voice trembled, and tears welled in my eyes.

I felt for him, somehow. I didn't believe his claim that he wasn't a monster—he'd killed two people, and meant to kill four, maybe five—but anguish, grief, and guilt had turned him into one.

He slipped off his jacket, groaning as the material slid past the wound. "It's okay." The comforting words automatically slipped from my lips, and he threw me another bewildered look as he went for his belt. But then he sucked air through his teeth.

"Here." I set the lighter and knife on the floor behind me, out of Andrew's reach, and unbuckled his belt myself. My cheeks went hot, more from mortification and discomfort than anything else, and I tried not to think of our kiss this morning. "A scarf or something would be better, to make the tourniquet tighter."

"I . . . I don't have one. There might be one upstairs—"

"It's okay." I yanked the belt from the loops. It was soft suede, flexible. "This might work, actually." I looped it around his upper arm, and rather than pulling the end through the buckle, I tied a knot like Mom had taught me. The tourniquet had to be tight, really tight, to work. I tied a second knot a bit above the first.

"Uh . . ." I glanced around, the room spinning faster than I turned my head. I was getting dizzy, so dizzy. "I need a stick or something to wedge between the knots and twist it tight." The knife was sturdy and straight, but I might cut myself by accident. Andrew was losing blood fast, so fast—his face had paled, and the puddle growing beneath him was startlingly large. I undid the second knot and tightened the first, straining to put enough pressure on the artery to stop the blood flow.

Andrew grunted in pain, but said, "I think it's working." He still looked perplexed—and there was something else. Regret, maybe? Or was that wishful thinking on my part? I wondered whether, if I'd opened up about Brady back in my room last night, Andrew would've cut the game short. If he knew how Brady's death truly tortured me, I might have become less of a flippant villain in his mind. Instead, I'd kept the secret bottled up, so worried he'd *judge* me. When really, he'd been judging me all along.

"I should've told you the truth last night, about Brady—" I started.

"I honestly don't think it would have changed anything," he said, like he'd somehow followed my train of thought. "You don't know what years of plotting revenge does to a person." In that moment, he didn't look afraid, or in pain. He just looked exhausted. And pale. So pale. I could almost empathize with his pain. *Almost.* What he'd been through—what he'd lost—didn't excuse torturing a thirteen-year-old girl. It didn't excuse *murdering* people.

I tried tying a second knot to hold the first in place, but couldn't manage it without the first knot loosening. "Shoot, I really need a stick or something." There must've been something I could use in the kitchen. "Be right back."

I dashed into the kitchen. There was a jug next to the stove filled with wooden spoons, spatulas, and a whisk. I grabbed the sturdiest wooden spoon and raced back into the foyer.

Andrew was holding the lighter.

Dammit, dammit, dammit. I wanted to clobber myself over the head. How could I be so foolish?

"It's time for one last game," Andrew said quietly.

"No. Please—"

"It's an easy one. Just a one-hundred-meter dash. Run. Run as fast as you can." He rested his thumb on the spark wheel. "You have one minute."

My jaw went slack. He was giving up. He didn't want to get caught. He didn't want to go to jail. So he was just ending it. Maybe he thought he was going to die anyway. "But where's my sister? Where's Caelyn?"

His expression hardened. "Just go home, Crystal. Fifty-nine, fifty-eight—"

"No. Don't do this. Don't end it like this."

"Stop trying to save me. It's over. Don't let me take you with me. Fifty-five, fifty-four."

My breath caught in my throat, and I looked at him one last time. His skin was sallow, his expression determined, yet utterly defeated.

And I ran. I ran because I didn't want to die, because I knew Caelyn wasn't in the house, because I didn't know how to save Andrew anyway, or if I even should. I ran like the earth had split open, and the ground behind me was falling into an infinite expanse.

I didn't even reach the end of the driveway before the house exploded.

CHAPTER 39

gripped my ears and ducked as an ear-shattering boom shook the ground, far enough not to be thrown from the blast but close enough to feel heat on my back. How much searing pain had Andrew just felt? Or had he died instantly? He'd be lucky, if so. Holy *hell*.

I was about to straighten when something huge crashed feet away from me. I cried out and covered my head, and after several moments without any other enormous objects dropping from the sky, I peeked at whatever it was, my breath ragged and uneven. The front door. Yikes.

Standing on wobbly legs, I took in the scene. The flames had already shrunk back inside the rubble, and thick plumes of black smoke billowed from the decimated house. Part of the outer frame remained intact, but most looked like it'd caved in, and pieces of siding and roof littered the lawn. I'd been lucky none of it hit me.

There was no way anyone could've survived that. Andrew must be dead.

Part of me wanted to cry out in anguish—the part still struggling to reconcile how Dylan and Andrew were the same person. Another part wanted to fall to my knees in relief. But I still didn't have my sister back. Where the hell could she be? Was Caelyn still in danger of bleeding out? Andrew had lost so much blood from a similar gash in his forearm, and fast.

I spotted his Jeep parked in the detached garage, which the explosion hadn't reached. I hadn't bothered looking inside earlier.

The doors were unlocked. Caelyn wasn't inside. That'd be too easy, right? Not that anything about the past twenty-four hours had been easy. Andrew's backpack was still in the passenger seat. I unzipped it. His main laptop and phone were likely destroyed in the blaze, but his school Chromebook was here. He'd sent me those first messages as AnOnymOus1 while in Mr. Richardson's class. Maybe this laptop contained some clue as to Caelyn's whereabouts.

I opened it with trembling fingers. The screen brightened, and an empty password field greeted me. Naturally.

I could hand the laptop over to the police, but God knew how long it would take them to crack the password. I had to find Caelyn *now*.

It was time to do what I should have done at the start of this twisted game.

It was time to ask my teammate for help.

Zoey sputtered and gasped as I untied the scarf binding her mouth. "Holy shit. You're *covered* in blood."

"Oh, don't worry, it's not mine," I said distractedly as I worked on the knot binding her right wrist to the chair.

"That doesn't make it any better!"

I winced, pausing on the knot. She already thought I was a murderer. This looked bad. Really bad.

"Whose blood is it?" she persisted.

"Dylan's."

"*What?*"

"Please, listen—"

"*What did you do to Dylan?*"

"Zoey, listen to me! Dylan's actually Andrew Cullen. He's the one who kidnapped my sister. He hacked my phone, installed that app I told you about—"

"Wait . . . Andrew *Cullen*? Brady's brother?"

"Exactly. I found his hideout just now . . . He, uh . . . I basically had to fight him off."

Zoey watched me for a long moment, then burst out in high-pitched, almost maniacal laughter. "Oh my God, you've totally lost it."

I wanted to scream in frustration. But also, I got it. Abject denial had been my first reaction, too. "It's true, Zoey. He blamed us for Brady's death. I mean, think about it . . . He has a legit reason to want revenge. This all had nothing to do with MortalDusk—"

"But I remember Andrew. There's no way in hell they're the same person."

"Do you remember him *that* well, though? It's not like we ran into him often."

"I guess . . . but Dylan would never do that. Never!"

"I'm sorry." I went to work on the knot again. "I know you like him."

"No, I don't," she said quickly. Too quickly.

I snapped my head up to look at her. "But you kissed him—"

"Oh, please. I was drunk." The moment I freed her wrist, she wiped her chin with the back of her hand. "Kiki and Randall had paired off, and Matty was obviously drooling over you, so I just . . ." She trailed off, shrugging. So she wasn't trying to swoop in and steal Dylan. Once again, she was simply afraid to be alone. How the hell had I missed this? I'd been such a self-absorbed twat.

Once her other wrist was free, she shoved me back. "Get away!" She doubled over to reach the knot securing her right ankle.

"I'm not going to hurt you—" I tried moving to her left ankle, but she swatted me away. "I'm telling you the truth!"

"Yeah, right."

"Zoey, *please.* I need your help getting into Andrew's laptop. Caelyn's injured, and I have to get her to the hospital—"

She eyed me suspiciously. "You have his laptop?"

"Yeah . . . well, his Chromebook." I scrambled to his backpack where I'd dropped it by the door.

"How'd you get it? How'd you fight him off? Where *is* he?"

"Never mind that. Will you help me? *Please?*"

"I still don't understand," Zoey said as she freed her left ankle and rolled both like they'd gone stiff. "If Dylan took Caelyn, why wasn't she there?"

My stomach sank. She'd better not have been there. "I don't

know." From the look on Zoey's face, I could tell she still didn't believe me. "I swear I'm telling the truth."

"Well, what makes you think getting into his laptop will help?"

"I'm hoping there's a clue on here about where she is. It's all I've got. I'm at a dead end otherwise." She still looked skeptical. "I know you have absolutely no reason to trust me. But Andrew really took my sister. He really made me do all those things. I swear it. I'm so sorry I tied you up. I'm sorrier than you can ever know. But *please.* Help me find Caelyn. I know you can get in here faster than the cops can." I brandished his laptop.

She poked her tongue into her cheek, considering me. She had to know the panic on my face was real. Finally, she grabbed the laptop. "Alright, fine. But first I need a fucking drink."

"*Thank* you."

I followed Zoey into the kitchen. She slid Andrew's laptop onto the counter and filled a glass with tap water, downing the whole thing in one long gulp. Then she filled it again before opening the laptop. Password required. She blew air between her lips. "Alright. This should be easy enough. I need to grab my laptop and USB. And . . . ah." She spotted her phone on the kitchen table where I'd left it earlier and pocketed it before heading upstairs. For a moment, I considered following, worried she'd call the police. But then I remembered . . . An0nym0us1 was dead. He couldn't hurt Caelyn anymore.

Zoey returned a moment later, her own laptop in tow. I sat across from her at the kitchen table as she got to work, first plugging a USB drive into her own laptop and typing away. "What're you doing?" I asked.

"Do you want me to concentrate or not?" she snipped.

"Sorry."

"I've written some scripts to crack passwords and stuff," she explained anyway, "just messing around. I need to make some tweaks first."

"Oh." As she typed, I wandered back to the counter and picked up a pen next to the Blooms' shopping list, absentmindedly twirling it. My stomach gurgled as I eyed a decorative bowl filled with apples and bananas. I hadn't eaten since lunch yesterday.

Zoey kept regarding me warily as she worked.

"I won't bite," I said.

She raised her wrist, showing the thin red line where I'd accidentally cut her, the skin around it swollen and pink. "Too soon."

I flushed. "Sorry about that . . ."

"Whatever."

After a while, Zoey pulled the USB stick from her own laptop and inserted it into Andrew's, fingers trembling. Then she crossed her arms. "Now, we wait."

I sat across from her again, each of us shifting our weight awkwardly as the minutes passed, avoiding eye contact. There was so much I wanted to say, but I didn't know if she'd believe any of it. Finally, I asked, "How long will this take?"

"I'm not sure. Depends how complex the password is—" But right then, someone opened the front door.

"Zoey!" her mother shouted. My heart jolted.

"In here!" cried Zoey. "Mom!"

Her parents appeared in the doorway, and Zoey stood and

raced into her mother's arms. "It's okay," her mother cooed, glaring at me over Zoey's shoulder. "You're safe now."

Mr. Bloom stood between us like a barrier. "The police are on their way."

My stomach plummeted. "What . . . *How* . . ." She must've texted her parents, either on her phone or laptop, and they'd zipped right home from their dental practice. She wasn't trying to unlock that laptop. She didn't believe me—not one bit.

And Caelyn was still out there somewhere, tied up and scared, and nobody was going to help me find her.

CHAPTER 40

Trying to explain everything that happened over the past day was like trying to teach a kitten to play chess, but way less cute. We all sat at Zoey's long dining room table, even Randall and Lucia, who'd shown up shortly before Chief Sanchez since Zoey texted Randall, too, in case her parents didn't get her message. Sanchez tried taking me to the police station, but the story started spilling out of me before anyone could convince me otherwise, even though Randall tried saying something about lawyers. But I was so desperate to find Caelyn, desperate for Sanchez's help, I raced through my account, incriminating or not. By the time I finished, Lucia's jaw was basically glued to the floor, and Randall and Zoey were pale as ghosts.

"So, let me see if I've got this straight . . ." Sanchez smoothed down his mustache, staring at his chicken-scratch notes. "You're claiming that Dylan was actually Andrew Cullen, Brady's brother—the boy who died in the Nelsons' storage unit about

five years ago. He enrolled in your school using fake documen-
tation—"

"Presumably," I said. Out of the corner of my eye, I saw Zoey
and Randall exchange a wide-eyed look. I couldn't tell if it was
shock over Dylan's true identity, or if they thought I'd lost it. I
hadn't yet explained *why* Andrew would have done all this, only
that he had.

"Mmkay. Presumably. He attended said school for six months
or so, then kidnapped your sister and texted you instructions—"

"It wasn't texting," I explained for what felt like the zillionth
time. "He installed some messaging app on my phone when I
wasn't looking. I think he controlled it on there." I motioned to
the Chromebook. Zoey's USB drive was still plugged in, but she
hadn't touched it since before her parents burst in. "Please, we
need to find Caelyn—"

"How could you let Matty eat those brownies?" Randall suddenly chimed in. "You knew what would happen, and you let it."

"No, I didn't know." I shouldn't have rushed through the
story; I was explaining this terribly. "It wasn't clear *why* I was
completing each task. I had no idea the brownies would be
tainted."

"You said Dylan told you to push Akira off the lookout
point," said Sanchez, flipping to the next page.

"Yeah, *that* time the instructions were explicit. But they usually weren't."

"But even though he instructed you to push Akira, she fell by
accident?" Sanchez asked. Randall clasped his mouth, watching
me with such a pained expression it tore my insides apart.

"Yes. She grabbed my phone to see one of Anon—Dyl—ugh, *Andrew's* messages, and I couldn't let her see what was happening. I tried getting it back, and we wrestled over it, and . . . she just fell."

"Why couldn't you let her see?" said Randall.

"I *told* you . . . Andrew said he'd kill Caelyn if I told anyone what was happening. What would *you* have done if it were Nessa instead?"

"I wouldn't have—" But he cut himself off, raising a fist to his mouth. The truth was, he had no clue what he would have done. Nobody can ever know what they'd do until they're in that position.

"Why'd you tie up Zoey, then?" Zoey's mom spat angrily. "You said you lost your phone by then. No one *forced* you to do that—"

I winced, but Sanchez lightly touched her arm. "Ma'am, please, let me handle this."

Oh, God. I was about to get *handled.* Arrested. Thrown in jail. Was the death penalty still a thing in Vermont?

"Why aren't you arresting her?" Mrs. Bloom jabbed a finger at me. "She killed two of her friends, and she tried to kill my daughter—"

"I *didn't*—" I started.

"Hang on." Sanchez raised a hand. "You should know— Akira's alive."

My heart jolted. "*What?* She is?"

"Holy shit." Randall flopped forward, putting his head between his knees as Lucia patted him awkwardly on the shoulder.

"It was a nasty fall," Sanchez went on. "She has some pretty bad injuries, and it might be some time before she can walk again. But she's alive."

"Oh, thank God." I clasped a hand over my heart.

"We found this next to her." Sanchez held up a ziplock bag with my phone in it. "It still works—"

"That's mine!" Relief washed over me.

"I figured."

I reached for it. "Here, I'll show you Andrew's app."

He didn't budge. "Now, this is evidence in an attempted homicide—"

"Please!" I stretched my hand farther. "Let me show you the app. I can prove *all* of this."

Sanchez's nostrils flared, but he passed me the bag, then stopped me when I started unzipping it. "Leave it in there." Oh. I swiped to the last home screen through the plastic, searching for the icon with the silver serpent snaking around a mic.

It was gone.

"Hang on . . ." I swiped through all the home screens. But the app wasn't there. Like it never existed. "No. No, no, no. Where is it?"

Had Andrew made the app self-destruct or something when he'd deduced it had sailed down the mountain with Akira? If so, he'd deleted any evidence that anyone had forced my hand. He knew he'd screwed me over even at the end as he thumbed the spark wheel, counting down, seeming to find some shred of humanity. He knew any evidence of my innocence would be destroyed with him.

He still wanted to punish me. As though what he'd already done wasn't enough.

Everyone watched me skeptically, expressions ranging from pity to fury. "I swear, it was there! The icon had a snake wrapped around a microphone. I swear to *God*—"

Sanchez took the ziplock back, shaking his head. "You didn't happen to record your conversation with Dylan, did you?"

"No," I whispered. He still wasn't calling him Andrew—that wasn't lost on me.

"Rookie mistake, boo," Randall said somberly.

"I didn't exactly have a way to record it, did I?" I snapped.

"Ah, well," said Sanchez. "If you recorded it in secret in his home, it wouldn't've been permissible in court anyway." Court. I was going to *court*. Next stop, jail. Do not pass Go, do not collect $200.

"I don't understand," said Mr. Bloom. "Why would the Cullen boy even do this?"

Randall, Zoey, and I seemed to hold a collective breath. But I had to tell the truth. My lie got me here in the first place, and I had to believe my truth would get me out. I took a deep breath and told everyone how we'd snuck out that night to play Manhunt. How we'd lied about it the next morning, and ever since. Zoey threw fearful glances at her parents, who watched me with stunned expressions. "But Andrew saw us all out there," I said. "He knew the truth the whole time."

"Whaaaaat," said Randall. I still couldn't tell if his reactions meant he believed me, or if he thought I'd concocted a wild lie.

"Now wait a minute." Sanchez scratched his cheek scruff. "You think he wanted revenge or something?" As the adults focused on me, Zoey surreptitiously started typing on Andrew's laptop, compressing her lips so all the pink disappeared. Had she unlocked it? Maybe she hadn't been faking her attempt.

"I don't just *think* it," I said. "He admitted it. All of it; how he sold his real passport to some kid going to Europe, how he lied to us about living with his dad. His parents died in a car crash months ago."

"Marcia and Nate Cullen?" Mrs. Bloom gasped. "What a shame."

"You didn't know?" I asked. "Weren't you Facebook friends?"

Mr. Bloom shook his head. "We're not on Facebook."

Useless, the whole lot of them.

"Dylan was an emancipated minor, I believe," said Sanchez.

"He did tell us about his father," said Randall. "That part's true."

"It's *all* true," I said.

"Well," said Sanchez, "he could've fibbed about that to fit in. Maybe he didn't want your pity." I cringed. Was he really so determined to believe some dead boy over me?

"But he even told me he was picking up his dad at the train station this morning," said Randall. "That's some serious fibbage." Hope filled my chest. Maybe he was starting to believe me after all.

"I'm in," Zoey said suddenly, pulling out the USB. "I had a program on here to crack the password," she explained to Sanchez.

Mr. Bloom's brow pinched. "How'd you get something like that?"

"I, uh . . . coded it myself." Zoey's cheeks flushed to match her pink ombre tips. If she could hack MortalDusk, writing a password hack must be child's play. But instead of looking angry, her dad looked impressed. Zoey bit back a hint of a smile.

Sanchez motioned for the laptop. "We should bring that in for analysis—"

But Zoey kept typing. "Let me turn off the password." She clicked around for a few seconds. "Huh."

My pulse sped up. "Huh? What's huh?" What had she found?

"Well . . . there aren't any files on here."

My stomach dropped. "Wait, *what*?"

She spun the laptop around to face me, showing me the main C drive files. Or lack thereof. "It's a wiped drive."

"What programs did he have installed?"

She shook her head. "There's nothing." He could've been using web-based apps the whole time, which he could access from either of his laptops or his phone.

"What about the web browser?" I asked, panicked. "Anything in the history?"

She swiveled the laptop back around. Sanchez looked conflicted, like he wanted to snatch the laptop and follow protocols. Zoey clamped her lips together tightly as she clicked around. I narrowed my eyes. "Nope," she said, "history's been cleared out. Looks like Chrome's the only browser installed . . ."

Over her shoulder, out the window, I saw Mom's car pulling into our driveway. Oh, God. How was I going to explain all of this to her? This would destroy her—

But then I saw something that made my heart go still.

Someone was in the passenger seat. Someone shorter than

Mom. Someone with two long braids that swung behind her as she leaped from the car.

Caelyn.

Alive.

"Oh my God." Before anyone could stop me, I was out the front door, sprinting across the yard. "Caelyn!"

She spun and spotted me. "Crystal! Oh my God, you'll *never* believe what happened!" It was like a story was bubbling up inside her, ready to burst. She was free. *Free.* But her eyes widened in fear when she saw the police chief following me. "Uhm, what—"

I barreled into her, my hug cutting off her question, sobbing into her hair, clutching her tightly. She was here. Really here. She smelled like strawberry shampoo, and her huge earring dug into my cheek, and she was real, alive, *alive.* I released her from my embrace to cup her cheeks, taking in all the little details—her slightly bugged hazel eyes behind her thick glasses, her button nose with a smattering of freckles, her full pink cheeks. "Are you okay?"

"Yeah," she said as I examined her arms. No gashes. No cuts. None on her neck either. Huh. She giggled like I'd tickled her and yanked her arms back. "Dork. Are *you* okay?" Her smile dissolved again at the sight of Andrew's blood on my hands, and she gasped. Caelyn wasn't covered in any blood at all. Her hair was frizzy as always, but in double plaits, which I knew she couldn't do herself; we always had to braid each other's hair. And she was wearing black leggings, but yesterday she'd worn jeans. And those earrings . . . I didn't remember those.

Mom slammed her door. "What's going on?"

"Mom?" My voice was strained. "Where did they find her?" But I knew. I knew, I knew, I knew.

"What do you mean?" said Mom. Sanchez merely watched, arms crossed. "I just picked her up from school. I almost had to take one of her new friends home with us, too. Tessa, was it?"

Caelyn nodded distractedly, still staring at my bloodied hands. "You were right, Crystal . . . about laughing it off . . ."

"You took my advice," I said. Her bully. Tessa. I'd told her to laugh off her insults, her pranks. And now, somehow, they were *friends*.

Because Caelyn had been at Frost Valley this entire time.

She'd never been kidnapped at all.

"What the hell is going on—" Mom's words evaporated as a high-pitched buzz filled my ears, and brown spots speckled my vision as I fell to my knees. Someone caught me before my head could slam into the ground—maybe Sanchez—but it might as well have split into a million pieces.

I killed Matty for nothing. I set a SWAT team on Randall's dad for nothing. I nearly killed Akira—and maybe permanently injured her—for nothing. I tied up Zoey like some monster for nothing. All of it was for absolutely *nothing*.

Had I made the whole thing up? Was Dylan—Andrew—even real? Or was he a figment of my imagination—a way to grapple with the guilt of killing Brady after Zoey blackmailed me? Was I so desperate to keep our secret, so traumatized that I sought revenge on my own friends? Had my brain concocted this wild scenario with An0nym0us1 to justify my actions?

The voices around me merged, and I shook my head, like that would somehow fit the scrambled pieces back together. Sanchez

was on his knees in front of me, gripping my shoulders and trying to keep me upright, saying something, but I couldn't hear
the words. I scanned everyone's faces until I found Zoey's. She
covered her mouth as tears streamed down her face. Even Randall's eyes watered.

"You guys . . ." I finally said. "Dylan was real, right? Tell me
he was real."

"Of course he was real," said Zoey. *Of course.* Zoey knew
who he was, too—so did Randall and Sanchez. He was real.
An0nym0us1 was real. It had all really happened. I didn't do
this myself. That was only what Dylan—Andrew—wanted me
to think.

He'd framed me. He'd faked Caelyn's kidnapping somehow.
"I swear to God, he did this. Somehow, he did this. There's a
tracking device!" I pointed to the gravel where I'd tossed the
tracker. "He was tracking me, but I found it on my car . . ." But
Andrew had been in my driveway earlier. He probably picked
it up and took it with him . . . and it went up in flames with the
rest of the evidence. Just as he'd planned all along.

"Will someone please tell me what the hell happened to my
daughter?" Mom cried.

"I'm sorry, Mrs. Donovan," said Sanchez. "We'll get her a
psych eval, and I'll explain everything at the station . . ."

I tuned them out, ignoring everyone except Zoey and Randall. "Please. You have to believe me. It was Dyl—Andrew. He
wanted revenge for Brady's death. He made me hurt the rest
of you. He installed an app on my phone . . . He somehow created these videos and pictures of Caelyn. She was tied up and
gagged. There was even a picture of him cutting her. Kiki saw

one of them." I gasped. "That's right! Akira saw one of the pictures! Right before she fell. You can ask her—"

"Akira's in surgery now," said Sanchez.

"But . . . but when she wakes up, she'll be able to tell you that."

"*If* she wakes up," said Randall. Any belief he'd had in my story had gone out the window when Caelyn appeared.

I gaped at him, helpless, until Sanchez helped me stand and unclipped a pair of handcuffs from his belt. Caelyn was crying now, and Mom screamed at him to let me go, that there must be some mistake.

"You have to believe me," I said, frantic. Suddenly, I remembered something. "Dylan told you I was paranoid, right?" I asked Zoey. "That I was mentally unstable. He told you that, right?"

Both Zoey's and Randall's eyebrows shot up. He'd said the same thing to both of them, playing us all like pieces on a chessboard. "Well, he told me *you* told him I was paranoid. He flipped it around. He was trying to turn us against each other, to make us suspect each other. To make me suspect *myself*. He gaslit me, Zoey."

The handcuffs were frigid on my skin, digging into one of the scrapes from Fishman's yard, making me squirm in pain as Sanchez led me toward his cruiser. "I wouldn't kill our friends!" I called back, more to Zoey than anyone else. "You *have* to believe me!"

But of course she didn't believe me. I'd tied her up in her basement. And I'd done it on my own, without following any instructions.

She had no reason to believe me.

Let's be honest—I had no reason to believe myself. I didn't even know what was real anymore.

All I knew was that my life was over.

CHAPTER 41

The thing about being obsessed with playing games your whole life is you know when someone's playing *you*.

It didn't take long to figure out what happened. And when Zoey came to visit me at the juvie detention center, backpack in tow, I knew she knew I knew. I just had to get her to *admit* it.

I'd been stuck here for four days, held without bail since my charges were murder, attempted murder, arson, kidnapping, and filing a false police report—and the investigators had a mountain of evidence stacked against me.

We're talking a mother lode of points here.

Ten points for triangulating the prank call's location to the park, twenty for the nylon bag at the bottom of Hanover Lake, and five for Jeremy Fischer's eyewitness account placing me at the scene. Ten points for my Instagram post of Hanover Castle and five for Mr. Ferguson placing me at Mount Morgan when Akira fell, *plus* bonus points for our li'l phone swap. Ten points for my fingerprints on the rake that broke the Nelsons' basement window, leading to the furnace room with the busted gas pipe. Tying up Zoey after threatening her with a knife must've been a gazillion points right there. And more points were incoming, since Matty's parents were having the brownies tested.

And let's not forget how I confessed to all of it. I just couldn't prove I'd done any of it under duress.

"How's Kiki?" I asked as Zoey sat across from me, her pink jacket overly cheerful in this gray, dreary room. She shrugged it off, scanning the other small tables dotting the room, some occupied by other teens and their visitors, then searched my face. I knew how I looked—pale and haggard beyond my years, eyes bloodshot and puffy from endless sobbing fits over Matty, my curls more mussed than usual without my anti-frizz cream.

"She's a trooper," said Zoey. "She's got this huge neck brace, and it'll be a few weeks before she can attempt crutches. But she's, like, more annoyed that Lucia keeps showing up with flowers and shit than anything."

I chuckled softly. "She wants to make amends."

Zoey rolled her eyes. "I know. Anyway . . . you should know, Akira's memory from that morning is shot. So she doesn't remember seeing anything on your phone, or whether her fall was an accident or not, or anything at all, really."

"Yeah, Mom told me."

She'd also told me about how she'd gotten an email from me while I was trapped in the back seat of Sanchez's cruiser, exactly twenty-four hours after the games began. In this email, I confessed to everything, apologizing to Mom and admitting I'd wanted the MortalDusk tourney prize for myself. My email to Fishman proposing an alliance—supposedly a last-ditch effort before going for my friends' jugulars—corroborated this. Mom had shown the email to Sanchez, thinking it was obviously fake and proof of my innocence—I hadn't had my phone nor access to a laptop while handcuffed.

But she didn't realize there were ways to schedule emails.

I actually laughed when Sanchez showed me and my lawyer how the email's originating IP matched the emails everyone else received: Mr. Chen, Fishman, even the one Randall's parents got from the no-show prospective client. I also recognized it as the IP I'd matched between Dylan and An0nym0us1. He'd been spoofing the same IP address the whole time, likely so the police *could* connect the dots—and I couldn't prove I wasn't the one using a VPN. More points for me, yay!

But I knew what evidence would exonerate me. And I knew it existed. All I needed was one conversation with Zoey. One conversation alone, just the two of us. And Chief Sanchez agreed to let her visit.

Zoey pressed her lips together as we each waited for the other to say something else. She wouldn't budge, so I spoke first. "I didn't hurt any of you on purpose."

Tears immediately sprang to her eyes. "You let Matty eat those brownies." But I definitely used the vanilla extract. I knew that now. Once the dust settled, and I had nothing to do but replay those awful twenty-four hours in my mind, I remembered the bottle of extract I used had been brand new. I'd had to peel off the plastic seal. I told Mom, and she found it in the trash. Proof. I'd only measured out extract from one bottle. Vanilla. That's it. Andrew had broken in when I went to the gazebo, tampered with the batter, then confiscated the EpiPens upstairs. He never had a real hostage to look after, so he was free to sneak around. He must've stolen Matty's EpiPens at practice that morning, or anytime at school. Later, as the paramedics whisked Matty away and we were all distracted, Andrew had slipped back upstairs to replace ours.

"I didn't know they were tainted," I said.

"You called in a fake tip—"

"I didn't realize it was Randall's address."

"You pushed Kiki off that cliff—"

"She fell by accident—"

"You tied me to that chair!" She was crying now.

"Andrew said he'd kill my sister if the cops found out!"

"You have an excuse for everything!"

"Because it's all true!"

She covered her mouth, tears spilling down her cheeks.

"Please, Zoey. Don't do what *he* did. Andrew knew the truth, knew *our* truth, and he didn't tell anyone. He let that grudge fester for years, and he got his revenge, but look where it got him. You know the truth. You *know*."

"Even so. You hurt our friends. You hurt *me*." Her lower lip quivered. "I never would have done that to you." *Even so*. She did know. "I would have told you what was happening. I would have found a way, any other way."

"Please understand . . . I was terrified for my sister. I'd do *anything* to protect her." Years ago, after seeing how devastated and helpless Andrew looked after Brady's death, I vowed never to let that happen to us. I vowed to always protect Caelyn, no matter what it took—even if it meant blackmailing my own drunken father into leaving.

As it turned out, that's exactly what whipped Dad into shape. He'd visited me yesterday, having flown in after Mom told him what happened. Apparently, he'd joined AA out in Vegas and had been sober for months, and recently got a marketing job at one of the big casinos.

"I need you to know," he'd said, "I left because I knew your mother would be better off without me. And I've left you alone because . . . well, because I'm a coward. I thought you hated me. But I never would've hurt you. *Never.* I tried coming into your room that night because your mom threatened to take you kids away, and I wanted to make sure you were still there. That's all. But I'm sorry I scared you. I never should have laid a hand on your mom. I never should have . . . spoken to you, the way I did sometimes. I should've been a better father, a better husband. I royally screwed up everything, and I'm so, so sorry."

Had I overreacted, driving him away? I always seemed to suspect the absolute worst in people. But if what I did helped Mom, and got Dad to clean up his act, I couldn't regret it. I'd go mad if I regretted all the ways I'd screwed up trying to help people.

"Everything I did," I said to Zoey, "was to protect Caelyn. You can't know what you'd do until you're in that kind of situation. You just can't."

Zoey's jaw hardened. "Just because I don't have a sister doesn't mean I don't know what it'd be like to make impossible decisions."

"I never said that—"

But she talked over me. "You and Kiki always do that . . . You've always kept stuff from me, like you assumed I wouldn't *get* it. She told me about her eating disorder, you know, after she started therapy. She told me how you convinced her what she was seeing in the mirror wasn't real, and to talk to her parents, and all that. *I* could have been there for her, too. I could have been there for *both* of you. But you never trusted me. Why?"

"I could ask you the same thing. I never knew you were struggling, because you kept it all bottled up. Why?"

She tugged at the ends of her pink hair. "That's fair. I . . . I guess I thought you'd think my problems were silly." She shrugged. "I was afraid if I seemed like a whiny bitch, you'd leave me out even more."

"That's why you cheated, wasn't it? And why you blackmailed me when I caught you. You were afraid to be left out."

She cringed. "I hate that I did that. I really regret it. All of it."

"I regret a lot of things, too. But we can't hold them over each other's heads forever. We have to forgive each other. For *all* of it."

She perched her elbows on the table and held her face. "You'll never forgive me."

"I already have." I reached over and took one of her hands, making her look at me. "We both hurt each other. I'm *so* sorry for what I did to you. I'm sorry for starting the lie about Brady, for pressuring you to go along with it. I'm sorry Kiki and I kept things from you. I'm sorry for treating you like a criminal for cheating. I'm sorry for not seeing all the pressure you've been under. And I'm sorry *beyond words* for tying you to that chair. I'm sorry, and I mean it. I mean it so freaking much."

Zoey clasped her mouth as tears spilled down her cheeks, letting my apology hang in the air between us like a balloon that could pop any second. Finally, she gave a great sniff and bent over to fish something from her backpack.

Her laptop.

She opened it, trembling, and clicked around for a moment. Then she spun it to face me.

It was a video of Caelyn. Tied and bound to a chair. Yelling for me to help her. The first video Dylan had sent me as An0nym0us1. I gasped—seeing it was still shocking as ever.

"Deepfake," Zoey explained, her voice shaking. "There were a bunch of videos and pictures like this on Dyl—Andrew's— Chromebook. All fake, all using deepfake technology. There are a bunch of apps that let you do stuff like this now; he basically just superimposed Caelyn's face onto videos of himself, pretending to be tied to a chair, saying those things." I knew it. Five years ago, we'd made him doubt his reality. He got revenge by making me believe a false reality. "And honestly," Zoey went on, "anyone could get her photos from her Instagram. He must've done the editing on his other laptop, but he was sloppy—one of the stock videos he used was on this one. Maybe he dragged the file in with the others by mistake, I dunno."

"On his Chromebook?" I prodded.

She visibly swallowed. "The—ah—the USB I plugged into his Chromebook wasn't just to crack the password. It . . ." She let out a shaky breath. "It extracted and deleted any document files behind the scenes. There weren't many besides these, so it was fast. By the time you finished telling everyone what happened . . . it was done. It's just . . . I didn't *trust* you. After you tied me up like that, I thought it was the other way around, that *you* were trying to frame *Dylan*. I thought you made up that whackadoodle story about him being Andrew and put something incriminating on his laptop. So I wanted to get it off there. But once I saw all this"—she motioned to the screen—"I knew. I knew you were telling the truth . . ." She trailed off, watching me closely. "Why don't you look surprised right now?"

I raised the corner of my mouth. "Because I already know all this."

Her eyes went wide. "*What?*"

"I knew what you did." I'd spotted her tell—the way she'd clamp her lips, biting back the truth. I knew when she was lying.

"But . . . if you knew . . . why didn't you tell the police? Why didn't you confront me?"

"What do you think I'm doing?" I thumbed toward the mirror to my left. "That's a one-way mirror. I'm wearing a wire. Wave at Chief Sanchez." I waved at the mirror.

Her jaw dropped, horrified. "But I thought . . . Sanchez said secret recordings weren't permissible . . ."

"In the target's home." I gestured vaguely. "Public space is fair game."

"You . . . you *played* me. You—"

"No! I *helped* you." I laughed and clasped her hand again. In her shock, she didn't pull away. "I told Sanchez what I suspected; that you took the files using that USB drive. I told him you probably thought I was trying to set Andrew up or something. But I don't want to press charges or anything, and I got him to agree that if you confessed to taking the evidence from Andrew's laptop—if you *admitted* what you did and handed it all over, you wouldn't get in trouble. This isn't a game. I'm done playing games."

Sure, Zoey should probably get in trouble for withholding evidence she'd been sitting on for days now, keeping me locked away, making me grapple with my grief alone. But I wanted to free us both—not just from imprisonment, but from the guilt, grief, and fear that drove each of us to make such terrible mistakes.

And I wanted to free us from each other. The main thing binding us all these years was a game and a lie. We'd clung together on such a shaky foundation, no wonder all it took to demolish us was a shitty dude with a grudge. If we'd confided in each other, trusted each other, been there for each other, none of this would have happened. But holding a grudge would only fester more misery and resentment. So forgiveness was my best hope at setting us free.

I hoped Akira and Randall would forgive me. But even if they didn't, I knew Andrew had forced my hand. I hadn't wanted to hurt them or Matty, just like I hadn't wanted to hurt Brady all those years ago. This time, there'd be no secrets to claw at my heart. This time, I'd forgive *myself*. And while I'd never stop missing Matty, and I'd need years of therapy to grapple with the trauma, my conscience was clear. I did what I did to save my sister, even if she'd never really been in danger. Andrew had planted the idea that I was paranoid, making me doubt myself, manipulating my reality, and that wasn't my fault.

All that mattered to me now was being with Caelyn and Mom. Dad offered to send more money each month now that he had a steady income, so Mom could pay the mortgage after all, but she'd likely put the house on the market soon anyway. But it didn't matter where we lived as long as we were together. I saw that now, even if Caelyn would still be fussy about it. I shook my head, thinking of what Caelyn said earlier this morning when she visited with Mom. "I can't believe you did all that, and it was just a *prank*." She snorted. "Shoulda just laughed it off." Little twerp.

Finally, Zoey heaved a heavy sigh, her shoulders hunched as she rubbed her eyes. "I want the games to end, too. And I *never* want to play MortalDusk again."

"Um, try telling that to Randall."

"Oh, I already did. He's not thrilled." Her lips quirked. "You know Fishman won the tourney, right?"

"Yeah, I heard." I also knew Jeremy Fischer had told the police he thought the email he'd gotten from me was fake. He said I'd been way too confused when he met me in the park, that he thought someone was coercing me on my phone outside his house. That cocky bastard actually showed up for me. He wasn't such a jerkface after all.

"Well, he's invited us to stream with him a couple of times a week."

"For real?"

"Yup. Randall's the only one who wants to take him up on it, though. They played together last night after Randall got home from the hospital. Lucia, too, though she always died within point two seconds." Lucia had also vouched for me, so I'd heard, telling Sanchez I'd asked her to look out for Randall—that I wouldn't have if I'd wanted to hurt him. "Our channel has, like, a bazillion subs now." But Zoey's smile quickly faded.

"What is it?"

"I still can't believe Dylan was Andrew. I can't believe he fooled us like that for so long."

"I know."

She screwed up her face. "I can't believe I *kissed* him." She stuck out her tongue, like, gross.

"I can't believe I did, either."

She raised her eyebrows.

"That morning, before he left—he kissed me." I grimaced. "And I kissed him back."

"Ugh. Hey, at least you didn't throw yourself at him."

"Don't feel bad. You had no idea."

"Thanks," she muttered. "But I'll never get to tell him off, or kick him in the face. He deserved what he got. He *deserved* to die."

My heart broke for her then. For all of us. "Oh, Zoey."

"What?"

I bit my lip, unsure how to break this news. Revenge wasn't always clean. Justice wasn't always swift. "The police didn't just let me talk to you to clear my name."

She blanched. "What do you mean?"

"They want any files from his laptop to try to find him. There were no human remains in the rubble." It was a flaw in Andrew's original plan, too, like I'd suspected. The police always would've known he didn't die in the fire. His game had too many glitches. "He didn't die. He's still out there, somewhere."

"But . . . how? Where could he have gone?"

"I wish I knew."

Andrew had clearly hatched some sort of escape plan, since his endgame was always to fake his own death and start over with a new identity. He probably had a car other than his Jeep hidden somewhere, primed to flee. He must've run out the back door as I sprinted out the front, then threw the lit lighter at the house and didn't get caught in the blast. The police had found traces of blood in the backyard, and then they just . . . disappeared. Maybe my tourniquet worked after all. Or maybe Andrew had somehow faked his wound's severity to get out of confessing to the police. I wouldn't put it past him—and let's be real, he'd probably do whatever it took to outsmart the police and start a new life. Hopefully, he wouldn't hurt anyone else.

But I remembered the shock in his eyes as I tried to stanch his bleeding. *I'm not a complete monster.*

There was a monster in each of us. The question was whether you managed to stifle it.

Maybe Andrew had finally locked his in a cage. Maybe he was now free from guilt and embitterment, and would move on from his thirst for vengeance. After all, in the end, he'd called a draw.

The problem for him was I never accepted it.

Brady's death was an accident. Matty's death was *murder.* There was no way in hell I was going to let Andrew get away with this. For now, my family was my priority. I'd clear my name. Apologize to my friends. Finish high school. Maybe even play in next year's MortalDusk tourney.

But someday, I was going to find him. Someday, I was going to beat him at his own game.

And I couldn't wait to play.

Acknowledgments

Thank you so much—yes, *you!*—for picking up this book, for choosing it, and for spending time with my characters. I can't even tell you how much it means to me. Okay, fine, I'll tell you.

My debut novel, *All Your Twisted Secrets*, launched six days after the WHO declared COVID-19 a global pandemic. On top of how terrifying the world was, bookstores shut down, and Amazon stopped shipping books that week, and since an author's debut sales often predicate future book deals, I was scared my author career was finished from the start.

But readers bought my debut online (or ventured out for curbside pickup), reviewed it, shouted about it on social media, told their friends about it, and sent me such kind words of encouragement. It's thanks to my readers *These Deadly Games* was possible. And thanks to *you*, my next stories will be possible.

So, from the bottom of my heart, in the absolute cheesiest way: *thank you.*

To my husband, Bryan, thank you for your unending support, for brainstorming with me, for bringing me lattes and pastries, for listening to me babble endlessly about publishing, and for *everything*. I love you so much.

To my parents, Lorri and Mark, to Grandma Gloria, and to all my family, thanks for your love and support, for rooting for me every step of the way, and for always believing in me even when I don't.

Thanks to my wonderful editor, Jennie Conway, who loved this book before it was even a book, and whose fantastic feedback made it shine. I've so appreciated your guidance along the way, and I adore working with you. Thanks also to my keen-eyed copyeditor, Sara Ensey; Kerri Resnick, who designed this book's stunning cover; Sara Goodman, editorial director; Eileen Rothschild, associate publisher; Elizabeth Catalano, senior executive managing editor; Jessica Katz, senior production editor; Lena Shekhter, production manager; Michelle McMillian, interior designer; Alexis Neuville, marketing manager and fellow *Shadow and Bone* fangirl; Mary Moates, publicist; Natalie Figueroa, assistant publicist; Brant Janeway, vice president of marketing, and everyone else at Wednesday Books/St. Martin's Press for all your hard work getting this book into readers' hands.

Thanks to my incredible literary agent, Jim McCarthy. I will never stop talking about how you seem to reply to my emails before I even send them. It must be magic. Thank you for selling this book two months into a global pandemic (again, magic), for loving my stories, and for talking me down from a panic more than once. I'm so happy to have you in my corner.

Thanks to my foreign rights agent, Lauren Abramo—it's

mind-blowing to see my words in other languages—and the team at Dystel, Goderich & Bourret. Thanks also to my film agent, Mary Pender, at the United Talent Agency for championing this book in Hollywood.

Thank you to my beta readers and friends Wendy Heard, Sonia Hartl, Megan Scott, and Elizabeth Schwab, and to my sensitivity readers, for helping me make this book even stronger.

Thanks to all of the talented authors who blurbed this book: Jessica Goodman, Emma Lord, Rebecca Hanover, Amie Kaufman, Tom Ryan, Sophie Gonzales, and Wendy Heard. It's such an incredible honor to have your support.

Thanks to my author BFFs: Mike Chen, Wendy Heard, Shana Silver, Hannah Reynolds, Sophie Gonzales, Erin Bowman, Jennifer Iacopelli, Alechia Dow, and Dan Koboldt, for always being there to confide in, for helping me navigate this wild industry, and for being such joys to chat with constantly.

Thanks to the entire author community for being so welcoming. I'm fortunate to get to call so many of you friends: Jessica, Claire, Karen, Rebecca, Aimée, Amparo, Demetra, Emma, Julia, Samantha, Ashley, Alexa, Intisar, Janella, Jordyn, Tom, Nita, Sarah, Tess, Julie, Jess, and everyone in Clubhouse (the writing group, not the app, no offense to the app). Thanks to the rest of my friends and my BookBub coworkers (you know who you are). Please know how much I appreciate you.

Thanks to everyone on my street team! It blows my mind that you want to be part of it. Every time I get an email notification that someone's joined, my husband hears me squeak across the apartment. It's *such* a joy to have our lil' community, to see your excitement, to have your support, and to gush about books we all love. And I so appreciate your help spreading the word. (New members can sign up at dianaurban.com/street-team; we'd be thrilled to welcome you!)

Thank you endlessly to the booksellers, librarians, teachers, bloggers, Instagrammers, TikTokers, and YouTubers who have helped more readers discover this book. I'm eternally grateful for your support and enthusiasm for my stories.

Thank you to the creators of *The Elder Scrolls V: Skyrim* (Bethesda) and *Fortnite* (Epic Games) for inspiring Mortal-Dusk and providing me with countless hours of entertainment. Actually, there's probably an exact tally of hours somewhere in the settings, but nobody needs to see that.

Thanks to Taylor Swift. You'll probably never see this, but I basically listened to *Folklore* on loop while drafting this book. Knowing you created it during lockdown helped give me the strength to finish this book during lockdown, too. So thank you for that.

Thanks to my favorite film score composers, Howard Shore, John Williams, Hans Zimmer, Ramin Djawadi, Sonya Belousova, and James Newton Howard, for all your music, the soundtrack to my life.

And, you know what? Yeah, I'm thanking my cat again. Kitty, thanks for being my coworker during the pandemic. A lot of this book was written with you on my lap—hence Whiskers, who plays such a vital role in this book.

If you enjoyed *These Deadly Games,* I would so appreciate it if you left a review on Amazon or your preferred retailer. Nothing sells books more than good word of mouth, and I'd be so grateful for any words you might be willing to leave. And again, *thank you.*